D1807414

"If you're an avid reader of all-male erotica and haven't yet discovered editor John Patrick's series of torrid anthologies, you're in for a treat. ...These books will provide hours of cost-effective entertainment."
– *Lance Sterling, Beau magazine*

"John Patrick is a modern master of the genre! ...This writing is what being brave is all about. It brings up the kinds of things that are usually kept so private that you think you're the only one who experiences them."
– *Gay Times, London*

"'Barely Legal' is a great potpourri...and the cover boy is gorgeous!"
– *Ian Young, Torso magazine*

"A huge collection of highly erotic, short and steamy one-handed tales. Perfect bedtime reading, though you probably won't get much sleep! Prepare to be shocked! Highly recommended!"
– *Vulcan magazine*

"Tantalizing tales of porn stars, hustlers, and other lost boys...John Patrick set the pace with 'Angel'!"
- *The Weekly News, Miami*

"...We guarantee you that this book will last you for many, many evenings to come as you relive your youth, or fulfill your fantasies with some of the horniest, hottest and most desirable young guys in fiction."
– *Blueboy*

"'Dreamboys' is so hot I had to put extra baby oil on my fingers, just to turn the pages! ...Those blue eyes on the cover are gonna reach out and touch you..."
– *Bookazine's Hot Flashes*

"I just got 'Intimate Strangers' and by the end of the week I had read it all. Great stories! Love it!"
– *L.C., Oregon*

"'Superstars' is a fast read...if you'd like a nice round of fireworks before the Fourth, read this aloud at your next church picnic..."
– *Welcomat, Philadelphia*

"Yes, it's another of those bumper collections of steamy tales from STARbooks. The rate at which John Patrick turns out these compilations you'd be forgiven for thinking it's not exactly quality prose. Wrong. These

stories are well-crafted, but not over-written, and have a profound effect in the pants department."
– *Vulcan Magazine, London*

"For those who share Mr. Patrick's appreciation for cute young men, 'Legends' is a delightfully readable book...I am a fan of John Patrick's...His writing is clear and straight-forward and should be better known in the gay community."
– *Ian Young, Torso Magazine*

"...Touching and gallant in its concern for the sexually addicted, 'Angel' becomes a wonderfully seductive investigation of the mysterious disparity between lust and passion, obsession and desire."
– *Lambda Book Report*

"John Patrick has one of the best jobs a gay male writer could have. In his fiction, he tells tales of rampant sexuality. His non-fiction involves first person explorations of adult male videostars. Talk about choice assignments!"
- *Southern Exposure*

"The title for 'Boys of Spring' is taken from a poem by Dylan Thomas, so you can count on high-caliber imagery throughout."
– *Walter Vatter, Editor, A Different Light Review*

Book of the Month Selections in Europe and the U.K. and Featured By A Different Light, Oscar Wilde Bookshop, Lambda Rising and GR, Australia and Available at Fine Booksellers Everywhere

When one orgasm is simply not enough...

COME Again
Volume 1

A Bold Collection
of Erotic Tales
Edited By
JOHN PATRICK

STARbooks Press
Herndon, VA

Published in the United States
STARbooks Press
PO Box 711612
Herndon VA 20171
Printed in the United States

Many thanks to graphic artist John Nail for the cover design. Mr. Nail may
be reached at: tojonail@juno.com.

Book and text design by Milton Stern. Mr. Stern can be reached at
miltonstern@miltonstern.com.

First Edition Published in the U.S. in Sept. 1997
Second Edition Published in the U.S. in Sept. 2007
Library of Congress Card Catalogue No. 96-070307
ISBN No. 1-934187-07-0

Books by John Patrick

Barely Legal (Editor)
Country Boys/City Boys (Editor)
My Three Boys (Editor)
Mad About the Boys (Editor)
Lover Boys (Editor)
In the BOY ZONE (Editor)
Boys of the Night (Editor)
Secret Passions (Editor)
Beautiful Boys (Editor)
Juniors (Editor)
Come Again (Editor)
Smooth 'N' Sassy (Editor)
Intimate Strangers (Editor)
Naughty By Nature (Editor)
Dreamboys (Editor)
Raw Recruits (Editor)
Play Hard, Score Big (Editor)
Sweet Temptations (Editor)
Pleasures of the Flesh (Editor)
Juniors 2 (Editor)
Fresh 'N' Frisky (Editor)
Boys on the Prowl (Editor)

Contents

EDITOR'S NOTE

Most of the stories appearing in this book take place prior to the years of The Plague; the editor and each of the authors represented herein advocate the practice of safe sex at all times. And, because these stories trespass the boundaries of fiction and non-fiction, to respect the privacy of those involved, we've changed all of the names and other identifying details.

Come out and play with me
C'mon, c'mon over
O Come let us adore him
Come to your senses
Coming together
Come again?
Come follow
follow
Coming all over me
Coming 'round the mountain
Every spring comes, then summer
Come if you can
Come if you wish
Come if you will
Come with me
Come now
Come later
Come again
Come let us be joyful
Come what may
Come and play with me again
Come with me
The best is yet to come
– *J. Blank*

INTRODUCTION:
THE MULTI-ORGASMIC GAY
John Patrick

"Multiple orgasms can be experienced by multiple people. The more the merrier." – *Star of the Golden Age of Porn Richard Locke*

Michael Segell, sex researcher, finds that, "Women seem to have much greater orgasmic potential than men, but many women (maybe as much as 20 percent of American women) never experience orgasm at all. In some cultures there's not even a word for female orgasm. Even women who are orgasmic don't come every time, as most men do. Of all the orgasms ever had, men have certainly stolen the lion's share.

"Researchers know more about orgasms today than when Masters and Johnson explored human sexual response in the 1960s. ...We now know, for instance, that the pursuit of pleasure motivates man to pursue many reproductive acts. His refractory period is also adaptive: Excessive sexual activity would cut into the time needed to replenish his sperm supply, causing his genes to suffer in their quest to make it into the next generation.

"The lack of any comparable spacing device is one reason why there are more multiply-orgasmic women than men.

"Just as a small percentage of women experience the kind of refraction more commonly seen in men, some men are capable of the kind of multiple orgasms that resemble a woman's. Ejaculation and orgasm are separate physiological responses, and many men, following the tradition of tantric yogis, have learned how to separate the two by 'pulling back' before the moment of ejaculatory inevitability. They can experience pleasurable contractions, then work toward orgasm again. This can be done repeatedly. Once ejaculation occurs, however, a period of refraction usually sets in.

"But a subset of multiply-orgasmic men can repeatedly reach orgasm and ejaculate without detumescing. According to a recent study, some multiply-orgasmic men claim to have had this ability since their first sexual experience; others discovered it later in life, usually within the context of a highly arousing sexual relationship. Still others developed the ability after practicing the squeeze technique to overcome premature ejaculation, or by following sex

1

manuals on 'extended sexual orgasm.'" Confounding common belief that Olympian sex is the province of the young, most of the men were in their forties, and a third were fifty-five or older. All of them reported an extremely limited, or nonexistent, refractory period. Most men reported between two and nine orgasms per sexual encounter – one man has had as many as sixteen (but who's counting?).

In the book The Multi-Orgasmic Man, Mantak Chia writes, "You may already have experienced multiple orgasms. Surprising as this may sound, many men are multi-orgasmic before they enter adolescence and begin to ejaculate. Kinsey's research suggested that more than half of all preadolescent boys were able to reach a second orgasm within a short period of time and nearly a third were able to achieve five or more orgasms one after the other. This led Kinsey to argue that 'climax is clearly possible without ejaculation.'"

In another groundbreaking work, Fundamentals of Human Sexuality, Dr. Herant Katchadourian adds: "Some men are able to inhibit the emission of semen while they experience the orgasmic contractions: in other words they have non-ejaculatory orgasms."

Chia contends that as men recognize that they also have this potential and learn some simple techniques, more and more of them will discover that they too can experience multiple orgasms. Chia says the secret is found in Taoist sexuality, also called Sexual Kung Fu, which began as a branch of Chinese medicine. The ancient Taoists were themselves doctors and were concerned as much with the body's physical well-being as with its sexual satisfaction. "Sexual Kung Fu," Chia says, "helps men increase their vitality and longevity by allowing them to avoid the fatigue and depletion that follow ejaculation – to stop them from, literally, going to seed."

Why do most men lose their ability to be multi-orgasmic? Chia suggests that it is possible that for many men the experience of ejaculating, when it happens, is so overwhelming that it eclipses the experience of orgasm and causes men to lose the ability to distinguish between the two. To become multi-orgasmic, you must learn (or possibly re-learn) the ability to separate the different sensations of arousal and to revel in orgasm without cresting over into ejaculation. Chia cautions, however, that all orgasms "are not created equal. Orgasm is slightly different for each person and even different for the same person at different times. Nonetheless, men's orgasms share certain characteristics, including rhythmic body movements, increased heart rate, muscle tension, and then a sudden release of tension, including pelvic contractions. They feel good, too. After noting that 'orgasm is the least understood of the sexual processes,' the thirteenth edition of Smith's General Urology explains that orgasm includes 'involuntary rhythmic contractions of the anal sphincter, hyperventilation [increased breathing-rate], tachycardia [increased heart-rate], and elevation of blood pressure.'"

For a long time orgasm was seen – and for many men is still seen – as strictly a genital affair. In the West, Wilhelm Reich, in his controversial book The Function of Orgasm, was the first to argue that orgasm involved the whole body and not just the genitals. In the East, the Taoists have long known that orgasm could be a whole-body experience and developed techniques for expanding orgasmic pleasure.

Many sex researchers are now arguing that orgasm really has more to do with our brain than our brawn. Brain-wave research is beginning to reveal that orgasm may occur primarily in the brain. That you can have an orgasm in your sleep – without any bodily touch – seems to confirm this theory. Further support comes from neurologist Robert J. Heath of Tulane University, who discovered that, when certain parts of the brain are stimulated with electrodes, they produce sexual pleasure identical to that produced by physical stimulation.

Chia believes that, with practice, you can learn to experience the peak feeling of orgasm without triggering the reflex of ejaculation.

Chia says, "Although sexual relationships between men were at times condoned and at other times discouraged by the imperial court – no doubt depending on who was sleeping in the royal bed – Taoism has never condemned homosexuality. Taoism avoids condemning any part of human sexual experience, since it is all considered a part of the Tao. Rather, Taoism tries to teach people how to stay healthy, whatever their sexual preferences. Gay men simply need to know the practices that will help them have satisfying and healthy sexual relationships.

Chia relates the story of a gay writer and activist who was doing a radio interview about his book on life in the pre-Plague bathhouses, where gay men often would have numerous sexual encounters per night. When asked about whether the desire for multiple sexual experiences is characteristic of gay men in general, the author shot back that it is characteristic of all male sexuality, but that straight men are influenced by female sexuality. If, he continued, we really want to know what male sexuality is like, uninfluenced by females, we need to look at gay men.

Chia says that the Taoist understands this characteristic of male sexuality in terms of the properties of masculine energy, or yang. Yang is active, volatile, and expansive. During heterosexual sex, the woman's yin receives and balances the man's yang. (Yin and yang are variable qualities that exist in both men and women. There are some men who are more yin and some women who are more yang.) According to the Taoists the universe always seeks balance in relationships as in nature.

In general, when two gay men make love, each man's yang charges the other's, increasing rather than diminishing their sexual desire. Gay Healing Tao instructor B. J. Santerre explains the value of multiple orgasms for gay men: "Gay men really need multiple orgasms. Most straight men are going to do it once or twice in an evening. For gay men it's really common that they need more than that in a night. With this practice you are going to be able to fully satisfy this desire whether you have a partner or not." The expansiveness of yang energy is hard to contain and often will want to escape through the most direct route – the penis. It is no surprise that the object of much gay male sexuality, according to gay sex educator and healer Joseph Kramer, is "to get it up and off." As Santerre explains, "If you conserve your semen, you are going to be able to go back to the heyday when people would go to the bathhouses and have orgasms all night long. When you learn this practice, you are able to do the same thing, but you won't exhaust yourself and you won't even need to leave home!"

Most gay men are aware of the pleasure potential of their prostate and their anus, yet some gay men still disparage men who are "bottoms." This attitude is not surprising given the negative stigma associated with "getting fucked" and the links in Western society between power and being on top. Taoism sees the person on top not as dominating but as healing his or her partner. The person on top (or the more active partner) gives more sexual energy (and healing) to the person on the bottom (or the more passive partner). According to the Tao, everything that is active must also be passive, and therefore it is recommended that gay men be versatile: both "tops" and "bottoms." As one multi-orgasmic man explained, the sexual benefits are obvious: "A guy who has been both a top and a bottom is a great

4

lover because he knows what it is like to satisfy his partner and to be satisfied. If you are only a top, you know only one version. The same if you are a bottom."

When you are the bottom, you also have the benefit of having your prostate massaged during anal intercourse. According to Stephen T. Chang in his book The Tao of Sexology, gay men who generally are bottoms have far fewer prostate problems than tops and heterosexual men. B.J. Santerre continues: "If your anus is really strong, you are going to be a great fuck for your partner. You are going to massage his penis as he is penetrating you. You are not totally passive and just waiting for it to happen. You take part in it by contracting and releasing the lower part or the higher part. You can contract it really fast two or three times in a row, or just let your partner get a little bit deeper and surprise him by squeezing it."

In his memoir Young Man From the Provinces, Alan Helms says he discovered his first multi-orgasmic man at the baths. Says Helms, "I'd always thought there was something desperate & sleazy about the baths, & in any case I'd always been able to get most of the men I wanted so I hadn't needed them. But my friend Seymour was right. Once I got off my high horse &, er, in the right frame of mind, I loved the baths – all those shadowy shapes moving along dimly-lit corridors, the naked men spotted in the showers, the sudden encounters with Mr. Right for the Night, then the tentative groping & quick seclusion behind the locked doors of a room whose claustrophobic dimensions focused the lust while the sounds of sex erupted into the halls, men making love in the sauna & the steam room & the orgy room, the living pornography of it all, the anonymity that gave greater intensity to the coupling, that sense of crossing a boundary into a world where knowledge of the other consists entirely of the body, seeing & touching the body, nothing but the single, well-hung, proportioned, beautiful body, all communication concentrated into physical response & the transported moans of excitement, surrender, gratification. Dispensing with as much of the cultural & psychological baggage as is possible for people of our time & place, the men in the baths embraced the purely physical & erotic ...I loved it, all those naked, responsive, beautiful bodies. ...A topsy-turvy world where customary values are inverted--Fire Island Pines, Mykonos, Alice's Wonderland, the Lenten carnival where jesters rule & outlaws set norms. You might think it was easy for me to enjoy such a world since I could compete with success, but men far less

5

desired than I was got their chance with a humpy guy so horny he couldn't see beyond the need of his tumescent dick, or so into the bacchanalian spirit of it all that one mouth or ass served as well as another.

"My first time, my friend Seymour took me to the Continental Baths where in the swimming pool I met up with a barely legal, pearly-skinned cowpoke from Montana. A couple of delectable hours later he had come three times, so yes, thank God, he'd really wanted me!"

Speaking of being wanted, one of the most desired porn performers currently, Drew Andrews, revealed to Manshots: "Even when I was really young, I knew what sex was, and I was one of these little boys who was always playing doctor or whatever little games I could figure out – any way that I could get into the other little boys' pants. And it was always the little boys. I knew really early – not that I was gay, but that I really liked little boys. And certain friends and I, we'd always play little games. It was nothing more than, 'You show me yours, I'll show you mine,' and a few touchy-feelies, and once or twice, at a very early age, a little oral, which did nothing – not for them anyway, but I loved it. And I was always the instigator. It was total manipulation. And I think they were just as curious as I was. I'd always start with little questions...kind of a 'Have you ever done...?' or 'Have you ever thought of...?' And it would go on and on and on like that.

"(The first time I jacked off) I was afraid I was going to get caught. Okay, here we go. This is awful. I'm in bed. It's late, late at night. The folks have gone to bed after the late news. At the time, I was sharing a room with two younger brothers. Well, here's the killer part, ready? I'm maybe like, nine years old. And of course, I'm lying there with a hard-on, and I'm playing with it. And I'm playing and playing, and of course, what happens is that I have an orgasm. Now, I couldn't come yet. I didn't ejaculate, but – (Makes a popping sound.) 'Oh, my gosh!' I had an orgasm that just shook the world. And those orgasms, to this day, I wish I had as strong. They were just body convulsions. Great! And it was like, constantly – six, seven, eight, nine times a day. And I remember the first time I actually ejaculated. By then I'd gotten my own room, and again, just like any other evening, I was lying there in bed jackin' off, and all of a sudden, it was just like, 'Bam!'

"When I first started ejaculating – I was almost like, 'Oh, man! I have to clean it up. Oh, my God, this sucks.' I shot all over my sheets. And then I freaked, because I thought, 'Oh, my God! My mother's gonna find out.' So, that's why it was so vivid. You know, to this day, I've only had two nocturnal ejaculations. The thing is, I've been getting off, literally, at least three times a day since I was twelve years old."

The spirit of this collection is best summed up by one of the hottest stars of the so-called Golden Age of Gay Porn: "'Sex ain't love,' they say, (but) I know better," Richard Locke said in his book Locke Out!. "When I began to love myself, I began to love others. I did it with my whole heart and soul. I have never been sexual with anyone I didn't love, even if only for a moment, or in a crowd, or on the screen, or on a stage. Multiple orgasms can be experienced by multiple people. The more the merrier. One of my best friends said to me the other day that I had 'built my life on sex.' My lover picked up on it, and every once in awhile, he uses it as tongue-in-cheek humor. It is not a nuclear power plant or a trip to the moon, but I have no regrets and I'm proud of my contributions."

Even today's porn stars have multi-orgasmic fantasies. Steve Pierce (aptly named, incidentally; check out all his piercings in "Straight Construction Site," especially his P.A.) has a favorite which he related to Ed Karvoski Jr. for The Guide. Steve said he dreams of going to the park just to get some sun, "and there's these guys with their shirts off, playing baseball, and they look pretty hot. So I lay my towel close enough to check 'em out. Well, sooner or later, the ball lands near me and I attempt to throw it back to them, and they start chastising me for throwing a ball like a fag. Pretty soon the group of them gangs up on me and grabs me and wants to teach me a lesson because they notice I've been checking them out. So they drag me behind the bleachers and start working me over." Not missing a beat, he continues, "First they piss on me and call me names. Since that only seems to excite me, they start shoving their dicks in my mouth and taunt me further. By that time, they're starting to get turned on, too.

"So since this doesn't seem to be producing the reaction they wanted, they decide, 'Well, since this guy is such a fag, why don't we just give him the baseball bat.' And then I take that and that gets me off, which sort of turns them on in a kind of sick way, so they jack off all over me and leave me lying there in the dirt, where I proceed to come again, just thinking about it!"

A more common multi-orgasmic experience is described by Peter Hunter in the book Boys Like Us, beginning with his first visit to a popular campus cruise spot: "Prime USDA sixteen-year-old chicken was not a commodity in great supply on that particular market, though the demand for it may have been as high there as anywhere else.

"Soon a man began to follow me. It was dark, he was too far away, my eyes were too shifty and timid for me to make out exactly what he looked like. I ducked into an alley formed by three buildings near the football stadium, with no way out but the way I'd gone in. Realizing my error, I leaned back against a wall and held my breath, hoping he would go away – but also, in spite of myself, hoping that he wouldn't. I had no idea how I was expected to act in such a situation, no idea what he might say or what I should say or what we would do if he did follow me. I realized the danger I had put myself in. He could have a knife, a gun. He could be a psycho, a cop. He rounded the corner and I was trapped.

"I could see him clearly now: in his late thirties or early forties, spare tire, sagging face, thinning hair – everything hideous and unattractive to a sixteen-year-old. We exchanged awkward greetings. He asked me my name, where I was from, what I was doing – innocuous questions that seemed as caustic and insidious as those of an interrogation squad. The spotlight of his eyes burned into me. I did the only thing that seemed logical, I lied. Lowering my voice to make myself sound older, I told him the first far-flung, improbable tale that popped into my head. My name was George; I was an art buyer from Washington, D.C., in town on business with the university, purchasing some late-sixteenth-century paintings for its collection. The man nodded in assent, playing along, interested to see where the game was leading. He continued to ask questions and I continued to dig myself deeper into my wild story. Finally, I excused myself, saying I had to get up early the next morning to report to the president of the university.

"(But now I) knew for sure that they were out there. I could return whenever the urge struck me.

"The urge struck me later that evening. I tried to sleep and couldn't close my eyes. A thousand little testosterone needles of curiosity pricked me. It was past midnight. I snuck out of the house and sped back to campus.

"The square was busy. I no longer recall how I met Arthur Brown, although I remember other things about him quite clearly. Later that night, in his bed, Arthur gave me my first blowjob.

"Then he gave me my second blow job.

"Then he gave me my third blow job.

"Arthur appreciated the fact that I was a virgin, and he swallowed everything I fed him greedily, as though he might never again have the chance to taste such a rare, sweet liqueur. I tried to reciprocate, but inexperience betrayed me and I choked on the sheer size of Arthur's equipment.

"The sun was coming up when I got back on my motorcycle and rode home. Arthur made me promise to come see him again. I promised, but I knew that I would not go back. I had already determined that what had occurred that night would never be repeated. I thought that by allowing Arthur Brown to suck my cock I had worked some kind of ritual magic to exorcise the bad spirits that lived in me. To use a more secular metaphor, I saw those blow jobs as a kind of immersion therapy."

Welcome to the world of the multi-orgasmic, dear reader! Sit back, now, relax, and enjoy a bit of "immersion therapy" of your own.

A HIGHER SENSE OF PLEASURE
John Patrick

"...He considered his degradation profoundly moral. And furthermore, he considered it his right. The purpose of it all was nothing other than the pleasure of the senses, of the body – in fact, to be precise and unequivocal, of his cock." – *Pier Paolo Pasolini, in "Petrolio," his unfinished novel*

You are dressed for a long night out. Dressed for turning on others. Your white satin shirt, unbuttoned to expose your magnificent pecs, opens even more invitingly as you dance across the floor in front of me – again.

I'm sure the mere sight of you has driven some to madness. And as I watch you closely I too am consumed with desire. My eyes travel hungrily down your body, to your narrow waist, and to your black jeans, the jeans that hug your small, rounded ass. But it is how those jeans hug your genitals that really gets me going. What a waste to have that cock and those balls hidden, locked away from all those who wish to sample them.

As the DJ switches to another song, you leave the floor, sweating profusely now, your dancing partner following closely behind you. Always behind you. I mean, I would too, just to keep my eyes on you. Now at the back bar, my gaze is boring holes through you, but you don't seem to notice. Even though I'm the one observing you, in a strange way I feel like I'm the one who is exposed. For once, I don't mind.

I watch as you make your rounds, speaking to your friends. You move in a smooth, fluid motion, like a cat moves, with ease, self-assurance.

Now I take in all of you – your hands, your arms, your fingers, your blue eyes, your long lashes, your neck, and, of course, your pecs, slightly hidden by the sweat-soaked shirt, darkened nipples peaking through the gaping of the fabric, at once seen and then hidden.

You are truly magnificent. Occasionally, you will push your damp, long blond hair away from your face and, up close, I see you are not really handsome. Your nose is too small, your mouth pouty, but it is a mouth made for sucking cock. The way you tease the men, I

11

know you must be inside their minds, understanding how much they want you. Or, maybe, they have had you already, for all I know, since I am a visitor here, and want some more of you.

I order another drink and I am soon moving beyond mere fascination. I'm clearly aroused, my cock hardening in my own jeans, my breath becoming shallow. The air in the back bar has become thick, closed in, claustrophobic. My cock begs for attention so I shift to a standing position, move closer to you. I rub my cock, rather blatantly, and it feels so good, but it would feel so much better if it was your hands or lips or tongue that was on it, moving slowly, taking your time. I would with you, you know, take my time.

And as I look up into your face, checking to see if you have noticed me yet, your lips curl slightly into a pleasant little smirk.

Oh, god, I love that smirk. You have noticed me and I want to wipe that smirk off your face by shoving my cock between your lips, sliding it into your mouth, down your throat. You look away, but I can tell you are not interested in the man who has captured you at this moment, because you turn your head to look at me, to see if I am still enraptured. I am, of course, and you smirk at me again. Damn that smirk. I really want to use force to wipe that smirk off your face. Real force. To smack your face with my prick, back and forth, harder, harder, slapping you silly.

But you turn your attention to yet another man, one who has bought you a beer. You aren't smirking now, just gulping your beer. You are a pig – and I love that. Yes, wipe the foam from your lips and look up, look up at me, still staring at you. You don't smirk this time. Instead you look quickly away, feigning interest in the man who bought you the beer. But from the way you are fingering that bottle, up and down, tightly, I can tell what you have on your mind. I turn a bit, to show you I have been thinking of you and getting hard. I stroke myself, lewdly – I have no shame. Finally I walk toward you, and just as I'm upon you, you turn your back on me. I stand behind you, waiting. Then someone moves from the bar and I move down to take his place. You turn and look down the bar. You find me. You are interested. The smirk returns, but you return to the man who bought you the beer. He hasn't stopped talking and you must be horribly bored by now.

Yes, you are – it's late and you are restless. You're saying goodnight. You're on your way out. You stand behind me, smirking.

There are no pleasantries. "I'm leaving," you say, confident.

I am supposed to follow, and I do.

You got a ride with a friend, you say, so I drive. You don't want to go to my hotel. No, you'd prefer it if we go to your place.

So near you now, I am frightened. Ordinarily, I have confidence in my lovemaking ability, but I have worked all day. Now that I am in the car, you don't say much, giving me time to pause to consider. Could I really fuck you, you who so clearly want it, and want it to last all night long? I know that I want to very badly. In a moment, I feel a rush of excitement pass through my body. My hard-on tells me I will be able to fuck.

I thought it might be a little room somewhere but it is a concrete condo on the beach. I am impressed. The elevator is brightly lit. As I lean against the back wall, I gaze at you in the light. On the way up from your booted feet, your black jeans, your satin shirt, I can tell your body will be a delight to discover; nice round hips and great pecs. The shock is your face. It is deeply tanned. In the light, I can see creases in your forehead. You stay too long in the sun.

You shift nervously but hold tightly to your offensive edge. "How old are you?" I ask.

"How old do I look?"

"Old enough."

"I am."

"Oh, good...at least, I'm not robbing the cradle. Me, I'm thirty-nine... " I let that information and your totally brazen style trickle down for a moment. How appropriate that in your prime I should meet you. I have to respond. Like taking a blind curve at high speed, I force my wandering gaze to turn directly into your eyes. I want you to know I will do whatever you ask and that I have a few ideas of my own. You smile, as if you know something that I don't.

As I am getting ready to kiss you, the elevator doors open with perfect Hollywood timing, and I follow you down the dark hallway.

Inside, you set the lighting, and we step out onto the ninth floor balcony. We stand at the railing looking down at the white crests of waves turning down on the dark water. I put my arm around your slender waist.

I tell you how nice it is, and you mumble something. I realize it is not really your place. Your lover is probably out of town, and now another out-of-towner has taken his place.

We kiss and you say it is time to go to the bedroom.

13

By the side of the bed, in the soft indirect light, you simply take off your clothes and let them lie where they fall on the floor. You crawl under the covers. It seems so blasphemous, so unromantic.

Standing awkwardly just inside the bedroom, where I stopped when I came in, I try to adjust to this strange turn of events. You stare silently at me from the shadows as I shift my weight from one foot to the other, waiting for some indication of what is expected of me. I am a rough character in many respects, but I have a few manners I trot out when I feel like impressing someone, and I never sit down in someone's house until I am invited. That doesn't happen too often, though. Either one. The impressing or the sitting. I am pretty much a loner, not given to visiting friends, even when I have them now and then.

"Why don't you come over here. I won't bite," you say, turning on your side and propping yourself up on an elbow.

You push away the covers, shift and open your legs, exposing your crotch. I am not sure if the gesture is an innocent one or you are setting a trap into which I, given half a chance, would easily fall into. Being locked between your thighs with that cock would be a wonderful fate.

Hurriedly, I take off all my clothes and step over to the bed. You lift up, start kissing my half-hard cock. "This is just too cool," I say, wondering if it is really happening, watching myself respond to your kisses, then your sucking.

You release my cock when it is hard. You don't say anything; you lay back and let me get into bed with you. The mattress is firm, the sheets cool. The first skin touch is warm and fragrant. I knew you would want me to explore your body. Although I have not asked directly, I think you wish to be fucked senseless. You sigh as I rub your smooth skin.

I slide over you, thigh to thigh, elbows up so I can see your face. We kiss. I let my knees slip onto the mattress between your legs and slip my cock into the crack. You move to make yourself comfortable with this position. I take a few rubbing strokes on your ass while I allow suck on your pecs for the first time. I sense you are smiling, knowing I've been waiting, saving it for you.

I take my sweet time exploring your perfect form, licking, kissing, nibbling. But I do not spend a lot of time with your cock. It is stiff, hot. I fear you will come too soon. I lift your legs so I can get closer, right at the entrance to you...then inside. I lick my finger before I start to fuck your anus.

I get in position to make a straightforward move for your asshole. As if you have been reading my mind, you catch my arm and motion to the nightstand. I see the grease and begin applying it. Then you apply the rubber.

You pull me down so that your face is very close to mine. You turn her mouth to my ear and whisper, "My lover doesn't fuck me. He only wants to get fucked. Please, be gentle." Your voice is soft, perhaps from the pain of that constant desire, but determined. I can feel my body tense with fear. In general, I like getting fucked – even rough fucked. Now I am expected to do the fucking, but it has been such a long day. Can I pull this off? I slip a finger inside you, then two. I pull them out and bring my cock to the hole. Much to my surprise, I am ready, as hard as I have ever been. I relax. You moan in recognition of my prowess and push me in. I move faster, and you open up some more. You want to be fucked, I find, but you want to control it. You do the guiding and I move without thinking. All feeling is blurred beyond recognition. All I can do is hold on tight to your body. I don't want to come. I want to stay here forever. You take me to a higher sense of pleasure than I have ever known. We fuck for what seems like hours and you come. I follow you, and only stop because I can't take another stroke. When I open my eyes, you are there watching. As my grandmother would say, "like the cat that swallowed the canary." I crawl into your arms and kiss you. You push my head down, down into your crotch. You want to come again. You want me to go down on you. I slide down. Even though I am not particularly good at oral sex, I am determined you'll never know it. Your cock is coated with the first climax. I bathe it with saliva, wipe it, then begin sucking.

On closer inspection, I see it is a lovely cock. Not big, but thick. Your lover wants it up his ass all the time, and I can see why. It would feel wonderful, all that thickness. You immediately start directing my suck as well, so it is easy to follow. When I stray, you push me back. I feel like an expert cocksucker now, and you come quickly and easily. We pull the covers up. You apparently want me to stay. You don't ask, so I presume. We will sleep close the rest of the night.

In the morning, you are businesslike, and I am in love. You want to be fucked again, this time in the shower. It has been years since I have done that, and I willingly oblige. In this heady atmosphere, it is even more intense. "You don't have to do anything you don't want to," you reassure me.

Oh, how I want to, I insist, crawling downward, opening up the lips of your ass and burying my face inside, sniffing, licking, drinking you in. I can't get enough of you! And you love it! As you moan and thrash, thrusting your magnificent hips toward me, I feel a surge of pride and power. My cock twitches in pre-orgasmic shudders as I place my hands on your hips and thrust my cock into your ass. You raise your arms over your head and I grasp your wrists in one of my hands. I am seized with an incredibly strong desire for which I am entirely unprepared: I want to fuck you silly.

"Oh, yes," you gasp, eagerly writhing beneath me. "Fuck me. Fuck me."

Released from fear and shame, I pump my cock all the way in and before I know it I begin to come. I let go of you and you quickly reach down and turn me around. I know what is coming. Thank god I like both roles, like the flexibility of this. But I don't know if I can handle you. The thickness of you, now, after I've come. I realize you are just as nervous. You take pains to prepare me, enter me slowly. The water cascades over us in this position, and I feel like I am being fucked in a waterfall. You are good, oh, so good. I can't remember a fuck this good. No wonder your lover wants it all the time. Your lover. Damn your lover. Your very lucky lover.

Now, over coffee, you are far away. I notice you aren't saying much. Nothing, as a matter of fact. I ask you questions like, Is everything okay? Are you upset? Still, you don't speak. Then you begin to talk about your lover, how he's taken a job in another city and you have to decide whether you want to move or not. I can tell there's desire there, but there's more, as if it's more in the mind. You really love him, I can tell.

I wish you well. When I leave, I know I won't see you ever again. I shouldn't really. It would be self-destructive and, thanks to you, I am finally growing out of that state of mind, to a higher sense of pleasure.

COME AGAIN
John Patrick

Peter's morning erection was thrusting the sheet into a comic tent. The day's heat was already building, and he felt swept away by it, sweat dripping from his body as he tossed the sheet away and he jerked his cock. As the cock began swelling ever larger, ever harder, it made him think of firm buttocks, of Barry's butt, his cock sliding between the crack and deep into Barry.

Furiously he worked his cock. It seemed that whenever he was gripped by sexual desire, which was very often these days now that Barry was gone, his desires were thwarted by the ringing of the phone or one of the workmen coming to the door early, wanting directions for the day. But that would not happen today since he had now run out of renovation money. Now the house looked as if it were in the early stages of demolition.

Peter came; it was a glorious orgasm, best he'd had in days. Breathing heavily, almost staggering, he made his way to the bathroom.

The bathroom was the best thing about the old house. It had a patterned tile floor in three shades of tan against black and white, an alcove behind the door housing an ornate cast-iron radiator where Peter could heat towels, high ceilings, sculpted cornices covered with three inches of yellowing paint, a huge cast-iron bathtub with ball-and-claw feet, with a chrome shower ring, and an old-fashioned flat shower head.

Peter shook the can of shaving foam, tested the heat of the water in the basin. He pulled flesh tight over the angle of his jaw. Even this reminded him of Barry, whose rosy cheeks looked as if they'd never known a razor.

He recalled how he had seen Barry flaunting himself shamelessly on the street in front of the bar. He was too young to get in, so he hung around outside to see who he could pick up. That night, Peter never even went in the bar, just took Barry home. All that night, Peter couldn't forget where he had met Barry. But one forgets what one was like when one was that age. He criticized Barry, but he knew full well he had acted like that when he was a kid, had gone to wherever gay men were and loved being picked up. But Peter was not the beauty Barry was. Peter was a tall man with large moist eyes, a full mouth and a thin, prominent nose. He was thirty-four but looked much younger. He was tanned with his brown hair coiffed over his ears. His face was unmarked by lines of worry, which was not surprising, since he had enjoyed a life of relative ease and wealth since the cradle. He had a softness of expression about his eyes and mouth; when crossed, his lip would begin to tremble and his face might dissolve into petulance.

It seemed Peter had found his match in Barry. Peter said it was a case of "the beauty and the beast." Barry moved in. He also joined the crew and helped with the renovation. During the day, while Peter was at his law office (he specialized in international litigation), Barry worked hard, learned a lot, and fell madly in love with six-foot tall, dark-haired stud Jason, whom Peter had managed to blow only once. Peter had thought Jason was happy with his girlfriend, but that was before Barry. Soon the crew chief was catching Jason and Barry in the act, and finally Jason had to go. After this, Barry began to drift. He was seldom at the house, and when he was he was moody, distant.

Finally Peter had to say, "I've got feelings, too. Okay?"

He stood looking down at Barry's bowed head.

"Look," Peter said, beginning to pace. "We've been having a pretty hard time lately, haven't we? Always arguing and squabbling about one thing or another. Getting on each other's nerves. And it's been making me very unhappy, Barry. But you know, for my part, I only criticize you because I want you to grow up decently and become a kind and considerate person. I don't enjoy fighting with you. Believe me. But think of it this way. If I didn't care about you, I wouldn't bother with you, would I? Shit, it'd be so much easier just to ignore you, let you go to hell. It'd be a lot easier for me just to shrug my shoulders, now wouldn't it?"

"But you don't do that."

"And I think, really, that you know why I don't."

But Barry left. Peter knew he'd go to be with Jason, but he tried to forget the boy and move on.

Now Peter hadn't finished shaving when he saw Barry's compact body in the mirror. The kid was soon at the door, seemingly contrite.

Peter breathed in deeply and then sighed profoundly. He had forgotten that Barry still had a key to the house.

"What happened?" Peter asked.

"I wish I knew. There's this girl, you see. He's been seeing her for a long time I take it. Anyhow, she didn't like the idea. Even with a guy. I was faithful to him, though. I was there for him, even if he was out fucking her, I was there, waiting."

"Oh, don't misunderstand me! I'm not being censorious. If anything, I'm envious, Barry. Jason was a hunk, no doubt about it."

"Yeah, he told me you blew him."

"That was before you."

"I know."

Barry came into the bathroom and took Peter in his arms, pulling Peter's ass into his crotch. Peter tried to finish shaving.

"I love you, Barry. It's just that it isn't so simple now. A lot of things have happened."

"Oh?"

"Yes. I've simply run out of money."

"Daddy's out of money?"

"No, not Daddy. But I have to go ask Daddy. I'm dreading it. So here I am living out of these rooms."

"Still, it's better than most people have."

"It's just that all this work is just so expensive..."

"I work cheap – "

Peter turned around and took the boy in his arms. Barry lay his cheek against Peter's hairy chest.

Peter tugged at the boy's blond curls. "It's an attractive thought. Very attractive."

"You know, you're so fuckin' tall that I don't have to bend over very far to give you a blowjob."

Peter pushed the boy away. "I just came."

But Barry would not be denied. "You can come again."

Barry stripped and began sucking his former lover. Eventually Peter put his hands around Barry's smooth asscheeks, and roughly pulled him forward as Barry took his cock further down his throat, back and forth, up and down.

Before long Peter had to put his hands around Barry's prick. Usually Barry found Peter a little too aggressive, almost dangerous, as if he tried to belie his scholarly appearance. But this time, Barry welcomed his roughness and urged him on with little shrieks and gasps. He responded by clutching Peter's hairy balls, but he refused to release his cock from his mouth. Soon he began to jerk the lower part of the shaft like a dog worrying a bone. He was going crazy with

19

desire, over and over again, he felt himself at the brink. But each time he pulled back and relaxed his grip on Barry's cock.

Peter knew exactly what he was doing. Young Barry was completely under his control. Peter knew well all of the vital signs, how Barry's asscheeks shook with a disco-like rhythm, begging to be filled. Peter looked into the bedroom and his bed seemed to quiver in anticipation: Barry was back!

Barry couldn't hold back any longer. Peter's jerking of him brought him on and his cock began to buck and spasm with a life all its own. Barry's cum spurted out of his cock and onto the floor.

Barry let Peter's cock slip from his mouth while he caught his breath. Peter drew him up and they kissed. It was a longer, lingering kiss.

"You came," Peter said.

"I can come again."

And so they went to the bed. Peter held back so he could watch the boy's ass. God, he thought, it's a very nice piece of boy flesh. But he was sad, because he realized now just how much he missed it – and how much Jason must have enjoyed fucking it. As Peter climbed on the bed, Barry's cock thrust itself towards him. Peter lubed it, then lubed his own cock, then Barry's ass. Finally ready, Barry pushed Peter onto his back and mounted him, slamming the prick into him and jumping up and down on it, jerking himself while he did.

They fucked in this position for several minutes; neither of them was in a hurry now, having both come. Finally, Barry got on his back and took Peter missionary. This too lasted several minutes because they were lost in each other's arms, kissing deeply, pledging their undying love.

Finally, Peter lifted himself up and jerked Barry while he watched his cock slamming in and out of Barry. This brought each of them off again within moments.

Despite the heat, despite the fact they were drenched in cum, Peter would not let Barry up.

"Was it worth it, Barry?" Peter asked, holding Barry down. "Looking at it now?"

"What a stupid question!"

"Of course it was worth it. You were living in a dream. What a hunk! Oh, don't think I don't understand!"

"I'm sorry. I never meant it to happen, believe me."

"I envy you that, Barry. You breathed an air I've never breathed."

"What air was that?"

"The air in Jason's apartment. On Mango Boulevard."

"You knew where I was?"

"Sure, but it's like my father, the philosopher, says, 'What can you do?'"

Barry took Peter's cock in his hand and squeezed it. "What you can do is fuck me again."

THE WORLD'S GREATEST BOTTOM
John Patrick

Thank you for your letter. You make love with your beautiful words, words that tantalize and titillate. But in your fantasy I am so passive. All that one-sided activity. You should know, or at least you will know soon enough, that I am very active, which makes me "the world's greatest bottom!" Arriving Friday as agreed. – Timothy Christopher

Cameron rolled out of bed. His bare feet landed on the cool carpet. Completely nude, he stood there momentarily dazed from having read the letter, which he still held in his right hand. He checked his watch: 4 o'clock. The odor of the cum on his fingers excited him again, for the letter had moved him to jack-off. He licked his fingers.

Despite the air conditioning, he was hot and his body was sweaty all over. He walked across the room and stood before the mirror. He was six feet of gym-built stud. Not bad for thirty. He was pleased with himself. He sighed deeply and lovingly he touched myself, then hurried to the bathroom. He could not wait around in the house. He would shower and dress and go to the airport, and hang out there until Timothy arrived.

There, amid the traffic on the highway, the potential of having this rendezvous with the boy that one of the video critics had called "the world's greatest bottom" invaded his senses. He felt his cock stirring again. He gunned the gas pedal, sending the big, air-conditioned Buick leaping toward the airport.

Cameron spotted Timothy as he came through the exit gate. The little blond boy snake-hipped through the crowd with great ease. Cameron blinked when he saw the kid wore a wanton-looking pair of Levis, with holes in all the right places, but he greeted him warmly and Cameron felt comfortable immediately. Although the walk out of the terminal took light-years, Cameron loved every step of the way. It was so good to finally be with the boy he had so often fantasized about. And to find him so charming, so disarming. He could hardly wait to get him home.

When they arrived at Cameron's condo, they went directly to the bedroom.

23

Naked, Timothy lay on his belly across the big pillow so his ass stuck up nicely. He held his head against the regular pillow. There it was: the ass. He wriggled and Cameron savored the sight. He kissed the bottom; the skin shivered under his lips. Timothy started playing with himself. His hips moved from side to side as he masturbated. Cameron kissed and sucked on the ass while Timothy rocked and shimmied. He felt Timothy's breath speed up. His bottom swayed slowly and sensuously. Cameron's short fingernails dug into Timothy's skin as he bounced harder and faster, faster, slowing down, then speeding up, faster and faster until he came. Cameron was overcome; he kissed Timothy's beautiful, naked ass, felt Timothy's cock. Timothy had come as well.

Trying to catch his breath, wiping perspiration off his forehead, Timothy rolled away, turned on his back.

"Now, it's your turn," Timothy said. He drew his knees up and opened his legs. "You didn't already come, did you?" he asked.

"Yes, but it was a small orgasm and I want a big one this time," Cameron said, his hands trembling a little as he talked. "Yeah, seconds are usually best for me," Timothy said.

He put his mouth on Timothy's cum-covered cock and gently sucked it, slowly and for a long time, the way Timothy had told him he liked it.

"Oh, kiss it, suck it."

Cameron's mouth moved to the ass and he began licking it, and Timothy's hips started grinding again, faster but with long pauses. Soon Timothy's ass was throbbing around Cameron's tongue.

Suddenly, Cameron got up and went to the bathroom. When he returned, he explained he had long been fascinated by Timothy's sex scene in "Cycle Sluts" with Johnny Harden. Harden was no longer in the business but the dildo made from his cock was still a best-seller and Cameron prized his. "Is this close?" he asked, removing the replica from its black velvet bag.

"God, how disgusting," Timothy laughed.

Still, the boy had never seen the Harden replica hard-on, so he examined it closely. "You know," he said, "I scarcely remember him. There have been so many since."

"The last one is always best one?"

Timothy chuckled. "I guess you could say that."

Timothy agreed to let Cameron insert the dildo. He wanted to take it doggie-style and Cameron greased the enormous thing eagerly.

24

To add to their amusement, he inserted the video into the VCR and the actual scene started playing. Timothy groaned, "I can't fuckin' believe this! I've never even seen this!"

As Cameron shoved and shoved, Timothy became enraptured watching Johnny fuck him on the screen. He reached for the remote control and rewound the tape, then started it again. Cameron reached under Timothy and fondled him while he continued shoving and shoving until he finally got the whole thing into Timothy.

After awhile, his questing fingers removed the dildo, or rather, received it as it fell out of Timothy.

"Oh, that was good," Cameron said.

Timothy's hand was moving up and down his cock. Cameron had never met a boy who loved handling himself so much.

It was not a large cock, but it was in perfect proportion to the rest of him. "C'mon," Timothy begged, "put your mouth here. If you don't make it fast, I might come in my fist, and all this good hot stuff'll go to waste."

While Cameron sucked, Johnny's vulgar words, interrupted by Timothy's sobs and soft cries of pain when he pressed his big cock into him, filled the room. "Jesus," Timothy cried as he came.

- - -

To defray the high cost of having Timothy visit him in Cleveland, Cameron had arranged a party for the second night of the porn star's visit. Timothy had agreed to it, realizing what he was making for the long weekend would mean he wouldn't have to take any calls for the rest of the month if he didn't want to. But it was agreed also that Friday night was to be Cameron's alone, and Cameron was not disappointed so far, especially when he got the letter from Hollywood the day before, something so unexpected, so thoughtful, so exciting. Timothy had sent the letter by Fed-X. When Cameron mentioned it, Timothy said, "I send everything Fed-X, so it gets there."

"Well, it was very nice."

"What was really nice was that you wrote that fantasy about me. It really turned me on. Do you write those stories for a living?"

"I write, but not those stories. I write copy for ads. I'm a copywriter."

"Whose ads?"

"Technical stuff mostly. Deadly dull. That's why I take time out to write some fantasy stuff."

25

"Bet there's money in the advertising business."

"Only if you own the agency. I don't."

Timothy was quiet, and Cameron assumed he was realizing for the first time that this was not his usual score. Most of the men who wanted him were wealthy, Cameron figured, and lavished gifts upon him. Cameron, although comfortable, was hardly well-to-do and he had to be careful with his finances. Dinner would not be at a fancy restaurant, but it would be pleasant enough because Cameron was a regular at Sneaky Pete's and he was guaranteed a table, even on the busiest nights.

Although it did not cater to gays exclusively, Sneaky Pete's

was owned by gays and all the waiters were gay. Cameron's favorite, Bobby, was still playing hard-to-get after three years, but Cameron enjoyed the teasing.

Cameron knew the party would be especially good because his pals hadn't seen each other for a few weeks. Bill was a sexy-looking man, standing about six-three and a body that looked like he spent hours each day sculpting his physique, which he did. Bill was the host of the event; he was known for his parties that turned into orgies. He had a three-bedroom home that he designed to put his guests in the mood. Two of his three bedrooms had king-size water beds, wall-to-wall mirrors, piped-in music, TV monitors that played porn videos, and subtle colored lighting.

Cameron threw himself into Bill's arms and kissed him. Then Bill threw himself into Timothy's arms and kissed him. Timothy smiled as they walked into the stunning living room, with its views of Lake Erie, and he saw another hot stud peeling his clothes off to the strains of a sensuous melody played softly in the background. The stripper began to dip and sway around Timothy, and Bill chuckled, "Takes one to know one." Bill was referring to the fact that the stripper, who called himself Storm, had once appeared in a video and based on that one performance was able to carve out a career as a stripper. He never made another video, but his incredible versatility (including a fisting scene for the mail order version) had made him infamous. His lover, Joseph, was also at the party and came into the room carrying drinks. "They've found each other," Bill explained, as Storm and Timothy began to dance together.

Joseph grinned. "The question is, what will they do with each other?"

"I'm sure they can figure something out," Cameron said, embracing Joseph. He had not seen the distinguished-looking gray-haired executive in almost a year. "Darling, you look fabulous," Cameron told him.

"All because of Storm. I've never gotten so much exercise."

They laughed conspiratorially and Joseph handed Cameron one of the drinks he was holding. "Here, I don't think Storm is much interested in this right now."

Cameron sat down with Joseph and he could see the silhouettes of the dancers in the mirrors, and the sight of them made him hard. Storm had taken Timothy's T-shirt off and began to suck and lick his nipples. Timothy's golden brown nipples stood up on his hairless chest in response to Storm's tongue. He cupped his pectorals in his hands and watched Storm suckle.

Joseph slid his hand down, down into Cameron's crotch. Cameron let out a moan, as he remembered how good this man was the last time they fucked. Joseph laid him down on the living-room floor and pulled out Cameron's throbbing erection. He licked away the pre-cum and began licking his cock in feather-like strokes. Before long Joseph had removed Cameron's clothes and he was moving his fingers in and out of Cameron's ass as he told him how he intended to fuck him. How he was going to start with him, go to Storm and then finish inside Timothy. This caused Cameron to come, but his cock remained hard as he watched Joseph strip. Joseph had the biggest cock in Cleveland, Cameron always said, and that was what kept Storm in line. Impulsively he guided Joseph's movements as he arched his back and Joseph rubbed his cock against the puckering anal lips. Joseph opened Cameron's legs wider and Cameron gasped with pleasure. Timothy came dancing over and became enamored of Joseph's cock. He licked and sucked like a cat licks a dish of milk.

"What do you think about that cock?" Bill asked, masturbating his own rather sizeable cock.

Timothy's eyes grew bigger as, as if drawn to a magnet, Storm joined Timothy in the sucking of Joseph. They both licked and sucked his cock while they played with each other. Cameron lay on the floor beside them and played with his cock as he watched Timothy open his mouth wide and take in all of Joseph's cock. Joseph was simply overcome with lust, and he started kissing and rubbing first Timothy's ass then Storm's. He thrust his tongue in Timothy's ass so deep that it made Timothy cry out. The sight of all this was

27

enough to take Cameron over the edge. He shot his cum and lay there in the midst of three beautiful men and smiled.

Before long, Joseph got up and Bill led them into his special water-bed room. Once in the room, Bill began to meticulously set the stage for the orgy. He put a plastic mat over the bed and dimmed the lights. He turned on the TV monitor, and instructed Timothy and Storm, the stars of the evening, to get in the bed and play with themselves. Bill left the room for a moment, and when he returned he had a gallon of oil. He poured the oil all over them, and rubbed them, as he described how good they looked.

At that point, Joseph, who had been having his cock sucked by Cameron, jumped in bed and formed a circle of bodies, each one going down on someone. Timothy responded to Joseph by opening the lips of his ass wider to allow Joseph free access to his ass. Meanwhile, Cameron was busy sucking Storm to full-hardness. Joseph tongue-fucked Timothy until he tightened his legs around his neck and begged Joseph to fuck him. Bill had been sucking Joseph while he was tongue-fucking Timothy and Bill now guided Joseph's dick inside Timothy's ass. Seeing it going all the way in without stopping Bill could hardly hold back, his passion was so intense. After a few minutes of a slow rhythmic rocking, Joseph pulled out of Timothy and slammed into Storm. Cameron didn't release Storm's cock from his mouth as Joseph fucked. Storm came and Cameron pulled back and caught the cum with his hands. Joseph pulled out and pushed Cameron over on top of Storm, then shoved his filthy prick into Cameron. Meanwhile, Bill was between Timothy's thighs, madly screwing him.

They went on like that, Joseph leading the way and the others following. Even Storm had his chance to fuck Timothy. At the end, they were all kneeling on the bed with Timothy in the middle, jerking off.

"Now this is a circle jerk," Bill gushed, pleased that the party had gone so well.

Dazed, Timothy lay on the bed for several minutes. He could hear guests leaving and then there was silence. He dozed off. When he awoke, Joseph and Bill were again in the room. Bill climbed on the bed and hauled Timothy closer to the foot of the bed. He bent Timothy's legs until his feet were in the air, then began to rub his hard cock over Timothy's messy asshole. For a few minutes, he fucked the crack. After a while, Timothy understood that Bill was teasing him, and that he wanted him to struggle to get his cock. After all those cocks, Timothy had never felt emptier. His battered ass was burning, but he moaned, "Please." He began writhing under him. "Please put it into me."

"You sure?" Bill teased.

"Oh, yes," he grunted.

Bill began sliding his erection into Timothy. Meanwhile, Joseph came around and got on his knees on the bed, his cock dangling in Timothy's face.

Gradually, Joseph's cock hardened and Timothy understood the man was enjoying what he saw. Before long, Bill had pulled out and Joseph had taken his place. "You want it?" Joseph demanded. "Here, feel how big it is." He thrust the head of his thick cock against the hole, not inserting it, but stretching the boypussy taut.

"Oh, yeah," Timothy said.

An inch at a time, each of them glorious, he stretched Timothy wide open, then he began to move. Timothy's eyes rolled back in his head. Bill had taken Joseph's earlier position and started jabbing his cockhead between Timothy's lips, and Timothy's tongue flickered out to service him. Timothy's head was turned sideways to accommodate him, and even shallow penetration put tremendous strain on his neck and shoulders. Timothy sucked him as long as he could before Joseph's pounding became too insistent and he again lost control over his mouth. But he still continued.

This was the very core of Timothy's eroticism. These two men had brought him to a point where there was nothing he craved more. There could be no self-deception, no lies about not really wanting it. And these men were incredibly good at what they did. They liked fucking and being fucked, they knew how to do it, and they wanted Timothy to enjoy himself. Joseph churned deep inside Timothy, speeding his rhythm. Timothy tried to spread his legs wider, to open his ass up even more, and Joseph pushed especially deep inside him, jabbing him sharp and fast, his hands digging painfully into his asscheeks.

"Oh, shit," Joseph snarled, and Timothy knew by his convulsive hip movements that he had come. Before long Joseph had removed his cock and gone to the bathroom.

Soon Bill was moving to the place where Joseph had been. Unlike Joseph, Bill went into Timothy in one vicious thrust, and Timothy screamed. Tears sprang into his eyes. Nevertheless, Bill wanted Timothy to have a good time; he began to fondle Timothy's cock until it was aroused fully. While Bill's penis moved in and out of his hole, Timothy started to spasm.

"Oh, yeah," Joseph said, returning to the bedside. He was playing with his cock, which, even limp, was stupendous.

Joseph put one foot up on the bed, then gradually insinuated the head of his cock into Timothy's mouth.

"This is something we've wanted for a long time. But we really do want you to enjoy it. That makes it better for us."

Timothy nodded.

Bill still hadn't come, he just kept on and on. Finally Joseph was erect again and Bill made way for him. For Timothy, there was no respite to gather his breath. Bill's cock was inserted in his mouth and Joseph returned inexorably to his ass. Oh, yes, he was good. Thorough, hard, unstoppable. Timothy had the feeling they could go on and on until he was dead. Under these circumstances, Timothy knew it was better to scream freely, without restraint, to plead for mercy, to cry, to struggle beautifully, to sweat and strain, to be fucked and fucked again, to ask them what they want, to agree to everything they say, to promise anything if only it will stop.

Watching Joseph, Bill could no longer hold back and he came. Timothy did his best to take it all. Bill disappeared and Joseph continued, but only for a few moments. Timothy's eyes were closed throughout Joseph's orgasm. At last there was respite from pain, but not from the tension. The only question was, when would it start again, and how?

Timothy rolled over and dozed. When he awoke, Joseph was lying at the far end of the bed; he was smiling sweetly.

"We've always wanted to find somebody who could do that," he said.

"Oh?" Timothy said, raising his head. His eyes were heavy; he felt drugged.

"Yes. And we're all alone now. I told Cameron I wanted you for another day. You can stay, can't you?"

Timothy nodded. He'd had no idea now what appointments he had made, and it mattered little as Joseph moved down the bed.

30

CREAM BUNS
Peter Gilbert

"A good day. He's coming along nicely," said Trevor.

"Why don't you write your diary earlier?" asked Richard from the other bed.

"I might miss something important. The most important things often happen late at night."

Richard lay facing the wall and wondering what Trevor had written on Sunday night, and how many of the earlier entries were actually true.

They had met in January. He had known of Trevor for some time. It seemed inconceivable that this six-foot-tall football playing hunk could be gay. Trevor was twenty two; a post graduate research student. Richard, two years younger, was in his second undergraduate year.

On that winter's evening, having nothing else to do, Richard decided to go to a meeting of the university Gay and Lesbian Society. "Not my scene at all but I might as well see what goes on there," he had said. Trevor was there as Richard secretly hoped he would be. He bought Trevor a drink. It all started from that. Richard, who came from an extremely conservative background, found Trevor's openness and frank conversation revolting but fascinating. Time and time again in the subsequent weeks he had walked away from his new friend in disgust but then, in the privacy of his bedroom, mulled over what Trevor had said. The boy in the photo copying room really did have a nice ass but there was no need to comment upon the fact. On their frequent visits to the photo copying room together Richard saw no sign whatever that the boy 'wanted it' as Trevor maintained he did. His name was Alan and he was seventeen. That had been left to Richard to find out. Indeed, the lad seemed to relate better to him than to Trevor. He dutifully made copies of the various papers Trevor produced. It was only with Richard that he smiled and, once or twice, chatted.

Trevor's account of Alan's seduction would have been disgusting if true. Richard was perfectly certain that there wasn't a grain of truth in it and listened with interested amusement.

"He's got a lovely cock!" said Trevor. "All of seven inches, maybe more. But his ass! Bloody breathtaking!"

"And you availed yourself of it, did you?" asked Richard, sipping his beer and crossing his legs at the same time.

"Did I ever! Right up. A bit difficult at first but he wanted it badly."

Richard made a point of going to the photo copying room the following morning. Alan, apparently unaffected by his traumatic 'experiences' of the previous night, was at work.

"Did you have a good time with Trevor yesterday?" Richard asked.

"Oh yeah! We went to the Hare and Hounds. It's a nice pub. When do you want these ready?"

"Oh, any time. They're not important,"

The holiday in Germany had been Trevor's idea. He knew of a little hotel; more of a pub with bedrooms really. He also knew of a travel agent who sold cheap air tickets. More important, he said, the area was swarming with boys and young men who would do anything. At first Richard declined. His parents expected him to go on holiday with them and he intended to find a job for the rest of the summer vacation.

Trevor's tales of Rainer, of Georg, and Peter, all aged from sixteen to eighteen and willing to do whatever the English guests wanted, weakened his resolve. Trevor had photographs of them. Rainer, Georg and Peter were good looking boys and the photographs, taken by a flooded quarry in which they had been swimming were interesting. There was no sign, in their faces, of the wildly improbable orgy which, according to Trevor, had happened in the bushes earlier.

Richard was not at all surprised to be told, when they arrived, that Rainer, Georg and Peter had gone away. Certainly there were numerous attractive boys around. They crowded into the bar in the afternoons and evenings but seemed far more interested in the various automatic machines than in the two Englishmen. It was certainly pleasant to watch them, clad in the briefest and tightest shorts Richard had ever seen, bending over the pool table and Trevor's comments, hopefully incomprehensible to them, were less embarrassing than they had been at home. There were three boys at the pool table that Sunday night.

"What wouldn't I give to screw that one with the blond hair!" said Trevor. "What about you?"

"No thanks."

"There must be one you fancy."

"Not really. Are you ready to eat yet? I'm hungry."

"So am I, but not for roast pork and bloody dumplings. Talking of which, I'll bet that tall one has a nice pair!"

It happened that Richard had been watching the boy for some time. He looked about eighteen and there was a distinct bulge in his leather shorts.

"Nice German sausage too, I shouldn't wonder," said Trevor. Richard, with an identical thought in mind, nodded. He really was a stunning looking boy. For another half an hour, Trevor and he watched the game – or rather the players – intently before going into dinner. When they came out, the cues were in their clips and there was no sign of the three lads. They had a few beers and then went up to their room. They hadn't been in bed for more than a few minutes before Trevor started.

"That blond one would screw well," he said.

"Mmm."

"Did you see that look he gave me?"

According to Trevor, the boy had made signals throughout the evening. Richard hadn't noticed as much as a glance.

"If only I spoke the bloody language!" said Trevor. "It would be easy then. Bring him up here, work him up a bit.. You know, feel around. He'd soon have his shorts off. What wouldn't I give for a chance to push my cock up his ass! I wonder if he's had it before. Probably has. Most of them do it."

Richard listened with equanimity. It was when Trevor turned his attention to the tallest of the boys that his comments had an effect.

"Those legs!" he said. "I've never seen anything like them!" Neither had Richard. Hoping that Trevor wasn't looking, he reached under the bedclothes and grasped his cock.

"So bloody graceful!" Trevor continued. Richard thought the same. "And those leather shorts. Just open the flap and it would jump out at you. I'll bet it's bloody enormous. You could see that when he stood up."

"I never really noticed," said Richard. In fact he could have told Trevor that the flap was secured by six buttons, one of which was not original, that a strand of cotton hung from the bottom of the shorts and that the side seam had been re-sewn.

"I'm not much into sucking cock myself," said Trevor conversationally. "A lot of people are."

33

Richard's cock was as hard as iron. "Do shut up, Trev," he said. "I'm trying to get to sleep." It wasn't true. If only Trevor would write his diary and then turn the light off, Richard could indulge in a pleasant fantasy. Trevor's comments were relevant but not necessary.

"I'm not a bit tired," said Trevor. "I think I'll have a wank."

"Please yourself."

"Not as good as having someone suck it and not as good as getting it into an asshole but buggers can't be choosers, eh?"

Richard heard him pull the quilt back. Surely he wasn't going to do it so openly? He turned his head towards Trevor. He was! It stood up rigidly from his groin. Richard had never seen it before. He had often wondered what it looked like. He'd watched Trevor playing football several times – just to get a good look at his friend's powerful legs and try to estimate its size. It was enormous!

"Good old John – Thomas," said Trevor, fondling it. "You're going to be a bit disappointed tonight, I'm afraid unless...."

"Unless what?" Richard asked. He hadn't wanted to speak but couldn't help himself.

"Unless you feel like helping out."

"What's the time?"

"Eleven thirty."

"Could do I suppose. We don't have to get up early." With what he hoped look like reluctance, he climbed out of bed.

"Looks like you need it too," said Trevor, laughing.

"Your fault. Talking about that tall boy."

"I thought I was right. Come and get a good mouthful of this."

It was the most enjoyable night of Richard's life. There had been incidents at school and one at university but a teenager with his pants round his ankles, terrified that someone would interrupt them or a student who came with enormous pleasure and then bundled him out of the house as if he had some dreadful disease couldn't be compared with Trevor! He got the impression that even if someone were to burst into the room, Trevor wouldn't mind. The feel and the taste of that enormous cock in his mouth were incredible and Trevor was so enthusiastic; so full of.... zest!

"Get down and lick my balls!" instead of "Hurry up. Someone might come!" – a remark which had amused Richard at the time. "Oh yes! That feels great!" instead of "Don't do that. It tickles."

He didn't really want Trevor to do what he did at three o'clock in the morning but it would have been churlish to refuse and Trevor had been, as he promised he would be, patient and gentle. It hadn't hurt nearly so much as Richard had feared. In fact, once it was in, it felt rather nice. There was something strangely comforting and amusing in knowing, as he climbed exhausted back into his own bed, that Trevor's sperms were in both ends of his alimentary tract.

The three boys were in the bar again the following night. Trevor started up again.

"That boy's ass gets more inviting by the hour!" he exclaimed. Richard had similar impressions of the tall boy but they were centered in his front rather than rear.

They finished one game. The tall boy fumbled in the pocket of his lederhosen and brought out a handful of change. Another did the same. The tall boy put down his cue and came over to them. He said something in German and held out a handful of coins.

"They want change for the pool table," said Rainer. Richard reached into his pocket.

"Oh! You are English?"

"Yes. What do you need?" asked Richard.

"Have you got a two Mark coin?"

"Plenty. How many do you need?"

"Only one for one game."

Richard handed over the necessary coin. The boy filled his hand with small change. "You also play this game in England?" the boy asked.

"Sometimes. We call it pool."

"Also us. You would like to play? My name is Michael."

Richard introduced himself and Trevor. "You also wish to play with us?" asked Michael. Trevor grinned and said he would watch. Richard knew what he was thinking.

The backside Trevor had so much admired belonged to Florian. He and Michael were seventeen. The other boy, Hans -Peter, was eighteen. The played and, foresee ably, the Germans won. They played again and the Germans won again.

"My friend knows three other boys from this village. Rainer, Georg and Peter. Do you know them?" Richard asked.

"Oh yes," said Michael. I know them good. They make holiday with their girl friends."

35

"I didn't know they had girl friends. How long have they known them?"

"Maybe two, maybe three years. Georg is, so to say, promised."

"Engaged. Well, wish them all the best when they get back."

Richard put his cue back into the rack and rejoined Trevor. He said nothing about Rainer, Peter and Georg. It was best, he thought, to let Trevor indulge in his fantasies.

"Invite them over to join us," said Trevor. Richard did so. Quite apart from the delights Michael and Florian sported under their shorts, they were good company. Hans Peter seemed somewhat taciturn but that, Richard thought, was probably a question of language. Florian and Michael spoke English quite well. He wondered how much they had understood of Trevor's conversation the previous day. Probably nothing, he thought, or they wouldn't have wanted to sit with them.

The conversation turned to music. It turned out that Florian and Michael shared Trevor's taste exactly. It was, thought Richard ruefully, the only taste they did share but he could hardly complain when Trevor invited them upstairs to listen to his portable C D player. Richard was left with Hans – Peter, and Hans – Peter was hard going.

"What do you do for a living?" Richard asked.

"Wie bitte? Say it again please."

"What is your job?"

"I am Kaufmann."

"What's that?"

"I am sell things."

"What sort of things?"

"Wie bitte? Say it again please." And so it went on. An hour went by at the end of which Richard knew that Hans – Peter was waiting to be called up to go into the army; that he was a salesman for an agricultural implements company and that he had three younger brothers.

Finally, Trevor and the other two re-appeared. "I think now it is late and we must go home," said Michael. Will you be tomorrow here?"

"Yes."

"Oh, that is good. I look forward on it. Good night."

They went upstairs. The C D player was still out on Trevor's bed. "That Hans Peter is a nice enough lad, said Richard, "but it was hard going talking to him. "I was praying that you would come back."

"Too busy. I had my hands full." said Trevor. He put the player back in a drawer and began to undress.

"You wish you had, you mean."

"No. Honestly. I had my hands on their cocks."

"I don't believe you."

"Please yourself but I did. Through their shorts of course."

"And they let you?"

"Sure. We were right about Michael. Florian's not got a lot up front but Christ, what an ass! Do you feel like it tonight?"

"Not really," said Richard. He was beginning to go off Trevor. He was bitterly disappointed but he knew he could never establish a relationship with such a born romancer.

"Please yourself," said Trevor. He got into bed and started to write his diary. Richard fell asleep.

Florian and Michael appeared at seven o'clock the following evening. "Where's Hans Peter?" Richard asked.

"He is with his girl friend out." said Florian.

"And do you have girl friends?"

"Of course." So much for Trevor's story! thought Richard. They played one game of pool and sat down.

"Florian, have you heard 'Lunatic Fringe' asked Trevor.

"No. I don't think so."

"I've got it upstairs. Do you want to hear it."

"Yes, please." Both boys stood up.

"Better for you to stay down here with Richard, Michael," said Trevor. "He doesn't like it." Michael sat down again.

"You do not like Trevor's music?" he asked.

"Not at all. Thank God he's got headphones." Michael laughed.

"But you enjoyed it yesterday afternoon?" asked Richard.

"Yes, it was okay. Florian like it better than I."

"You couldn't have heard a whole C D surely?"

"Oh, no. Two tracks only."

"What else did you do? You were upstairs for an hour."

"Only talk."

"About?"

"Oh many things. Trevor is a nice person. We like him. You too. You are also a nice person."

"Trevor gets carried away at times," said Richard.

"Please?"

"Oh, nothing. Another game?"

Michael agreed. They played. Richard won. They played again. Michael won. A third game was necessary. Richard looked at his watch. Almost two hours had elapsed since Trevor and Florian went upstairs. They played – and Richard won again.

"That was good," said Michael.

Richard excused himself to go to the toilet but, in fact, took the other staircase. He stopped outside the door to their room. He could hear no music but it was possible, he thought, that they were using the headphones. He was about to open the door when he heard Trevor's voice.

"That's right. Put your legs wider apart. Yes. That's just right."

Richard let go of the door handle as if it had been electrified. It was, he thought, just possible that Trevor was showing Florian some position connected with football. Surely he couldn't be...

Bed-springs creaked loudly. He heard Florian gasp and then cry out. Trevor murmured something. Florian replied but so softly that Richard couldn't hear what he said. He went downstairs with his mind whirling. Could it all be true after all? It certainly sounded like it.

"Sorry I took so long," he said. "I nipped upstairs to get a map but Florian and Trevor seemed to be busy so I didn't disturb them."

"What sort of map?" asked Michael.

"Oh, just the one of the local area. I was going to get you to show me the best places to go."

"What do you like to do?"

Well, thought Richard, here we go.... "Drinking cream," he said.

"There is a very good dairy in the town. I could show you where it lies."

"No. I mean, er, sort of sucking cream out of long German cakes."

"Eclairs. There is also a cake shop. We also have very good buns in Germany."

"Yes, so Trevor said."

"With cream it is important that it is fresh I think," said Michael.

"Absolutely right. As fresh as possible."

"Oh, good!" said Michael. For an instant Richard's heart beat faster. "Here is Florian," Michael added. Trevor and Florian joined them.

"Nice music?" Richard asked.

"Very nice," said Florian. "I think we must go home now. He turned to Trevor. "In the afternoon?" he said.

"Sure. I'll be waiting for you."

"Meaning?" Richard asked when they had gone out.

I was going to ask you to make yourself scarce for a couple of hours. That lad is coming on nicely. I think I might be lucky tomorrow if I take my time."

- — -

"Yes... a good day. He's coming on nicely," Trevor repeated putting the diary away.

"So what did you actually do?" asked Richard.

"Oh, not a lot. Got his clothes off, felt around a bit. Showed him the erotic possibilities of his asshole. He's never been fucked, which is a bit of luck."

"That sounds like a lot to me."

Trevor chuckled. "It was," he said. "Hang on. It must still be here. Ah, yes."

Something flopped moistly against the wall by Richard's bed.

"What is it?" he asked.

"My handkerchief loaded with Florian's spunk. God! Does that boy come!"

"I don't think I want it on my bed, thank you," said Richard. "You can have it back." He got out of bed, picked up the handkerchief by its corner and carried it over to Trevor. He dropped it onto the bed cover and stood there.

"Actually...." said Trevor.

"Yes?"

"There's a lot to be said for a twenty year old British asshole as well."

"And for twenty-two-year-old British cock," said Richard, peeling back the quilt and climbing into the warmth of Trevor's bed.

- — -

39

"Florian is listening to music all the afternoon," said Michael.

"I know."

"What shall we do?"

"Trevor told me there is a flooded quarry near here."

"Oh yes. It is not far. You wish me to take you there?"

"Why not?"

They set off. At times the path was narrow and passed between dense bushes. Richard let Michael go first. Those shorts, he thought, were an utter delight. They might have been molded onto the boy. Every contour was clearly visible. When Michael stood to one side to hold a branch back the enticing bulge in the front seemed somehow even larger in the daylight.

"Here it is," said Michael as they pushed through the last bush. It was huge. Great granite cliffs on the other side rose above the dark surface of the water.

"We swim here sometimes," said Michael.

"So I heard." Richard sat down on the grass and threw a pebble into the water.

"What shall we do now?" asked Michael.

"I don't know."

"We could swim."

"Not me. I haven't got my things with me."

"Nor I also, but there is nobody to see."

"You swim. I'll watch."

He did! Michael peeled off his tee shirt. Richard had never seen a torso so beautifully suntanned. Michael's sneakers and socks joined the tee-shirt on the grass. Michael grinned and then began to unbutton the shorts. He turned, modestly, to face the water and let them fall. Richard hoped that his heavy breathing was inaudible from that distance. The boy was absolutely beautiful. His honey, colored torso and darker brown legs contrasted wonderfully with the milky whiteness of his butt. He stood poised on the edge for a split second and then disappeared with a splash into the water. Richard watched him. He was a good swimmer. Once he turned over to wave allowing Richard a brief glimpse of a dark patch at his midriff and something large which flopped from one thigh to the other as he turned over again.

The minutes went by. The only sounds were Michael's splashing, the song of birds in the bushes and the distant hum of traffic. Richard chewed a piece of grass, folded Michael's clothes, and then had an idea. He didn't fancy swimming. He wasn't very good at it. He could sunbathe though. There wasn't a soul around. He peeled off his clothes, rolled his jeans to form a pillow and lay down. High above him a skylark sang. He wondered what Trevor was doing at that moment but such thoughts were likely to have a noticeable physical effect. Wondering about the maximum depth of the water made him think about Michael. That was worse. He turned his head to one side. Michael's folded shorts came into view. That was worse still.

A few spots of water landed on his legs. "Ah! That was so good!" He looked up again to see Michael towering over him.

"So you enjoy the sun bathing?"

"Yes," Richard replied shading his eyes to catch his first good view of a German penis. It hung limply between Michael's legs and swayed gently from side to side. It wasn't so much its length but its bulk which impressed Richard. It must, he thought, be an inch thick.

"How are you going to dry?" he asked lazily.

"The sunshine will do that." Michael lay beside him. "It is good here, you think?" he asked.

"Very good," said Richard. He was dying to turn his head towards the boy but continued to look at the sky.

"There is nobody to disturb," said Michael. "All the people who come here make holiday."

There was a long pause. Richard wondered if he should correct the sentence and decided not to. He was, after all, not an English teacher and 'on holiday' was just as odd when one stopped to think about it.

"Nobody at all," said Michael. There was another pause.

"Here you could eat the cream éclairs and nobody to see," Michael continued.

"Save that the cake shop is about a mile away," said Richard. Michael said nothing. He didn't have to. Richard felt wet fingers go round his wrist, lift his hand and deposit it on something soft, damp and surrounded by wet, bristly hair.

"I think you do not have to go that far," said Michael and the softness began to harden almost immediately. Richard wrapped his fingers round it. He could feel it pulsing.

"I shall come nearer," said Michael. He stood up and arranged his clothes in a line down Richard's right side. His cock pointed outwards and cast a shadow on the grass. It was huge; bigger,

Richard thought, than Trevor's and, somehow, much nicer looking. As Michael lay down again he could see the pink tip poking out from the puckered foreskin.

"There!" said Michael. His left leg pressed against Richard's. It felt cool and damp. Richard's cock rose. Michael laughed. Richard grasped his cock again. "A good éclair?" Michael asked.

"Delicious!" said Richard. "Just how I like them." It was his turn to change position. Michael opened his legs and Richard lay between them so that his head was above Michael's navel. With his hands on the boy's damp thighs, he lowered his lips on to it. Michael said something in German. Holding the skin between his lips, Richard slid his mouth down the stiff shaft. Michael sighed. He tasted superb. The slightly brackish, muddy odor from the water gave way to a healthy, male taste. It was strong, slightly musky and unbelievably exciting. He put a hand under Michael's balls. Michael groaned and spread his legs wider apart. Richard let his cock slip out of his mouth and moved downwards slightly so that he could press his head as far as possible into the boy's damp crotch. Blades of grass got into his mouth and on one occasion he had to spit one out. The boy at school had tasted good but was hardly responsive. The student had been responsive enough. Michael tasted better than both and, even in those first few seconds, proved his enjoyment. He drew up his legs, spread them outwards and put his hands under his butt to press himself on to Richard's searching tongue.

Once again Richard took his cock between his lips and let it slide into his mouth. He rubbed the inside of Michael's thighs with the palms of his hands and sucked on it. Michael gasped and then groaned. It hammered at the back of Richard's throat.

"Ah! Ah! Ah! Ah!" Michael panted. Desperately, Richard tried to hold him still.

"Ah! Ah! Ah! Ah!" he continued and then.... surely not? It couldn't happen quite so soon – not after last night. But it did. He felt it, warm and wet on his thigh. Damn! He thought. But it made no difference to Michael who writhed, heaved and gasped and who might, if it were not for his distinctly human taste and smell, have been an animal. Trevor had been good. Trevor had been excellent but Trevor had been nothing like this. Richard held on the boy's thighs with his hand. He felt Michael's pubic hair against his nose.

Michael gave one huge upward heave. Richard choked slightly as it flooded into his mouth. He tried to swallow but couldn't.

It dripped out of his mouth and fell in long streams onto Michael's still belly. Michael lay passive and smiling.

"That was good!" he said. "You like our German cream?"

"Delicious!" Richard replied, wiping his mouth on the back of his hand.

Michael got to his feet. Richard clambered up and began to brush the grass from Michael's back.

"Tomorrow..." said Michael.

"Yes?" Richard wiped away more grass, lingering slightly on Michael's firm, round buttocks.

"Maybe you like to try German buns," said Michael.

Richard, kneaded them gently, "And fill them with cream!" he said. "That sounds like a very good idea!"

JUST THIS ONCE...
Leo Cardini

"Gee, Eddie. I don't know about this."

"Aw. C'mon, Wally."

"But I don't think we should be in here."

At Eddie's insistence, we had just entered the old science building. Not the new Eisenhower Science Center completed three years ago just in time to usher in the sixties, but the original red brick building that's hardly used for anything anymore.

"Listen, Wally. I'm telling you we're not going to get into any kind of trouble. I mean, if we weren't supposed to be in here, why would they keep it unlocked?"

"Then how come you were so careful no one saw us enter?"

"Heh, heh. You'll see. Now just stop whining and follow me."

"Well, maybe just this once."

"Good. See, while you were in the library last weekend, too busy studying to hang out, your good friend Eddie did a little snooping around."

"But you don't even go to college here!"

"Yeah? Well, I could've. If I wanted to."

Which wasn't quite true.

It was really kind of spooky walking into the old science building again. Dust hung suspended in the air, and the worn, warped floorboards creaked with every step we took.

Eddie turned up the collar of his tan Barracuda jacket – which he thinks makes him look cool – and led me down the left arm of the wide, high-ceilinged central corridor that ran at right angles to the front entrance. Wordlessly, we walked past the old wooden doors of the labs and classrooms with the room numbers stenciled on their large, opaque windowpanes.

The only sign of life in the building was the thin, tinny sound of a radio news broadcast issuing from behind one of the lab doors – something about what President Kennedy had said that morning.

At the end of the corridor we were forced to turn right where it elled into a shorter, narrower corridor, until we reached dead end at the entrance to the first floor men's room.

Eddie opened the men's room door and entered. Surprised that I was actually doing it, I followed him in. Strange, but the lights were on, although the four dim white globes hanging high above us didn't provide much illumination, since two of them had burned out.

The men's room was even creepier than the corridors. The sound of our footsteps seemed magnified as we walked across the white-turned-grey tile floor with years of dirt ground in between each small, six-sided tile. To our right, five porcelain sinks with mirrors above them stood silently, except for one leaky faucet whose persistent poing-poing-poing echoed throughout the room. Beyond them, two old-fashioned urinals going all the way down to the floor rested in disuse. Five wooden stalls ran along the opposite wall, all with their doors ajar, except for the one in the middle.

"Okay, Eddie, what are we doing here?"

Eddie raised his right index finger, pressed it vertically against his lips, and silently mouthed, "Shhh!"

He very quietly walked over to the middle stall – the one with the closed door – until he was about two yards away from it. He bent over and looked under its door. Then he moved to the stall to the left of it, pushed its door all the way open, stepped in, and gestured for me to follow.

I scrunched my face up into a question mark, and mouthed, "What?"

Eddie scowled. I could tell he was getting impatient with me.

I practically tip-toed over, though I had no idea why we were being so quiet, and entered the stall.

It seemed kind of perverted to be in a men's room stall with another guy – even though he was my best friend – especially since in order to shut the door behind me, I had to almost press my body against his. I came so close to him I could practically feel the space between us.

And when he leaned forward and reached behind me to lock the door, I could actually feel his chest pressing against mine. His belt buckle rubbed against me just above my navel, since he's six-two and I'm only five-eleven, and his crotch pressed against my lower abdomen. I was so embarrassed, I could feel my cheeks flush.

Then he stepped back as far as the toilet would allow. He pointed at the graffiti-covered partition that separated this stall from the middle one next to it.

Waist high, there was a crude-cut hole in the middle of it, about eight inches in diameter.

"Look," he whispered, with a smirk on his face.

I peered through the hole. From where I was standing, I could only make out the right leg and lowered jeans and briefs of someone seated on the toilet.

"Eddie, what the heck are we doing in here spying on someone taking a crap?"

"Look again, kiddo."

This time I bent forward when I looked. Whoever it was, not only did he have his jeans and briefs down all the way to his ankles, but he had his legs spread wide open, and he was sitting there stroking his cock! His swollen mushroom of a cockhead capped a long, rock hard cockshaft that curved slightly inwards like it was trying to reach above his bush of dark brown pubic hair to kiss his belly button. He was stroking it with long, slow strokes. His two big balls, enclosed in their brownish ballsac, followed the course dictated by his cock-clenched fist, ascending and descending between his spread apart, muscular thighs.

Not that I pay much attention to guys' crotches, or stuff like that, but how often do you find yourself watching someone masturbate in a men's room?

"Eddie, let's get out of here."

I felt bad for the guy because I know how hard it is for me to find privacy whenever I want to jack off at home. You see, I share a bedroom with my younger brother, Teddy, and he seems to have the knack of walking into the room at just the wrong time, like that afternoon he almost caught me experimenting by rubbing my cock with his old Davy Crockett cap. And I swear whenever I try to lock the bathroom door, my father's always there knocking on it with his, "You all right in there, son?" like he knew exactly what I was doing.

"Relax, Wally. Watch this. Heh, heh."

Eddie might be my best friend, but I hate the way he goes "Heh, heh" when he laughs. It always makes him sound like he's trying to put something over on someone, which he often is, except it usually backfires on him.

Eddie unbuckled his belt and lowered his polished chinos and BVDs all the way down to his ankles.

When he stood up again, his over-sized cockhead poked out between the front of the shirttails of his madras shirt, looking like an actor peeking from behind a closed curtain to check out the audience.

He unbuttoned his shirt all the way down the front, exposing his tall, wiry body without an ounce of fat on it. A sparse fuzz of curly, golden blond hair covered his chest, descending in a narrow line to his tight abdomen, and below to the overgrowth of pubic hair above his huge, heavy-hanging cock. Like I said before, it's not that I go around looking at other guy's cocks or anything, but Eddie's is so large you can't help not noticing it. It was like his cock had taken over his body and drained it every ounce it could spare until it had grown into this huge, swollen monster several sizes too large for its master. Even his balls were big, and they hung low in his pale, practically hairless ballsac.

Eddie saw me staring at his cock. I got really embarrassed, because every time he catches me doing it, he gives me one of those nasty "heh-hehs" of his, like he'd caught me doing something perverted.

The truth is, though, that he loves it when guys stare at his cock, and he takes every opportunity to show it off. Well, he's kind of a jerk and a loser, so I guess it's one of the few ways he can feel superior to the rest of the guys.

Anyhow, Eddie took his right hand and started yanking on his cock, stretching its soft, rubbery length. I was beginning to feel real creepy about being in there with him, but I couldn't help watching as his cock stiffened. You know, it's so big that when he gets hard, it still hangs down in front of him. Not like mine, which stands at attention, which can sometimes be embarrassing if you get hard at the wrong time, like in the locker room after gym class. I mean, when the guys start talking about girls, or stuff.

Once Eddie got his cock as hard as it gets, he let go of it so that it flopped down in front of him.

He looked at me, smiled, and then pointed at the hole again.

Whoever was in the next stall, he had moved his face close to the hole and was looking in at us.

Then I saw who it was!

Bud!

That was all I needed! Now, Eddie's always getting me into trouble, but this took the cake.

You see, Bud and I are both freshmen, and he shares the dorm room right next to mine.

I mean, supposing he went blabbing around that he'd seen me crowded into a men's room stall with another guy! It did look kind of suspicious, you know – like we were fooling around with each other, or something.

But before I could figure out what to do, Bud put his free hand up to the hole and waved his fingers in this beckoning gesture.

Did he want me to put my ear to the hole to tell me something? But he wasn't looking at me. He was looking at Eddie's cock!

Before I could figure things out, Eddie shifted his position so he was facing the hole, and Bud moved his face even closer until his mouth was dead center in the middle of it.

Eddie slowly pushed his cock forward until the first several inches of it entered the hole. And do you know what Bud did? He took it right into his mouth and wrapped his lips around it!

"Ooh!" Eddie moaned as he pushed a little more of his cock into Bud's mouth. I heard a muffled gag issue from Bud's throat.

Now, if you'd ever told me that Bud would do a thing like that, I wouldn't have believed you. I mean, he's just as regular a guy as you'd ever hope to meet. He's always working on his old jalopy, or playing basketball, or joking around with the guys in the dorm. And there's nothing effeminate or soft about him. I mean, I'd seen him countless times in the buff toweling himself off after a shower, and I'd always admired the way he kept his trim, compact body in shape.

Come to think of it, he spent an awful lot of time in the shower room horsing around with the other guys. And then he was always running around the dorm wearing nothing but his briefs, and bursting into your room unexpectedly, trying to crack you up by breaking into a song like "My Boyfriend's Back," though I gotta admit his high-pitched Angel's imitation wasn't bad.

And there he was, sucking off my best friend.

Eddie looked over at me and winked.

"Didn't I say I had a surprise in store for you? You're next. And believe me, he's really good at it. It's a rare guy who can take every last bit of good ole Mister Ed into his mouth."

He calls his cock Mister Ed because he says it's large enough to be a horse's.

Then Eddie pulled his cock almost all the way out of the hole again. It flopped out of Bud's mouth and he pulled his face away from the hole. With his free hand – the one that wasn't still working on his cock – Bud reached through the hole, grabbed Eddie by the balls and pulled them through. Eddie's body yanked forward, like his cock was an arrow shot out of the bow of his body, until his abdomen was pressed flat against the partition.

"Woah!" Eddie exclaimed. "Hungry little cocksucker, isn't he?"

To keep his balance, Eddie raised his hands up along the stall partition until he could curl his fingers over the top of it. But his chin forced his head backwards, so he turned towards me, pressing his left cheek as close against the wall as the rest of his body.

Then Eddie closed his eyes. I could read in his face the pleasure he was receiving from the other side of the partition. First, he just stood there with his mouth open, looking blissful. Then a prolonged, practically silent "Ohh!" streamed out of his mouth. Gradually, the muscles around his eyes and mouth tightened as his face contorted into a grimace, reflecting that odd mix of pain and pleasure you feel as you approach orgasm.

The meandering "Ohh!" turned into an urgent, steadily increasing "Ahh!" as his facial muscles strained all the harder. He tightened his grip on the partition, and tensed his ass and leg muscles, pressing his hips all the more forcefully against the partition.

"Yeah! That's it! That's it! All the way down your throat! Ahhhh!"

That last "Ahh!" seemed to last forever, and it was so loud I was afraid someone might hear us.

But Eddie wasn't finished! He'd come once, yet he couldn't stop! Now the "Ahhs!" became intermittent, stabbing the silence of the men's room again and again as Eddie tilted his head backwards and violently jerked it back and forth. In each toss of his head I could glean the excess of pleasure that exploded throughout his body with every new spurt of cum.

For a while there he seemed so out of control that I was afraid he'd damage the partition by yanking it out of place, but when all the unbelievable orgasms worked their way out of him his body finally ebbed to a restful state once more. I was speechless. My mouth hung open; I'd never seen anything like it.

When he disengaged himself from the partition and pulled his cock out again, it was still half-hard, lazily flopping down in front of him.

He turned to me with a, "Heh, heh," as he lifted his chinos and briefs up again. "See. Didn't I tell you I had a surprise in store for you?"

"My god! But what'd he do when you were coming?"

"What do you think he did? He swallowed it."

"He swallowed it!"

"Of course he swallowed it."

"Down his throat?"

Eddie tossed me one of his "How stupid can you be?" looks.

"Gee," was all I could manage to say.

The image of Bud's Adam's apple bobbing up and down as he swallowed volley after volley of Eddie's spurting cum flashed into my mind. As did the quick conjecture of how it would feel to stick my own cock in some guy's mouth.

"By the way, Eddie, how'd you find out about this place?"

Now, for once in his life, Eddie was speechless.

He stalled with "Um," while he zipped and buckled and buttoned himself back into place all the faster.

"And what did you mean when you said its a rare guy who can take all of your cock into his mouth?"

Well, Eddie, face turned red and he put on this big act of anxiously looking at his watch.

"Cripes! Look at the time! I'm gonna be late for work! So I'll leave first, okay? You stay here for a couple of minutes. We don't want anyone see the two of us leave this stall at the same time, you know."

"But, Eddie, there's no one else in here except for Bud, and he knows we're in here together!"

"No. Let's not take any chances. See ya later, Wally."

By then, he had his shirt and pants in place again and he rushed out, leaving me there alone to puzzle what the heck was going on.

Well, I felt kind of funny just standing in the stall like that. Supposing someone did see me come out just after Eddie? So I turned around, faced the toilet, and unzipped my chinos. I snaked my cock out of the front opening of my Jockey shorts and held it in my left hand, aiming it at the toilet bowl.

51

I could see out of the corner of my eye that Bud was staring at me through the hole. I felt as conspicuous as could be and my cock got this tingly feeling, like I could practically feel his eyes running up and down all over it.

You know how sometimes when you have to piss, the piss just won't come out? Like when you're standing at a urinal and there are guys on either side of you? For me, it's like the more I don't want the guys next to me think I'm standing at the urinal just to peek at their cocks, the more the piss won't come out.

A lot of times I just give up trying to piss, shake my dick like I'm jiggling off the final drops, and zip up. But you know, once when I did that, I had to piss so badly I went into the next men's room I came to. And the guy who entered next and stood in the urinal beside me was the same one who was pissing beside me in the other men's room. I recognized him instantly because he was wearing a maroon Barracuda jacket. Yeah, not tan like the rest of the guys, but maroon – and you know what they say about guys who wear maroon Barracuda jackets, especially on Thursdays.

Anyhow, this was one of those occasions when the piss wouldn't come out.

You know how sometimes your cock starts to get hard just when you don't want it to? Like during class three minutes before the bell's going to ring to signal the end of the period? Well, standing in that stall with Bud's eyes glued to my cock, it started to stiffen right then and there, like it was playing a dirty trick on me by pretending to advertise that I wanted my cock sucked, too.

At first I tried to hide it by just holding it aimed at the toilet, but as it kept getting harder I couldn't do that anymore. You see, when my cock gets hard, its gets absolutely rock hard. Not like Eddie's. And it sticks straight up. Well, it got to the point I couldn't hide it anymore. I mean, there it was, curving upwards, battling against my hand, and my hand was losing the battle.

So I finally let go of it.

I heard Bud say, "Jeez!"

I turned my head and looked at the hole. His face was still close up to it. And he had his free hand there beckoning me to stick my cock through!

"C'mon, Wally. Do a fellow frosh a favor, huh?"

I couldn't believe he was actually talking to me! I mean, it's one thing to suck someone's cock – I think – but another thing to talk to them about it. It just seemed to strange that someone like Bud was doing something like that.

I mean, was this the same Bud Anderson I always saw outside the dorm working on his car, lying on his back underneath it hidden from the waist up, chanting some top-thirty song like "Duke of Earl"? Who'd ever have thought looking at him at a moment like that he'd rather be between some guy's legs than under the chassis of his car, and that he'd prefer cum down his throat to grease on his hands?

I just stood there and my erection wouldn't go away. I looked at Bud. His eyes caught mine, he smiled – gosh, he's handsome – and he coaxed me with a nod and a "C'mon."

I couldn't believe it when I actually turned towards him. It was like I had stepped out of myself. Against my will, I felt my cock moving towards Bud like iron towards a magnet.

Bud's eyes focused right on it. His mouth fell open with awe as he lost himself in contemplation of my hard-on.

I looked down at my cock and tried to imagine what there was about it that he enjoyed so much. Its thickness? The prominent blue veins that meander along its underside? Its eight and a half inches?

Yeah, I measured it once. Well, both Eddie and I did together. He kept suggesting it until I finally gave in one afternoon when we were at his house and his parents were out. We went up to his bedroom, pulled down our pants, played with our cocks until they were hard, and measured them with a wooden ruler. And I know he's never going to let me forget he's got nine and three quarter inches. Only Eddie would count the quarter-inches in order to brag.

Seeing Bud looking at my cock, it involuntarily twitched.

When it did, Bud stretched out a slow, whispered "Wow!"

So then I deliberately made it twitch.

This time Bud's eyes opened wide as he inhaled a slow, audible "Ahhh!"

Through the hole, I could make out Bud moving off the toilet to reposition himself on his knees in front of me, all the time still stroking his cock.

I let my cock bob up in front of him with another twitch.

Bud slowly stuck out his tongue and then, without moving his face, looked up into my eyes.

I felt weird looking into his eyes at that moment. It just seemed too intimate, you know, to have a dorm mate silently begging you with outstretched tongue and eyes glued to yours to stick your cock in his mouth.

But still, I moved forward until my cock was dead center in front of the hole. Then I slowly inched it in.

I felt the tip of Bud's tongue against my piss slit. It was like a little pinprick of pleasure that caused my cock to jerk upwards. Bud continued to tease it again and again with the tip of his tongue. Soon he had it bouncing helplessly out of control, like the way you get when you lose your balance on one of those trampolines next to the miniature golf course.

He brought it to a halt by suddenly capturing my cockhead tightly between his lips. I could tell he wanted more of my cock, so I gradually arched my body forwards, feeling it slip into his warm, wet mouth.

He slowly moved his mouth up and down my cockshaft. Not all the way, though, because it seemed like there was about an inch too much of it for him. He just couldn't get it down his throat, probably because of its thickness.

Then Bud made one final effort and pushed his mouth onto my cock until I could feel it enter his throat. I heard him gag a couple of times, but that didn't stop him from keeping it there for a few seconds. The pleasure of my cockhead in his throat networked throughout my body and I involuntarily moaned.

When he resumed sucking on my cock, now taking all of it in with every suck stroke, the sensation was so overwhelming I could feel myself getting weak at the knees. Now I knew why Eddie had gripped his fingers over the top of the partition for support, and I did the same.

As soon as I did, I felt Bud's mouth dismount my cock. I remained in place pressed against the partition for a little longer, but, puzzled that his mouth didn't return to my cock, I stepped back, pulled my cock out of the hole, and peeked in to see what Bud was up to.

He was seated on the toilet again, still stroking his cock.

"C'mon over in here," he nodded, indicating the stall he was in.

"Gee, Bud. I don't know. Supposin' someone comes in here?"

"They won't notice. C'mon."

"Well...okay."

I had a hard time getting my cock back into my pants and zipping them up because it wouldn't go down. It tented out below my belt, threatening to announce my erection to anyone who might walk in.

I slowly opened the stall door so I'd have time to see if anyone one else was in the men's room. I heard Bud's stall door creak open and I quickly exited mine and slipped inside his. My heart was pounding as I closed the door behind me and locked it.

I turned and looked down at Bud. He had slipped off his tee shirt. Since his jeans and Fruit of the Looms were down to his ankles, I could see the whole of his fine, lean, young adult physique. I always figured he had a big cock when it was hard but seeing it close up like this, I appreciated just what a whopper it was. I would never had believed it could've grown so long.

He looked up at me and smiled, flashing his perfectly white teeth at me.

Then, as he unbuckled my belt, undid my chinos and slid them and my briefs down to my ankles, he said, "Oh, Wally. You don't know how many times I've looked at you and imagined what it would be like to have you rock hard in front of me like this."

Next, he unbuttoned my shirt.

"There," he said, indicating the hook on the back of the stall door. "Take it off and hang it on that hook."

"Are you sure we're not going to get into any trouble, Bud?"

"Listen. I've been here lots of times."

"You have?"

"Yeah. No one comes here unless it's for the same reason we're here."

"Now, wait a minute. I just came here because my best friend Eddie brought me here."

"Yeah. Sure."

He smiled and winked at me like we were co-conspirators.

I didn't bother to defend myself.

I twisted my upper body and put my shirt on the hook.

When I faced Bud again, I saw that his eyes had returned to my cock. It had remained hard all this time.

Then he put his right hand up to my ballsac and started fondling it with his fingers as he closely examined my balls.

55

No one had ever played with my balls before. And I'd always been a little embarrassed about them since one's slightly larger than the other. Not by much, but it's noticeable. Even when I'm hard and my ballsac contracts around them, pulling them close against the base of my cock, you can make out the difference in size. Now, subject to Bud's appreciative scrutiny, my embarrassment slipped away.

The novelty of the pleasure I was feeling between my legs as Bud stroked my balls caused an involuntary "Oh!" to issue from my mouth.

"You like that, huh?" Bud asked, looking up at me.

My cock jerked upwards in acknowledgement, pulling Bud's attention away from my eyes again.

He moved his face forward, opened his mouth, stuck out his tongue and slowly licked up the underside of my cock. When the tip of his tongue had reached my piss silt, he wrapped his lips around my cockhead and then gradually descended on it. I watched as my cock disappeared inch by inch into his mouth. I heard him gag again as I felt my cockhead in his throat.

I guess he really liked having cock in his throat because it was then that he started stroking his own cock all the faster.

He moved up and down my cock, slowly and steadily. Then, while he was still sucking me off, he took both hands and placed them on my thighs. He slowly moved them behind me and slid them up across my asscheeks.

I had never had another guy touch me like that before. I mean, I was used to horsing around with guys, and feeling them smack me on the ass, and stuff. I'd never had any guy's hands actually dwell on my asscheeks, evaluating them the way Bud was. His hands felt so firm and so sure of what they were doing that I think I actually liked it.

He molded his hands around the curvature of my asscheeks and pulled me towards him. At the same time, he repeatedly pushed his mouth all the way down on my cock until his nose was buried in my pubic hair.

Sandwiched between this embrace of mouth and hands, I could feel the cum churning up under my balls in no time. I closed my eyes to enjoy it, just the way I do when I jack off and I'm getting ready to come.

Then I heard the stall door next to ours shut! My eyes shot open as a lightning-quick wave of anxiety sped throughout my body. I hadn't even heard anyone enter the men's room! And to make matters worse, someone had cut out a hole on the partition separating these two stalls also, so anyone who was interested could see exactly what we were doing.

Bud took his mouth off my cock, looked up at me, and whispered, "Relax, will ya? No one's coming in here just to take a shit. They're coming in here for some action. So let's give him a helluva show and maybe we can get a group thing going."

Well, I didn't know if I wanted someone actually watching me get my cock sucked. And I was even less certain about getting a "group thing" going.

Before I could figure out what to do, you know what Bud did? He started licking my balls! I mean, with no embarrassment whatsoever, he just opened his mouth wide, stuck out his tongue, planted it way underneath my balls and gave them one slow, slurping lick after another while his left hand instinctively went back to his still-hard cock.

I must admit it felt good, though I'd never heard of anyone doing that before.

Meanwhile, whoever was in the stall next to us had finally sat down on the toilet and peeked through the hole.

Bud was still licking my balls when he looked towards the hole out of the corner of his eye.

When he saw who was there, he froze, his tongue halting midway up my ballsac.

He withdrew his tongue, sat up, and moved his own face close to the one staring at us through the hole.

"Jeff!" Bud exclaimed in amazement.

Yeah, Bud's roommate! Mary's kid brother.

"What the hell you doing here?" Jeff practically hissed at him.

"What am I doing here! What are you doing here?"

"Boy, what a big phony you are! After all your talk about us being faithful to each other, here I find you cheating on me with Wally. Hi, Wally."

"Uh...hi, Jeff."

"But I should've known," he continued. "It's always 'Isn't Wally good looking?' and 'Boy, that Wally sure has one hell of a body.' What a fool I've been not to suspect something like this was going on behind my back."

"Pipe down, huh? This just kinda happened."

"Well, it wouldn't have just kinda happened if you hadn't been here in the first place."

"Yeah? So what the hell are you doing here?"

"Oh...well...uh..."

"And I wouldn't be here if you'd let me chow down on your cock more often than you do. Every night it's the same thing. 'Oh, please! Stick the big cock of yours up my ass and fuck me real hard!' I'm tired of fucking you. I want to suck some dick!"

"That's all you ever have on your mind, sucking cock."

"Look who's talking! If you had your way, you'd even find a way to have cock up your ass while taking your final exams!"

"Yeah?"

"Yeah!"

"So?"

They'd reached an impasse and silently glared at each other. I stared in amazement at their two fuming faces as I thought of all the things that must have gone on in their dorm room while the rest of us just thought they were quietly studying.

Looking like they'd just read each other's thoughts, they both turned and looked up at me. I had lost some of my erection and my half-hard cock, eye level with their faces, was pointed at them like a nosy eavesdropper.

Then they turned back to each other and smiled.

Jeff's face left the hole, and from what little I could see, I could tell he had got up and put his jeans back into place, quickly exiting the stall.

Our stall door opened and in he squeezed.

"Hey, fellas," I said. "I think we're going to get in a mess of trouble if anyone walks in here."

They didn't seem to be bothered the way I was.

Jeff removed his tee shirt and put it on the hook over my shirt. Then, while lowering his jeans and briefs, he wedged himself in between Bud and me.

Bud took Jeff's cock in his mouth while Jeff put his left hand to his mouth, got his middle finger all wet and moved it down to his asshole, sticking it in to give it a lube job.

When he was done, he pulled his asscheeks apart, turned his head around to me and said, "Go ahead."

"Huh?"

"Stick it in."

"Won't it hurt?"

Bud took his mouth off Jeff's cock to say to me, "You kidding? He could take that friend of your's cock up his ass with room to spare."

"Yeah?"

"Yeah."

Then he resumed sucking on Jeff's cock.

My father always says that sometimes the most educational experiences at college happen outside the classroom. I don't think he ever had anything like this in mind!

Jeff pulled his asscheeks apart all the more and rotated his hips until my cockhead was pressed against his asshole.

"Go ahead. Push it in."

One slight push and it slid in easily. Now, I thought Bud's mouth on my cock felt good, but this was like nothing I'd ever experienced before. For one thing, Jeff's asshole was tighter than Bud's mouth.

"Just slide it in and out."

This wasn't as easy as I'd imagined, until Jeff helped out with, "Here. Put your hands on my hips, so you can keep your balance."

He reached behind himself, took my hands, and planted them on his hips. I was hesitant to hold him in such an intimate way, but it did make it easier for me to move my cock in and out of his ass. Before long, I was fucking him with smooth steady strokes. With each plunge into his asshole the sensations in my cock networked throughout my entire body.

I felt the steady bump of my abdomen against his asscheeks as I pushed him slightly forward with each cockthrust, forcing his own cock all the further down Bud's throat. Bud just took it in with funny mmph-ing sounds while he ran his fist up and down his own dick.

All this time Jeff had his eyes closed and his head tilted so far back it was resting on my right shoulder. His mouth was open and he kept moaning a soft, steady "Ohh!"

Soon I was close to coming, but I was enjoying myself so much I didn't want to yet. Without really planning what I was doing, I came to a stop with my cock all the way up his ass. I don't know what came over me, but my hands started to roam over his tightly-muscled, smooth-skinned body. They admired the tautness of his abdomen, brushing across the thin line of hair that descended from his navel into the fullness of his black pubic hair. Then they ascended up above his waist to his practically hairless chest – just a sparse bush of hair between his pectorals – until they reached his nipples. With my thumbs hitched under his armpits, the flat of my hands molded themselves to the contour of his pecs, brushing against the hardness of his nipples.

Jeff moaned all the louder and then, turning his head toward me, whispered, "Pinch them!"

"What?"

"Take them between your thumbs and forefingers and squeeze."

When I did, he closed his eyes again and continued moaning, forcing his chest out while grinding his ass against my hips.

All this time Bud never let up sucking on Jeff's cock while stroking his own.

I started pumping in and out of Jeff again while continuing to squeeze his nipples. This time my ascent to orgasm came all the faster, taking me by surprise. I lost control and I knew I was about to come at any second, so I placed my hands on Jeff's hips again to steady myself.

Jeff scrunched up his face and his prolonged "ohh!" increased in volume and intensity. He took Bud's head between his hands and directed his cocksucking with long, slow strokes. When he did that, Bud accelerated his cockstrokes and I could tell from the urgent, muffled sounds coming from his throat that he was on the verge of coming, too.

Suddenly, the three of us were coming! I felt the cum explode out of my cock and into Jeff's ass. The pleasure was so great it flooded my entire body. My cum seemed endless. Spurt after spurt overwhelmed me, each spurt firing a gunshot-quick "Ah!" from of my mouth, until I could feel myself getting weak at the knees.

Jeff held Bud's head firmly on his cock. His body kept jerking and I knew that every jerk told of an explosion of cum down Bud's throat.

When Jeff had finally come to rest and allowed Bud to remove his mouth from his cock, I saw that Bud, too, had indeed shot his load. His cum oozed down his cock and onto his fist, which was still wrapped around it. More was slowly dripping down his chest, proclaiming what a powerful cum-shooter he was.

After a pause, Bud said, "Whew!" and got all business-like about wiping the cum off him with toilet paper.

Jeff and I followed suit by pulling up our pants and briefs again

Now that we were done, I felt embarrassed about this situation all over again.

"Gee," I said, "It's a good thing no one else was in here, what with all the noise we made."

Jeff turned around and reached behind me to take our shirts off the hook. While he did, he pressed his body against mine, and before I had a chance to turn my head, he kissed me right on the lips.

"Yeah, it is," he said, after he'd kissed me, handing me my shirt, "but I'm still glad we risked it."

Jeff was the first of us to squeeze out of the stall. He walked over to the middle sink, pulled a out a pocket comb, wet it with faucet water, and combed his hair, nonchalantly whistling "I Will Follow Him," which struck me as funny, considering what had just gone on.

Bud followed, washing his hands at the sink to Jeff's left.

By the time I had gotten myself together again and left the stall, the two of them were arguing in whispered voices.

As I moved to the vacant sink next to Jeff and turned on the faucet to wash my hands, I heard Bud say to Jeff, "I guess we're just not compatible."

"Heck, fellows. You sure looked compatible in there."

"Yeah," Jeff said, "but that was just because you were in there with us, and..."

He stopped mid-sentence and turned towards Bud. Then they both turned towards me with wide grins on their faces.

"Say, Wally," Bud said. "Any plans for tonight?"

"Not really. Just hitting the books."

"Well, you could sure do us a favor if you drop by our room before going to bed."

"Gee, fellows. I don't know. I mean..."

But if you could only have seen the look of eager expectation on their faces.

"Well...maybe just this once."

RIDE WITH A STRANGER
John Patrick

We drifted to the dance floor. The music swept through me like the heat from my third beer and I swayed hypnotically to the music. I glanced to the man who had bought me the beers at the bar. He smiled.

It was a slow dance and he held me with intention, held me like a lover, held me like I, and no one else, belonged in his strong arms. I pressed into him, floated into the alluring scent of his cologne. Brut. I hated Brut, but on him it was perfect.

"Take you home?" he finally whispered in my ear.

"Ride with a stranger?" I murmured. After all, he was indeed a stranger. Never ride with strangers, never take their candy. The voice of my mother still haunted me twenty years later. "Do you also offer candy?" I had an impulsive urge to flirt with danger. Out-of-town boy climbs in car with butch stranger and disappears – tomorrow's headlines didn't faze me. In fact, at that moment, that headline seemed like good news. I thought my interview for a new job had gone badly and my only recourse was to return to New Mexico.

"Don't worry, pretty boy, I'm a cop." His tone blended reassurance with provocation. Stud man with a police badge was offering to take me home. I had a sudden fantasy of leaning over his car, legs spread, as he searched for illegal contraband. Then I wouldn't be stepping out on my lover back home. Then it wouldn't be cheating. I'd simply be a kid in town for a job interview, wrongly accused, victim of a corrupt cop. I hoped I looked suspicious.

He drove an old black Corvette ("undercover," he said with a wink) and we rode fast into the muggy night. At the beach, he showed me the restless ocean. A storm was blowing in. We stood there, in the moonlight, he behind me, grinding his hard-on into my ass. I thought for a moment he was going to take me right there, but, no, he was a gentleman. He wanted me in bed. "Should I take you home?" he asked, his voice cool as the night air had become.

"Yes, I suppose that would be the best," I said vaguely. I didn't want to go back to the hotel but the brisk air had a sobering effect and the hope of a police search was a fading fantasy.

He took me home all right, his home. A stained-glass lamp lit the small living room; otherwise the house was dark.

He slammed me up against the wall and held my face in front of him like he was going to kiss me. He was so close, I could feel his teeth on me, but he sideswiped my mouth and swung low with his head and sucked at my nipples through the T-shirt I was wearing.

He left me and went over to the couch, fluffing the pillows. Then he stared silently at me from the shadows as I shifted my weight from one foot to the other, waiting for some indication of what was expected of me. I was a rough character in many respects, but I did have a few manners I could trot out when I felt like impressing someone, and I never sat down in someone's house until I was invited. That didn't happen too damn often, though. Either one – the impressing or the sitting. I had been faithful to my lover.

"Have a seat." He motioned to the overstuffed couch, then went to the kitchen.

"You want another beer?" he called to me.

"Sure," I said, although I'd had enough.

When he returned to the living room, he had removed his shirt and unfastened the top button of his denim shorts. His massive, deeply tanned, hairy chest glistened with sweat. I wanted to lick every inch of his skin, but I sipped my beer instead.

We sat there on the couch, gulping our brews, not speaking. I asked myself what was I doing here with this stranger, a man who said he was a cop. What a difference between now and the good-nights only a year ago. Those were the days when Bob, my lover, fucked me before he left on one of his trips and our love-making lingered through days apart. Now, with the stud next to me, I wanted to be elsewhere, preferably with Bob, but only the way it used to be, not the way it had become, with no fucks, no love, no nothing. Bob had made too many trips, I figured. He didn't trust me, didn't think I was being faithful during his frequent absences. Bob was not a man of fantasy. He dealt with the reality that he could control. What he couldn't control, he didn't want to deal with. I could no longer be controlled. And he could no longer deal with me.

To me, silence creates a tension so my mind began to sing. As the song, "50 Ways To Leave Your Lover" started playing in my head, I smiled. "So, you're really a cop?"

"Would I lie to you?" He flashed me the badge. I saw his name was Dennis.

"Neat," I said. "Vice squad?"

He chuckled, laid a cool hand on my thigh. "Internal affairs."

I laughed out loud. I don't know why I found that so funny but I did. I guess I supposed that before long he would be having an internal affair with me.

I finished my beer as his fingers moved up my thigh, under the tight white shorts I'd bought just for the trip to Florida and tugged at my balls. I dropped the empty beer can on the floor and took him in my arms. I kissed his handsome face. Slowly my lips left the stubble of his beard and moved down his chin and neck in a path aimed at his massive cock – gently licking and kissing – along the way. As I approached sacred ground, I dropped my left hand down toward the cop's sex and brushed my hand across it. A slight quiver greeted my attention and I slyly finishing unbuttoning his shorts. Realizing my intentions, the cop pressed his body tighter against me. My mouth engulfed the cop's tit, sucked on the nipple. The cop breathed a sigh of pleasure. I went to the other tit, licking the sweat, sucking the nipple. God, he tasted good. He began running his fingers through my blond hair while my head traveled south, stopping to play along in his hairy naval. My hands took over what my mouth had been doing as I passionately manipulated the stud's body.

My hands seem to set off orgasmic tremors in him.

He could hardly wait to get me on all fours, thighs spread, my ass spread wide so he could play with my dangling cock while he prepared my entrance with spit. Then he stood and he told me to open up my mouth. He fed me his cock, exploring every hollow of my wide open mouth, holding me by the hair.

He would get none of that hacking and spitting you usually get from other cocksuckers trying to take a cock that was at least ten inches. No, if there was one thing Bob taught me it was how to suck a big cock. Dennis was even bigger than Bob, and my face became one big fuckhole to hold his cock. I can hold it down my windpipe for an incredible amount of time. After awhile, I knew he was ready. I didn't want him to come until he fucked me, but he couldn't hold it. I let the cock drop from my mouth and cum drooled down my chin.

He moved round to my backside and gave it a slap.

"God, what a pretty ass. Now I can take some time with it."

"Please..." I begged.

"Yeah, show me that virgin hole, boy. Spread it real wide."

He nudged the head of his prick into the crack.

65

Reaching under me, he palmed my quivering nuts. My hard little cock stuck up next to my belly.

He jammed it home, pressing it deep into me. It was what Bob called a "split-butt fuck." He rode me as if I was one of the burros we used back home to go up into the mountains. He slammed it into me all the way to the balls and I squealed.

I gritted my teeth and took it all. Every single inch. He guided me a little by my tits, pulling my right and left nipples like they were bits, yanking my balls, making me come, not once but twice.

When he had his second orgasm, he hugged me to him and kissed my shoulders.

I collapsed into the cushions of the sofa. He lifted himself off me and said he was going to the bathroom. I lay still. As I slipped further into the music of my mind, I returned to a place where I often journeyed in moments of darkness – when Bob fucked me the first time, in the mountains.

This place was every bit as heavenly.

What just happened was real.

Maybe it would happen again.

Maybe I should make it happen.

COME BANG MY BOYFRIEND
John Patrick

"Bang My Boyfriend. Sexually insatiable couple seeks jocks for fun and games. Call 823-0069."

When I hear my boyfriend's footsteps, a quiet seems to settle in the air. A stillness blankets my frenetic mind. Momentarily, I am seduced away from my obsession with myself. I let go of my cock and await David. I have been thinking about sex with others, and have a big hard-on. I am shocked by my actions when David is away. Even when he is in town, I dream of others.

David comes into the room, finally. He is nude. He smiles when he sees I have an erection. He gets into bed, closes his eyes, spreads his legs and arches his back. I kneel behind him, gently slide my fingers into him. He moans. Softly. And pushes back so that soon my fingers are all the way in. I pull them out and stick them in again. His face disappears into the pillows. He turns his head to the side and begs me to fuck him.

I tell him I will if he will consider running the ad, the ad that will broaden our horizons. We have to have the courage to explore new things, I tell him. We know each other inside out; that's the armor we wear in the world. The secret familiarity between us protects us. What we do, we do because it makes us happy. It is our fate, I believe, to be men who can love one another and have sex with others.

David says none of his friends can ever talk to their lovers in this way. "None of them has me as a lover," I say.

We often talk about why it is that two men can be lovers but we have found no answers – yet. Maybe it's because this feels so damn good, as now, when I slide my thick nine-incher into his tight ass.

It isn't long before he's saying it again: "Please come. I'll do anything to feel you coming inside me again. You know that I'm your slave." I hold my cock inside him, letting him push backwards just a little, which starts me coming.

After I've come, he drops to the bed, exhausted, and we kiss. We stay close to each other, as close as two people ever get. His is a beauty I am so privileged to share. It is always enough to put me over the edge. Yes, it is true what they say about him: I am Mediterranean fire; he is blond ice. It makes me think how lucky I am in this world.

He looks at me, slowly pulling my hand to his uncut cock, still erect, throbbing. I know what I must do, and I don't mind a bit. It is impossible to deny our need for each other. My tongue laps something far more substantial than any I've ever made love to – because that's what I do I do to my lover's prick, make love to it. I hold back, staying the impending flood that threatens to inundate me at any moment, portending the release of the cum. Such is our passion.

- – -

"I'll show you how." Those were the most comforting words I ever heard. David lay down on the mattress, and pulled me on top of him. "Feel how I'm moving? Move with me," he said. I did. Then he rolled me over and began unbuttoning my shirt, leaving my T-shirt on. He got up on his knees and slowly fingered the button on my pants. He slid my pants off but left on my BVDs. The way he touched my cock mesmerized me.

"Feel how I'm touching you?" he whispered with a smile. He ran his nails down the sides of my T-shirt and up my thighs. His mouth was very near my cock. "If you're going to fuck me with this," he said, stroking it, "then I want you to feel it. This is an act of sweet imagination." He took the head of my cock in his lips and began to move his mouth up and down the length of it. When he finally spoke, "Now," was all he said. He rolled over on his back as I fumbled with his clothing. I touched him with an adolescent's lack of grace. At first I thought he was being very patient about it. Then I wondered if my clumsiness allowed him to be more excited with me than he could have been if I was experienced. When I was fearful or unsure, he became more present in our lovemaking, encouraging me. When I got excited like a colt, he guided me back under control.

No, nothing I had ever done had prepared me for the moment when I knelt between David's thighs and had no idea of what to do. "Wait," he said, pressing his fingertips against my thighs, "let me." He gently guided the cock inside him. "Wait," he repeated, "don't push. Be gentle. Let me get used to this big dick before you start fucking." I lay carefully on top of David. After a moment, his long, lean body relaxed against me. "Yes," David said as I moved with him, following his lead. I found if I tried to think about what I was doing, I lost the rhythm of the fuck. So I stopped thinking.

"Yes. Oh, my big stud!" David grew more excited; he became wilder in my arms. It scared me, I didn't know what was happening. Suddenly he stared to cry out and yanked my hair. I stopped moving. There was a long pause. His body slumped beneath me. One of his arms flopped over his head against the pillow in annoyance. "Why did you stop?" he asked quietly.

"I thought I was hurting you."

"Hurting me?" His voice rose a bit.

Ashamed, I turned away from him but I was still inside him. "Fuck it," he demanded, putting his hands firmly on my ass. And I did, for what seemed like a good ten minutes of vigorous screwing.

After we'd come, I lay quietly in his arms. I'd fucked my first man, and he was satisfied.

- — -

At the party that night we saw them: the innocent couple. There was something spiritual about them, I could tell right off. A beautiful bond existed between them, but I doubted they knew it, at least the extent of it. I doubted they realized just how sweet they were, how childlike. It was this purity that excited David. At first we stood off at a distance, watching them. When we came closer, we couldn't believe they didn't know how extraordinary they were.

Finally when we walked up to them I said: "You two make a wonderful couple. I just wanted to tell you that."

They smiled but I could tell our interest made them slightly uncomfortable. But it was too late, we had spied their secret from afar: they were uninitiated. And we could well imagine them doing things they'd never imagined. Yes, it would be good for them, liberating. Their innocence made them the most appetizing specimens. They were ripe for it. We'd have to get them interested somehow. After some small talk, we realized that they were adults after all, not dreamy children. Though from across the room they had appeared so blissful. We had to focus on their innocence, we had to catch the scent and drink them in because we felt we owed it to them. After all, they were not children – how had they managed to retain their innocence for so long? It was abnormal....

The older, shorter, heavily-muscled one, John, was dark, dressed in black, with large doe eyes that seemed in constant fear or awe. The taller one, who said his name was Mark, was slender, with short blond hair. No nonsense, secretive. Mark was at the moment unemployed; he was, he said, "working on my tan." I started calling him the Sun God, which seemed to amuse them. John was finishing his junior year in college. John's father, we assumed, supported the both of them, although he probably had no idea that's what he was doing. We saw between them a love so intense we couldn't help staring. But they knew nothing, so absorbed in themselves they were. We almost expected Mark to lift his fork and start feeding John, who was the younger of the two we found, from his plate as they huddled together, chatting with us.

After the buffet table had been cleared away, my lover said, "Well, let's get it over with," proceeding to laugh and talk his way into their innocent hearts. He couldn't resist now, after I'd pushed and pushed. It had become sport. Our host saw what was happening and drew me aside. "How can you do that to a pair of people who have nothing in common with you, whom you've just met?"

"Oh, we have enough in common," I retorted.

They agreed to follow us to our place for a "nightcap." John rode with me; David went with Mark. John got amorous right away, snuggling close and rubbing my groin. "Of course we're going to separate you." I said. "You come with me. He goes with him."

"I can live with that," he said, pulling down my zipper.

It was too easy. Things were not as blissful as I had imagined. This was hardly a seduction.

"Come in, make yourself at home." Seeing how Mark clung to David, I became filled with contempt. I realized it had taken over, slowly, inch by inch, all night. David had had his eye on Mark all along. Mark was like a much younger version of David; John was a boyish version of me. Somehow the opposites-attract thing wasn't working here.

The two of them smoked. Our living room became filled with smoke. Ordinarily, this kind of thing drives me crazy, but it was right tonight, a full moon night, and the scent, the haze, the ambiance was utterly erotic. I made this observation aloud, and David looked at me like I'd lost my mind. Maybe I had.

"Who's fucking whom?" I asked, trying to keep my voice steady, feeling John's strong hand on my calf. John kneeled on the edge of the sofa, towering over my face. I smiled and said, "I'll fuck first, then David can fuck next, and so on – " He chuckled, and leaned down and stopped any more nutty remarks from me with his mouth. I was startled and for a moment uncertain how I wanted to respond. I thought we'd pair off first, then join up later. But John wanted to put on a show right in front of his cute boyfriend. We'd not been here before. I wanted this kiss. I'd known it as soon as I felt John's hand on me, felt his lips kiss my cock through my shorts in the car. I felt torn between so many things: David's shame, for instance, of having me the object of desire instead of him. John held his mouth pressed to mine until he felt a response. He then pulled back and said, "I've wanted to do that all night."

I shook my head and looked across the room. David had left us, had taken Mark out on the porch. Mark held on to David as if he was about to fall down. John brushed my hair away from my forehead and pulled his mouth back down to mine. I caught his breath with the excitement. The scent of John's sweat and the leather jacket he wore filled my head. John straddled my lap, pinning me against the back of the couch in a supple movement that didn't even break our kiss. I strained upwards, against John's weight, reaching out for the heat I felt.

"Lift up," I said.

As John raised himself a little from me on the creaking sofa, I was able to free my swollen cock. John stood and dropped his pants. As he climbed from them, I could see his cock, average in size, but thick, was erect. He straddled me again and my cock slid softly up and down his crack as he sucked in my breath, kissing me deeply. His tongue touched my teeth then sought out my tongue while his hand reached back to squeeze my cock. I pressed forward, loving the touch of John's mouth and tongue. I drew back only to catch my breath, but John pursued my mouth, grasping my head with his hand.

I felt lotion being applied to my cock and I opened my eyes. David stood over us, preparing my cock to enter another man. Mark moved to the other side, watching as David guided my cock into his lover John's ass. Deeper and deeper I pushed. "Oh, God! John," I said, not believing the joy I felt at fucking this boy. I kissed the side of his face, his hair, his ear, finally resting my forehead on John's chest as all of my energy went through my cock into John's body. I pushed hard, the full force of my body inside John.

As I worked deeper, I felt only the desire, like a tide wiping out any misgivings. I wanted John as I'd never wanted anyone before. "Please, baby," John moaned in my ear as I thrust inside him, almost swooning at the feel of John straining downward to take in more of me. John's voice was hoarse with desire as he tried to hold in his

71

screams as I battered his ass. "Yes, yes," he said over and over again as he came.

We sat sprawled silently for a few moments until I caught my breath. Now Mark climbed over me, his little cock jutting out from his body at a rakish angle. I had the biggest cock in the room, that was certain. No wonder they all wanted it. Mark smiled and looked into my eyes. I wrapped my arms around him, kissing him with a feeling that let him know this was going to be just as good for him as it had been for his lover. I rubbed my hand across the broadness of his back, enjoying the feel of his tender skin and the pale color of my hand against the deep tan of the youth's flesh. I could barely breathe just watching the contrast and feeling the suppleness of Mark's body as it began to respond to the pressure of my own.

I kissed the back of Mark's neck and sensed his breath beginning to come faster as he lowered himself atop me. David moved in again to slide one hand down to spread Mark's legs farther apart, then rubbed his thighs methodically.

Mark moved slowly at first, then pushed it all inside, fulfilling the desire I'd had since I'd seen them at the party. I had wanted to fuck them both and here I was, doing it.

"Oh, fuck it," David cried out, jacking off and coming more quickly than he'd ever come before. Mark saw what was happening to my lover and came himself. I let my body relax against Mark, but then I saw that David was not weakened by this explosion of energy. Neither was Mark. Mark rolled off and onto his back. His lover held him and began playing with his tits, finally taking the small pink nipples into his mouth, one by one. He rolled his tongue over them, sucking them in as deeply as he could, then nipping at them.

David climbed over me next and gasped as I got close to the lips of his ass. He glanced up at my face. His eyes opened and closed as if he could not believe the pleasure he felt as my cock sank deep inside him. I smiled as I watched the rush of red to David's face as he moaned and groaned.

I realized that in all of their lovemaking, these boys, David included, never wanted to fuck as much as they had wanted to get fucked. Mark flicked his tongue across the pointed hardness of John's cock, then drew it inside his mouth as he'd had John's nipples, sucking it and then pressing it between his teeth, gently, then harshly, until John's body was again convulsed with the coming orgasm.

David began pushing rhythmically, unceasingly, until he screamed wildly. After his body shook with the final wave of yet another orgasm, he pulled himself up so he lay next to me, allowing my sopping cock to wave in the air, as if beckoning Mark to move away from John's and onto it. Mark did this, without hesitation, and began sucking me while his hand continued to stimulate John. David caressed Mark's hair while the boy blew me. Because Mark would stop occasionally to return to his lover's erection, David was able to lower his head and suck me. David knew just how to get me off, and before long I was coming. Mark returned to my cock to share the cum with David.

The lovers went to the bathroom together and when they returned, they dressed. We agreed to meet again, and David accompanied them to the door.

When David returned, I pulled him down to me and kissed him solidly on his mouth. "It's just not fair," I said.

"What?"

"It's was supposed to be you getting banged, not me doing all the banging for chrissakes."

"Oh, there'll be another time."

I sighed. I knew he was right. I'd just have to bide my time. Maybe run another ad.

I WAS A SEX SLAVE TO A PERVERTED TEEN BOY BAND
Dan Veen

Paparazzi light the way for the Boyz to their stretch-limo. Teenyboppers scream for a soiled article of New Boyz underwear. Adrenaline and hormones flow around them like Ecstasy. Girls throw themselves on the Boyz' limousine like it was a phallic symbol instead of a status symbol. Their teen acne smudges the limo's smoked-glass window. They hold up signs like : RICKY RICK I SAVED MY CHERRY JUST FOR YOU!"

Poor lovesick fish sticks. If you only knew the truth about the New Boyz.

Ricky Rick – he's the hot husky one with the gold earring – hops in the limo slinging sweat like a mutt out of his bath.

"Dude! We really had'em pumpin' and humpin' out there tonight!" Ricky Rick high fives Joe-Joe who's already opened the beers. "Fuckin' bitchin' cool as shit tooooooonight!"

"Chillin'! Fuckin' chillin'!" Joe-Joe (he's the cute one) slaps back. "Waxin' to the max!" He whaps Taylor's cap down, boying around. Taylor's the tall sensitive one. Your Dreamboat Mystery Date. Taylor lobs a beer across the car seat to Sean (he's the impish troublemaker one, the hand-in-the-cookie-jar kind of kid.).

People have the hots for different boys. I'm glad I don't have to choose. I love 'em all.

Worship them, in fact.

Have to.

I am naked in their stretch-limo. My stretch-ass is high and wide, waiting for the junior gods to notice me.

I'm their groupie.

Their slave.

The girls throw hotel keys at the limo's smoked glass windows. Hopeless. Their fans can't see what the Boyz do in here.

Ricky Rick yanks down his baggy pants. He sticks his hand in his shorts. He yanks out his penis; it's thick even when it's soft. He sits up in his seat. He puts his cock against the mirrored windows where a girl outside is pleading for an autograph. He says, "Here, bitchie, bitchie, bitchie! Is this what you want? You want to suck my famous fucking cock? You want a mouthful of my celebrity studmeat?"

He wags his famous fucking cock at her unsuspecting face. I'm jealous.

"That's what you hormonal cum-catchers want, isn't it? You want this dick, don't you, you fucking cheerleader, you slutty prom queen?" He sticks his tongue and his cock out at her.

It turns me on when Ricky Rick gets crude. He's a foul-mouthed, ball-banging, rude, crude dude. What Ricky Rick wants, Ricky Rick gets – NOW.

He won't take `maybe' for an answer. He's a storming-butch-meatloaf number with a quarterback's shoulders tapering down to a young waist and muscley butt. He'd be rough trade on Sunset Strip if he hadn't lucked and fucked his way into the singing racket. Ricky Rick loves to fuck. Just loves it. Can't fuck enough. Especially me.

The other boys laugh with Ricky Rick. They're swigging the beers the manager has thoughtfully provided (along with me) for their relaxation.

"Yo, Ricky, roll down the fuckin' window and fuckin' stick yer cock in her mouth – maybe she'll run alongside the car sucking it all the way to the fuckin' airport!" Taylor sneers. Taylor looks sensitive and poetic in all the interviews where he denies all those rumors. But Taylor digs down-and-dirty rauncho-sleazo stuff. You should've seen the way he dicked my ass last Saturday night. "Poor babe looks like she really wants a taste of it bad!"

Joe-Joe goes, "Yeah, them boob babes are almost as bad as our cocksucker here!"

Ricky Rick plops back down, looks me over, the `cocksucker' here.

Me they don't usually notice till their hard-ons bother them. They treat me like doo-doo. Boyz will be boys. Remember all those fantasies you had when you were a kid? All those nasty sexy things you wanted to try with everybody and everything? All those people you wanted to catch and do nasty things to? Well, the Boyz have the star power to do all those things. Usually to me.

When their four pairs of young pink balls need unloading, that's when they'll start playing with me.

I know their teen hard-ons by heart. When they're ready for a fuck, the `Cocksucker' here will have them all to myself out there in the Embassy Suite of the Holiday Inn by the Airport. Me and the

Boyz will lock all the doors, check the windows for photographers. One by one those incredibly hot teenage heartthrob boys will place their hard young 'n throbbing cocks in my mouth to get blow jobbed by me.

This cocksucker is looking at Ricky Rick's cock. Ricky Rick's uncut meatus flushes day-glo pink with after-show energy. His cock is fattened up with his power play, it trees up out of his lap through the pissflap of his white undershorts which I tongue-washed for him this morning, blow-dried with my own devoted breath.

"How's my biggest fan doing tonight, huh?" Ricky Rick grins me that famous gap-toothed grin, the wholesome All-dimpled-American grin gushed over by so many teenyboppers – and mature bachelors who like to bop young male teens. Ricky Rick's flicking his cock in his lap. "Yeah, we had a great show tonight. They loved us. Open up. Let's see."

His finger sticks itself into my mouth, uninvited but always welcome. His finger retrieves from my mouth a deposit of cum, like phlegm, dripping from his finger. It's been stored right there where his cock had put it this afternoon before the show. The boys laugh at the way I lunge after it to lick it back off Ricky Rick's finger into my mouth. Rick teases me with it. He offers it up to my mouth. I snap at it. He pulls it away. He offers it. He pulls it away.

"Here, cocksucker," (Ricky Rick's putting on a show for the other Boyz.) "I'll give it back to you. I know how much our cum means to you."

He takes the dripping cum wad, daubs it right on the enlarged aching glans of my toad-stool-big dick. I start to wipe it up before it drools off the crown.

He stops me. "No, sucker! Suckers are supposed to suck! I want you to suck it off with your mouth. Use your tongue! See if you can suck it off your own dick!"

They all laugh and taunt my engorged penis. Damn, my dick hurts, standing out there like that, all stiff and big and hard! They haven't let me jerk off since their last concert a week ago in Phoenix.

As the official slave groupie of the New Boyz Tour, I'm responsible for the care and feeding of the New Boyz hard-ons. I am always hard. It always hurts. They know it's hard. They know it hurts. They see to it. They like it always hanging out from my body in perpetual desire for them. "Our biggest fan" they call my dick.

They tell me that's how I won the privilege of going on The New Boyz nationwide "2 Big 4 U Tour".

They say they wouldn't think of honoring me with their cocks if my dick wasn't so goddamn humongous, so outrageously bigger than any dick the boys have ever seen before. They say their cocks wouldn't even touch my worthless holes if it weren't for my freak-meat.

It's true. My meat is very big. The Boyz are fascinated by it even though they seldom touch it – except to make it hurt. They've never seen an adult boner the size of mine before. They're young; cocks are new things to them. Like playtoys. What kid wouldn't take advantage of all that power, all that fame, to get a look at every adult dick he could command?

- – -

Six other men were in the hotel room that day I auditioned for the New Boyz "2 Big 4 U Tour".

We were just what the agency asked for: Unemployed Actors. Healthy. Well-Built. Thirty something. Male. Just what the Boyz liked. We were all handsome lean adult males. We stood there, standing servilely in front of a bunch of snickering kids. The Boyz stretched out on the sofa like four spoiled princes nonchalantly popping bubblegum.

Ricky Rick. Joe-Joe. Taylor. Sean.

I couldn't believe I was actually seeing these pin-up dreamfucks live, in person. I used to put their rock videos on Pause and jerk off to them.

Ricky Rick, my teen stud hero, propped his spiffy Nikes on the hotel's glass coffee table. He laced his hands behind his head and looked beneath his ball cap at us grown men awaiting to obey his orders.

"Okay, kiddies," Ricky Rick talked down to us adult men like we were boys sent to the principal's office for discipline. "Me and my guys need ourselves a cumdump for when we go on tour. Some hole who'll keep us entertained on our private plane and take care of our cocks at night – especially numero uno here."

Ricky Rick pointed to his meat packed box. That famous dick basket of his looked even bigger than the billboard underwear ads he did.

My mouth watered. I felt my dick sprout. The same was probably happening to the five other potential cocksuckers. If I was going to win the honor of Official Cocksucker for the New Boyz 2 Big 4 U Tour, I'd have to beat off some stiff competition – competition that was growing stiffer by the minute.

We lined up.

They told us to strip to our shorts – fast.

Clothes flew. Once we men got totally bareassed naked, they told us to turn around. They told us to bend over. Wiggle our butts. Spread our legs. Spread our legs wider.

"Wider," Ricky Rick snickered, enjoying our struggle to please them. "I wanna see those balls dangling down."

I swear, it was like an erotic Simon Says.

I couldn't believe sensible mature men could be made to act so monkey-like in front of a bunch of mocking, snickering schoolboys. But there we were, brought low by our servile lusts, stripped to our bare nuggets, enslaved by these irresistibly studly chickens toying with us like we were chorus boys in a Chippendale strip show.

Not that I minded. Degradation sets me free. They asked which of us liked to suck cock and which of us liked to take it up the ass. They made us shuck our shorts and do jumping jacks naked. Six sets of cocks and balls flapped in the air.

The Boyz started hooting and jeering. They pointed.

One poor loser had a teeny-weenie three-incher of a dick. Hardly worth getting up. Looked like a worthless baby butterbean. You could barely see it through his pubic hair -- and it was already hard!

Boy, did the kids have a field day with that tiny worthless pea dick of his!

They poked it and tweaked it and called it names. They humiliated the hell out of this poor guy who could've been their dad. He had such a puny nothing dick, you couldn't blame him for blushing from head to toe. He had a damned decent body, the type that tries to overcompensate for micro-genitalia. His hard-on looked like a bright-red berry after they got done punching it around. I think the poor dude was sniffling some when they got done with him.

They Boyz said they wanted to see how a guy with such a little dick could jerk it off. They taunted him. They ordered him to jack off in front of everybody. They said jerking off was probably all he ever did with it anyway. No way that Tic-Tac dick ever saw any real fuck-action. Let's see if it can cum, they jeered. Yeah, shoot that little squirter for us!

Peanut-Dick got to work on his baby pud all right. The Boyz had a ball tormenting him. They enjoyed having adults rush to do their bidding, making them strip, jumping through hoops, no matter how demeaning or impossible their commands.

I couldn't help but watch the poor underhung guy with the red gumdrop dickhead. He tried desperately to get his Vienna sausage to spit. Panting and huffing in a jerk-frenzy. He tried to stretch it longer, but the poor nub just popped back into place. It wouldn't grow anymore. He stuck his crotch out like he was some he-man. It was laughable watching him pinch his baby-size dicklet between his thumb and pinky, then shake his wrist like he was getting ready to roll dice. Frig as hard as he might, his useless thingy just wouldn't shoot. It just got redder and rawer while he stood there, rubbing the clit-meat for dear life.

The Boyz snickered. They rubbed their big teen hard-ons in their baggy pants. Just seeing the outlines of their cocks made me sprout some wood in my own jockstrap. My extraordinary dick's dimensions immediately became...extraordinary.

"Yo! You! Yeah, you! The hairy one!" Taylor sized me up, watching the elastic ballooning in my jock. "Looks like we got us a big one, dudes!"

I watched them all play with the flap in the fronts of their Hawaiian boxer shorts, playing peek-a-boo with their cocks. I told them they'd always turned me on ever since I'd seen them on the Tonight Show. I went to one of their concerts. It was so wall-to-wall on the floor that I could take my dick out right there, right beside the stage with nobody noticing. I jerked off right out in public, at the feet of the New Boyz, among those screaming fans, looking at the New Boyz half-hard cocks flopping around in their pants and I just knew they didn't wear any underwear because I could see the outlines of their cocks so well, could even tell which of their cocks was cut or uncut, and I jerked off and came splat on the back of some kid's New Boyz T-shirt. I bought every Tiger Beat magazine with the Boyz pictures in them and tailed them around the country whenever I could. Being their groupie had always been, like, my dream, they were so, like, clean-cut and young and fresh and sexed up and -

"Yeah, yeah. Just let's see that meat yo-yo of yours fuckface!" Taylor's boom box voice made us all jump. "I'm fucking fed up with our fucking fans fucking ga-ga yackity-yak about us and how they fucking adore us! I want some fucking action! Now strip!"

Even the loser with the gumdrop dick stopped tweaking his meat for a sec. They all watched my super-length of beef unfold from its jockstrap container.

Sean whistled. "Dude! Whoa! Check it! Is that rocket for fucking real? How the fuck do you handle that?"

Ricky Rick came over to it. Without asking me if he could, like it belonged to him already, he felt around the heavy knob of my inflated dick.

"Shit! This is one cool crowd-pleaser!" he chuckled approvingly, a hint of envy is his whisper. "Bigger'n anything I've ever seen in those cocksucker movies!"

The five other guys stared at my attention-getting schlong. Even Ricky Rick looked at it for a minute with a kind of awe, like he wanted to borrow my dick for a little while just to wear it out somewhere. The usual disdain for his fans was gone from his face. This was something even Ricky Rick could respect.

"This one oughta be in the Book of World Fucking Records." Ricky Rick wrapped both fists around my dick. A large portion of my baseball bat still stood out.

Of course the Boyz were impressed with it. They had to see it in action. Just like the little guy, they wanted to see me jerking it off. The logistics of sex still titillated these kids. I gladly jacked my cock for them. They asked if I ever sucked myself off, it being so damned long. How far would it go in my mouth? Did I ever try and fuck myself with it? Did anybody ever really let me fuck them with it? Did I ever fit it inside a girl's pussy? A guy's ass? What did it feel like to be up in there so deep?

The Boyz wondered how anybody ever sucked my dick or took it up the ass.

Truth was, it didn't happen much – not often enough. Most people couldn't fit the head of it into their mouths. Try putting a tennis ball all the way in your mouth, and you'll get an idea of the size of my dickhead. Most guys ran screaming whenever my meatbat got near their assholes. Most times I had to settle for an enthusiastic lickjob. Otherwise I would suck the other guy's average cock. I also learned to take it up the ass. Learned, in fact, to love it. It still seemed strange that the guy with the biggest dick didn't dominate in bed. But you know what, some guys spend so much time craving big dicks and wishing they had one, I think they welcome the opportunity to release their pent-up frustration on a big boner like mine. The New Boyz obviously took to the idea of using my dick for a punching bag.

Taylor immediately muzzled my dick like it was a dangerous animal that shouldn't be loose. He said that was how my dick was going to be for the rest of the 2 Big 4 U Tour. I was so elated that they chose me, I nearly shot my cream right there. He said that with a dick like mine I would be their perfect private mascot for the 2 Big Tour.

"I'd say it was too fucking big for anybody." And Sean playfully put one of his socks on it.

- — -

The Boyz have a ritual that they make me do in their dressing room before every show. A humiliating ritual. A private ritual.

The boys stand in a circle around me. The young men drop their drawers. They turn around. They present their boy buns to me.

"Now kiss our asses, asskisser!" Ricky Rick orders over his shoulder. "Open 'em up." he snarls. "Stick your tongue in there!"

He instructs me to spread their asscheeks one by one. I have to insert my face between their beautiful teen-muffin asscheeks. I have to kiss each of them, each of their hot buttholes. I have to taste each boy with my tongue.

This I do eagerly. I always give each butthole such loving care, too. Taylor's ass was always sweaty-soapy, well-washed and scrubbed. Joe-Joe's ass sprouted curly fuzz which I loved to delve my tongue into and swish around. Sean's asshole looked like a bright pink peppermint – tasted like one too!

But Ricky Rick's asshole, ah, it was just right! Kissable, lickable, tongueable, edible in every way! Deep between the crack of his hefty buttcheeks gaped a big funky boyhole ripening into a manhole gummy with hot testosterone and musky anal smells tucked in the folds of his assring. When Ricky Rick's ass was done with my tongue, they turned around so all four of their hard, dripping teenage prongs surrounded me.

Ricky Rick told me to kiss each one of them right on the peckerhead, for luck, he said.

I was the lucky one, getting to kiss the New Boyz's goodies. I loved it as much as I loved tonguing their asses. Taylor's cock is a swaggering microphone of flesh. It's long and floppy when it isn't hard. You can see it sweeping the front of his pants when he break dances on stage. Joe-Joe's cock is still growing. It gets bigger every time I see it or suck it. He has this theory that the more suckjobs I give him, the bigger he gets, so naturally he keeps me real busy sucking him off as much as I can. I think it will eventually be longer than any of the other Boyz's cocks when he grows up. Sean has got a peppermint candy cane to match his peppermint ass. It's a thin long red cock, red as a dog's dick, with strawberry-blond pubic hair to match. I always feel like I'm sipping a cherry cream soda whenever I blow him.

Now Ricky Rick has got the cock and balls. It's a big coarse-looking thing. It's got the rumpled and rubbery formations of a turkey head, chewy waddles and surprises of flesh, noodly veins and nodules of knotted ribs and flanges flapping around my lips as I suck. Actually it's kind of ugly-looking. But can it fuck! Yessir, you learn to love a tasty cock like that! It looks kind of strange, dangling off his smooth tight trim body, like this horse-schlong was grafted on him. God, I love kissing on it. though! It always treats me to a string of pre-cum trailing like cotton candy from my his cock to my mouth.

I want to suck it more, but he won't let me. The rest of the pre-show ritual is jerking off all over my body. Besides my giant unleashed dick, they like my hair-covered body. I'm a fairly bear-ish man. The contrast between me and their nubile pink smooth bodies turns them on. They like to see their spritzing cocks mat the fur on my chest and back, and drip through my shaggy chest rug right down to my pubic patch. After all four of their cocks shoot, I feel like a Jackson Pollock spatter-painting. They command me to clean the residue from their cocks. Young cum is usually dripping off their cocks like leaky faucets. I especially love to lick the remains from Ricky Rick's cockspout. I dig my tongue underneath the hood, delving around his helmet to get me a tongue full of hot slimy cream cheese.

I'm not allowed to swallow any of that cum while they are performing onstage. That's part of the good luck ritual. It insures that they have a terrific night. I stay cumloaded the entire time. I look chipmunky with both cheeks full of their combined boyloads of cumbroth.

Should the Boyz happen to have an off night, they accuse me of having swallowed some of their cum prematurely. Then I know I'm in for a painful, sleepless, memorable night.

Sometimes – if I feel especially horny – I gulp some of the prime Boyz jism just so they'll give it to me good.

Tonight, however, the randy little lambs are frisking for a fuck. I know I'm going to get it anyway. I wish I had a camera for the tabloids tonight. The Boyz have me suck their cocks, slobbering in their limo seats, passing me around from crotch to the other, along with a six-pack of beer.

When their show has been a superhit, when everything clicked, their school kid prongs get hyper stimulated. Overheated. The only way they can find some release is to get their rocks off with me. It's up to me to do it. I sense a crazy night ahead of me. I especially look forward to Ricky Rick's cock.

I had learned to take the rough ride Ricky Rick gave me on his bumpy cock. When Ricky Rick shoves it up me, it feels like a dozen French ticklers gyrating up inside my ass. One time that cubfucker was so turned on, he rode me down the hallway of the hotel. He had his cock inside my ass the whole way, scooting and nudging me on my knees. My favorite celebrity top teen dicked me all the way to the stairwell. He made me crawl several flights down the stairs without letting his cock slip out of my ass.

"You lose it, motherfucker, you hairy-assed freak-meat sonofabitch, and you won't sit down for a month!"

Ricky Rick didn't need to worry. My ass had a suction grip on his cock. He deliberately flexed his cock inside my star-fucked pussy, making me feel it.

Flopping between my knees, my own bedraggled dick snuffled snail trails of pre-cum down the stairs to the fifth floor landing where he stopped and fucked me hard. He liked me with my elbows on the lower step. Nothing but my asshole stood up in the air for him to screw. His cock already arched up, so he really dug it into my ass at this angle, skewering my coccyx with his rippling prong. We made a racket fucking there in the concrete stairwell. I couldn't touch my own dick. I had to use both hands for support so Ricky Rick's cockthrusts wouldn't send me flying headlong down the stairs! He took his own sweet time coming inside me. As if he liked to hear me howl and yip with every thrust. When he got done coming he turned me around and made me crawl back up the steps on my bare sore knees. He demanded that I tell him how wonderful a fuck he was all the way back up. With every step I had to thank him. I tried to tell him what a terrific feeling his fat meatfucker was.

"Yeah, the acoustics were great, weren't they!" Ricky Rick slapped along with his freshly spent cocktube still squishing inside me like a loofah. "You screamed great too. A high B. I do like to see a grown man cry! Now hold on to my cock in there, dude, till we get back to the room. Hurry, and I'll let you wash it off for me with your tongue."

That was how they got the idea for our private recording sessions. The Boyz actually taped their midnight fuck bouts with me. All my cries and sighs. Later, in the studio, they'd re-mix our fuck-noises into some of their songs. Nobody could tell exactly what those moist squealy exhalations were, but the subliminal sounds sure turned people on and kept the New Boyz topping the charts.

- – -

So tonight my hot slot feels ready for anything.

I sense a crazy night ahead of me.

Back at the hotel, the New Boyz and me make our way through the back entrance. They lead me out of the limo naked by my hard-on.

The Chauffeur only smirks at my discomfort and humiliation. He tells me he is writing a tell-all book on the kinky sex-lives of teen celebrities.

The boys sneak me into their hotel suite. Naked and hard, I'm left to stew and simmer, subservient and horny there on the carpet, while they bullshit around and bust up some hotel furniture. (They wouldn't be a proper rock group if they didn't.)

Once in awhile one boy grabs hold of my dick like it was a slot-machine handle, pulling it down to try to hit the jackpot. Taylor, the little sadist, even swings me around the room by it. I can barely run fast enough. When he lets me go, I topple on to the bed. They all like to torture my big dick. They know I can't help it. They know I haven't come in weeks. They rub my huge polished hard-on like a talisman, a good luck stone. They treat it abrasively, derisively, but that's their own Boyz's way of showing affection. My dick is as big as their egos, and that's what they like about it.

Tonight, they treat my giant whang like it was a goddamn pinata, batting it all about with their own cocks, taking potshots at it, spitting on it, kickboxing it. They like making it big and hurting and sore.

The Boyz' cocks are all rock hard now, looking like sweaty tag-team wrestlers. They don't even want to take turns with me. They want a free-for-all. They want to fuck me all at once.

85

"Yo, hold it, guys!" Ricky Rick stands in the middle of the naked boys with his quarterback body commanding us. He stands over my face. He strokes his craggy meat, looking like a blue-veined stalactite hanging temptingly above my mouth-hole. Ricky Rick is their natural leader through sheer Neanderthal bluster and bestial exuberance. "We work as a group. We sing as a group. Now we're gonna fuck as a group." He gets that devilish twinkle in his eyes. "We're gonna try for two dicks in each of his holes!"

I never attempted rauncho-pervy shit like this before. Leave it to a wholesome American teen idol to come up with something so fucking twisted-sadistic!

Nights like this, I wish I had a few extra holes to accommodate all their cocks.

I'm ready for anything. I'm steaming for it. Ricky Rick practically guides me by my prick. My poor prick is so hyped-up since Phoenix that the steering of it is automatic.

He tells Joe-Joe to lay back on the floor, his prick in the air. Joe-Joe is a tasty piece of youth too. You could see he has a way to go to be a full-grown man -- be he isn't far from fucking one.

I am more than ready when Ricky Rick leads me over to Joe-Joe's prick. Hotter than ever. Joe-Joe's cock stands straight up in the air like a newly sprouted pink tulip. God, do I want to sit on it! Fortunately, that's exactly what Ricky Rick wants for my ass, too.

Joe-Joe sighs and blows into the crack of my ass that's receiving his cock. The head of his cock nuzzles around into the fur of my asscrack, lost in my hairy cleft. I open wide my haunches. I aim my butthole for him. Ricky Rick eases me down onto Joe-Joe's crotch. There's no pain at all. Only the smooth pleasure of my man's butt snarfing up Joe-Joe's boydick like it's the most natural thing in the world. Our balls rest atop one another. My back is to him. I can't see how Joe-Joe is taking this fuck. He probably has his eyes closed dreaming of dicking some pussy. Joe-Joe's cock quivers up in me, taunt, probing, stirring up my insides. Ricky Rick makes me lay back, covering Joe-Joe's chest. His chest heaves beneath mine.

Ricky Rick tells Taylor to come over, tells him to fuck my mouth, fuck that mouth since it's already open, open and drooling with pleasure. Yeah, look at the way he sucks your cock. Feed him your meat, shovel it in! I really did like sucking Taylor's dick. Taylor always gets a kick out of how my tongue snakes around his fucktube.

I have such a long tongue that I can slide it up under his balls and tickle Taylor between his legs.

Ricky Rick gets down close to my working jaws to watch me swallow Taylor's cock.

"Mm, you suck cock like a pro, fuckface. Would you like more cock in there?" Ricky Rick pulls Sean's cock close to my face so that I'm eye-to-eye with it.

Of course I moan and shake my head yes as best I can. I've taken turns sucking all their cocks before, but never together at one time. I know I can do it. Even if I get lockjaw, I'll take one cock in each cheek. I hawk up a lot of spit, filling my cheeks with it just in time for Ricky Rick to guide Sean's stiff sweet-tasting candy cane into the other side of my cheek. Their cocks are touching, sliding together inside my mouth. Sharing my mouth and colliding on my tongue. Soon as their cockmeats mesh together inside my mouth, Taylor's cock stiffens, his balls dance around my lips. His cock floods my mouth with his warm spermy juice.

The other kids laugh at Taylor's jism drooling out the side of my mouth, coating me and Sean's cock as well. Both their cocks are swimming in Taylor's cum. It puddles up in my throat. I gargle what I can, letting the rest spill out. His teen milk makes my mouth more receptive for sucking. Ricky Rick isn't about to let us up yet even if we wanted to, which we don't. Taylor's trigger-happy cock is stiffening for another go around anyway.

Down below, biting at the edge of my asshole, I can feel Ricky Rick working his way into my fur-lined hole. He sticks his finger into my hole, alongside Joe-Joe's cock. He wiggles it around down there, while the two boys writhe on top of me, feeding me uncut cock.

Ricky Rick strokes the dark hairs on my legs. He plays with the curly shorthairs around my timber-prick. He yanks them like a bully yanking a girl's pigtails. My cock flops. Pre-cum bubbles in it.

Yes, Ricky Rick is working that fat uncircumcised gristly knob of a cock into my already penetrated asshole. He's determined to double-cock me. I've never tasted so many cocks in all my holes in all my life. I'm a one-man orgy.

Ricky Rick spreads my legs wider.

There it is, his marvelous cock, feeling as wide and prickly as a pineapple, scrunching up into my tight ass with a delicious sloppy prong of meat. He moves it right alongside Joe-Joe's supple cockpiece. I take a deep breath. It slithers up farther. It feels tighter and juicier than it felt before.

The folds and contours of Ricky Rick's cock are feelable to the very last inch. I'd scream if I didn't already have a combined total of sixteen inches of svelte young male meat brushing in and out of my mouth like electric toothbrushes.

Watching Ricky Rick fucking me in the ass turns them on. Taylor nearly shoots off again, but he holds it, saves it, hoping to cum with the others.

Ricky Rick's dicking dick is breaking me open. My balls start to spill sperm when Ricky Rick jabs his cock all the way in.

"Hey guys! Look at that thing go! Stand back! This big fat fucker's coming just because we're fucking him! Yeah! Hole! How do you like that star-cock now!"

Ricky Rick heaves above me, careful not to soil himself with my blobbing spunk-cream.

I love being made into an altar of orifices for the New Boyz cocks. I live for their sweet cum, and that's exactly what they are going to give me.

Joe-Joe pipes up below me: "Ricky – his ass feels so tight now that your cock is in there – I'm gonna – gonna blow my wad!!" Joe-Joe squirms on the floor beneath me. He clutches at my bear chest.

"Well, shut up and shoot your load then, fucker!!" Ricky Rick keeps plunging his cock. "Cream that wad in his hot fucking pussy-ass! Shit, man, that's what it's fucking made for! Hell, I can feel it creaming! Oh, make it nice and warm and slick for my big fucker!"

Ricky Rick pinions me to the floor. His knobby cock slides in and out of my ass all the easier as Joe-Joe's load lubricates my ass-passage. These kids are true musicians all right. They rock and roll my holes in perfect sync, cumming on the downbeat almost together. Taylor and Sean shoot off into my mouth. Frothy teenage cream bubbles up out of my mouth like all their throat-drilling has finally struck oil. They take turns fucking my soft throat socket until each is satisfied that his balls are drained. Both Taylor and Sean collapse together on the floor. My mouth dribbles their mingled cherry jizz.

I can see Ricky Rick riveting my ass above me now. His pecs flex. His ass rears high in the air. His thick cock pulls out of my ass to the very ring of his foreskin. He slams it back into me, his fierce bull boy balls slamming my buttcheeks. He gives each of my double-poled asscheeks a squeeze. His cock barrels in ramrod straight, jostling my fuckhole. It stays there, cumming, creaming and unloading for what feels like hours.

My poor cockboat ass overflows with Boyz cum. The stuff is everywhere when Ricky Rick finishes dicking me.

Finally Joe-Joe and Ricky Rick both slip out of me together, leaving my gaping spread hole full of cum and fond memories. That's a wrap.

- - -

At the end of the tour and our last wild night in the hundredth hotel room, Ricky Rick hands me a ring. He doesn't say so, but I notice it is the twin of the famous ring he keeps in his ear. I thank him and say I'll have to get my ear pierced when I get home.

He says in his own gruff, lovable way, "Me and the Boyz want you to hang around for awhile. You've been lucky for us so far. And I want you to wear this ring down here." He flicks my fist-size dickhead with his finger. My dick drools at the thought of sporting Ricky Rick's other earring in my pierced cockhead. "I gotta admit. It's sorta hard to find a guy with a dick this big who's as fun as you."

I'll gladly wear the ring wherever Ricky Rick tells me to wear it. I accept Ricky Rick's business proposal. I drop to my knees to finalize the deal inside Ricky Rick's shorts. Me and the Boyz will make beautiful music together.

SATIN
John Patrick

I lose out on the dark, sexy hunk and I don't think my luck can get much worse, but I am wrong. I offer to give Eddie a ride home from the bar. He too lost out on the one he'd been pursuing and, as always, I take pity on Eddie. Once I took so much pity on him I let him blow me in the john. It wasn't a bad blowjob; rather good, as a matter of fact, but nothing I want to repeat. Nelly Eddie simply is not my type.

"Steve-ie," Eddie says softly. I turn and look at him. His face is a crumbling, ashy white, except for the reddened lips. He's sunken down in the leather seat of my black Lincoln Town car and he has the most bizarre expression on his face; it is hard to place at first, looking up at me, eyebrows raised, hint of a smile, hint of a tongue at the back of his open mouth, until I realize that he has slipped into his drag scene again. Then I see the rest of it. His shirt and pants are open and he is wearing red satin panties, which are too small to hold his balls, which are slipping out the sides, and the head of his now hard uncut cock seems to be winking at me. He's fingering the satin. "I put these on just for you," he says.

"C'mon, Eddie," I say.

"Tell me what you're wearing," he says.

"Eddie, this isn't my scene." I'm edging myself as close as possible to the door.

"I bet you have on those same white cotton Calvins you had on that night you let me – " He puts a hand around my wrist and locks on. With the other one he's rubbing himself. "Just touch it. Just touch it and see how much I want you."

"Eddie, you're really fuckin' out of line," I shout.

"I just want yah to touch it, Steve-ie." He's strong as hell, for a nelly shit, and pulls on my wrist. I yank back hard, dragging his body closer to mine. He starts to half-slide, half-crawl toward me. I'm practically up on my feet in the back of the car to avoid having to touch him. Eddie slides down into my lap with a kind of whining and grunting noise, like an infant. I slow the car to a crawl and yank him off me. He slams against the door, stunned. I hit him in the rib cage, hard. He's still making that noise, like a child; it enrages me. I hit him again, and again, just bringing my fist down like a gavel on his side. Something seems to crack a little bit. He groans. I pull the car to a stop. I reach over him and push open the door. I shove, hard. It takes some doing but I manage to get him off the seat and onto the soft shoulder of the road. He cries out, begging me not to leave him.

Suddenly a car passes, its lights putting Eddie in the spotlight, as if back at the bar, on the stage. I gasp at the pitiful sight. He reminds me of that dethroned queen Cookie, sitting alone night after night, having seen far better nights, waiting for a pick-up. I made the mistake of sitting down next to her (or, rather, him, because his real name is Clyde) when I first moved down here. In those days I hadn't made up my mind about drag. I was both fascinated and repelled. Maybe it went back to when my dad paid for me to see a psychiatrist. The doc said, "You should be seeing a boyish girl, not a girlish boy." Well, I tried that, but it didn't work out. My dad said the girl was a lesbian.

Cookie seemed to have more brains than any psychiatrist I saw. She told me about the guy who wouldn't take her out because she was from London. "Honey, a queen is a queen," Cookie said, lighting up a Marlboro Light with a theatrical flair, "no matter where you're from." I told her about my bad times with my dad. She said, "When I told my parents I was a drag queen, I could just see their faces over the phone. Being gay is one thing, but a drag queen on top of it!"

Cookie tried to set me straight, as it were: "Drag is an art form," she said. "And just the same as an artist paints a picture, we paint and present ourselves as a form of art, our canvas being ourselves."

Eddie does not look at all artful now, on his knees in the gutter crying out to me. Maybe if he were in full drag I'd like him better. A kinda cute boy in some respects, but he's wearing red satin underpants.

But there I go making judgments again. "Let's not criticize all the time," Cookie had said. "Let's harmonize." I'll always regret never letting her harmonize over my body.

I blink back to the present. I am out of the car, standing over Eddie, and for some reason I am unable to move. Then he grabs my legs. "Please, Steve-ie," he coos.

"Okay, bitch. I'll take you home. But I want you to put on a show for me. I want to see you in drag. None of this half-assed playin' around in satin underpants."

"Oh, no, Steve-ie, no more half-assed anything."

Fucking can lead to enlightenment, Marco Vassi said once. Fucking can lead to many things. It can also be a bummer sometimes. I am thinking this is one of those times. I am waiting for Eddie in his bedroom, sitting on his brass double bed with the red satin sheets. It's all very comfortable. He says his parents pay him to stay away. A dress like something Carol Channing wore in "Hello, Dolly!" is hanging in the closet. I remember what someone at the bar had told me that Eddie played a great Channing. He lip-synched to "Till the Parade Passes By," won second place. That was his night in the spotlight. Nothing since. A year in hiding, because he didn't win.

I strip to my briefs, begin to wonder what's taking him so long. I get up and go into the bathroom. He shuts off the water and reaches over the stall for his towel. He emerges from the shower wrapped in terrycloth from his armpits down.

"You want the shower?" he asks.

"No," I say, "I want to talk to you."

He looks at me with his large brown eyes. He's taken his shiny brown hair out of the ponytail and it now frames his face. He flutters his long lashes at me and slides a hand across my arm. "What, Steve-ie? What did you want to talk about?"

I feel a silly thickness in my throat as I eye this boy, who is a boy but not really a boy. A thing. I lean forward and take Eddie by the shoulders. I kiss him quickly on the lips, just to see what it would be like. He's got sweet breath and there's a strange shudder between my legs, one that I immediately feel guilty about. This is a queen, I tell myself, what the fuck am I doing?

Eddie giggles and I watch his butt as he drops the towel and walks away, his firm, hairless little cheeks moving in a disturbing rhythm. I stand looking after him for a few moments, even after he's gone.

- – -

I can't believe it but my tongue is up Eddie's butt, or what he calls his pussy, and he is groaning in gratitude. This is an acquired sensation, but a delicious one. I must admit I really like licking between his legs, first the butthole, then the balls, then the cock. Then back again, deeper and deeper. Until he's begging. I can't imagine any of my friends would understand this. It's a rush that I can't quite comprehend myself. But it's hard to concentrate on such questions when Eddie is sucking your cock. He makes me come, but he isn't done. Not by a long shot. And thank god because, as exquisite as the blowjob was, I do want to fuck him. This is raw, vital sex. Pure sex.

Desire from a bottom, waiting for me, eager for me, has always gotten me hard and kept me hard. But this is new to me, talking sweetly to a boy as if he was a girl. He's on his knees, presenting his glorious ass, "Fuck my pussy," he begs. "Fuck it."

My dick slides into him as if we were built for each other. No one has ever appreciated my cock more than Eddie, if all his moaning and groaning can be believed. He comes, but tells me to stay in, to keep on, come myself. And I do.

I feel the satin sheet under us become steadily more soaked with sweat, saliva, and cum. Eddie gets up, "just for a sec, Steve-ie," and goes to the bathroom.

My heart is pounding in my ears as he gets into position again. There is no end to this, I have found. Eddie can take it all and beg for more. The head of my dick pops into his ass and he whimpers, as if it's hurting him, and slowly, carefully, I press my entire length into him again. I pull almost all the way out, then slam back in. He's stopped whimpering; now he's crying, but still begging for me to continue. We're like a fucking machine, two parts moving together perfectly. His hands are all over me now as he begins to come. He has a fierce, shuddering orgasm that seems to go on forever as I stare into his eyes.

"Yeah, come for me, Eddie." Eddie. It's the first time I've said his name.

"Steve-ie!" he shrieks as the last of the cum is pulled from his little cock.

But damned if he's still not through. He wants to suck me again. I love having him on his knees in front of me, his throat milking me. I grab his hair, relax with his incredible ability. He can take the full length of me without gagging. He watches me the entire time, lets me see the tears that fill his eyes and roll down his cheeks as he sucks. Where it comes from I have no idea, but more sperm eventually spurts from me and he takes it all.

"Maybe I'll see you again?" Eddie asks hopefully as I pull my clothes on. I shrug, as if not to rule out the possibility.

- – -

I see him leave the apartment building, follow his Volkswagen to the bar. They let me go backstage. I am transfixed. He has transformed himself into Carol Channing again. The Channing of the '60s, not the '90s re-run. Now that I have seen him in full drag I am impressed. "Eddie," I finally manage to whisper.

He is surprised to see me, interrupts his primping. "How do I look?"

"Fine, hon- – ," I say, terrified now. I nearly called him "honey," a term I despise. I have come too close to the scene. It is a nightmare from which I must awake. I run out of the room, out of the bar, into the street.

I sit in my car smoking a joint, coming to terms with this crazy attraction we have for one another. I decide I will go back to the bar, take him from that place and bring him back to his room. And we'll fuck again there in that satin-sheeted bed. And we'll sleep together this time. And in the morning we'll talk about what it all meant. Yes, that's what we'll do.

SATIN II: EDDIE'S STORY (OR, HOW I LEARNED TO SUCK OFF REAL MEN)
Jay Greene

My parents were going at it again. Even from upstairs in my bedroom, with the door closed and my radio on, I could hear them yelling down in the kitchen. Probably half the neighborhood could, too. With my mother's Irish temper and my father's Italian machismo it was always high drama played to the hilt whenever they had a fight. And, as usual, this one was about me.

"He's a fag!" my father roared. "What do you expect me to do about it? It's too late now!"

"It wouldn't be, if you were half the father you should be!"

"What the hell can I do? Beat the shit out of him every time you find him with another guy?"

"Maybe that's why he's the way he is! You only know one way to deal with him – beat him!"

"So now it's my fault!"

And on and on...

I turned the radio up a little louder, trying desperately to block them out. There's nothing as wonderful as having your parents broadcast to the world at large that their son's a queer. Especially when you really can't help the way you are or do anything to change it. I was born gay; I'm certain of it. And although I try my best not to advertise the fact, it must be obvious to a lot of men just by my appearance and the way I act naturally, that I'm interested in cock and probably could be had.

I know my features are effeminate. I've got a pretty, almost girlish, face, with long eyelashes, a sensual mouth, and rosy cheeks that don't show the slightest hint of beard stubble. I shave only twice a month, and that's once more than is really necessary. My hair is very blond and naturally curly. I keep it cut short – at my father's insistence – but I still look more like a punk female rock singer than your average football player. Add this to my tall, thin figure and my delicate hands, which have a way of fluttering out of control, in spite of my efforts to restrain them, and I guess you've got a sitting target for any guy who's ever thought about sticking it to a queer if the opportunity presented itself. Because that's always the way It's happened. I've never been the one to initiate the situations that have gotten me in so much trouble all my life. It's always been the other guy, coming on to me. For instance, take the specific situation that was causing such a volatile outburst down in the kitchen that afternoon.

To the best of my knowledge, I hadn't done a thing to provoke it. I'd stayed home from school that day, nursing the tail end of a bad cold. My father was at work and my mother had gone out shopping, so I was all alone in the house. About two o'clock a man from the electric company came by to read the meter. He was new on the route and didn't know how to get into the cellar. When he rang the front bell, I went down to answer it. I didn't think twice about the fact that I was wearing only a thin pair of pajama bottoms. I mean, who expects a sex-crazed rapist to come ringing your doorbell in the middle of a sunny spring afternoon?

I let him in and showed him the way to the basement and was just standing around minding my own business while he took his readings, when suddenly I became aware that he was staring at me. Not just casually looking, the way one person does at another, but in a way that seemed all too familiar. From the time I was very young I've had men look at me in that other way and I've come to recognize it so well that it's almost an instinct. The hairs on the back of my neck started to tingle from the recognition and I began to flutter. I can't help it. Whenever I get nervous, I lose control of my hands. They move around like newly-freed birds trying their wings. "The – uh – next time you come," I said, trying to avoid those piercing dark eyes of his, "you can get in the cellar through that door over there. It's always open." I pointed, meaning to do it with just one finger, but the other three somehow got into the act too and they all wriggled in a different direction. He looked toward the door and then back at me. His hand went down to his crotch and began to slowly rub it. "Oh, yeah? Always open, huh? At night, too?"

"What – uh – what do you mean?" As I became more nervous, the pitch of my voice always rose. He was smirking now.

"I mean, if somebody needed to get in here at night, the door'd be open?" His rubbing was getting more forceful, and as were the results it was causing in his pants. From where I stood at the bottom of the cellar steps I could see a lump growing in his uniform. The sight of a man's cock has always excited me and this one had something in his pants that definitely commanded my attention.

He wasn't much to look at himself. He was balding and his face was more coarse than handsome, but that lump he was rubbing had all the earmarks of a true beauty, as though nature had concentrated all of its attention between his legs and done a slapdash job on the rest of him. Somehow, the very notion that a sub-average slob like that might have a gorgeous piece of meat on him made it all the more exciting. I mean, you expect a gorgeous man to have a cock that matches the rest of him in attractiveness, and it's a disappointment when he doesn't. But when someone as forgettable as that meter man starts flashing a spectacular piece of pork it can't help but arouse your interest. The lure of the cock takes on a force all its own; drawing you to it in spite of the person it's attached to. At least that's how it is with me. Begging the obvious, I asked him, "Why would you want to come here at night...?"

"To give you some of this." He took a firm grip on his cock through the loose trousers and pointed it at me. "Maybe you'd like to have some of it right now, huh?"

"I – " I gulped. "I don't know what you're talking about." I tried to look away, but that enormous, throbbing bulge he was holding out to me kept calling my attention back. I was fascinated by the thickness of it alone. Would I be able to get my hand all the way around it, I wondered? Or my lips...?

"Come here," he ordered. With a flick his belt buckle was open and he was starting to take down his fly. "Come on over here and see what I got for you." Those were the operative words. For me. As though is was some treasure meant to be mine alone. How could I resist? Nervously I started toward him. He grinned and reached into his pants to pull it out. "That's right. Come on over here and look at what I got for you."

When he finally pulled it out, I almost fainted. It was every bit as big as I'd thought it would be...and then some. Fat and long and hard and uncut. His foreskin was a thick ridge around the middle of the plum-shaded head. When he stroked it back, I saw a trickle of juice run out of the wide hole in the tip. I swallowed hard.

"C'mon," he said holding it out to me, "it won't bite. If you don't!" He laughed at his own joke, then reached for my hand and brought it to his cock.

I couldn't help gasping with amazement as he curled my fingers around the enormous shaft. It was as hard as a bar of iron, but the skin on it felt like satin. So smooth and shiny and soft to the touch. I swallowed again, hearing the gulp in my throat.

"You like that big, fat cock, don't ya, boy?" he said. He dropped his hand from mine and widened his stance, spreading his legs apart so that his prick stood up between them like a pole waiting for a flag to be hung on it. "Don't you? Huh? You got an eye for a big dick."

My tongue licked nervously across my lower lip. "Wh-what do you want me to do?"

"Whatever you feel like," he said matter-of-factly. "But I think you really wanna kiss it, don't you?"

Of course I did. I couldn't have denied it if I'd tried. My mouth was watering to not only kiss it but taste that gorgeous piece of manflesh. It didn't matter that he was slightly repulsive. His sex organ was one of the most beautiful I'd ever seen. Perfectly shaped, with no ugly veins or bumps to mar the smooth perfection of the fat shaft. A heavy sprout of dark brown hair stuck through his open fly around the base of his cock, and that turned me on, too. I've always been excited by the sight of pubic hair on a man. Perhaps it is because I have so little of my own and it seems like the mark of true masculinity if a man's bush is a thick, wild tangle for me to bury my nose in while I'm holding his cock deep in my throat. I saw him glance at his watch.

"Come on, kid. If you're gonna blow me," he said although it was all my idea, "go on and do it. I don't got all day." His hands came down hard on my shoulders and pressed me to my knees. I dropped without the slightest struggle, as though mesmerized by the winking eye of his cockslit as it opened and closed in response to the throbbing of the shaft below. There was a faintly stale, sour odor to his crotch when I got close enough to smell it, but even if I'd tried to stop from sucking him at that point it was too late. The moment my head was level with his cock, he took a grip on the back of my head and pushed me into it. His huge prick rammed through my lips and so deeply into my mouth on the first thrust that I gagged and almost threw up. I put my hands on his thighs to push him back. "You gonna play with it or suck it?" he grunted. "Come on. Do it."

I've had a good share of cocks in my mouth during my lifetime, but none as big as his. It stretched my lips so far apart that the corners felt like they were going to split. My tongue had very little room to wriggle under the weight of that fat shaft as he drove it back and forth at my throat. I tried to gather as much juice into my mouth as I could, knowing it would go down easier if was slick and wet. It wasn't the best blowjob I'd ever given, but it turned him on like crazy. As I gulped and swallowed, taking him down as far as I could without tearing apart my throat, he moaned and tightened the grip of his hands in my hair. He started to fuck my face with a fury. His knees trembled and the paunch of his belly shook, thrusting at my forehead while I drew him in and out of my mouth. I sucked hard on his foreskin, pulling it as far up on the bulbous head as I could and then teasing it back down the shaft with my tongue. He loved it. His moans got louder and his breath more ragged with each bobbing movement of my head toward his open fly. I knew he was going to cum in a matter of moments. I felt the shaft swelling against my lips and the heavy tube running up the underside of it pulsing with juice that needed to be spilled and swallowed. My lips moved faster, working for the reward I deserved. I could feel the first trickle of it running over my tongue – sharp and slightly bitter – and I milked him furiously with my mouth for the full flow.

My own cock was standing straight up inside my pajama bottoms, jerking fitfully back and forth with anticipation of that moment when he would fill me with his seed. Flood my mouth with the hot explosion of his cum. Pour it down my throat as fast as I could drink it. Drown my tongue in the wash of salty sperm. It was coming. Closer now. Quivering in the tube. Bubbling up from his balls. Ready to spill into me. Right on the brink of shooting.

Then, "Eddie? Are you down there?" My mother was on the cellar steps, her heels clacking against the wood as she took them two at a time, and then her cry of surprise and scream of disbelief split the air like a knife.

The meter man pulled his cock out of my mouth at just the moment when he began to shoot. His cum fired at my face in thick volleys that splattered across my nose and dribbled down my chin while my mother watched in horror and I tried helplessly to scramble to my feet. There was quite a scene down there in the basement for a while. My mother started to run back up the steps, crying for the police at the top of her lungs, and I half-ran, half-fell after her in total panic. She carried on like a wild woman, screaming that she was going to have the man arrested. He put an end to that notion in an instant by swearing that it was all my doing. "Honest to god, lady, he grabbed at me before I knew what was happening! Hell, I'm a

married man myself. I got three kids! You think I'd want to do
something like this? It was all his idea, lady! I couldn't keep him off
me!"

Considering the number of times she'd caught me in similar
situations – or heard about them from neighbors and officials at the
high school – what he said seemed to make perfect sense to my
mother. Not withstanding the fact that the guy out weighed me by a
hundred pounds and could have put my lights out with just one punch
if he'd really wanted to resist my perverted advances, I immediately
became the guilty party. I guess it was a little late in the game for her
to think of me as a victim.

"Get out of here!" she yelled at the man. "And if you show
your face here again, I'll have you arrested on the spot!"

Then she turned her wrath on me. "You get back up to your
room and stay there. When your father gets home, you'll wish you
were never born."

Well, that was something I'd wished quite a few times, so it
wasn't really such a threat. What could he do, I thought, that he
hadn't already done – or tried to do – before? Beat me up again? Cut
off my allowance? Confine me to the house? Put a chain around my
leg like a wild dog and keep me locked in my room for the rest of my
life? Whatever the punishment, it wouldn't – and couldn't – make me
any different than I was. The same thing was bound to happen again
and again' as long as there were other men like the meter man who
recognized what I was and knew I couldn't help myself from being
used whenever they wanted to take advantage of me.

I'd never seen such a look on my father's face, though, as
when he came to my room that afternoon. His cheeks were almost
purple with barely suppressed fury. When he spoke, his lips were
tightly pursed, and his eyes glared with hatred. He looked like if he'd
thought he could get away with it he'd have me killed on the spot.

"Your mother told me what happened today," he said, making
it sound like he had no part in my parentage himself. "It's just lucky
for you that it wasn't me who caught you! If It was up to me, I'd
throw you outta the house right now and wash my hands of you
forever, but she says I gotta try. So I'm gonna try. One last time. And
if that don't work. No, I'm fuckin' finished with you. Understand?"

I nodded my head yes, but I didn't understand him. No more
than he did. All I saw on his face or heard in his voice was
undisguised hatred. That, and the complete inability on his part to

accept a child he had sired who was so different from himself. Who found love in a way he thought was repulsive, just because it was with someone of my own sex. I saw in my father's eyes the total refusal to accept me for what I was, not what he would have liked me to be. That fact alone blinded him to any sense of justice and made me guilty of the worst crime he could imagine: not being a man. If I'd been caught screwing an Avon lady who'd come to the front door, or jumped on a Girl Scout peddling cookies, he probably would have clapped me on the back in congratulations and offered me a cigar. Because that would have been something he could understand...

But sucking on the meter man's dick was something so alien to my father's own instincts that he rejected not only the idea of doing it, but the son who found it so attractive. I didn't see anything wrong with what had happened in the cellar that afternoon – or in any of the similar situations that had preceded it. I'd only done what I thought was right. I'd been attracted to the man's cock, so I'd sucked it. To me, that was a perfectly natural and normal thing to do. I'd only followed my instincts. Many years later, I finally realized how much my father might have helped me at that point in my life if only he'd loved me enough to try to understand the way I was and overcome his prejudice toward my way of life. If he'd been at all concerned with my emotional growth, he might have tried to teach me the difference between love and lust. He might have explained that what I'd done in the cellar was wrong because the man was only using me. Taking advantage of my vulnerability to satisfy his own desires, as so many others had already done in my life. If sucking cock or even taking it up the ass was how I expressed my sexuality, he should have been wise enough to tell me to do it only with a man who loved me and meant something important to me; not with anyone who waved it in my face. But that was a lesson I'd have to learn for myself, the hard way, after years of letting myself be used and abused because I didn't know any better.

My father was too bigoted and close-minded to deal with my differentness in any way but to try to stamp it out. And the way he chose to do it really floored me. My father's solution to the problem of my homosexuality was to take me to a baseball game. "Your mother says I should do things with you," he grunted. "So I'm gonna take you with me to the Sox game on Saturday afternoon. Maybe if you see how real men act, you'll get these fruity ideas outta your head." To me, that was the worst punishment he'd ever devised. I couldn't think of anything worse than having to sit through an entire game of baseball in person. I loathed all sports, but especially baseball. Whenever he watched a game on TV, I got as far away from even the sound of it as I could get. It seemed asinine to me. Grown men yelling their throats raw while they watched other men swing sticks at a ball. What a true test of intellect and human creativity that was!

I cried and begged and pleaded for the rest of the week to get out of having to go, but come Saturday I had no choice but to get in the car and drive down to the stadium with my father. Even a severe bout of self-induced vomiting that morning held no sway with my parents. They were determined to make me a man, and what better way to do it than inflicting the all-American sport on me?

We took our seats in the bleachers and I tried my best to stir up a glimmer of interest in the game, but it was hopeless. I didn't understand any of the rules in the first place, and my father was too busy yelling at the top of his lungs and shaking his fist at the umpire to explain anything to me. In fact, he acted like he wasn't even with me. When I tugged on his sleeve and tried asking him a question, he brushed me aside like a fly on his shirt. By the fourth inning, I was really getting nauseous. The nervous strain of just being there was bad enough, but I'd also agitated my stomach by throwing up so many times that morning. The afternoon heat, mixed with the smell of cigar smoke and beer and rancid popcorn butter and cheap hot dogs was making my bile rise all over again. I knew if I sat there much longer I was going to vomit all over myself. "Dad, I've got to go to the toilet," I said. "I think I'm going to be sick again."

"Huh?" he grunted, not even turning his eyes from the field to look at me.

"I've got to go to the men's room. Where is it?"

He looked around with annoyance all over his face. "I dunno. Down there somewhere." He jerked his thumb toward the exit stairs.

"I'll be back in a couple of minutes. Okay?"

"Yeah, sure," he said, then suddenly leaped to his feet and started screaming obscenities at one of the players.

I slipped out of the row and went toward the exit. One of the vendors gave me directions to the men's room, and as soon as I was inside I felt waves of sickness hit my stomach like an iron fist. The place reeked of stale piss and ammonia. There were three toilet stalls opposite a half-dozen urinals and I raced toward the farthest one at the end. I reached it just in time. Slamming the stall door behind me, I dropped to my knees beside the crud-covered toilet bowl and threw up until my insides were sore from heaving. I'd never felt so miserable in all my life. I flushed the toilet and tried to stand up' but my knees were too weak. I crouched alongside the toilet' trying to breathe deeply and get control of myself. My face was covered with sweat' but there wasn't even any paper in the dispenser to dry myself. As I fumbled for my handkerchief, I heard the outer door open and a sudden rush of loud, laughing voices filled the room. There must have been a break in the game, because at least a dozen men came in all at once to take a piss. To my horror, the lock on the stall door where I knelt gave way as one of them banged against it and stumbled inside. The man's fly was already open and his cock half out of his pants before he realized I was there.

"What the fuck – ? " He gaped down at me through glazed, half-drunken eyes, then started to grin. "All right'" he said. "I didn't count on this, but what the hell! Just lemme empty this beer first, huh?" He yanked his cock all the way out and aimed it at the bowl, letting fly a stream of piss. I cowered helplessly against the wall, my hands fluttering in all directions as some of his urine splashed up on me while he unloaded. I'd never been that close to a man while he pissed.

Despite my fear, I felt a knot of excitement tightening in my stomach as I stared at the long, fat hose of cock hanging out of his pants and the bright yellow fountain pouring from it.

He was very good-looking. About thirty, with dark wavy hair and a thick moustache. He had a baseball cap pulled down over his forehead at a rakish angle and wore a Sox T-shirt that had wide rings of sweat under the armpits. The kind of man you'd see driving a truck during the week, or maybe working on a construction site. The kind my father would have been proud to call his son. All the while he pissed he kept looking down at me and grinning. I didn't know why...until he'd finished and shook off the last few drops. Then, as I watched him start to play with himself and take a few uncertain steps closer to where I knelt, it suddenly dawned on me. How dumb could I have been? Of course that's why he thought I was there? What other reason could there have been?

"Okay, sister, it's all yours now!" he said, waving his semi-hard cock at my face. "But do it quick, huh? I don't wanna miss too much of the game." He cupped his hand on the back of my neck and brought my head forward. The moment his penis touched my lips I didn't have to think twice about opening my mouth and taking it inside. I gulped it down feverishly and began to suck on it with a skill that astonished and delighted him. Within seconds, his cock was hard as the bats they were swinging out on the field – and nearly as long.

"Hey, Mike!" a voice called from outside the stall after a few minutes. "You fall in or what?" The man laughed and jabbed his prick harder at my drooling mouth. "Stick around, Tony!" he called. "I got a surprise for you in here!" He nudged my shoulder. "You wanna blow my brother, too, when you're done with me?" he whispered.

Without missing a stroke, I nodded my head yes. Why not? Let them all come in and have a turn, I thought. I'd take on as many as wanted it. After all, wasn't this just why my father had dragged me here against my will? So I'd be around real men? To watch how they acted and share their interests? I felt the first hot spurt of cum hit the back of my throat and swallowed it hungrily, already for the next big cock to be shoved in my mouth. I sucked a total of eight different men – one of them twice, a horny bastard he was – before I left the toilet and went back to join my father in the bleachers. Actually, I could have stayed longer and blown another two or three, because Dad hadn't even missed me.

On the way home in the car, he asked how I'd liked the game. "Oh, it was great!" I said, with genuine enthusiasm sounding in my voice. "Will you take me again next week?"

He looked at me in surprise. "Sure, Eddie."

"Do they play baseball all year, Dad?"

"No. After the season ends in September, then there's football. And after that, there's always basketball."

"Will you take me to those games' too?"

"Sure, kid! We'll go every week, if you want to!" He reached over and tousled my hair. It was the first time I could remember him touching me with any show of affection in years. "You know," he said, "I think we just might make a real man of you yet!"

I didn't say anything to that, but I couldn't help but smile, thinking of all the real men I would be making in the months to come.

- This story originally appeared in the late, lamented HEAT magazine.

SEDUCING THE STARS
Keith Davis

I'd watched him for a while. Teenaged boy down the street. Basketball player. Track star. Baby face and a man's body. Only 18. And the easiest piece of ass I'd ever had.

Oh sure, at first he wasn't gay, but he might let me suck his dick. Arrogant son-of-a-bitch. I had his legs in the air and his cherry hole split wide open in no time. So guys, if you want a few pointers, this is how it happened:

Step one: Get the dude alone in your house at night. Ask him over to help you with some manly task like putting up shelves or helping with the yard work. Make sure he works up a sweat so he'll peel off his skin-tight T-shirt and, flash, you a look at the tits you'll be abusing later in the evening.

I asked Ben over to work in my yard. I live in Mississippi, so sweat dripped off his pumped body in no time. Sure enough, he peeled off his little frat T-shirt and gave me an eyeful of bulging biceps, slick, bronzed pecs and washboard stomach. Now if I'd been your average neighborhood, I'd have of just sniffed his sweaty shirt until I shot a load in it – content to let the boy wear my spunk home.

But I'm not your average neighborhood.

Once your boy's teenaged muscles are aching and his lean body is glistening with sweat – invite him inside. Insist on it. Yeah, so what if he's got to meet Susie later or he's going to the movies with friends – once he's in your house, you own him.

Offer him a beer. If he's under 21 he'll appreciate the booze and it will lower his inhibitions.

Ben didn't have any plans and jumped at a free drink. Both shirtless, we kicked back on my sofa with our Buds and talked about pussy. I had the air conditioning on full blast. The cool air made his little nips rigid.

You've got to be able to talk nasty about pussy. If they think you're faggy, they'll disappear out the door in a second. So yeah, I talk to him about cunts. Wet, dripping, smelly cunts. While Ben got off talking about some cheerleader's snatch, I brought out the dope.

Grass is vital to getting these young bucks in bed. They fucking want it. They just need the pot to help get past all the societal shit they've learned since birth. Face it, they're men. They live to get their rocks off.

Ben freaked a little at first. I was his Dad's age – a little older in fact – and here I was offering him smoke. He didn't freak long. Young guys will whore themselves for a lot less than my potent Thai weed.

Now your boy should be right where you want him. He's drunk from you beer. He's stoned from your grass. He's hard from your talk about pussy. He's yours. And Ben was mine. He got all giggly and so I asked him when he last had some of that sweet snatch. Of course he lied.

"Oh, uh, well, uh, last week."

Yeah, right.

Ben. Ben. Ben. He was a feast all right. His button fly cut-offs barely restraining his fat boy cock. His teenaged prick begged for release.

At this point, you lean your head back, you sigh, and you ever so subtly stroke your big dick. The boy will look. Always. At the beach. In the gym. Young guys all wonder what kinda meat their buddy's got swinging between his legs.

As I rubbed my meat, I said, "Man, this talk about pussy's getting me so fucking hot."

"Me, too, man," Ben said, shifting, trying to reduce the strain on his bulging fuck toy.

"How 'bout another beer?" I offered.

"Great, man."

At first, young guys are way too cool to touch themselves in front of you, but the second you leave the room their paws are all over their bulging baskets. Warning: Don't, whatever you do, disappear for too long or that sweet load will be on their Calvins instead of down your throat.

"Ben, ol' bud, you'll never guess what I found." I had two beers in one hand and a video cassette in the other.

"What's that?" he asked squirming with anticipation.

"I don't know if I should show you. Your parents would kill me."

"I'm over 18. I'm an adult. What is it?"

"Well, you know all that talk of pussy got me to thinking..."

"Yeah what?"

"Well, its a film called 'Riding Miss Daisy.'"

"Wow! Fuck, man. Put it in."

"I don't know if I should." Make the little bastard beg to see your fuck film.

"Come on, man."

So you pop the tape in. You can feel it in the air that, quickly, the kid's really hot to trot. But no need to rush. After a few minutes of twat you make the first move.

"God, Ben, don't think if I'm fucked up or what, but I can't watch her in these pants. I mean fuck we're both guys. We might as well be comfortable." Ninety-nine percent of the time you don't even have to ask the lads to do the same. By that time those perpetual hardons are screaming for release.

Then something strange happens. That hetero porno movie disappears and your own homemade video of some young trade – preferably the boy's peer – beating his meat appears.

Oh, my God, you don't know how that got on there. You've been helping guys like him make some extra cash with mail order videos. You didn't mean for anyone else to see them. You're not gay, but it's a great source of income for you both.

You fumble with the remote, giving your new boy plenty of time to see their naked friend jacking his swollen young prick, full balls bouncing against the crack of his bubble butt. Their immediate thought – I can do that.

After Ben had an eyeful, I shut off the video. "Oh Ben, I'm too stoned I didn't mean to show you that. He was just earning some spending money. Let me find another film. I'm sorry."

"It's okay." The inevitable pause before the kid asked, "How much did he make?"

"Oh, him? Hundreds. Not as much as someone like you would make, though. You're much better looking. Anyway let me find another tape."

"Where'd you film him?" Ben asked.

"In my bedroom. I've got a camcorder set up there? Why?"

"Oh, I don't know. It's just that..."

"What, guy?"

"I don't, that is, I could use some extra money."

"Ben, what are you saying?" Make the little fucker beg to show you what he's got. He wants to, you know. And he's so proud of it!

"I think I could do something like that."

"No way. Ben are you crazy. I know your parents."

"They wouldn't have to find out. It could be our secret."

"Are you sure it's not the booze and grass talking?" Of course it is. That and his throbbing boner. But who the fuck cares?

"It's not. I know I could do a better job than he did."

"I don't know." Always make 'em beg again.

"Come on. Please!"

"You realize I'm going to sell the tape. Other people WILL see you naked. They'll see you playing with yourself."

"I don't care. In fact, it kinda turns me on, ya know?""

"Yeah, I know. And you've got a nice package, why not show it off?"

"Yeah, why not."

"You know fags are gonna see this. They're gonna see you naked. They're gonna be jacking off thinking about doing all kinds of nasty things with your asshole and your cock and balls. Is that what you want, Ben?"

He hesitated a moment. The idea of people – even fags – fantasizing about him obviously made him hot. "I want the money," he said.

"All right, Ben. I'll make you a star."

So, stripped to our jockey shorts, we went to my bedroom. What an ass, I thought. I couldn't wait to sink my ten-inch meat between his virgin buns.

Ben turned around. "What should I do now, Sir?"

I tossed him another joint. "Smoke this while I set up the camera." What a liar. I'd set the camera up that afternoon. But I know how tight a cherry hole can be. I wanted Ben to enjoy giving up his ass as much as I'd enjoy taking it. He looked so sweet and innocent flopped on my bed. His leaking dick peaked over his elastic waistband. I always love this part – taking a basically straight, upright young guy and initiating him the secret pleasures of gay sex. Man to man. Cocks and balls dueling. Ass holes stretching. Yes, Ben's life was about to change forever.

I turned on the TV. Young studs get off seeing themselves on the screen. Ben looked great! So sweet and eager. So trusting. Waiting for ME to tell him what to do.

"Okay, Ben. Start rubbing your dick through your briefs." He responded stoking his fat eight inches slowly and deliberately – tracing his big mushroom crown. Without further direction, one hand went to his nipple and started twisting and turning it. He peeled off his shorts.

"Okay, now wad them up and sniff them," I ordered.

Ben hesitated for a second before slowly raising his pre-cum soaked briefs to his puppy-dog face. After a few cautious sniffs, convinced that it wasn't so bad, Ben really began smearing his used shorts in his face.

"Oh, yeah, that's it. You're a natural kid. Oh, fuck, yeah."

His hand worked his meat like a jack hammer.

"Chew it a little bit, Ben. Chew that shittin' underwear."

The straight boy opened his mouth and stuck his pink tongue through the open, piss-stained fly of his own drawers – alternatively watching himself on TV and staring straight into the camera – working it for his unknown audience.

"Now turn over. I want to get some shots of your ass."

Ben was a natural. He rolled over and lifted his track-star firm buns in the air, grinding and wiggling them for the camera. His low hanging balls filled with teen cream swung obscenely between his muscular thighs.

"Spread those cheeks, kid. I've got to get footage of your hole."

Ben reached behind opening his virgin ass up for me and the world, his light curly hair-lined his crack – a trail leading to the cutest pinkest little pucker ever captured on film. I zoomed in close, capturing every drop of sweat, tuft of hair and wrinkle and ridge of his unexplored anus.

"Now I want you to wink it at the camera."

"What?" Ben asked, a little confused.

"Your hole, wink it at the camera."

"How do I do that?"

"Thrust. Release. Thrust. Release."

Ben knew what I meant. He pushed and retracted his sphincter making his pink asshole blow kisses to the camera. I love putting guys in touch with their glorious holes for the first time.

"Play with it, Ben. Explore it. Run your fingers up and down your crack. Play with your opening."

He'd caught on now and was soon slapping and poking and teasing his hole like a professional porn star. One thick digit, wet with spit slowly began exploring his hole. First one joint. Then the next.

With a moan Ben was inside himself up to the knuckle. The first time ever something went into his hot little hole instead of coming out.

"Beautiful, Ben, That's it. Fuck yourself with your finger."

"Oh, God, Sir. It feels so fucking good."

"That's it, boy. Fuck yourself. Get that finger deep inside you. Show me your insides." When Ben rammed a second finger into his hole and I knew he needed something more substantial. As his two fingers spread to show me deep inside his shit chute, I reached for a dildo I just happened to have on hand. It was a medium. Perfect for eager beginners. The exact object to prime the boy for the real thing. I tossed it on the bed.

"Here, boy. Put some spit on this and shove it in that hot ass of yours."

With one hand deep inside his hole and the other pulling his pud, Ben didn't know what to do. He let go of his engorged dick long enough to shove the dildo in his mouth. Yeah. He was gonna get it nice and slick for his hole. The dildo looked so natural in his mouth I made a mental note to film him sucking on the real thing soon.

Ben rolled on his back, briefly sniffed his dirty fingers and then with a scream of delight – slammed the dildo in his ass.

"Lift those legs in the air, boy," I commanded. "I want to get a good shot of that dildo going into your ass."

Ben was happy to oblige. He lifted his strong legs in the air and continued to fuck himself. Long strokes. Pulling all the way out before slamming it all the way back in. Spanking his hole with it. "How do you feel, boy?" I asked.

"Wonderful. Shit, man, I've never felt better."

"Think you can handle something bigger than that little dildo, son?"

"You bet I can. You got a bigger one?"

"Sorry, kid. I don't."

"Too bad," Ben said dejectedly.

"But, I... well no, you wouldn't go for that."

"What is it" he asked.

"Well – this."

Ben looked at me for the first time since beginning his film career. I stood before him. Twenty-five years older. Graying. With a long, thick beautiful hard-on dripping with pre-cum waiting to violate his ass.

"Fuck me!" Ben screamed. "Fuck Me."

"Who's in charge now, boy?"

"You are! Fuck, what ever you say, stud. Just keep raping my ass."

"You love it don't you? You love being a faggot. You love having your ass dicked by a real man."

"Yes, Sir. I never thought anything could feel so good."

"You know, boy, I'm gonna make a shit load of money off this tape. Hot boy like you giving up his cherry!"

The idea of me fucking his ass on film sent Ben bucking into another orgasmic frenzy. His second load of teen cream splattered on his own jock-boy face.

With one hand twisting his titties, and my other hand forcing his own spunk down his throat I shot rope after rope of man cum up his ass. Finally we collapsed into a sticky heap of sweat, spunk, and spit.

Now, guys, once you've filmed and fucked the little bastard, before any Catholic guilt sets in, have them sign a model release. Take identification from their wallets to copy. This way you're still able to make money off their sexual humiliation long after they are married with children. Ben, however never married. Being a cock slut on video became his vocation. But that's another story. Before he left town for good, he brought me new "stars," friends, classmates, even his younger brother. Yeah, he wanted me to film his little brother at midnight – the second he turned 18. But that too is another story!

So remember, with a little planning – and a little film – you can turn even the straightest, butchest jock into your personal porn star.

SNAKE COUNTRY: A COUNTRY BOY STORY
Tab Lambert

Back when I was young and naive I used to make fun of guys from the country. In my situation I really shouldn't have been making fun of others, but I didn't know any better back then. After all, I was still in high school in a small consolidated school district in southern Indiana. I told everyone Coach saw to it that I was kept back a year so I'd be older and bigger for the football team, but the truth was freshman math held me back that one grade.

I mean, it wasn't like my high school was in some urban combat zone, or anything, but the school building was in the small town where I lived. We were the type of school where the homecoming queen's float was dragged around by a tractor and no one saw anything weird about that situation. Anyway, I lived in town of 3,000 souls and the school was in town, so I saw myself as a city kid and I saw them as country bumpkins.

I don't know where I got that idea. Actually, some of our best players were from the old coal-mining villages and the small farms way out in the sticks. We called it snake country back then. Like I said, I was acting like a teenager -being stupid. I made fun of all those country boys when they came into town in overalls and baseball hats, but after I met Billy Joe I stopped being such an asshole.

Billy Joe was a good ol' country boy from Georgia who was up north helping out on his uncle's farm in Indiana. To him, what I was calling snake country was overcrowded. Where he came from 10 or 20 miles away was a close neighbor. To everyone's surprise Billy Joe and I hit it off right away and, even if he was a fuckin' redneck, he was a hell of a blocking back!

We started off just as buddies, but after I got to know him a lot better I discovered that we had something in common.

We were both closet fags!

Back in 1973 you didn't admit to being gay. We all joked about it in the shower, but no one ever came out and said he liked dick better than pussy. When I tried joking with Billy Joe, though, something about the way he looked at me told me this country boy was different. We started hanging around together, staying late after practice so we could shower together without any of the team

113

watching. That's where I discovered something else about old Billy Joe that I learned to respect and desire, like the fact that Billy Joe had a solid nine inches of rock-hard, thick, beautifully uncut dick between his legs.

It wasn't hard the first time I saw it up close, but it got that way in a big hurry as we rubbed against each other in the team shower room. I'd never seen an un-cut one before, and that nasty looking dick fascinated me. My new buddy really was from snake country! I mean, there were a dozen nozzles in the shower room, but there I was right up next to Billy Joe, my dick as hard as his as we turned on more hot water to steam it up.

He was the first to touch me, his soapy hand finding my dick in the midst of clouds boiling up from the six nozzles we had running. When I found his dick, we started a mutual masturbation, our private jack-off session ending a few frantic seconds later with two very clean dicks and a duel blast of hot cum that splattered over the shower walls.

I'd never touched an uncut dick before, and the sensation of that velvety softness wrapped around a core of pure steel was such a turn-on to me. I wrapped my fingers around that erotic rod, rippling like I do when I play with myself, wanting in the worst way to please my new lover. We pressed tighter together, both glancing towards the shower opening, the fear of being discovered making us hurry, the thrill of this shared lust making us want it to last and last and last.

I used both hands on that un-cut whopper, cupping his heavy balls. Billy Joe did the same, but then he turned his hand and pushed one finger up between the cheeks of my ass, bringing my orgasm on in a flash, and bringing Billy Joe's cum up from those heavy nuts I was still holding.

That was when I discovered something even more amazing about Billy Joe's big cock. That revelation was that the country boy's big dick could shoot like a machine gun. Once was never enough for my country lover. I kept jacking and Billy Joe kept coming. I got him off three times in a row lots of times, and the last squirt was as wet and juicy as the first!

Even soft Billy Joe's dick was at least 5 inches long and as thick as most guys get when they're fully erect. I was almost 20 then, so I got hard at the drop of a hat. Once I knew how much fun it was to play with his dick, every time I saw Billy Joe I sprang a woodie. That was a real problem! I had to be careful around the rest of the team.

You know what I mean, playing at being a straight stud and all that, but when the two of us were alone we worked on being gay.

We did it after practice, under the stands after games, and in the boys room at school whenever we could both sneak off. We carried lit cigarettes whenever we were playing our jack-off games, figuring that any principal or teacher who caught us would believe we were sneaking out for a quick smoke.

It wasn't long before secretive hand jobs weren't enough for either of us, even when I was making Billy Joe come two or three times in a row at lunch. I was dying to taste that uncut dick, and from the way he was shoving fingers up my ass I knew that Billy Joe was anxious to become my asshole-buddy. Billy Joe invited me out to his uncle's farm for the weekend to help stack bales of straw up in the loft after his uncle did whatever they do to wheat to harvest it. The uncle hauled away the good stuff and left Billy Joe and me in the field. Our job was to pick up an endless row of straw bales out there and haul them to the barn on a flatbed truck.

The farm was eight miles out at the end of a pothole-filled gravel rode, desolate and deserted after his uncle left, perfect for what I had in mind. I went along more to be close to Billy Joe than to actually help, but Billy Joe made me work! God, did he make me work! I was swore everywhere, except where I wanted to be! Oh, we had fun, but not until after the chores were finished. We piled what seemed to be tons of straw bales on the truck, ran them up a little escalator into the hay loft, then took off for a pond under a spreading tree to wash before supper.

Once we got naked and semi-clean Billy Joe grabbed for my dick. I remember thinking it's about fucking time as he pulled me into the deeper water and then up under the roots of the Weeping Willow. Inside there was six feet of sand making a private beach, and just enough room for both of us to lay side-by-side out of anyone's view.

As I slipped up beside him, Billy Joe bent and took my dick into his mouth. I gasped in awe, never having felt anything that good in my life. Billy Joe and I might have both been closet fags, but he had a lot more practice than me when it came to actually doing something about those gay urges. He wolfed down my dick, taking me in until his nose was buried in the soft curls of my pubes, my balls squirming against his chin.

As you can probably guess, it didn't last, or rather, I didn't last. I came quickly, filling my new buddy's mouth with a huge load of cum. To my amazement, Billy Joe let me come in his mouth, not pulling off as I filled him to the brim with creamy white goo. Then, after I thought I was through, Billy Joe swallowed it all in one Adam's apple-bouncing gulp.

I said I was finished, at least for a few minutes anyway, but Billy Joe had other plans. He must have decided to see if I could have a multiple orgasm, too. I came in his mouth. Billy Joe swallowed. But then he just kept on sucking!

My cock softened slightly, rising back up as it slipped deep into his throat. It was just soft enough to bend. As he deep-throated me, I groaned and fucked his face.

Building to my second orgasm took a couple of minutes. Billy Joe sucked and squeezed and swirled his tongue, and I rewarded him with a second mouthful of jizz.

Now really finished, I collapsed. He came up over me, wanting to kiss me, but afraid of going that far with another jock like me. Instead of kissing me Billy Joe pushed me over onto my belly and got behind me, spreading my legs. As I realized what he was going to do, I shivered, but I was too exhausted to resist.

"No way it's going to fit," I panted. "It's too big. Man, it's way too big!"

"It'll fit," he whispered.

"I'm afraid," I admitted in a gasp.

"I'll just put the head in," Billy Joe whispered as the burning cap of his dick touched my winking asshole.

"Yeah, right," I laughed.

Suddenly I knew how girls felt when guys said that to them. I groaned, but I didn't stop Billy Joe as he spat on his hand and wiped the juice across my asshole. He rubbed my crack, sticking a finger up into my virgin asshole, and then he nudged the crown of that big dick into the pucker of my asshole.

My poor cherry asshole! Man, Billy Joe's dick burnt as he shoved it up inside my anus. This was like a dream come true for me, taking it up the ass from my best buddy, but for a few seconds it hurt too much to be any fun. Then Billy Joe began slowly sliding his dick in and out, humping me with inch-long strokes, making me love it as he screwed my ass with that lovely uncut dick.

The fact that Billy Joe's dick was a snake made my first shafting go easier. That steel shaft rode easily back and forth through the extra skin, making a natural lubricant. Even though his dick wasn't moving much on the outside, where it counted, Billy Joe's whopper was getting the job done.

That country boy fucked me so good he made my cherry hole spasm around his driving dick, drawing the cum from Billy Joe's balls in a hot wave of lust. The slippery juice squirted up into my clutching asshole, making it buttery and slick.

Billy Joe got off big, but he just kept fucking. I rolled over in his embrace, wanting to see him as he fucked me. We ended up with my knees up in the air, ankles around his neck, my asshole snapping at his big cock. I grabbed my buddy by the shoulders and pulled him to me, mashing my lips to his, feeling the bristles of his beard scratching my chin.

Kissing another guy was neat; we both took to it immediately. We shared spit as we pawed each other. But there was so many other things that both of us were dying to do, and after way too short a time that hot kiss broke. Billy Joe flattened me out on the sand as he pushed down with his chest.

The second time Billy Joe came inside me I came with him. Two prior orgasms might not be much for a man like Billy Joe, but mine was more mental than actual.

My ass was getting sore, but Billy Joe was still hard and raring to go. What did I do? You know the answer to that one. There was nothing left for me to do but suck his dick!

I got down between Billy Joe's legs. I wiped his cock off with a rag and got down to business, drawing his un-cut dick into my mouth, my lips nibbling further and further over that thick tower of manhood. As I pushed my tongue out, the tip slid under the cowl on his dick. I moaned as I swirled in that loose skin, the flat of my tongue swiping across a spot that I knew felt really nice, that magic inch just under the piss-slit, and as I sucked his dick Billy Joe did some moaning of his own.

God, I loved giving him head!

That marvelous dick throbbed in my mouth, the foreskin sliding as my fist moved up and down in time with my mouth. My chin whiskers left a rash on his balls, but Billy Joe never complained. Now I know that he likes a little pain as I scrape my chin across his tender scrotum, and as my tongue swabs eagerly over the oozing tip of his dickhead. Then, like now, the second another drop of that sweet sap came pouring out, I slurped it up.

I worked the rubbery head of his dick to the back of my throat and then tried for more, eager to take him all the way into my oral cavity. I didn't think about breathing. All I cared about was stuffing more of that giant snake down my throat. When I finally came up for air it was a groaning, gasping rise, and then a quick dive back down over the thumping mass in my mouth.

"Get ready, Tab," Billy Joe whispered as he raised his hips, driving his dick deeper in my mouth. "I'm fixin' to come in your mouth, buddy. Ooh, man. Here it comes. I'm close. Ooh. Ooooh! Oooooh, here it comes!"

I slid my hands under his hips, grabbing those buns of steel, and as I sucked the swollen head of his dick it exploded, sending a musky jet of cum across my tongue.

My reaction was to pull up, but I caught myself before my mouth came completely off Billy Joe's dick. As it worked out, that movement was pretty neat. I got to slide back down as more of my buddy's cum came rushing out across my tongue, and as I swallowed my first load of man-juice, Billy Joe arched his back and gave me his third climax in a row, this one filling my mouth with hot love.

- — -

It went on like that all through our senior year of high school. I turned twenty before graduation. Billy Joe's 20th birthday was a month after we got out of school. We moved south and got jobs, and we lived together.

Our lovemaking hasn't changed much in the years since we discovered our passion for each other. We never ask about other partners; we never ask each other about much of anything at all. Our love is our great secret, and the sex is always the same: We suck each other until we're good and ready, usually in a long 69, and then I take it up the ass from my best buddy until we both come C me usually once C Billy Joe never less than twice!

A PRACTICAL DEMONSTRATION
Carl St. John

We started on the mall outside the chemistry building, but as the demonstration picked up steam and grew, the mass of chanting, singing people flowed over to the administration building.

"No more war! Nixon out of Cambodia!" It was May of 1970. We were on the verge of shutting the college down in the aftermath of the Cambodian incursion and the deaths at Kent State. What I didn't know was that I was also on the verge of making one of the hottest discoveries of my life C a discovery which had nothing to do with international politics, anti-war demonstrations, or peace movements.

It started when I went to piss in the bushes between the Ad Building at the parking lot. I barely had my dick out when a solidly-built black guy in a psychedelic tank-top pulled up alongside me, grinned and nodded, and snicked his zipper down.

I gasped. I've never seen such an immense slab of manmeat in my life. The guy wasn't particularly tall, but the cock which flopped out from the front of his faded jeans looked like it belonged on King Kong. It was fat and long and loose, the head clearly defined by a deep groove separating it from the wrinkled, dark shaft.

"Holy shit!" I said, and then shut up, embarrassed. I heard a low chuckle. The stream of my piss arched up and out, hissing against the bark of the tree. I looked hesitantly at the man beside me. His teeth flashed in the smooth darkness of his face.

"It's OK," he said. "I'm used to it."

I looked away from his face, staring frankly at the meat he was shaking slightly as he prepared to urinate. It looked bigger around than a ring of polish sausage, and it appeared to hang at least eight inches out of his fly.

"I'm sorry," I said. "I didn't mean C I mean, I just C well, I'm sorry. I've just never seen a cock so big."

He chuckled again, and then the stream of liquid sparkled out in a sudden jet from the head of his tool. His piss mingled with mine on the tree. "It's nothin' I did," he said. "But I guess it's better than small, huh?"

"I can't believe anybody could take that," I said. "It must be like a fucking telephone pole when it's hard."

My own dick was stiffening as I hungrily gobbled up every possible visual impression of that monster. I knew damned well I would be fantasizing about it the next time I jerked off C and the fire which was beginning to glow in my cock and balls told me that I was going to have to make an opportunity very quickly to bring myself off.

The pause seemed long. I was suddenly nervous again; had I gone too far? Stepped out of line? I let my eyes go back up his body. His face was taut, hesitant. Without repeating that wonderful smile, he said, "Well, I guess you could find out, if you wanted to. You want to see what it's like when it's hard?"

The universe stood still, even the noise from the demonstration disappearing. Oh, God! I thought. It can't be. It's too fucking good to be true!

It was too fucking good to be true C but it was true just the same. We left the protest of the war in more capable hands, and headed for Calvin's place. Ten minutes after I had stepped into the bushes to piss, I was trying to get my lips around the biggest knob of the biggest cock I have ever seen.

Calvin's dong didn't grow proportionally much longer when it got hard. But it was an incredible mass of manhood, just the same, a solid seven inches of warm flesh which was so thick that I truly couldn't get it all into my face. It was the first time I had ever sucked a cock which I couldn't deep-throat.

Not that he was objecting to my technique. I had my jaws stretched wide and my mouth fixed hot and sucking over the fist-like knob of his crank. My tongue was playing with the cord under the head while my fingers squeezed and yanked the flaring base of his tree. When I tickled his nuts while jacking his shaft and sucking his glans, his whole body shook in a spasming shudder of pure delight.

It was my first experience with interracial sex, but the color didn't mean a thing beside the overwhelming fact of this gigantic pecker that more than lived up to the myth. His dick was leaking pre-cumlike a faulty faucet, the gentle tang of that clear juice filling my mouth with a taste which made my cock eager to shoot.

When the work my mouth was doing made his erection start to twitch in rhythmic preparation for eruption, Calvin began to moan quietly. "Oh C ohhhhhhhhh, man!" The sound was a low rumble of satisfaction trickling from his throat the way the peckergrease was leaking from his dick into my mouth.

I tightened my fingers on his shaft and jacked harder, sucking the knob and flicking steadily with my tongue. My other hand was tickling his nuts, but when Calvin shoved forward to put more of his cock into my face, I let my fingers trail back along the ridge behind his balls.

When I stabbed my forefinger into his asshole, Calvin gasped, then yelled "oh yeah! C oh, fuck, man!" The fat cylinder of his stiff dick swelled in a giant twitch of pleasure. I yanked hard, pumping his crank in time with the sucking and licking I was doing at the end of that flagpole.

With a wailing cry, Calvin orgasmed. The first shot of his spunk into my mouth came so hard and thick that it took me by surprise. My head bobbed backwards, Calvin's cockhead popped out of my mouth, and a heavy squirt of thick white jizz splashed against my face. I dived fast, gobbling his crank back between my lips before the height of my sleek lover's joy could be reduced. A third huge gob of sperm hosed against my tongue as I sucked his tool back into my face.

My hand was jacking his dick steadily. I could feel the pulsations as his jizz surged through his tube. His asshole was clamping tight around my finger in rhythm with the passionate explosions of his ecstasy. He was grunting, whining, gasping, as the sizzling sear of his juice scalded through the tingling passages of his magnificent meat. He was experiencing the ultimate in ultimates, the perfect orgasm.

When the wild frenzy of his climax had expended itself C in about ten hard, heavy shots of thick white sperm which filled my mouth with the slick hotness of his lust C he sagged, a long whimpering sigh whistling from his throat.

"Oh, man!" he gasped. "Oh, fuck, man!" His voice was ragged, uneven with the aftershocks of his soul-wrenching passion. "Oh, fuck, man, can you ever suck cock!"

It was one of the great tributes I had ever received. I grinned at him, running my spunk-slick tongue around my jizz-smeared lips. His face had changed, been softened by the power of the ecstasy which had jetted out of his immense prick and into my mouth and throat.

His sleek chest heaving, Calvin reached a big hand and caressed the side of my head gently. "I want you in my ass, man. I want you to fuck my ass."

He climbed onto the bed and pushed the hard curve of his lean butt into the air. I could see the glistening sheen of the light coating of sweat which glossed his smooth skin. His asshole seemed to wink at me, its dark pucker flexing and twitching as the aftereffects of his orgasm rippled through his body.

I gazed in complete awe and wonderment at his body for a moment, my cock twitching against my stomach in little jumps of pute lust. My swollen dick was leaking pre-cum, and the fur on my belly was matted from the flow of my lubricant.

Calvin's balls were fairly tight against his body, the wrinkled bag of his scrotum dark, mysterious. His prick was still rigid, and I could see the immensity of his flaring cock-base even from this angle.

"Come on, man," he gasped, his fingers waggling at me from between his legs as he invited my stiff manhood into the hot clutch of his secret fuckhole. "Give me that cock, OK?" He was shaking with his continuing arousal.

There was a jar of Vaseline on the nightstand. I scooped out a glob of the yellowish grease and smeared it lovingly on the gaping crack Calvin was presenting to me. His body shivered as my finger probed the tight opening of his butt. The tight ring of muscle around his ass seemed to want to grab my finger.

After I had lubed his pooper, I ran my hand downward, feeling the tight warmth of his bag, the big firm stones pulled up so tightly they were almost inside his lean body. I let my fingers slide along the bottom of his stiff dick, and I pinched hard on the loose skin underneath the head of the prong I had been sucking the spouting juice from just a minute before.

Calvin groaned, his ass pushing backwards in a spasm of excitement as I revivified the nerves in his crank. I tickled back down the shaft of his rod, rubbed his balls, then got into position behind his taut ass.

I was panting, almost out of control, as I slid the knob of my tool up and down the valley of his asscrack. The tight hotness of his hole tried to suck me in – and I didn't resist.

I shoved the whole length of my hard prick into the clutching sheath of Calvin's asshole with a long, smooth stroke which left me jammed hard against the firm warmth of his buns. I felt my balls swing against his, and the grip of his ass clenched in an involuntary spasm of excitement as he felt me buried in his bung.

I grabbed his hard hips in a wild surge of overwhelming lust, yanking my big new lover hard against me. He moaned, his body shaking almost as much as mine was. He wasn't three minutes past blowing one of the biggest loads I'd ever seen, but his body was responding with the kind of hot ardor you would expect from a man who hadn't cum for a week. Calvin was one hot fucking dude!

"Fuck me, man.! Fuck me good!" He was a huge, beautiful stud with a cock like the Washington Monument, but when he felt my meat jammed into the tunnel of his bunghole, he was like a baby begging for candy. "Do it. Oh, come on, man! Fuck me! Oh, Carl!" His hips were swerving and grinding as he tried to make the swollen shaft of my hard on rub every nerve in his back door.

I had envisioned myself fucking Calvin's ass with the cool smoothness of a connoisseur, the placid restraint of an old hand who could control every tingle of his cock. But the picture of my big face-fucking black stud with his horse cock and his eager asshole set fire to the short fuse of my passion. There was no way I was going to be able to hunch his butt through the long, varied fuck that I had fantasized.

I fucked him like a cock-machine gone crazy, slamming my pork in and out of his tight-clutching fuckhole with a pistoning power which set the bed to squealing almost as loudly as Calvin was crying out from the friction and pounding pressure of my fat crank rubbing his nerves into an insane frenzy of lust.

"AHHHHH!" he yelled, and I felt his asshole clamp tight around my crank. His body went rigid, and then suddenly his butt was flexing in rhythmic spasms of climax. He was coming again, his body jerking in convulsive eruptions of ecstasy from the rubbing intrusion of my cock in his ass.

I yanked him against me, shoved my prick so far into his ass I thought it might come out his mouth, and geysered a fountain of sticky spunk into the grasping python of his butt. The world was spinning around me as though I were drunk; my orgasm was so intense and so all-consuming that I never knew exactly when Calvin collapsed forward onto the bed. I rode him down, my spurting prick buried in his hole and filling his rectum with my cum.

Calvin had shot two huge loads in just a few minutes! And before that long sweet spring afternoon was over, I coaxed three more loads out of his fat sausage! Then he took a couple of my loads; I came so hard each time that I was afraid I might actually faint.

So the protests went on out in the streets. I don't want to make light of the causes and issues I was involved in, but I have to say that "Make Calvin, Not War" became my slogan for the rest of that school year.

TOMCAT
Buddy Hopkins

I never planned to own a cat. If anything, I would've gotten a dog. Would have. But it hardly seemed compatible with my lifestyle. An active jock, on my own for the first time in my life, I spent many nights in many different beds. And when you're out banging a different pussy every night – or very nearly – you can't always get home in time to walk the dog...if you get home at all. It seemed every girl I met wanted to take me to bed. I gave off a scent, according to one of my co-workers at the hotel where I work when I'm not attending junior college. In fact, he took to calling me Tom, as in tomcat.

So there I was, without pets...well, without the four-legged kind, at any rate. And with no plans to own one. Then one cloudy Sunday afternoon I heard this plaintive meowww.

At first I ignored it. The second meow was harder to ignore. And the third was most insistent. Getting up, I walked to my open window. There, outside, was a scrawny, scruffy, orange-and-tan refugee from some cat-war. Underfed and over fought, it was definitely the worse for wear. And clearly it had decided I was the one to help it out of its predicament.

"Go home," I said with some measure of annoyance. It was the first time in five days that I'd been home for more than long enough to change clothes, and I wanted to pay bills, do a load of wash, and tidy up. I didn't need interruptions. But my exhortation was met with a more insistent, full-throated Meowwwww!

There was nothing to do but open the door and survey my visitor. The cat seemed tame, letting me pet its ruffled fur, but there was no collar or tag. Lifting the animal up, I held it upside-down and checked. A tom. "I'll call you 'Scruffy' -temporarily," I said, setting the cat down gingerly. "But mind you, you're going home as soon as I can find who you belong to."

Of course I hadn't a drop of cat food in the house, and Scruffy – despite an evident limp – seemed to be suffering more from hunger than anything else. His ribs showed. If he had a home, he hadn't been there in a long time. Searching my cupboard, I found a can of white meat tuna and put the contents down on a paper plate for Scruffy. He wolfed it in three seconds flat.

Still annoyed at the intrusion, I called up the town's animal regulatory agency. Had anyone registered a lost cat fitting Scruffy's description? No, they had not. The agency could send a truck to pick Scruffy up, of course. Could I hold him there for a few hours?

I inquired what the procedure was from that point. They'd hold him at the shelter for a week, I was told. Then, if no one claimed him.... Long sigh.

I couldn't be the cat's executioner. "Oh, never mind," I said. "I'll hang onto him. I'll put up signs."

There was a vet two blocks from my house, and I decided I'd better take Scruffy in. I'd walk over. I hadn't a carrier, so after calling to book an emergency appointment, I picked the bedraggled animal up in my arms...and had the misfortune to run into my neighbor.

Smash was a punk type who rode a motorcycle, probably derived actual pleasure from squooshing bugs, and no doubt did unspeakable things to small animals as well. He wasn't too kind to his fellow humans, either. "Pussy-boy!" he exclaimed on seeing me holding the cat.

Unfortunately, we shared a destination. It turned out Smash was headed to the vet's too, with his – what else?! – pit bull, and with a friend for company. Riding in his friend's car, he got there first, greeting me with more derisive cries of "Pussy boy!" when I walked in. A young man in a blue uniform looked up at the exclamation.

I didn't know why I took it so hard, but the name-calling really got to me. "The tech will look at the cat first. Then the vet will be in," the receptionist said after showing me to an examining room.

The tech turned out to be the young man in the blue uniform. MARC, VETERINARY TECHNICIAN, his tag read. I was still shaking from the run-in with my neighbor. "Don't let it get to you," Marc said, laying a kindly hand on my arm."

"Want to talk about it? The vet's got an emergency and won't be in for a while yet."

It turned out Marc had assumed, from the remark, that I was gay. "But I'm not!" I protested too vehemently.

"Are you sure?" he asked, his eyes probing into my soul.

"I'm currently dating five different women!"

"You sound like a man who's trying to prove something."

Why did my stomach flutter, ten minutes later, at this offer of dinner that night? He had qualified it, "So I can teach you the basics of cat care."

Surely I recognized Marc was gay – he was pretty open and evident – yet I cancelled a date with Rhonda "for the cat's sake." Now really! Some part of me must have known what the score was.

The rest of me learned the score quickly, when Marc's arm went around me at the front door, when he toasted me with white wine and looked deep in my eyes, and finally when he kissed me, his tongue questing deeply in my mouth.

I pulled back in fright. "Don't run away from yourself," he urged me in a soft, yet strangely compelling voice. And kissed me again. His hand stroked the back of my neck, and his body closed in on mine, his hard lump sending burning shivers through me as it pressed against my equally hard boner. (Now why had I thrown a rod? Why?)

"We could finish the wine in the bedroom," Marc suggested, still using that low, hypnotic voice. "C'mon in." His hand stroked lightly across my denim-covered bulge, lingering at the apex of the protrusion, where my dickhead was leaking lube like a faulty faucet. I felt his fingertips tickle my dicktip through the denim, and gooseflesh rose all across my body.

In the bedroom he took command again, undressing me. I neither helped him nor protested, just allowing him to do as he wished with me. When he had me naked, he removed a rubber from the night table, slipped it on my dick, and dropped to his knees.

I was still standing, reluctant to commit fully by getting onto the bed, but at the feel of his lips enveloping my dick, I felt weak-kneed and staggered sideways to the bed and fell on it, my legs still dangling over the edge, as if still preserving my ability to flee by retaining contact with the floor.

Who would flee with lips like those sucking heartily on my hard cock? Marc's mouth had ovalled around me and was coaxingly tempting my dick to show him if it could add that extra inch to its already-impressive length and girth. I don't know if I succeeded in adding an inch to my size, but his insistent suction certainly fuelled the fires that were powering my pistoning hips.

As Marc's marauding mouth did a sensuous number on my amazed dick, I began pumping up and down, shoving my meat down that gulping throat as if trying to fuck his asshole from the top down.

That mental picture exploded in my brain in bursts of red-orange: Fucking his asshole! Gay guys did that, I knew. Would Marc let me fuck his ass? There were so many new things to try! But right now I was enjoying the tight grip of his mouth as it rode up and down my quivering stalk. His tongue did neat tricks too, flipping along the bottom of my dick, flicking at it, tantalizing it with promises half-kept.

I burrowed full-bore into his mouth, driving down his gullet, ramming inward with hard-charging strokes. Marc managed to keep up with me all along the way, gulping me in and out insistently. No matter how sloppy my strokes, no matter how wildly I rampaged in and out, he never lost his suction on my dick.

Now he added another touch, hefting my balls and squeezing them gently while he sucked. And then, just to really ice the cake, his other hand slithered up my chest, making contact with my brown button nipples, tweaking and tugging at each in turn.

So there I was, hunching up and down on the bed, my legs still dangling to the floor, as Marc molested me delightfully, his mouth working over my hard-driving dick while his hands tickled and tugged and tweaked and tormented. My dick-drool was lubing the inside of the rubber while his spit greased up the outside. I was almost ready to come when Marc said, "Want to learn what else gay guys do?"

I figured I knew the answer to that one already, but knowing it wasn't the same as experiencing it. I was ready to try! Marc scrambled off me and assumed the position on the bed. I got behind him and positioned my spit-lubed, rubbered dick at the puckered portal to his assvault. Then I pushed forward slightly. Nothing happened.

I pressed some more, but his anus was clenched tightly shut. I didn't want to push too hard and hurt him--or myself. "You don't have to be gentle. I won't tear--and you won't break," Marc laughed. He seemed to understand my fears. Maybe he'd had the same thoughts, himself, his own first time.

I put more muscle behind my thrusts, and this time I breached his entryway. As Marc grunted a gentle oof! I felt his anal sphincter stretch and accommodate my eager meat. Then he backed up, his anus swallowing more of my rod in the process, and now I gained enough confidence to really press forward.

This time I buried a good third of my seven inches in his humid interior, and I kept going when I didn't hear any protests from him or feel any pain on my own. All I felt was a wonderful warmth and a terrific tightness. His assguts were wrapped snugly around me, his sphincter gripping me in an intense hug at the point of entry, and every inch of my dick that was inside his rectal tunnel was bathed in a moist warmth that seemed to make it tingle.

We both began chugging back and forth, my balls slapping up against his rump with every in-stroke. The sweaty thwack of my balls against his butt cakes was an erotic sound to my virgin ears, and it inflamed my balls every time I heard it. "You can fuck me faster! Harder! It won't hurt me," Marc panted, as short of breath from his excitement as from his exertion.

As I speeded up my strokes, I took a leaf from his book and reached around to molest one of his brown nips. It toughened beneath my fingers' insistent pinching, becoming a stiff little finger of granite, rigid and protruding, pointy, responsive. Every time I stroked the pad of my thumb across that nubbin or pinched it between my thumb and forefinger, I elicited a groan from Marc.

Soon we had both broken out in a sweat that had nothing to do with the temperature of the room. "I'm gonna come," I warned Marc, unable to hold back the tide in my full balls any longer. "What about you?" I was still thinking in man-woman terms--make sure your partner is satisfied first.

"Don't worry," Marc chuckled. "I'll get mine--in spades." The words sent a shudder through my frame. I had the feeling he meant to pork my butt next! Could I take it? Would it hurt? Fear notwithstanding, the mental image was enough to drive me over the edge, and I dumped my balls' creamy cargo in Marc's receptive anus with one last, violent thrust inside him.

As he felt my dick pulsate wildly in his asshole, then start to shrivel rapidly, he instructed me, "Pull out before the rubber slips off. Hold the base while you slide out." I followed instructions, then waited while he disposed of the rubber. What was he going to do to me when he got back from flushing the rubber? The question made my dick start to rise again.

All my body hair was standing on end when I saw Marc return from the bathroom, his massive dick leading by what suddenly looked like a foot. I knew, rationally, that his dick was not a foot long, of course, but picturing it sliding into my never-entered anal clench, I winced and cringed at the apparent size of that monster. How was that thing ever going to fit inside me?

"Are you ready?" Marc asked with a wink. I noticed with some relief that he was carrying a tube of lube with him. "I have a little of this left in the drawer, but I think you're going to need a lot, so I brought a fresh tube with me," he said. "For sure, spit alone won't do it for you."

I got on my forearms and knees, but Marc rolled me over. "Get on your back. I'll take you that way," he said. Then he lubed his fingers with a generous dollop of grease and proceeded to grease up my reluctant entrance.

The feel of his fingers was both thrilling and scary. As he slicked in and out of my back door, he touched nerve endings that fired off horny responses. Too, the mere feel of him there reminded me of what he was about to do to me...and that both thrilled me and scared me simultaneously.

He had two fingers in me, and he crooked them both so that he hooked the inner grip of my rim each time he slid out. He straightened them out for the re-entry and then crooked them again as he slid out.

Now I felt a third finger join its compatriots in plunging into my asshole, and finally the fourth finger made its presence known. He was fucking me with four fingers. How much bigger could his big dick be?

I found out a minute later, when his fingers slid out, and I felt the solid presence of his love muscle nudging its way into my anal clench. I humped forward, as if to get away from the invader, but he followed me forward, whispering, "I won't hurt too much, I promise." Then he nuzzled at my neck, first kissing, then nibbling.

A shiver ran through me at the feel of his warm lips and hot breath, which made my neck hairs stand on end and brought gooseflesh to all my body. Without thinking, I backed up again, and I unwittingly impaled myself on Marc's solid flesh pole. "Owww!!" I yelped as he breached my entryway and spread my asslips wide.

He froze in place. "Get used to it," he said soothingly. "I'll wait." He stroked my skin with his gentle hand, so used to soothing animals at the vet's office, now taming me instead. "The pain will recede in a minute or so."

And in truth it was ebbing already. "OK," I gulped. "I'm – I'm almost all right now." It still hurt, but less and less, and I suspected that the worst was behind me. He was in me now. I was spread. Even though he was going to plunge in deeper, it stood to reason that he wouldn't spread me much more, and it was the spreading that was what hurt.

Gradually, easily, slowly, carefully, Marc inched forward, slipping in quarter-inch by quarter-inch, till I felt his dickhead snugging deeply up in my bowels. "You've got more than half, babe," he whispered in my ear. Then he began to twist and pinch my nips again. While I was distracted by his fingers on my nipples, he skewered the rest of the way into me with one sharp thrust that surprised me, filled me, even spread and stretched me, but didn't hurt any worse.

My asshole was burning, but it wasn't any pain that I couldn't handle. Now he was in me to the hilt, and he began to fuck deeply in and out of me, while I fucked up and down beneath him. The hand that had been on my nips slipped down to my dick, which I was amazed to realize had grown rigid again. He jacked me in perfect rhythm with his fuck-strokes, and we quickly crested toward climax again--his first and my second.

"Gonna spray you, babe," he grunted after just a few minutes of relentless fucking.

"Do it!" I urged. "I'm gonna shoot too."

We came in synch with each other, my spray warmly pelting my smooth chest as his outpouring filled the rubber in my assguts.

"I'm one up on you," I said, hoping he'd let me suck him off to even the score. Indeed he did, but then he insisted on sucking me off, and I was ahead again.

"Well, if you insist on keeping score, you'll have to come back one night soon to even things up," Marc said with a twinkle in his eyes. "Is that OK with you...Pussy Boy?"

Somehow the name didn't sting anymore. In fact, coming from Marc as a private joke, I liked it fine. And I thanked Scruffy, the stray cat, for bringing us together.

Scruffy is still very much a part of my life six months later, and Marc is still very much a part of my life too.

FLORIDA CRACKER
Thomas C. Humphrey

"Come here and take care of this, Teach," the kid ordered. He straddled the corner of my desk, his long legs splayed, feet on the floor, a broad, hungry grin dominating his plain face. With one hand he bunched his tight jeans and slowly traced the thick cylinder running down his left thigh halfway to his knee.

I moved to the window at the opposite end of the desk and closed the miniblinds to block the view from the sidewalk. My hands trembled so much I could hardly grasp the wand, and my throat was so tight it hurt to swallow. As I turned to face this cocksure youngster, I wasn't sure I wanted this. I did not even know his name, had never seen him until a few minutes before, and yet... .

His eyes locked into mine and led them down to where his thumb traced the tight bulge against his inner thigh. I forced another swallow and shifted my focus upward to take in a full view of him. He was the kind of nondescript kid, neither handsome nor ugly, who normally arrests my attention only for a second, if at all. And yet... .

Fifteen minutes before, I had been going through the uneventful routine of my professorial life, with no thought of anything as daring as this. I had come down the stairs of the antiquated Rathskeller at the University of Florida after a brief coffee break and turned right through the open doorway into the basement men's room, intent only upon relieving myself and then going to the library to complete some research.

Just as I rounded the turn, the kid scurried into view, moving from the vicinity of doorless stalls to one of two urinals against the wall directly opposite the doorway. It was the speed of his movement, and the direction, that caught my attention and made the moment stand out from the hundreds of happenstance occurrences which register briefly on our senses and then vanish into oblivion. People do not usually move so rapidly in a men's room, and they do not move from stalls or washbasin to urinal; the movement pattern was all wrong. As I registered this incongruity, it was strengthened by another sense impression, a faint rustling in one of the stalls.

The kid raced me to the urinals and chose the one on the left. I stood practically brushing shoulders with him, unzipped, and strained unsuccessfully to urinate. As seconds of inactivity lengthened, I glanced around for something to focus my eyes on, and they drifted down and leftward. The kid, also having difficulties, was holding his cock in his left hand, giving me a clear view. It was almost obscenely long and broad, obviously partially distended, and its crown and retracted foreskin were gorged and reddened, as if from recent stimulation.

Just as the thought that I had stumbled upon something illicit prickled the hair on the nape of my neck with excitement, my attention was drawn to movement at the stalls. A soft, round-faced kid moved toward the door, glancing apprehensively at us as he exited. He had not even bothered to flush the toilet.

As my flow finally streamed heavily into the urinal, I shifted my focus to take in the kid's rangy, rawboned physique, his long, stringy reddish hair, his pale, freckled face and arms. He caught me studying him, and our gaze held a second or two longer than usual. He emitted a long "Whew," bent slightly at the waist, and crammed himself back into his jeans without having urinated as I turned to the washbasins. He soon joined me, again practically shoulder to shoulder, and I lingered longer than necessary rinsing my hands, which trembled slightly under the stream of cold water. My pulse was speeding and my breathing was short and labored. We again made eye contact, and he grinned knowingly before leaning to splash water on his face. As I dried with a paper towel, I caught his reflected stare in the mirror. Again he grinned, this time lasciviously.

"Did I interrupt something just now?" I blurted out, not believing what I was hearing myself say. My legs suddenly were so weak I had to brace myself on the basin.

"Yeah," he said, tossing a wad of toweling at the trash bin. "You got here about a minute too early." He stared at me intently for a few seconds and cupped his crotch in one hand. "You interested in finishing the job?"

I could not believe the kid was being so ballsy with a professor, and I also could not believe what an intense turn-on it was for me. Completely caught up in the excitement of the moment, I answered, "Maybe, but certainly not here."

"You got an office?" he asked, giving his crotch another squeeze.

As excited as I had been during our silent walk across campus, once inside my office, I began to have second thoughts. For six long months since the breakup with my lover, I had immersed myself in work and suppressed my sexual needs. Now, by offering himself to me so blatantly, this audacious youngster had reawakened those needs, and the surge of lust I was experiencing reminded me just how strong they were. Throughout my career, I had had a cardinal rule against any involvement with students, and I was reluctant to break that rule now, no matter how fired up I was.

"I don't know, maybe we should just forget this," I stammered.

"Come on, Teach. You can't back out now," he said. "Since you got me in here, you sorta owe me." He gestured me over with a toss of his head. "Come on and get me off. You know you want it."

I did want it, and we both knew it. I moved between his legs and reached to trace the outline of his stiff cock down his thigh. With trembling hands, I mastered his heavy belt buckle and unbuttoned his jeans. He raised his ass off the desk, and I tugged jeans and underwear down below his knees. As his cock was freed, it sprang up and slapped against his abdomen.

My mouth fell open in awe at what I had exposed. In my fairly extensive experience, I had run across mostly six-and- seven inch dicks, with a smattering of eight-inchers. Nothing had prepared me for the monster cock which now confronted me. As the kid leisurely leaned back on the desk and pulled his shirt up, his thick rod pulsed against his abdomen and completely obscured his navel. I grasped it at its base and stacked my hands up the shaft.

"Good god! How long is this thing?" I blurted with disbelief.

"Got a ruler, Teach?" he grinned.

I fumbled in the drawer for a plastic ruler. The kid stood up and forced his pole straight out. I laid the ruler on top of it and discovered its tip at the eleven and a half inch mark. I broke a rubber band and, careful not to stretch it, wrapped it around his shaft at about the midpoint and then measured the band at six and a quarter inches. I stood fingering his timber in awe.

"See how it fits your mouth," he said, pressing my head downward.

I bent over and licked around the plum-sized head and then took it in my mouth. The corners of my lips stretched painfully as I mastered just the huge crown. I had no idea what I could do with the rest of it.

The kid grabbed me by my upper arms and twisted me around and then pushed down on my shoulders until I knelt directly in front

135

of him. He locked his hands behind my head and slowly pulled me forward onto his pole. I opened my mouth wider and wider to accommodate him until I was afraid my jaw would become unhinged. The muscles and ligaments in my neck strained painfully, and I hurriedly worked my jacket off and loosened my tie. I suppose knowing what a colossal cock he was driving into me, the kid very patiently pressed my head into his crotch until he reached my tonsils and I struggled to back off. He held me tightly, the tip of his rod lodged in my throat, until I overcame my gag reflex and opened up a little wider. Then he pulled my head closer and closer and worked a couple more inches of his dick right on down my gullet. When he had fed me as much as I could handle, he started gently thrusting his pelvis, withdrawing from my throat and then slowly driving in again, his big cockhead shoving my tonsils aside each time. As I became more and more used to it, his thrusts became harder and quicker until my eyes teared over and I pushed against his thighs, unable to breathe.

He released my head and stepped back, popping his dick out of my mouth. "You did good, Teach," he said. "Most people can't handle that much." He walked around the desk and sat in the swivel chair. My heart drummed in my chest and my own hard-on threatened to tear through my trousers as I watched him pry off his sneakers and slip off his jeans. "Come here and get back on it," he ordered.

Although I'm pretty versatile, basically I've always been a top. After two years of that role with my ex-lover, this kid's arrogantly domineering attitude and his countrified Florida Panhandle speech turned me on something fierce. I imagined him and his cracker buddies driving around some small town in mud-splattered pickups complete with gun racks, guzzling beer, and dragging some gay kid off into the piney woods to use until their lust was satisfied. The thought made me want to be mastered completely by this towering dick in front of me. Conscious of precum soaking through my briefs, I knelt before him, eager to service him.

"I always have wanted to be on this side of the desk," he said. He reared back in the chair, spread his legs, and pulled my face into his crotch.

I squeezed his handball-sized nuts with both hands and licked and slurped and sucked on that big whanger, gradually taking more and more of it until again it was sliding past my tonsils.

For awhile the kid just leaned back and sighed and moaned as I serviced his rod, occasionally hunching deeper into my throat. He swiveled around and threw both legs onto the desk and slid forward until his ass was hanging over the edge of the chair. "Oh, yeah, chew on my balls," he instructed.

I licked and nibbled at his ballsac and managed to get one of his nuts in my mouth, where I sucked on it with as much pressure as I could muster.

"Oh, shit, that feels fucking good," he moaned, hands tracing idly through my hair. Then he pulled me off his balls and shoved my head lower. "Get down there and eat my ass," he ordered, cramming my face between his cheeks. I spread them wider and went to work on his tight, rosy pucker. I reamed his ass good, driving my tongue as far up him as I could.

"Oh, god, yeah! Fuck that hole! Get your tongue in it!" he groaned.

I lifted his ballsac and kneaded his balls as I shoved my tongue deeper in his ass and swirled it around. He sat trembling and moaning with pleasure until the sensation became so intense he couldn't stand it anymore. His ass ring clamped down on my tongue and stopped its movement. "Shit, I'm about to blow my load," he said. He jerked my head back up to his cock. "Get your fucking mouth back on it," he growled.

I grabbed his cock at the base, squeezed hard, and began rotating my hand around it. At the same time I took a little more than his huge head in my mouth and gave it all the tongue action I knew. His thick rod began jumping and bucking, and he started whimpering and tried to shove more of his pole into me. He slid his legs off the desk and wrapped them around my back, grabbed both hands full of hair and raised his ass off the chair, humping my mouth. "Don't quit! Don't quit! I'm about to pop!" he groaned. His body went rigid and all movement stopped. His shaft swelled and jerked, his knob flared and blasted thread after thread of thick cream down my throat, practically drowning me.

The kid didn't move for several minutes, just kept his legs tight around me and held my head on his cock as his abdomen heaved and he gasped for breath. When he began to soften in my mouth, he loosened his legs and sat up, pushing me off his dick. "Whew!" he sighed as he reached for his clothes. "You suck cock a hell of a lot better than that other guy," he said.

I just knelt behind the desk and watched him dress. When he was finished, he moved toward the door. "Thanks, Teach," he said. He flipped the dead latch, stepped through the door, and closed it behind him.

Immediately, I ripped my pants down and savagely worked on my aching cock, reliving the sensation of his huge tool sliding in and out of my throat. In no time, I spewed out the biggest supply of spunk I could recall. Then I cleaned myself up and continued my professorial routine.

- – -

A few nights later, just before closing time, I was leaving the musky stacks of Library East after chasing down an obscure reference I needed for a paper I was writing. Library East is used primarily to house seldom used materials of interest mostly to grad students and instructors. It does not have a heavy volume of student traffic. It does have a reputation as a gay cruising area. Over the years, people have managed to gouge three-inch holes through the solid marble partitions in the men's rooms, and it is rumored that some kids unscrew the light bulbs and fuck in the upper stacks, reasonably confident that they will not be caught.

As I started down the narrow stairwell between the fifth and fourth levels, I almost bumped into the cracker kid with the gargantuan dick. He flashed a broad grin of recognition and, without saying a word, grabbed my hand and pushed it into his crotch. "Let's go to your office," he said.

In the office, I turned on a small lamp on a side table and tilted the shade to throw most of the light against a bookcase. When I turned around, the kid had taken off his shirt and sneakers. "Get your clothes off," he said brusquely, unfastening his belt.

I quickly undressed, excitedly watching his gigantic cock spring out as he slid his jeans down and stepped out of them. He stood slowly running his hand up and down his shaft until I was completely naked.

"Come over here and suck my dick," he ordered.

I walked toward him, my throbbing boner pointing skyward. When I stood in front of him, he grabbed my head roughly and shoved it down. "Get on it," he snapped. I dropped to my knees and tugged and squeezed on his big balls as I forced my jaws and throat to expand to handle his thick rod. When I was ready, he grabbed my head with both hands and started fucking my mouth, rougher than before, shoving well past my tonsils on every thrust, until my eyes were streaming tears and I was half delirious from lack of oxygen. My cock was so hard it ached, and I began stroking myself in rhythm with his thrusts into my throat.

He stopped his movements and loosened his grip on my head. "Get this sucker as wet as you can," he said. "I'm gonna butt-fuck you now."

I licked up and down his long shaft, slobbering and drooling as much as possible, getting him ready, but my ass was protectively clenched tight, and I was more than a little anxious knowing I was about to be invaded by this mammoth cock.

He jerked me to my feet and shoved me down across the desk, scattering a set of student papers beneath me. As I trembled with fear and expectation, he pried my legs farther apart, spat on his hand, and worked one and then two fingers up my ass and frigged it for a few seconds. Then he leaned down and spat in my crack.

I looked over my shoulder as he dribbled spit along his huge ramrod. "Go easy," I begged.

"Ain't no easy way to get this fucker up in you," he said, as he pressed it against my opening.

When my ass ring finally parted enough for the huge head of his cock to pop in, the searing pain was like somebody had given me an enema with scalding water. "Jesus Christ, take it out!" I said, raising my upper body off the desk and trying to twist out from under him.

He roughly shoved me back down and threw his weight on my shoulders. "Lay still," he said. "I'm gonna fuck your ass, and if my dick comes out, it'll just hurt again going back in." Oblivious to my agony, he rammed another three inches of cock in me.

I lay half sobbing and begging him to stop, at the same time trying to relax enough to make his assault on my insides a little easier. As he kept shoving more of that gigantic dick up my chute, I worried that he might seriously damage something deep inside me.

Finally, his legs rested against me and his big balls bounced against my inner thighs. "You've got it all, Teach," he said. "Now you're gonna get fucked."

He leaned over and rested his chest on my back and reached under to massage my pecs and pinch my nipples. He slowly ground his pelvis into me and rotated his cock in broad circles, with almost no in-and-out thrusting. The pain in my bowel lessened, gradually giving over to a warm, tingling excitement. After awhile, I began pushing back against his cock and rotating my ass to match his movements.

"Oh, yeah, Teach," he moaned. "Move that ass around, make it good for me. I could fuck your tight hole all night."

He broadened his movements, and his thrusts became deeper and deeper. At the same time he nibbled at the back of my neck and gave my tits a workout with his fingers. My cock, which had shriveled from fear when he first shoved into me, sprang back to life and throbbed demandingly as his movements slid it back and forth across the slick papers beneath me.

As I got more and more excited, I reached back with both hands and pulled his ass cheeks toward me, encouraging him to pile-drive me.

"That's it, kid, fuck me hard," I urged.

He raised up off my back and lifted me up until I leaned on my arms. He wrapped one arm tightly around my chest, grabbed my dick with his other hand, and began jacking it, matching his strokes to the movement of his cock in my ass. Before long, we both were moaning and squirming with approaching orgasm. His hand was flying up and down my dick, and he was driving his huge timber full-length up my ass on every thrust.

Then he gave a few short, spasmodic jabs, pulled almost all the way out, and buried his full ten-plus inches deep in my gut. His hand on my cock slowed as his rod swelled and pulsed and delivered a load of jism that hit my gut in wave after wave.

I snatched his hand off my dick and gave it a few final frantic strokes and blasted my cream all over the scattered papers below me. I collapsed onto the desk and he sagged on top of me, both of us gasping for breath.

We lay quiet and still for a few moments. I could feel his heart thumping against my back and his cock slowly softening in my ass. I expected he would withdraw, but no, he simply started humping me again.

His cock was hardening again! I couldn't believe this. He drew back so that he could watch his cock impaling me again. "Oh, that's nice," he kept saying, "so nice!"

Then he came again, not as spectacularly as the first time, more leisurely, as if he was savoring this one more than the first. I think I enjoyed it more myself because it was so unexpected, like getting a second dessert on the house.

Finally, he stood up and gingerly pulled his long pole out of me. I was almost sad to hear it plop from my anus.

"Man, what a fantastic fuck," he said.

"Better believe it," I agreed.

I turned over and leaned against the edge of the desk and watched as he picked up my briefs, wiped his cock off on them, and tossed them to me. I wiped away his cum, which was dribbling down the back of my thighs, and watched him get dressed. When he finished, he turned to the door, flicked the dead latch, and opened it.

He turned around and grinned broadly. "See you, Teach," he said. He stepped through the door and closed it behind him.

As I watched him leave, I was pretty confident that he would make it a point to run into me again pretty soon.

Maybe next time, I'd at least get around to asking his name. As I thought about another session with that monster between his legs, my cock boned up again. I stood up, faced the desk, and stroked my rod until I sprayed another load of my own across the already ruined papers beneath me. To hell with how I would explain it to my students.

DAVID
Bud O'Donnell

I began my sexual activity with others at age ten, when I received and gave my first blowjob with a fellow eighth grader. He was nearly fourteen. I got my first piece of female ass, that same summer when I was most willingly seduced by a 17-year-old girl. I learned that she had been fucked by my four older brothers, and she was curious as to whether my dick was growing as big as theirs. It wasn't at that age, but it was long enough to satisfy me, and I guess her as well. But, other than that, the opportunities for further sexual education did not present itself until I started college in Detroit.

I lived with my maiden aunt for the first semester and then she passed away. I was shocked to discover she had left the house to me in her will. I really liked the place and figured I could live with her furnishings until I could afford to decorate it to my own taste. My aunt's furnishings were ancient, but they were like new.

Given this great independence for the first time in my life, I started to trick. One of them was an older guy who was connected to one of Detroit's most prestigious auction dealers. He seemed more interested in my aunt's furniture than he was in my athletic body and nine-inch dick. The deflation to my ego, by his raving about the house's furnishings instead of my body ones, however turned to be a bit of the luck of the Irish.

He convinced me to allow his company to auction off the furnishings. Since there was nothing in the will which said I had to keep the furniture, only the house, I agreed, and it was one of the best financial moves I could have made. Even after the auction house took their percentage, and taxes were paid on the profits, I ended up with over fifty grand. It was obvious my aunt had not furnished her house from the Salvation Army's Thrift Shop. That took a tremendous strain off my income in trying to keep up with taxes, insurance, and utilities on the place. It also allowed me to begin furnishing it to my liking.

Although my aunt had maintained the house well, after nearly 50 years of hard and cold Michigan winters, parts of the house began showing signs of age. One such area was the large slab of cement which leads to the big front porch. I call it a "stoop" for lack of a better word. Three steps lead to that wide stoop and one step higher puts you onto the big open porch. The "stoop" was nothing more than a big cement slab that sets on a 24-inch-high, rectangular, brick retaining wall. The spring of my second year there, I noticed a large crack down the middle of that stoop, and it was beginning to sag in the center. It obviously needed to be replaced. Like most neighborhoods, ours is inundated with solicitors and handbills. I remembered seeing one that advertised all kinds of cement and brick repair work. Knowing I had kept it, I dug through my files until I found it. The ad gave a phone number with the name DAVID on it.

One Wednesday afternoon in August, after I got home from the clinic, I called the number listed and talked with a women, who said she was David's wife. She said she would have him call me when he returned from work. She referred always to her husband as David, not Dave.

At about five thirty, the phone rang. It was David. The voice at the other end spoke with a very clipped British accent.

I was hoping my Irish parents wouldn't be too pissed off, if I hired an Englishman to do my cement work. My parents had a lifelong dislike for the British. I explained the problem to David and he said he would be over as soon as he could shower and change his clothes.

It took about 45 minutes when I heard the front door chimes. I was shocked when he introduced himself as David. He was almost ebony in color, yet he had features, more delicately shaped than other black men I had seen. I hoped my expression did not offend him. I was not upset, just surprised. David's color and extraordinarily good looks and clipped British accent, fascinated me. He was wearing a very baggy shirt and loose fitting slacks, making him look on the thin side. He had a delightfully warm personality, and his accent added to his natural charm. I stepped out onto the big porch and I noticed a big dump truck at the curb, with the words DAVID'S HOME REPAIRS, printed on the side of the door.

He told me what I already knew; the slab would have to be replaced. Using a measuring tape, he took the dimensions, checked out the bricks in the wall that supported the slab and began figuring on a pad of paper. He explained what had to be done, and then told me he could do the job for about $600. I had visions that it would cost a great deal more. He guaranteed his work and was willing to put that on paper, so I told him he had the job. What amazed me was after we had written up a small contract and we both signed it, he walked out to his truck, climbed up into the back and began tossing various tools out. I had no idea he was going to start that very afternoon. I watched him from my dining room window as he climbed down from the back of his truck. David stripped off his shirt and my jaw dropped down and my dick jumped up. Under that loose fitting shirt had been hidden the most amazingly muscled upper body I have ever seen. David was physical perfection. Not a big man, he stood about five- eight, but every muscle that I could see above his waist was developed to the fullest.

I thought I had a "hot" body, developed from 12 years of gymnastics training and competition, but I felt like an anorexic when I stared at David's magnificent muscularity. He seemed to be oblivious of his physical beauty, as he nonchalantly hauled his tools up to the front of the house. He walked up on the stoop and with pure muscles, began whacking away with a heavy sledge hammer.

It was such a turn-on just watching his body work like a well oiled machine, that my cock began oiling itself. David knew just where to lay that hammer and soon I saw massive cracks all along the top of that slab. Using a huge crow bar, he began prying sections loose. He took a special hand saw and begin cutting through the reinforcement wires in the cement.

His upper body, naked to the waist, glistened in sweat. His name was perfect. I've seen Michelangelo's David in Italy. This living David's body was far more beautiful than the cold, white marble of which the Italian David is made. I hurried into the kitchen, readjusted my straining cock and then whipped up a batch of lemonade. I put it in a big thermos and, carrying one of my back patio tables and a glass, brought the drink out front. I called David to take a break. He had been working for close to two hours.

His pleasure in my taking the time to fix him something to drink was obvious. He couldn't thank me enough. While he downed two full glasses, we talked. He was from Trinidad, had come to the United States when he was 18. He became an American citizen, married an American girl when he was 28. His wife was expecting their fifth child. He worked for a cement company, but since he hoped to one day own his own business, he moonlighted with odd jobs to earn extra money. He was thirty-five, but looked like a muscle-bound teen.

I did not hesitate to tell him that he had the most beautifully developed body I had ever seen. He actually blushed, and the shining black skin took on a purple hue. He told me that it was very kind of me to pay him such a nice compliment. He worked until it got too dark. I sat in the dining room watching him through the window, rubbing my hard dick through my slacks. I was so turned on, I walked into the bathroom and jacked off. When I returned, I saw David climb into his truck and drive away. He had placed a barrier around the stoop to keep people away. I noticed that most of the slab, was laying in hunks in the hollow between the walls. I walked out the back door and there were the table, thermos and glass along with a brief note stating he would be back about five the next day.

That night, I lay in my bed, fantasizing what it would be like to make love to that bundle of black muscle, and jacked off twice before I finally went to sleep. I rushed home early the next day, and David arrived promptly at 5:30. By the time it was dark, he had the old slab completely removed from the brick walls. His strength amazed me as he hoisted those pieces of concrete, put them into a wheelbarrow, and threw them in the back of his dump truck. As strong as I knew I was, I was sure I could not have done it. I had taken him more lemonade, which he seemed to favor over other cold drinks. He was personable and chatty when he would take a short break. On Friday, I didn't have a chance to see him, because I had a couple of emergency appointments at the clinic. By the time I got home David had been there and gone. But he had the hollow between the support walls filled with sand. He arrived Saturday morning while I was fixing my breakfast. I asked him in to join me. He seemed very hesitant, but finally agreed. He quickly put on his shirt and it was a turn-on just to watch him eat. God, he was a hot-looking man.

David began building the frame for the new slab. I saw him putting wire meshing on the bottom and then aluminum support bars. It was about one when he rang the back door bell. He was dripping in sweat. It was a very warm August day. He explained that he would not be able to get the cement poured until Monday afternoon. I invited him in, but he was hesitant because he was all sweaty. I told him not to let that bother him, and as he stepped inside, I walked into the bathroom off the back entry, and got a towel. Instead of handing it to him, I walked up behind him and first draped it over his head and vigorously rubbed his wet hair. He laughed. I took the towel and dried his shoulders and his arms.

With his clipped accent he joked about how nice it was to have his own personal valet. Standing about four inches taller than him, I swung the towel around and gently wiped his face, then his neck and down his chest.

When I got to his rock hard pecs, I could feel his nipples through the terry cloth towel. They were almost as big as the end of my little finger. As I rubbed over them, they grew stiff, and I heard him try to squelch a moan. I was so turned on, and knew I was talking one helluva chance, but, through the towel, I took hold of his nipples and rolled them between my thumb and forefinger.

He sucked in a deep breath and thrust his head back until it was against my shoulder and neck. He was breathing hard and made no effort to stop me.

I leaned down, and whispered in his ear. "You are so beautiful, David." His whole body shivered when I kissed the side of his neck, and continued to play with his nipples. My cock, straining against my fly was pushed against the crack of his cloth-covered ass. Looking down over his shoulder, I could see his own pants tented out at the fly. I ran the tip of my tongue inside his ear, and his voice chattered a staccato, "Oh, oh, oh, oh."

His body smelled of an erotic combination of fresh sweat and cinnamon. I slid my hand down the front of his pants and wrapped my hand around the long, hard tube of his cock.

I quickly loosened his belt, popped open the buttons and his baggy pants slid to his ankles and lay in a heap around his work boots. I shoved his boxer shorts down and his cock slapped up against his belly. His prick was longer than mine, but not quite as thick. The shaft of his cock was jet black, yet the exposed corona was a bright pink, the same as my own. David is the only black man with whom I've ever had sex who was circumcised.

I felt nothing but pleasure as he reached back and rubbed my dick, which was straining against my slacks. His words, however, jolted me more than a current of electricity. "Will you bugger me, mon?"

"Oh, I'll do anything! Whatever you want me to do." I turned my head and kissed his temple. Then I spun him around, leaned my face down and kissed him on the mouth. I was surprised when he rammed his tongue into my mouth and then sucked on mine with a passion I didn't expect.

I ran my hands up and down his back and then wrapped my palms around the cheeks of his ass. They were as solid as rock and about the size of two cantaloupe. I eased him down on the bench behind him and knelt between his legs. I removed his work boots, pants and underwear.

I didn't get up, but leaned forward and buried my face in his crotch. The odor of fresh sweat, male musk and cinnamon filled my nostrils. I don't know what kind of deodorant or soap he used, but that combination sure turned my crank.

I captured the end of that gorgeous pink cockhead in my mouth. As I closed my lips around his shaft and sucked, he came. This was too much! His juices were so copious that they began to flow out of my mouth and down his cock. I couldn't swallow fast enough.

When his body quit shaking from that intense orgasm, he began to apologize, repeating how sorry he was for coming so quickly, and then he slid down to his knees and we faced each other.

"Would you keese me again, mon?"

We clung for long minutes, swabbing each other's tonsils with our tongues. He pulled his mouth away and asked if he could take a shower before I "buggered" him.

I said yes, if he'd let me shower with him. Never in my wildest fantasies as I jacked off every night thinking about David did I ever believe anything would actually happen between us. We were all over each other in that shower. I admitted how pleased I was that he liked getting it on with another guy, but how surprised I was too. He began talking a blue streak, and explained how when his wife got pregnant, she would not allow him to have sex with her until the baby was born. He said during the eight years he was married, nearly five of them had been spent with nothing more exciting than jacking off.

He told me how one of his older brothers began "buggering" him when he was only nine, and he got so he liked it but he hadn't had his "arse buggered" since he left Trinidad.

He never used the work fuck, but always "bugger". He said men in Trinidad did not have the sexual hang-ups that American blacks had about having sex with a buddy. He said he enjoyed sex with his wife, but also like to suck cock and get "buggered". The latter two actions he could not get from his wife. And once she got pregnant he didn't get anything at all from her.

It wasn't until we'd dried off and found ourselves naked in a spare bedroom that I learned just how good a cocksucker he was. We sucked each other off. I was so turned on, my dick didn't lose its erection after I came.

When I got David off, and he saw I still had a hard on, he rolled over onto his belly and hoisted his ass in the air. I got some KY from the bathroom. While he lay with that gorgeous ass in the air, I crawled on the bed behind him, reached up and grabbed hold of his asscheeks. They were so muscular that I had trouble prying them apart, but I managed to lap my tongue up and down the length of his crack from his balls to the bottom of his spine. I think that was a new experience for him. His head snapped up and he turned to look back at me. I winked at him and pushed my tongue back into his ass crack. He lay his head back down on his arms and whimpered like a baby. I flicked my tongue back and forth over his asshole, and then rammed it inside. He squealed, clamped his ass cheeks and nearly crushed my nose. I greased my dick, moved up behind him and lay it up along the crack.

When I released his cheeks, they pinned my cock tightly in the crevice. I slid my boner up and down his ass valley. I raised up, and pushed my dick into his crack. I wasn't too sure I was going to get my cock into that tight little ass. David reached back and spread his buns with his hands. It was easy finding his hole, as it was a little pink ring in a sea of black. As I pushed the strawberry-shaped head of my cock against his pucker, it was like trying to force a baseball bat through a key hole. My dick began to bend in the middle. Suddenly, I watched that little rosette flutter open like a camera shutter and my cock began to disappear inside. David grunted as the thick head of my cock popped into his ass.

The heat, the pressure and the pleasure were almost more than I could take. I felt my balls tingle. I held still for a long moment, but then David began pushing his ass back, swallowing more and more of my cock shaft. He sounded like he was gargling mouth wash. I leaned forward and David pushed back until our balls were swinging against one another. I lay my chest against that hard muscular back.

Reaching under him and with one hand, I played with his nipples and with the other I stroked that long, black cock until it was rock hard again.

His moans and encouraging dialog made me feel like I was the stud of the year. His hands would reach back and pull on my ass or fondle my balls. He worked his fingers underneath him and tickled my cock as it slipped in and out of that fantastic ass. I was in no hurry, and I fucked him slow and easy. That's the way he seemed to like it best. Every time I would deep dick him, he would gurgle in his throat and wiggle his ass around my embedded dick. I jacked his cock and played with his balls as I continued to fuck. It was a marvelous position and penetration was deep. After several delicious minutes in that position, I rolled us over onto our sides, and fucked him spoon fashion, stroking his cock as I fucked. When I asked if he would lay on his back and put his legs over my shoulders, he answered. "No, mon, I'm not a womon."

I did not challenge his argument. He definitely was not a woman!

We eventually rolled until he was flat on his belly and I was laying full length on top of him, and moving nothing but my hips, I pounded my cock into his tight ass. I would feel myself close, and I'd slow down. I fucked David for almost an hour before I came a second time that afternoon. His ass seemed to suck my load right out of my balls. I jacked David off and he shot just a few seconds after I did.

We showered again, dressed and talked.

On Monday afternoon, David arrived and, shortly afterwards, along came a huge cement truck. It was the only time that David had some help. The men backed part way up my driveway and then extended and angled the cement shoot to feed the fresh concrete into the frame for the new stoop.

When they were finished and David had put up the barrier again, I asked if I could treat him to dinner. He seem genuinely pleased, but hesitant because his clothes were covered with cement drippings. I offered to let him shower and loaned him one of my warm up suits. He looked better in it than I did. He said he liked Chinese restaurants, so I took him to one that I knew had excellent food.

When we returned to the house, I asked if he had to leave right away.

He smiled and asked, "Why? Would you like to bugger me again?" I nodded my head, but told him I wanted him to "bugger" me first. He seemed a little reluctant, but once he buried that long black cock up my ass, he demonstrated his expert ability. I came twice without ever touching my cock.

For the next couple of weeks, David found reasons to stop by and "check" on the cement work. We always ended upstairs fucking and sucking each other through at least two orgasms.

A few weeks later, a friend of mine, who is the director of one of our local art schools, and I were having lunch and he mentioned his difficulty in getting "good" models for his life study classes. I thought immediately of David. I told George about this "workman" with the fantastic body. He asked me to see if the man might be interested in "posing" a couple of nights a week for two hour sessions. The pay was a hundred an hour.

I called David and told him about the modeling offer. He came over and although he was nervous about the idea of modeling, the money sounded too good for him to pass up. He felt better when he learned he didn't have to model "completely" nude, but could wear a bathing suit or a "posing strap," David didn't know what a posing strap was, so I went to the local gay "boutique" and bought him one. I had an erotic ball fitting that on him. I also registered for the classes where he would be modeling. For the next two semesters, David and I got together for a pleasing mutual fuck twice a week.

Early the next summer, David had the chance to buy a partnership into a small cement company located out of state. It's what he had been working for. The last I heard from David, was a Christmas card with a photograph of his wife and their eight kids. I have no idea if he ever found another man to "scratch the itch," but I know I'll never forget the year he allowed my dick to scratch it for him.

WREN: TODAY'S PICK-UP
Frank Brooks

On a late-summer afternoon in the 1970s I was sucking some stiff college cock at my friend Ted's place as Ted simultaneously fucked the teenage stud's ass and an eight-millimeter straight fuck-film flickered on the home-movie screen in front of us. All three of us were naked and sweating in the muggy afternoon heat. Ted's big deal was picking up straight college boys, getting them drunk and horny, then fucking them silly. Ted wasn't much into sucking cock himself, so he invited me over to heat the boys up with some fellatio, thereby helping to prime them for a fuck. Once I got a boy squirming and Ted got him tipsy, Ted had little trouble getting his cock up the kid's ass.

Today's pickup, a gangly, long-haired blond, was on his hands and knees on the rec-room floor, panting as Ted plugged his heretofore virgin butt from behind and I crouched with my head shoved up under his belly, sucking him like a calf sucking a cow's teat. As Ted banged him, the half-drunk, gasping teenager gawked up at the movie screen, watching a woman taking it up the ass doggie-style just as he was.

"Fuck!" the boy muttered. "Shit! Oh shit!"

He'd already shot two loads down my throat, and, when the phone suddenly started ringing, he went off again. As I gulped cum, Ted, cursing, popped his cock out of the kid's contracting asshole and staggered toward the phone. After draining the last jismy drop from the boy's cock, I got up behind him and slipped my cock up his ass. He mumbled drunkenly and stared up at the film, rotating his ass as I plugged it. For a so-called "straight" kid, he sure loved getting screwed. When Ted returned from the telephone, his big cock still hard and slick, he pulled me off the kid and stuck his cock back in where mine had been.

"Thanks for keeping him warmed up for me, cocksucker."

"My pleasure," I said.

As Ted humped, he told me about the phone call: It had come from Roger, who'd called to brag about the "baby-faced cutie" he'd just had down at the fairgrounds. (Roger was one of our cronies, a connoisseur of public sex, glory holes, and young meat.) Roger claimed he'd just "sucked off the horny little devil three times in a row" through a glory hole at the county fair. And not only that, but

153

the kid had returned the favor by sucking off Roger's over-sized, 47-year-old fucker not only once, but twice! Roger hadn't come twice in a row like that in years. And, get this: the kid had swallowed every drop.

"I don't believe it," I said. "Roger is full of so much bullshit."

"He sounded convincing to me," Ted said. "Why don't you go down to the fair and check it out?"

"Maybe I will, if you think you can handle things here alone."

"Get out of here!" Ted said.

I knew right where to go. The glory hole in one of the fairgrounds restrooms was notorious. It had been cut probably in the 1930s and, over the decades, had seen thousands, if not tens of thousands, of stiff cocks of all ages slide through it during countless county fairs. Graffiti going back to the 1930s adorned the stall walls. Due to the push-and-shove traffic in the restroom on a hot August afternoon on the busiest day of fair week, I had to wait my turn to get into one of the two stalls that shared the glory hole, but I finally got in.

The walls were an exciting mess of incredible graffiti and encrusted jism. It was a shame that the restroom was only open during the fair once a year. The glory hole was a four-inch by four-inch square. The moment I peeked through it, my heart started thumping wildly.

The smooth hand that I saw stroking a stiff, six-inch cock was young – no doubt about that. The kid wasn't looking toward me, but was peeking through a peephole in the other partition, watching the line-up of men and boys pissing at the urinals outside his stall. He was a baby-faced, all right, at least in profile, with thick, light-brown hair that fell forward into his eyes, a cute up-turned nose, and flushed, downy, slightly chubby cheeks. The moment he noticed me watching him, he stood up and shoved his cock through the hole. For one so young, he knew exactly what he wanted. I opened my mouth and took it.

The young cock was velvet-skinned, sizzling, and hard as bone, and had a mild, uncut tanginess although it was circumcised. As it slid in and out of my mouth, it flexed and squirmed, responding to every tug of my lips and wiggle of my tongue. I could sense him straining against the partition, trying to shove his cock deeper into my face. When he soon started making rapid little thrusts, I knew it was all over. I'd been sucking him less than a minute when he went off.

He shot a sweet, mild-flavored jism, like hot sap, and I savored it before swallowing it. I extracted every last sweet drop and released the beautiful young fuck-tool, but the boy didn't pull back. His cock remained thrust through the glory hole, gleamed with saliva as it twitched excitedly. I kissed it and nuzzled it, worshipping one of the prettiest young cocks I'd ever seen. Despite its bull's-horn hardness, its skin was soft as silk. After kissing and licking it until it looked as if it would split out of its skin, I took it back into my mouth and resumed sucking.

It took very little effort and very little time to get him off again. In less than two minutes, his cock was flexing between my lips, spitting its jism again. His new load was just as profuse and sweet, and I guzzled it as if I could never get enough young sperm. His cock remained rock-hard and stuck through the hole, so I kept sucking even after I'd drained him and within another minute or two he was unloading for a third time. The kid was phenomenal. I'd sucked off multi-orgasmic boys before, teasing three loads out of them in fifteen or twenty minutes, but I'd never before sucked off a boy three times in less than ten.

Even more incredible was that he still wasn't satisfied. He still pressed against the partition, offering me his randy young cock. I probably could have sucked him off yet again, but I needed a break. Standing, I touched the tip of my maroon-headed, eight-plus inches to the tip of his rosy-headed six inches and I stretched my foreskin up until it ensheathed both our knobs so I could masturbate us both. I was oozing lubricant, and soon his cockhead was slick with it. After letting me play around like this for a minute, he pulled his cock away and perched his downy-cheeked face in the hole.

Some boys have "Fuck My Mouth" written all over their faces, and he was one of them. Roger hadn't exaggerated, he was a baby-faced cutie, with a freckled nose and pouty lips. He showed me his fat little tongue and I shoved my veiny tusk of man-meat through the hole and into his waiting mouth. He managed to swallow two thirds of it before I hit bottom. He sucked vigorously and rapidly, as if starved for cock and jism.

Some boys have a knack for fellatio and he was one – a natural cocksucker. He wiggled his tongue under my foreskin and around and around my fat dickhead, driving me crazy. I clung to the top of the partition, trying not to groan out loud, trying not to start ramming and alert the entire john as to what was going on. His talented sucking sent daggers of pleasure not only through my cock but through my asshole as well. I wanted to bellow out, "Yeah, yeah, yeah!" – but I chewed my lips and controlled my breathing as best I could. He got me off almost as fast as I'd got him off. I closed my eyes and saw stars as I exploded into his mouth. I knew he was swallowing every drop.

I pulled my cock out and dropped down to kiss him, but I wasn't fast enough. He was already standing, shoving his cock back through the hole for another blowjob. To call the kid insatiable would be an understatement. A drop of lubricant oozed from gaping slit of his boy-cock, and I licked it off. His young phallus flexed insistently and I had no choice but to go down on it again. As if he had a time bomb in his loins, he came again within minutes.

And he wanted still more! Incredible! If we'd been some place safer, I'd have obliged him, but I was getting increasingly nervous as the men lined up outside the stalls and waiting to get in were getting increasingly impatient. I'd heard "What the hell are they doing in there?" uttered more than once, and a few times somebody had rattled the door of my stall. Before I could leave I literally had to take hold of the boy's hard cock and force it back through the glory hole. I'd never done anything like that before! Then I split in a hurry.

Forty-five minutes later I was back. After wandering the midway and thinking about nothing but the multi-orgasmic teenager, I grew hungry for another taste of him. But I was too late. He was leaving the restroom just as I was arriving, and I followed him out of the building and to a nearby concession tent run by a local church. There he put on a cook's hat and went to work selling hot dogs. I watched him for an hour before leaving the fairgrounds.

"That's my church!" Ted said when I gave him my "fair report." He was relaxing nude in his living room, trying to replenish his strength with a beer after his tussle with the tight-assed college boy. "Describe the little slut again." As I described the boy, Ted got up and pulled out a church membership directory and handed it to me. "See if you can find him in there."

Ted's church wasn't a large one and I spotted the boy without much trouble. "That's him."

"Are you sure?"

"I never forget a face I've plugged my cock with."

"I never forget an ass I've plugged with my cock with." Ted looked at the picture. "That's Wren what's-his-name. Used to be an acolyte – you know, a candle snuffer in a skirt. You sure that's him?"

I reassured Ted that Wren was indeed our boy, but he had to check things out for himself. Wearing dark glasses, he went to the county fair the next day – Sunday afternoon after church – and found the former acolyte at his glory hole post.

"He gives some of the best head I've ever had," Ted told me later. "I wonder where he learned to suck dick like that."

"How many times did you get him off?"

"None. You know I'm not a cocksucker. As soon as I shot my wad, I split. Sex in places like that makes me nervous as hell. I can just see the headlines: RESPECTABLE CHURCH MEMBER CAUGHT FELLATING TEENAGE ACOLYTE IN FAIR RESTROOM! It would ruin my reputation."

"Or add to it," I said.

The fair was over with and I feared I'd seen the last of Wren. I considered visiting Ted's church, but thought that trying to pick up the kid after a Sunday service might draw some stares, and I could do without the attention. Ted refused to assist me and kept his distance from the boy at church. So Wren became a jack off fantasy. Then, on a drizzly afternoon a month after the fair, I got lucky.

The basement of the old hotel downtown contained a public restroom where all manner of sleazy business had been going on for four decades. From time to time over the years the glory holes between the three stalls were patched over, but the patches soon sprang new holes. Cops ignored the place, as did the hotel management most of the time. As I came in out of the drizzle and entered the restroom I was glad to see that one of the three stalls was available. I was not glad to see, as I slipped into my booth, that a plywood plate had been bolted over the glory hole. Undeterred, I leaned over and peered under the partition.

The sight in the adjacent (middle) stall, nearly made me cream! Staring me in the face was the baby-smooth ass of a stark-naked boy who was crouched on the floor and sucking a kneeling man who had shoved his cock and thighs under the opposite partition. The kid's head was bobbing, his lips smacking, his throat growling with satisfaction. The boy's asscheeks had spread as he crouched, and I could see his moist pink asshole quivering. His bare toes and the pink soles of his feet were inches from my nose. Unable to control

157

myself, I stuck my head under the partition and kissed the kid's asshole, then licked his ass, feet, and fat balls.

The boy didn't even flinch as my tongue suddenly started sampling his luscious parts. He didn't miss a stroke of his cock-sucking, munching away on the veiny tusk of man-meat before him. He was jerking off as he sucked the man, and he wiggled his ass as I rimmed him. The kid's sucking got juicier and the man's breathing louder. I stuck my tongue up the boy's ass as deep as I could and twisted it back and forth.

The man started to grunt. "Take it, baby!" he whispered. "Yeah!"

I could hear the kid gulping, sucking down mouthfuls of man-spunk. At the same time, his young asshole started gripping my screwing tongue. As he grunted with youthful pleasure, I reached forward and caught the cum that was squirting out of his cock. I brought a handful of the slimy fluid to my lips and sucked it up. The sweet, alkaline, peppery taste got me high.

As the man left, I peered through the door crack. I recognized him as a trucker I'd sucked off a handful of times myself. He had a thick, uncut cock at least eight-and-a-half inches long. The lucky kid had enjoyed a mouthful.

"I'll suck yours," whispered the kid.

Looking back up under the partition, I saw him sitting naked on his heels, stroking his stiff cock as he looked down at me. He looked more naked than naked, perched there on the floor of the public restroom without a stitch on. My excitement surged when I realized I was looking at Wren himself.

"I'll suck your dick," he repeated.

"I'd love to have you suck my dick," I said, "but let's go some place safer and more private. I've got a van parked two blocks away. It's got a mattress on the floor in back. We can have more fun there."

"I can suck it here too."

"My van's a lot more comfortable and cozy."

"Come on, let me suck it!"

It took some fast talking, almost begging, to persuade him. He wanted to suck cock now! He didn't want to get dressed and leave. He failed to smile at my joking tone. I know that if another guy had walked in just then and wanted a blowjob, Wren would have turned his back on me and gone to work on the newcomer. But luckily nobody did come in, and after I'd teased him by letting him sniff and lick, but not suck, my blood-engorged eight-plus inches, telling him he could suck it in my van, he grudgingly got dressed and followed me.

The van was parked on the all-but-deserted top deck of a parking ramp. On a rainy day like this one not a soul would come up here to disturb us. I had curtains over the windows of the rear compartment and a mattress on the floor. I locked us in and we both tore off our clothes.

I pushed the sex-flushed teenager down onto his back and climbed on top of him. Grinding my cock and belly against his, I kissed him. He really was a cutie, and trembling with excitement under me. My tongue teased his lips apart and he clung to me, returning my kisses. His tongue slipped into my mouth, sliding against my tongue, and I sucked on it. We were both sighing and squirming against each other. In no time, his fingers clawed my back, his eyes rolled back, and he started jerking under me, spurting hot cum between us.

"Ohhh!" he moaned, twisting his head deliriously from side to side as I covered his hot face with kisses. As he continued spasming, I stroked his forehead, pushing the thick hair out of his eyes, delighting in the ecstasy evident in them. I sucked on his freckled nose and licked out his ears. As his orgasm subsided, I slid down to lick the cum off his belly. His slight chubbiness made me think of him as Cupid and added to his unique appeal.

His groin was as smooth as the rest of him, his pubic hair apparently shaved off. His armpits were equally smooth. He had ripe, plump balls, with pink, silky-smooth skin pulled tight over them, and a boyishly sweaty, sexy aroma that went to my head. I lapped at the fat nuts, teasing under and all around them. I kissed and nuzzled his perineum, then sucked on it. He pulled my head up and pushed his lube-oozing cock into my mouth. I sucked slowly, wanting to make the experience last. He gripped my head, rocking his loins, working his cock in and out. Before long he had his arms around my head in a hug, his hairless groin crushing my nose, his fat balls contracting against my chin. His cock was buried so deep in my throat that as he came he fucked his boy-spunk straight down my gullet.

"Yeah!" he whispered. "Yeah!"

After I'd caught my breath I asked him, "How many times a day do you get off?"

He shrugged. "I dunno – ten – twenty? Depends."

"Depends on what?"

"It just depends. Hey, you said I could suck your cock!"

I straddled his neck and let my eight-plus inches, foreskin peeled half back, throb in his face. He opened his mouth, tongue extended, and I slid my cock into it, rubbing the underside of the knob against his wet, wiggling tongue. With a vein-bulging cock nearly dislocating his jaws, he looked even cuter. I wanted to lean over and kiss him as he sucked me, but I wasn't flexible enough for that.

His eyes crossed, watching my cock slide in and out of his mouth. As he sucked me, using his tongue and lips in ways that sent electricity all the way to my toes, his right arm jerked rhythmically. I reached back with one hand and played with his balls, pinching the velvety sac skin and pulling on it. His hand jerked faster. His loins began to rock. I watched his eyes, excited by the way they registered his pleasure. When I saw them roll back, hardly more than their whites showing, I fucked my cock rapidly between his lips and brought myself to a climax.

We grunted in unison. Wads of boy-jism pelted my ass as I fucked my cum into his mouth and down his throat. It was a gorgeous sight, my pulsing, vein-bulging cock stuffing the kid's face as he greedily consumed my load and writhed with an intense orgasm of his own. No matter how many times he came, his orgasms seemed to be just as intense. Sometimes he appeared to nearly pass out.

I'd already lost count of his orgasms. I'd encountered multiply orgasmic boys before, boys who could hardly get enough of "the feeling," but never one who came so quickly and easily again and again, and who kept spurting. I expected him to dry up, but Wren's well of jism seemed bottomless. His repeated orgasms seemed not to cool his desire in the least, but, if anything, to increase it.

He lay there sighing in post-orgasmic bliss, slowly working his cock as I licked the melting cum off his belly and chest. Just as he couldn't get enough orgasmic pleasure, I couldn't get enough of his young spunk.

"When you come, what's it like?" I asked.

"What's it like?" He shrugged. "Cool- neat – I mean, it feels great!"

"So great you can hardly stand it, right?"

John Patrick

"Yeah," he said, pointing his toes in a luxurious stretch and stroking his cock faster.

"You jack off a lot, huh?"

"Sure," he said.

"I like watching boys jack off. Will you jack off while I watch?"

He shrugged. Squeezing his legs together, pointing his toes, he pumped his boy-meat, watching the tip of his cock as if it were already about to open up and spurt. As he masturbated, his balls pulled up even tighter in their pink sac, squirming to the rhythm of his cock-beating. When his loins began to rock and his eyes to get glassy, I knew he was close. Suddenly his head craned forward so he could watch the spunk shoot across his heaving stomach. He gasped, his toes clutching with each spasm, until he'd squeezed it all out and fell back panting. His performance for me had taken all of two minutes.

"Beautiful!" I said, sliding down beside him to lap yet another load off his smooth stomach. I was going to lie on top of him for another round of kissing, but he rolled out from under me, pushed me onto my back, and straddled my face. With his ass pressed to my mouth, his balls were draped over my nose and his six inches of stiff boy-meat throbbed over my eyes.

"Lick me like you did before," he said. "Like in the bathroom. That was cool! Lick my asshole!" He pulled apart his asscheeks and rubbed his sizzling young pucker against my lips.

Moaning, I kissed the delectable pink orifice and tickled it with the tip of my tongue, then sucked on it. The boy sighed, wiggling his ass. My tongue slipped inside him, twisting, working in and out. His cock flexed with each tongue-wiggle.

"Neat!" he moaned. "Wow!"

I love eating out young ass. I've rimmed some boys for hours at a stretch. But Wren got me too excited too fast, and soon I wanted to stick more up his ass than my tongue. Maybe the boy's own insatiable desire for climax was catching. In any case, before long I toppled him off me, onto his back on the mattress, and jack-knifed his legs to his chest, determined to fuck him and get off inside him.

I slurped up and down the length of his delectable ass-cleft, sucked his perineum, licked and nibbled his balls. He was jerking off, but I stopped his hand and held it off his cock as I sucked each of his fat nuts, then drilled his asshole once more with my tongue.

"Man!" he said. "Yeah!"

161

I slipped my tongue out of him. "Have you ever been fucked?"

He shook his head "no."

"I'll bet you'd like to be."

"Maybe," he said.

I moistened my middle finger with saliva and slipped it up his ass. He squirmed as I finger-fucked him. I stopped his hand when he tried to masturbate, fearing he'd pop off in two seconds and cool on the idea of getting fucked.

"You like that? You want something bigger in there, baby?"

"Yeah," he said.

He kept his knees jack-knifed to his chest as I got out the lotion and greased my eight-plus inches with it. He watched me grease up, breathing rapidly, his asshole twitching, his rigid pecker glued to his stomach. I smeared some Vaseline on his anus and down into his hole. I shoved one finger inside him, then two. He sighed, gyrating his butt.

"Feel good?"

"Wow!" he said.

"If you like that, you're going to love this." I pulled my fingers out of him and pressed my naked cockhead to his pucker. "Relax, baby. Take deep breaths and relax." I leaned into him, keeping the pressure on gentle and steady. It seemed impossible that my thick cock could penetrate his small anus, but gradually the tight little bud opened and suddenly I was sliding into him.

"Yeah!" I sighed, and he moaned "Yeah!" with me. The ecstatic look in his eyes as we coupled nearly brought me off.

"How is it, baby?"

"Great!"

Bridging myself over him, pressing my shoulders to the backs of his thighs, I eased the last few inches of my hard cock up his butt. As I pressed down on him and kissed him, my cock flexed inside him and his asshole responded by contracting. He stared into my eyes as I sucked his tongue and began to slide my cock in and out of him. He squirmed under me, wiggling his smooth, virgin butt as I screwed it.

"You like that, baby?"

"Yeah," he said. "Feels good."

I kissed him, sucking on his lips, feeding him my tongue as he fed me his. His asshole was incredibly tight, but incredibly elastic as well, and soon I was plunging in and out of him nearly eight inches at a stroke, nearly coming each time I rammed in. He clung to me, his hands caressing and clawing my back, then sliding down to press on my ass as if trying to get me to fuck him deeper. I was close to orgasm. A few more thrusts and it would have been all over for me, but I wanted this fuck to last.

I pushed up off him until I was kneeling, with my cock still anchored inside him. From this position I could play with his legs and feet as I fucked him and I could delight in the sight of my over-sized cock working in and out of his tight, clutching boy-hole. He rolled his head from side to side against the bare mattress, his arms thrown out to the sides as if crucified, his untouched cock flexing against his hairless groin and stomach with each fuck-stroke I delivered. I pressed his feet together and sucked his pink toes. The combination of my fucking him and simultaneously sucking his toes made his eyes almost pop out. He started to moan and writhe. Suddenly, his eyes rolled back with delirious ecstasy and the jism shot from his untouched cock and across his stomach. I caught up a handful of the fresh, hot spunk and smeared it on his toes, then sucked his toes clean as his pulsing cock oozed it last few drops.

He was showing me new tricks all the time. Not only could he come repeatedly, but he could come no-handed, at least with a cock reaming out his virgin ass.

"You're an incredible boy," I said as I rolled him onto his stomach. I pulled him up to his hands and knees and slipped my cock back up his half-open asshole. Holding his hips, I resumed fucking him, enjoying the delicious hotness, tightness, and slickness of his throbbing rectum. He had a beautiful round butt, one made to be fucked. It was a joy to watch my cock plunge in and out. I wished I could have got our fucking on film. Ted would have come in his pants watching it. I knew he'd have a fit of jealousy when he heard that I'd taken the boy's cherry.

I could have humped the kid's sexy ass all day, but my balls had swelled like over-ripe plums and were ready to burst. When the boy started rotating his ass as if trying to excite me, I went bonkers. Hunching over him, humping rapidly, I licked his back and the nape of his neck. God, I was close!

"Fuck me!" the boy said. "Fuck me!"

"Oh baby, get ready!" I straightened up, kneeling, pulling the boy up with me, my arms around him, my hands rubbing up and down his stomach and chest as I rammed his ass. He turned his head to the side so we could kiss, our tongues dueling. My right hand slid down, feeling his smooth groin, then wrapping around his stiff cock. My other hand squeezed his plump young nuts. I was fucking so hard and fast that my belly smacked his ass like a clapping hand. My hand pumped his wildly throbbing cock.

"Yeahhh!" he moaned, a pained, whimpering tone in his voice. "Fuck me-ee!"

His nuts contracted. His cock leapt in my jerking fist. My cock flexed inside him. He gasped as the boy-spunk spurted from his cock and splashed across the mattress.

I grunted as my cum shot up his ass. We writhed together, firing our loads and humping until the last drops had been squeezed from our aching rods. I gave his cock a few flicks to knock the cum off the tip, as if it were my own cock, then I pulled out of him.

Instead of licking up his load, I left it to dry on the mattress as a souvenir. The mattress was covered with souvenirs shot from the cocks of other boys, and now Wren's would be added to the collection.

I'd have enjoyed Wren for hours longer, but unfortunately I'd made a dinner date I couldn't easily cancel. Wren wouldn't give me his phone number and wasn't interested in taking mine. He wouldn't accept a ride anywhere and said he'd "see me around."

I last saw him jogging in the drizzle back toward the hotel, where the basement john was always a smorgasbord of cock sucking during evening dinner hours.

As luck would have it, that was the last I saw of the multi-orgasmic wonderboy.

I traveled nonstop for the next several years and, during my brief visits back in town, I never ran into him. I kept up on his activities, though, through Ted and our cronies, who enjoyed his fantastic blowjobs in restrooms around town from time to time and who saw him at the county fair each August, where he sucked glory hole cock when he wasn't selling hot dogs at the church concession tent.

Ted claims to have fucked him through a glory hole. For awhile he had a boyfriend his own age and was out of circulation.

Then came the big news.

"What's the latest on the candle snuffer?" I was talking to Ted long-distance, catching up on the local gossip.

"You won't believe this: He joined the Marines."

"What!"

"I told you you wouldn't believe it. Joined the Marines. He was home on furlough a month ago, wearing his uniform at church. No more acolyte drag for him."

"But why in the world would he join the Marines?"

"Guess," Ted said.

SECOND COMING:
The Use and Abuse of a Butch Marine
By William Cozad

I'm not much on tradition, so when the invitation came to my high school homecoming game and the alumni party afterward, I casually tossed it aside. Then I got to thinking about just who might be there. That got my cock to throbbing – all those jocks. What did they look like now, five years after our last game?

And, what the hell, it would be a nice drive with all the leaves changing color.

As I drive through the old town square, on that crisp autumn Saturday, I remembered my last days at high school, a sad time with my folks packing up, moving away shortly after my graduation.

Since I wasn't a jock I wasn't real popular or a member of the gang. It wasn't until I got to college that I found my niche, coming out and having my share of horny studs, even if they were only quickies or one-night stands.

That last year in high school I'd had a terrible crush on Steve. He was voted the best athlete in class, playing on both the football and basketball teams. He was a tall, muscular, dark-haired stud with blue eyes. I'd seen him naked in the locker room after gym class. He had a fat, clipped hose and big balls.

Once his locker was left open and I swiped a pair of his skimpy yellow bikini briefs, with piss and cum stains on them. I must have jacked off a hundred times while sniffing them, and I chewed on them till they lost their scent and were full of holes. The last I'd heard was that Steve had joined the Marines and just thinking about him fucking every girl in sight when he was on leave made my balls tingle.

The homecoming game was a humdinger. The Bulldogs were awesome, on top of their game playing to the rowdy alumni crowd. Three minutes into the game they made a touchdown. At the half it was 14-13 Bulldogs. In the second half the Wildcats got their act together and led 20-14 in the fourth quarter. The Bulldogs made a long ground drive and scored in the final minutes of the game. The extra point kick was good and the Bulldogs won 21-20 in a dramatic finish. The crowd went wild. I saw some familiar faces, smiled and gave high-fives.

167

COME Again, Volume 1

Swept up in the excitement, I decided to go to the alumni dance party. It would have been a bummer if the team had lost. At the American Legion hall someone had spiked the punch with booze. There were a lot of people I didn't recognize, but I'd been away for almost a decade, not going back for previous homecomings.

At the party, I was a loner just like I'd been in high school. Several cups of punch later, I was feeling no pain. "Bill, how the hell are you?"

I'd recognize that deep, sexy voice anywhere, even after all this time. When I looked up, there he was; Steve, in his drab green Marine uniform with the sergeant stripes. "Oh Steve, great to see you," I gushed. He shook my hand firmly and held it. I gazed into his steel blue eyes. I got goose bumps all over, just like I had when I saw him naked after gym class. Damn, I couldn't think of a thing to say. Not even small talk. He just took my breath away. "How do you like the Marines?" I finally blurted out.

"I'm a lifer. Found my calling. What about you? "

"Still working in the bank," I said.

"Making money the old-fashioned way, stealin' it?" he teased.

I laughed nervously.

"Figured you were a junior exec with those fancy threads."

He didn't know it but I was still paying for the Armani suit on my credit card. I was lucky to have a job at the bank now, what with all the mergers and staff cuts.

"It's nice to see you, Steve. You look good!"

He smiled and waved at people milling around, who probably didn't remember me. "Let's sit down and talk," he said.

I figured some ex-cheerleader would latch onto him and drag him to the dance floor, like in high school. He was considered a hunk, not just by me.

I gawked at Steve, I couldn't help it. He didn't wear a wedding ring and said that he was married to the Marine Corps. "This is a drag," he said finally. "I don't want to be in this crowd. Come back to my motel room with me for a drink. Let's talk about old times."

I couldn't believe it. I was now the center of his attention, like he'd been the center of my fantasy life back in high school. Weaving through the crowd, loud music blaring, Steve led me to the parking lot. I followed him in my car to his motel by the interstate.

168

In the no-frills room at the Motel 6, Steve poured us Seagram's Seven on the rocks. We sat at the small table, and he rambled on. He was on leave and decided to return to his old stomping grounds, said he'd hoped he'd see me. I was flattered, to say the least. "The Bulldogs got all the right stuff, just like when you were on the team," I said.

"Back when my pussy was tight."

I didn't think I'd heard him right. He must have meant when he was banging cheerleaders. I took a gulp of my drink. "You had quite a rep, the big man on campus."

There was no reply from Steve. He sat across from me at the small table, staring at his drink. The silence lasted for what seemed like hours. Without looking at me, Steve finally spoke. "You wanna do it, don't you?"

"Do what?" I asked.

"Give it to me."

"Give it to you?" I tried to shake the cobwebs out of my head. If I didn't understand him right he might kill me with his bare hands, this macho Marine. I was even hotter for him now than when we were teenagers, if that was possible. The fire of lust had been smoldering all those years. Feeling embarrassed, I looked away for a second. When I turned back, his eyes were locked on me. He was dead serious. "Oh God, yes, Steve. I've wanted you for so long."

"Well, then, let's get undressed."

I was still in shock as I watched Steve slowly take off his Marine uniform. My cock began to ooze as he watched me take off my expensive suit.

He was down to his skivvies. When he peeled off his white T-shirt, his chest was smooth and chiseled, like the statue of a Greek god. Both of us lay down on the bed, which he stripped back to the sheet, wearing only our shorts – his were boxers, mine briefs. His dog tags dangled on a silver chain around his neck. When he put those strong arms around me I felt warm and secure, like I'd never felt before. I thought of that slogan about the Marines having landed.

Both of us peeled off our shorts. Our stiff pricks dueled against each other. I couldn't believe this was happening, me and Steve after all these years were going to do it. Reaching down, we felt each other's boners. Steve's big cut dick was just like mine, a tad longer but not quite as thick as mine. Steve rolled over onto his belly. He looked over his shoulder, his blue eyes glassy.

"C'mon, fuck it, stud."

I was stunned. Here I had been fantasizing all along that he would want to fuck me. This macho Marine was begging for my dick up his ass.

He reached into the drawer of the nightstand where he had stashed condoms and lube. "Do it to me, Bill. Fuck me. Fuck my Marine butt."

I was so excited I was afraid I'd cum just putting on the rubber. Steve reached back and spread his ass cheeks invitingly. His crack was smooth. I swear it looked like he shaved it. His brown pucker winked. I managed to suit up and smear lube on my rubbered dick. I couldn't resist, leaned down and kissed both of his smooth, muscular ass mounds.

Then I slapped my cock against them. "Do it. Shove that hard dick up my ass. I train Marines to be lean, mean fighting machines. But I need to be disciplined myself once in a while. And that time is now – "

I couldn't believe it: Here was this macho Marine, a man's man, who wanted to be dominated. Well, I decided, I'd show him a thing or two about the real world, the dog-eat-dog banking business, where people had hearts of stone. "You fucking wimp!" I shouted.

"What did you say?"

"You heard me. Playing toy soldier games. Turned you into a pussy."

"Whatever you say. Just fuck it."

"Bet you're the base slut where you're stationed, Camp Pendleton, did you say?"

"I'd never do it with another Marine on the base. 'Don't ask, don't tell' don't mean jack squat. They'd throw my ass out of the Corps, medals and all."

"But you want my big dick, don't you?"

"Oh yes, Bill. Give it to me."

I was no longer drunk with whiskey, now I was drunk with power. I just kept slapping my hard dick sheathed in rubber against the Marine's buns of steel.

"Stick it up my ass, man."

"Why should I?"

He rolled over, stroked my cock.

"Because it's hard and you wanna get off. Besides, I've been waitin' five years for you."

I laughed. "You hardly knew I existed in high school!"

"Oh, I knew. You were a brain, but you weren't too bright. You didn't think I noticed the way you looked at me. I knew you wanted my body."

"You never said a fucking word."

"I let you steal my briefs, man. I let you. I knew it was you. C'mon. Let's make up for lost time." He rolled over, lifted his ass to me.

"Right on," I yelled, sinking it in to the hilt.

He screamed, then shivered and moaned as I settled in.

I hadn't fucked anybody in so long it took me a few strokes to get into the groove but he loved it anyhow.

"Oh, Jesus. Never knew a dick that big could get so stiff. Bang my butt. Tear it up. Hurt me. I'm a Marine, I can take it." Boy, could he ever! I humped the sergeant's fiery butthole for all I was worth, and I worked up quite a sweat.

He grunted and bucked back. "God, man, keep fucking my ass. Don't stop. God, you're even better than I thought you'd be. Such a hard dick! God, I love a hard dick!"

I crammed his ass fast and furious, but I couldn't hold out. Seemed like hours but it was only minutes before I felt the cum boil in my balls that slapped against his butt and erupt into the rubber.

"Oh, fuck yeah. I can feel it squirting up my ass. Oh, sweet Jesus! That's the best fuckin' feeling in the world, man!"

I'll say one thing, it was the most powerful orgasm I can ever remember.

His butt muscles spasmed. "I'm comin'! Holy shit! Comin' with your big dick up my ass! Aw fuck! Keep it in me, stud boy!" I collapsed on top of the sweaty Marine sergeant, hugged his shoulders and kissed his neck until my cock fell out. The powerful Marine bucked me off. Turning over on his back, I could see his belly slick with his own slime. "Put on a fresh scumbag," he barked.

I snapped off the spunk-filled rubber, which belched onto the nightstand. I threaded on another condom, not sure what to expect. The sergeant spread his sinewy thighs. He reached up and felt my rubbered cock that refused to go down.

"I'm your bitch. Fuck me some more!"

I couldn't believe how great the second time around was. It was slower, with deeper prodding. I loved looking into the fire of desire in Steve's blue eyes, into his very soul. With his ankles on my shoulders, I plowed his ass.

He cried, "Never felt like this before. Fuck me hard! Grind your dick up my ass. Oh yeah, that's it."

I fucked like a pile-driver, slamming my cock up the stud's asshole. I don't know how he took the heavy-duty pounding that had to turn his guts to mush.

He just kept on jabbering: "Oh, yeah. Do it. Cum up my fucking ass!" Steve's dick was hard and pulsing when he wrapped his fingers around the shaft and jacked it with a blurry fist. We finished at the same time, me squirting into the scumbag up his hungry Marine butthole and him spraying gobs of pearly white jism all over his rippled torso. His contracting hole siphoned my nuts. Lying on the bed beside him, I caught my breath. He moaned and smeared his ball juice into his leathery skin until it glistened.

We drank some more whiskey, sent out for pizza, and stayed naked. I fucked him again until his ass was raw and my dick was limp.

At gray dawn we showered together, his dog tags clanging against his thick chest as I blew him with the hot water cascading over us. This was the fantasy I had held since high school, of taking him in the shower, and it was actually happening. He was really getting into the blowjob action – even if it was going to give me lockjaw. At that point, I didn't care. All I wanted to do was suck this Marine's prick and finger his hot butthole while I did it. This finger-banging really got him going. He rammed his cock all the way, right down to the dense pubes. But the problem was I couldn't breathe. Sensing my distress and not wanting to choke me to death with his dick, he extracted it and slapped my face with it, while I continued to finger his hole. I watched as he stroked the shaft until he was screaming, "Oh, yeah, here it comes!" A big glob of jizz flew from the head and landed on my tongue. Naturally I clamped my mouth around his exposed glans and got every drop of the cum. It was a perfect ending to a perfect homecoming.

Then we hugged and kissed each other as if we were long-time lovers, which in a sense we were.

We promised to keep in touch, and somehow I just knew his butt was gonna need another good ass-pounding – sooner than later.

THE SECRET OF HIS SUCCESS
An Erotic Novella
By John Patrick

"Having all America think you are either hot, happening or sexy would make life intolerable. Imagine: endless requests for photographs, the importuning of movie agents, distraught women hurling themselves against your door, sneering jokes from friends, relatives, the mailman. Down that road lies madness. Had fate actually made me hot, happening or sexy, having the news publicized would be so hateful that TV Guide would find itself in court answering invasion-of-privacy charges. Yet it is faintly galling to be left off the list. A slow checkout cashier allows time to scan TV Guide's gallery cost-free. All are fine-looking men and women, apparently in the entertainment business. 'Hot,' 'happening' and 'sexy'? These turn out to be mere show-biz talk, meaning that these particular performers are having successes this winter. Envy gives way to sadness. Sadness for all beautiful young actors who each season receive these embarrassing media accolades. Before they have time to grow their first wrinkle, most will be has-beens, forgotten by the hypemeisters." – *Russell Baker, New York Times*

PREFACE

I confess that sometimes I fall in love with a character while I am recounting his story. Such was the case with Angel, of course, who was based on one of the great loves of my life, but there have been others. Donovan in "Boy Toy" always excited me. I kept picturing the cover boy doing all those nasty things and I came...and kept coming. Another of my favorites was Bobby Richards, who was discovered by Kyle Cartwright in "The Boy from El Dorado" and told his story in the sequel, "Teen Idol." Bobby was just too delicious to let go. I always wondered what happened to him after the hugely-hung New York photographer, Ben, moved in with him at Bird's Eye in Malibu, rebuilt after the wildfire that took Kyle's life.

So here is the rest of the story. The '70s are over and some are sobering up, Bobby included. But you'll find Bobby's need for constant affirmation hasn't changed, and the fact that no amount of money and celebrity can satisfy such a basic craving remains one of life's bitter ironies.

And to those of you who may question the true "secret" of young Bobby's success may find validation in a passage from Julia Phillips' memoir Driving Under the Affluence: "It was generally acknowledged that Crackers, who would turn ten this Christmas, gave the best damn head in Hollywood." – *John Patrick*

ONE

Stuart could have posed for any magazine he wanted to – he was that kind of beautiful. Straight men envied and hated him. Gay men envied him but they also adored him, some to the point of obsession.

Stuart's face was perfectly formed for one so young and his eyes were stunning – alive and sparkling with mischievous energy, greener than the glass of a 7-Up bottle. But his most striking feature was normally hidden from view. That is, unless you were willing to pay to see it. Stuart was known for having the biggest, most beautiful cock on the Strip. After a few weeks of working the streets, Stuart hooked up with Darrell, an older man who acted as his pimp. Darrell let Stuart stay at his apartment, even entertain tricks there, with only the pleasure of having sex with the boy twice a week in payment. But occasionally Stuart was drawn back to the street – just for the thrill of it.

On this clear, cool night in the early spring, Stuart's eyes scanned the approaching traffic warily, searching for the police cars he knew enough to avoid and the customers he hoped to attract. A dusty old Nova slowed for him; it was at least ten years old and wheezed blue smoke. The driver was not a day under fifty; even in this light Stuart could see how disheveled the driver looked, as if he'd slept in his clothes. His eyes were wide and his mouth leered. Stuart tossed his long blond hair and looked away. A guy in a car like that wouldn't be good for more than a twenty, and he didn't look like he was worth taking for less than his usual street rate of fifty or sixty. Besides, a guy that creepy sometimes made Stuart physically ill. There were times when he first came to Hollywood from Ohio that he was so desperate that anyone would do – but tonight he didn't need the money. He wanted to do something exciting.

He passed a couple of other street boys and he knew they were whispering about him. Everyone was trying to figure him out. He didn't mind if they talked about him. Everywhere he had ever gone, people had done that. He let people think what they wanted; he didn't care. His mother said he was anti-social and he guessed that was true enough. He was polite when spoken to, but very close-mouthed. Mostly he didn't stay in a conversation long enough for anyone to learn anything about him. He had no obvious needle tracks on his arms, legs or neck, so people assumed he smoked grass or crack or did pills or drank. Yet he hadn't asked anybody on the Strip about getting drugs, so everybody assumed he had his own connection, that he probably traded his ass for what he needed. Truth be known, the only thing Stuart was addicted to was sex.

Ten minutes after he brushed off the Nova, Stuart's patience paid off. A guy in a metallic blue Mercedes cruised him.

Stuart ducked down a side street. The Mercedes turned, followed him at a discreet distance. Stuart stood still under a streetlight in a parking lot and the Mercedes pulled up next to him.

The driver lowered the window. "Don't I know you?"

"Not yet," Stuart said, shoving his hands in the back pockets of this jeans. His basket, he knew, became nearly obscene when he did this.

The driver, an attractive guy in his early 30's, looked Stuart up and down. "Can I give you a lift?" he asked.

Stuart nodded. The driver unlocked the passenger door and Stuart looked left and right out of habit to make sure no cops would witness this, then gracefully slid into the passenger seat and shut the door. Soon they were cruising down the street at fifteen miles an hour.

The man couldn't keep his eyes on the road. "I can't believe a boy as pretty as you is working the streets."

"I like being my own boss," Stuart said, "and I'm not cheap."

"How not cheap are you?"

"Well, we can do a quickie right here for sixty, or you can take me home for a hundred – for an hour."

With a slight quaver to his voice, the man asked what they could do for that long.

"Anything you want," he smiled. "I'm open-minded."

"All right," he said.

175

The man said he was visiting from New York; the car was a rental and he was staying at the Beverly Hilton. He told Stuart he had given up hope of finding anyone on the street he could bring back to the hotel without causing a stir and had decided to go to Numbers bar when he saw Stuart.

As they parked in the underground garage the man asked, "How long have you been doing this?"

"All my life, man," he replied.

"Okay. But why? Why do you do this? You are such a pretty boy."

The man caressed Stuart's cheek, touched his hair.

"Like I said, I like being my own boss. Nobody tells me what to do and I come and go as I please. I can pick and choose who I date, and I do okay."

"Where are you from?"

"Ohio. I didn't get along with my folks. Besides, a boy can't stay at home forever, you know?"

"I guess," he said, and let it go at that.

The guy opened the door and ushered Stuart into the hotel room. Stuart had been to the Hilton several times and liked it. It wasn't terribly expensive, but it was comfortable. He sat on the edge of the bed, kicked off his sneakers, took off his T-shirt and tossed it on the floor. He sat there waiting for the man, who said his name was Ben, to come out of the bathroom. His libido in overdrive, his cock stirred in his jeans.

After a few moments, the trick came back into the room wearing only his boxer shorts. His body was nicely toned; he was the best-looking trick Stuart had had in weeks. He stood before Stuart and pulled down his shorts. His cock was cut, semi-hard. Stuart was stunned: Ben's cock appeared to be larger than his own. He had never seen any cock as big as his. Ben took Stuart's head in his hands and drew it to his crotch. This was unusual, and excited Stuart. Normally, the trick was all over Stuart, tearing open his jeans, feasting on his cock. Apparently this guy just wanted a blowjob. Ben's cock grew and grew as Stuart sucked it. Hard, it appeared to be as long as Stuart's, and thicker. And it was delicious. Stuart sucked and sucked. It wasn't often that a client affected him like this. Occasionally Stuart had a john who was a good lover, but that created problems for him, especially if the guy lived in Los Angeles.

As Ben pulled himself onto the bed, Stuart fell back. Ben stuffed Stuart's mouth with cock and began face-fucking him. Stuart choked on it, but let Ben continue. Stuart was so aroused, it hurt to have his cock trapped in his jeans.

Ben started doing push-ups over Stuart's face. Stuart amazed himself that he could do this and enjoy it so much. This man was using his mouth like an ass, or as Ben said, a "fucking pussy." Ben repeated the disgusting phrase over and over. Stuart had never been a pussy. He hated the thought of pussy.

Stuart put his hands on Ben's thighs to get him to slow down but it was no use. Ben was loving this and couldn't stop. His orgasm was incredible and took Stuart by surprise. He had not wanted to take it but he had no choice, he couldn't get the cock from his mouth in time. And Ben held Stuart's head as he came down from his high, forcing him to swallow it all, and keep the cock still imbedded in Stuart's mouth.

"Oh, yeah," Ben said. "Damn sweet boypussy."

Slowly Ben pulled his cock from Stuart's mouth. Then he lifted himself off the boy and, without saying a word, went directly back into the bathroom and shut the door.

Stuart lay on the bed, stunned. He reached down to his crotch and realized he had come in his jeans. He hadn't even touched himself there. He'd been on a few bizarre calls but never had he been treated like this.

The strange treatment continued when Ben re-appeared, started dressing. Stuart sat up. He didn't know what to say, so he didn't say anything. He let Ben lead, as he had done from the beginning.

There was no disguising the look of disappointment on Stuart's face when Ben said, "Get dressed. You want me to drop you where I picked you up?"

"Ah...yeah, I guess," Stuart stammered.

Ben zipped up his pants. "C'mon. You can probably get still another trick tonight."

Stuart sat still. "You mean we're done?"

Ben pulled his wallet from the back pocket of his pants. "Yeah, you took good care of me. I'm giving you a tip."

"Thanks, but I thought... " Stuart gulped, looked away.

Ben counted out five twenties. "You thought I wanted to suck you off? Or fuck you? Or have you fuck me?"

Stuart sighed.

"Look," Ben said, stepping over to the boy, shoving the dollars in his face, "I'm straight. I just do this when I'm here in L.A. I've a got a wife and two little kids at home."

"Where is home?" Stuart asked, taking the money. He was still not making any effort to get off the bed.

"New York," Ben said. "Now, you'd better get a move-on."

Ben went back into the bathroom. Stuart finally stood, wiped his mouth. Ben's cum had dried on his face. He picked up his T-shirt and slowly made his way to the bathroom. He stood at the door, watching Ben piss.

Ben looked over his shoulder. "You're the saddest-lookin' kid I've ever met out here. What the fuck's wrong with you?"

"Nothing," Stuart said, his eyes downcast.

Ben shook his cock, but he didn't put it back in his pants.

"You wouldn't be wantin' more of this, would you?" He turned and waved his cock at Stuart.

Stuart stared at the cock. It was bigger than his – longer by maybe an inch and thicker. Impossibly thick. It was enormous, and it tasted so good. Stuart was growing hard again.

"Well, come over here and show me how much you want it."

Stuart tossed his T-shirt on the tile floor and slowly walked toward Ben, as if in a trance, his eyes fixed on the cock that Ben was stroking.

With his free hand, Ben took Stuart by the shoulders and forced him to his knees. Stuart opened his mouth, and Ben began feeding him the cock. By the time he had three inches inside Stuart's mouth, the cock was hard again.

After a few minutes of fucking Stuart's face, Ben changed his mind. There was something about this one that made Ben want to do something he hadn't done in a long time.

"You wanna get fucked by that?" he asked as Stuart applied his best efforts to the cock.

Stuart didn't remove the organ from his mouth; he simply nodded.

"No extra charge?"

Stuart shook his head. Certainly not.

Ben sat on the edge of the bed. Stuart slipped out of his jeans. His erection bobbed deliciously in Ben's face as he stepped toward his john.

"God, that is a mean dick," Ben said.

"Not as mean as yours," Stuart said, stroking Ben's erection. He backed onto it, wiggling it to tease Ben, not that the stud needed any encouragement. Ben pushed up his pelvis and his knob came into contact with the pulsating sphincter. Ben then let Stuart slowly lower his ass over his cock. Ben felt as if he were playing with weights, bouncing Stuart up and down along his rigid cock length. Stuart grunted and puffed. "You like that, you pretty boypussy? You want more of it?"

"Yeah, ram it all the way in," panted Stuart. The cock was stretching his asshole like it had his mouth.

Ben let go of Stuart, who promptly succumbed to the full force of the savage impaling. Ben pushed vigorously into Stuart. He stabilized the sun-bronzed hips and Stuart soon began to meet each of Ben's thrusts, matching their intensity. Now that Ben's hands were free, he grabbed the boy's smooth shaft and pulled it hard while his other hand twisted each erect nipple in turn. "Oh, God! I'm going to come!" warned Stuart, squeezing his muscles on Ben's cock. Ben jerked faster, plowed harder.

Stuart gasped, squirmed, and soon Ben could feel the warm wetness on his hand and the spasms of Stuart's ass contracting ferociously around his cock.

TWO

Ben could not let Stuart return to the street, at least until he had shared him with his lover, Bobby. He insisted the boy come home with him.

"Home?"

"Yes. This isn't my room. I rented it for someone who had to go back to New York. I used to live in New York, but I live here now, out in Malibu."

"You mean you don't have a wife and kiddies?"

"I have a kiddie, let's put it that way. And I want you to meet him."

"Oh. Okay." Stuart was in no hurry to leave this man's company. He would stay with him for free if he asked. No problem. But Stuart was hungry. The ferocious sex had made him ravenous. Ben was happy to buy him dinner.

While they ate, Stuart opened up. "I was just a kid and I was watching television and there was a prostitute in this old movie. It was about a brothel. When I saw that, I decided that was what I wanted to do. I want to do that! Not for the money, I would have done it for nothing. It just really appealed to me. Having sex with all the men really appealed to me. And I didn't even know what sex really was.

"I knew one of my aunts was a prostitute. My cousins used to call her a 'fucking prostitute.'. But I loved her. She'd been selling herself for years and it never seemed to be so bad. She was the funniest person. Whenever she used to come into town from Atlanta, we always had a good time. She used to bring all this money and treat me to candy and movies and we even went bowling once.

"My cousins were so mean. When I was young, they would to call me a bastard, saying I hadn't got a dad. It wasn't really a big thing, but by the time I was twelve I started thinking a lot about it. I knew I wanted a dad. I knew I liked men. I guess I was very mixed up, but I really didn't know it! My aunt used to tell me when I got older that men are only good for money and sex. I really thought a lot about that idea. I really did like the idea of sex with men. That's when I started thinking about wanting to have a man to buy me things; this is what it meant to have a dad.

"It got so I was arguing constantly with Mom. She said I was a pervert, liking men. She made me think I was the one and only kid who felt like this about other men. But then I'd see my aunt and she'd tell me I'd be fine, but to always remember men were good for nothing but sex and money!"

Ben laughed. "Do you still think that?"

"I'm beginning to see men are good for more than that, but not much."

"We didn't discuss money. I want you to go home with me. There's somebody I want you to meet."

"Is he as handsome as you?"

Ben smiled. "You'll see. But you should know you have to be discreet."

"Discreet?" Stuart thought a moment. "Oh, you mean, I'm supposed to keep my mouth shut?"

"Yes."

"Or something terrible will happen to me?"

Ben chuckled. "Not exactly. Let's just say, it might get unpleasant."

"Money keeps my lips sealed."

"Have you ever been with a celebrity?"

"No, not that I know of. I mean, I don't get to see many movies or shit. I've met people who said they were in the movie business, but I only believe it when I see it, you know?"

"Yes, I know. How well I know."

- – -

On the way to Malibu, Stuart couldn't keep his hands out of Ben's crotch. He had agreed to $500 for the overnighter but he would have gone for nothing. For one thing, Ben was a dream lover and, for another, Stuart could hardly wait. After being in L.A. for a six months, he would finally meet his first celebrity.

It was near sunset as they turned off the Pacific Coast Highway and began the steep climb up Malibu Canyon Road. Ben soon saw the gray-blue fortress of a house perched on top of the granite outcrop and said, "There it is."

"What?" Stuart asked.

"Bobby's little house."

"That's a house?"

"Yeah, just a house," Ben chuckled. "But a guy who's been here a lot says it's always reminded him of a UFO, in more ways than one."

"Wow."

The house, which Ben explained to Stuart, Kyle Cartwright had named Bird's Eye for its unobstructed one- hundred-and-eighty-degree view of the mountains and the Pacific, had been completely rebuilt by his lover Bobby Richards after the devastating fire that took Kyle's life.

"And you were lover to both of em?"

"Yes, I guess you could say that."

Ben went on to relate that while still in mourning, Bobby rarely left the place after the crews had finished. But finally he went to New York and again saw Ben, a photographer he had met a couple of years before, and eventually Ben moved to L.A. to "try things out," as he said, knowing full well that he fit very well with Bobby. As Bobby was fond of saying, they were a "perfect fit," the tight ass and the long, thick cock.

THREE

Stuart was seeing Bobby for the first time in the most favorable of conditions. In the light of sunset, the Speedo-clad Bobby, with his oiled body, seemed to glow. Stuart found Bobby incredibly sexy. Bobby was, like Stuart, slender and fine boned, but while Stuart was blond, Bobby was dark and had large glittering eyes, accentuated by thick expressive brows. And although Stuart had been told he was handsome, he felt himself wanting compared to Bobby. Ben had said that Bobby was so extraordinarily handsome as a boy that people would stare at him on the street. His features were, Ben thought, perfect, as if carved, and he was so diminutive, he had a vulnerability that had excited Ben from the beginning.

"Who is he again?" Stuart asked when Bobby left the chaise by the pool where he had greeted them and went to make drinks.

Ben chuckled. "Bobby Richards. Did you see 'Space Travelers'? Or 'Back Into Space'?"

"Yeah, I think. Couple of years ago."

"Well, he's the kid in the movie."

"I don't remember. I'm not really into kids, you know."

"So I noticed," Ben said.

Stuart moved over to the edge of Ben's chaise. He had been hesitant, not reading the lovers' relationship fully, but Ben had made room for him. Stuart's hand slid up Ben's thigh.

Just then, Bobby was back, carrying three tall bourbon and Cokes.

Stuart left Ben alone and began to drink. Bobby sat next to them.

"So, you're really famous – "

"Famous for being able to please rich old men, mostly," Bobby said.

Ben got up, set his drink on the table. "I see you have a lot in common. I'll let you get better acquainted."

Bobby smiled as he watched Ben go through the sliding glass doors into his bedroom. Then he reached over and stroked the bulge in Stuart's pants. "Oh, god, not so much in common," he gasped. "You have a lot more in common with Ben than me."

Stuart parted his thighs to allow Bobby access. He was curious as to how Bobby had become so famous for pleasing older men, and ended up with the lead role in a sci-fi blockbuster.

It wasn't long before Bobby had Stuart's cock out and was sucking on it.

Stuart braced a hand against Bobby's shoulder, and managed to catch his breath. Bobby's hunger for his cock amazed him. Bobby wiggled his tongue over the huge head naughtily. The heat spreading throughout Stuart's cock felt too good to ignore. Just then Ben returned, nude. He kissed Stuart, spreading that sexual heat throughout Stuart's body and causing his pulse to flutter.

Bobby let go of the cock and, finally freed, it began throbbing violently before their faces. "God," Bobby gushed, delighted with it.

Ben experienced only a twinge of jealousy seeing Bobby suck the cock again. But that jealousy was washed away by Bobby's insistence on sucking each of them in turn, then trying to take both of them together. To Bobby it felt entirely weird, but still sort of nice. And it was good to have an understanding guy like Ben around whose penis was already hard for him, and whose moans seemed to indicate that Bobby was doing something incredibly right.

It was Ben's turn to squirm, and soon Bobby could feel the tension in Ben's thighs. Ben pulled away; he wasn't ready to come just yet. He ached to see that monster dick of Stuart's enter Bobby's ass.

Stuart was intrigued by the possibilities. Possibilities he hadn't even considered; possibilities that made his head spin.

Ben was a tremendous stud and Bobby was an insatiable bottom. They were a team made in heaven. He turned impulsively and kissed Ben, dizzily. Ben laughed, his eyes sparkling. "What was that for?" he asked.

"Just because," Stuart said.

In his bedroom, Bobby flexed his little, hard body up as Stuart knelt down in front of him, an act that could never be called embarrassing or clumsy, just part of the act, part of the preliminaries to fucking. Stuart tugged and pulled and finally slipped the bikini trunks off Bobby. Bobby fell to the bed and spread his legs wide. He watched the frozen smile of Ben as Stuart eased one, then two, then three, fingers into Bobby's warm asshole. Inside, back and forth. Stuart was practiced at this. This was what the customer wanted, this is what the customer ordered, this was what the customer was going to get – and more. Bobby's ass was used to this, and he opened up. Ben sat there for a while, watching Bobby's face as Stuart eased the fingers into his lover. But soon Ben could take no more; he had to be in there himself. He pushed Stuart away and became that fine fucking machine Bobby so adored.

Ben came deep, a quickie, true. It was sudden, true. But it was only the first one. Bobby knew that, after a rest, Ben would be back. Ben lifted up and let Stuart in. But Bobby wanted a breather in the action. He wanted to suck Stuart a bit. He had become fascinated with Stuart's good nine inches of curving dick.

"Oh, yeah," Stuart said, "Play with it. Make it real hard." When it was hard enough to suit Bobby, he guided it to his asshole. As Stuart began to fuck, a savage heat entered Bobby's skin. He cried out with the pain, with the pleasure of it, and Ben was everywhere at once, climbing over Bobby to put his cock in his mouth while Stuart fucked, bringing his lips to Stuart's for a long kiss, playing with Stuart's cock as it slid in and out. Bobby was feeling a strange, familiar, exciting, new touch on his thighs, parting them. Stuart rubbed his thighs, a touch so different and so familiar. His thrusting was familiar, because Stuart fucked him the way Kyle fucked him, with a certain gentleness, a certain responsiveness that only a bottom can provide when he tops.

Ben and Stuart were now pushing at each other in their greed to touch Bobby. Something shattered inside him; he came without touching himself.

He pressed his body against Stuart's and they gasped together as Stuart came. No sooner had he come that Ben pushed Stuart aside again, wanting to be inside Bobby again. At the same time, Bobby's hips surged up and he swallowed Ben's cock.

Soon they became swept upon the wave of desire, Ben pushing into him, Bobby feeling Ben grow bigger and bigger, shoving himself deeper in. Bobby cried out for more. Ben pressed his hands hard against Bobby's hips to still him as he finished. Slowly he spread Bobby's cheeks and Bobby felt the head of his cock hang at his asslips, not ready to leave. Bobby groaned as he felt Ben's cock rubbing rhythmically against his anus, and he pushed up to get the cock back into him. He couldn't begin to count how many times they had made love in the past and felt shattered and spent and warm in his arms afterward, but he did know now that rarely had it been this good.

FOUR

As they stepped from the Mercedes in front of the mansion in Beverly Hills, Bobby smiled and gripped Stuart's hand. They were both nervous. "Shit, you'd think I'd be used to meeting celebrities – especially since I'm considered one myself," Bobby said.

But meeting the members of Razor – the band with the number one hit on the rock charts at that moment – was disconcerting, regardless of how famous Bobby was.

Bobby pulled Stuart along behind him, whispering assurances to him, and reassuring himself at the same time: "You'll do fine. They'll love you."

They brushed past the multi-colored balloons that filled the entryway, left over from a party the night before and lolling against the molded doorways and fluttering softly up to the ceiling. A poster of the new album cover, "Desire," was taped to one wall. It showed the four studs – Joe, Pete, Mark and Jimmy – totally nude with Keith Haring-style arrows pointing to their cocks. Mark was the most flamboyant one, winking at the camera with an almost evil smirk, and rubbing his hands together with glee. Joe, who was part Cherokee, was the handsomest, but he looked dangerous, mean.

"That's the uncensored version," Ben said.

"You'd know," Bobby said. "You were there."

"Yeah, I snapped the picture."

Stuart stared, fascinated by show of limp rock star cocks. Joe was the one he would have done in a moment. But Bobby pulled on his hand, leading him into the sprawling living room. The lights were dimmed, and Ben stumbled over a white cat walking up to greet them. "Hey, Ben-baby," Joe said, picking up the kitty. "I'd like you to meet Pussy."

Ben shook a fuzzy paw, and Joe said, "Where are your manners, Ben-ny? We introduce our pussy to you and you don't introduce your pussy to us?" Joe's eyes were feasting on the two adorable youths trailing behind Ben.

Ben chuckled. "Everyone, I'd like you to meet Bobby and Stuart, my two pussies. Boys, this is everyone."

Ben looked around the room. "Well, almost everyone. Where's Mark?"

Tall, skinny blond Pete, obviously out of it, reclining on a red leather couch, said, "Lost somewhere in the kitchen." He was covered by a petite Asian girl, draped casually over him like a shawl. She appeared to be in another world altogether.

"You should check out the spread," Joe told the boys. "We've got all kinds of goodies left over." Ben had been invited to a private "brunch" after the "public" party of the night before.

They turned just as Mark appeared in the doorway, caught beneath the iridescent light filtering through a gathering of balloons. Mark was a true Irish redhead, his ivory skin sprinkled with millions of freckles that seemed to sparkle across his nose and shoulders and over his naked upper torso. He was wearing white briefs and came up to the boys carrying a glass of champagne in each hand. "Hey, Big Ben, who are these two beautiful babes?"

Mark took the boys on a tour and when they returned to the living room, Ben was already occupied on the couch with Pete and the girl. It was the first time Bobby had seen Ben with a female and he wanted to linger, but Stuart pulled him away, saying he didn't want to pee alone. They found the bathroom and relieved themselves. He did a double-take when they re-entered the bedroom and saw Joe, Jimmy, and Mark standing naked and stroking their cocks.

"There you are," Mark said. "Now we can really party!" Mark had the most body hair, a massive triangle of reddish curls covering his chest and pubic region, and he seemed to favor Stuart, as the three of them converged on the two younger guys. Mark reached down to touch Stuart's cock, still covered by his pants. He was already stiff. While Mark unbuttoned Stuart's shirt, Joe worked on Bobby's pants, and Jimmy planted a wet and sloppy kiss on Bobby's lips. Their tongues danced greedily together while Joe stroked Bobby's shaft, careful not to make him come too quickly.

Mark and Stuart were getting better acquainted, embracing and kissing like long-lost lovers while stroking each other's pricks. As Bobby stood closer to Joe, fondling his throbbing prick, he inhaled his pungent sweat, so sensual and powerful. Joe got Bobby out of his shirt and bent to kiss his belly all over, his tongue flitting into his navel and digging inside it for a while. No one had ever paid attention to that part of him before and it turned Bobby on. Meanwhile, Jimmy moved behind Bobby and began kissing his asscheeks. Joe moved in a straight line down to Bobby's curly pubic patch. He concentrated on licking inside Bobby's thigh. Bobby tensed as Joe's tongue touched the tip of Bobby's cock. He licked the salty residue from Bobby's slit, while Jimmy was lapping contentedly at his ass.

Bobby looked across the room to see Mark on his knees, gorging himself on Stuart's huge prick. Then he began sucking each testicle. It seemed he was going to swallow Stuart's scrotum whole.

Jimmy and Joe finished their foreplay, and Bobby felt warm rushes, not only from having his ass so expertly prepared and his cock licked, but also from playing voyeur to Stuart and Mark. Jimmy and Joe led Bobby to the bed, urging Mark on as they passed him. Stuart ran his hands through Mark's long locks as he continued his oral assault. He was greasing the meat with liberal amounts of saliva. Up and down his head plummeted, forcing Stuart's prick deeper into the back of his throat.

"Make me come," Stuart grunted, yanking his hair.

The other three stopped to watch the spectacle as Stuart's body stiffened as it neared release. Mark pulled back to watch himself as the cock shot blast after blast, each diminishing in intensity but still packing a punch. As the last blast of cum was released, Mark went back to sucking the heavy ball sack.

"God, what a load," Joe said.

"He's good for another," Bobby said, licking his lips as he sat on the edge of the bed. In moments, he had Jimmy and Joe's cocks in his mouth. He alternated them, letting each sample his cocksucking skills.

Meanwhile, Stuart kissed Mark's hairy chest, taking each nipple into his mouth, playfully biting on them as he felt them growing harder. He worked on his upper body until his body hair was soaked with spittle. Then Stuart eased down to Mark's throbbing cock and sucked him deep into his mouth. Mark began to jackhammer around on his tongue. Mark was so horny it was merely a matter of minutes before he was ready to blow. Stuart squeezed the base of his cock firmly to suppress his orgasm. "Hey, what are you doing?" Mark asked with a tinge of anger in his voice.

"Sorry," Stuart grinned, "but you're going to want that – " Mark turned to see that Bobby was now on his knees on the bed, his ass raised into the air and spreading his buttcheeks. Jimmy climbed on the bed and began by rubbing spit on his stiff rod, then kissed Bobby's ass all over, even plowing his tongue into his hole and rimming with no hesitation. Jimmy was very methodical, scouring Bobby's asshole until Joe pulled him off.

"Come on, Joe," Bobby begged. "My ass needs your cock real bad. Hurry up and fuck it!"

Joe laughed and moved his massive shaft toward the butthole. He began spearing Bobby with a quick and precise thrust. Then Jimmy took his place; the transition was so smooth it almost took Bobby's breath away. Jimmy fucked for only a few moments before Mark demanded entry. But even Bobby's practiced ass muscles were really no match for Mark's rampaging cock. His nuts swung wildly, hitting Bobby's nuts with jarring blows as he picked up the pace.

"Come on, Mark," Bobby cried, "give it all to me! Fill my ass with your cum!"

Bobby would have kept urging the others on, but Stuart had moved to the bed, stuffing his half-hard cock into Bobby's mouth. Seeing Bobby sucking Stuart excited Mark and he came with five hard, wicked explosions, and by the final one, he had his cock out, and cum dribbled back down Bobby's legs right down to his knees. After Mark pulled out, Jimmy was in again, loving it, and he came almost immediately. Bobby didn't let up on Stuart as Joe got into position, but as the thrusts began, he couldn't keep sucking. Instead he hung onto Stuart, kissing his erection while the ramming continued.

While Joe was taking his sweet time, Jimmy and Mark left the room, and when they returned they had bottles of champagne. Mark tipped the bottle over Bobby's prone body and let the liquid flow over his back and run down to his ass, where Joe's cock was still going full bore. Joe licked Bobby's back and Mark and Jimmy did the same, taking swigs from the bottle. Then they poured the wine on Stuart. Mark licked his belly, and Jimmy licked his upper torso. Being so close to his belly, Mark couldn't resist running off course a bit and joined Bobby's mouth at sucking Stuart's cock. Finally Joe came and then they all stood around the bed while Stuart climbed over Bobby and screwed him masterfully, his massive meat filling him as none of the others had.

Later, back at Bird's Eye, Bobby sighed in his sleep and pulled the sheets away from Stuart, mummifying himself in cotton and leaving Stuart naked and alone. Bobby muttered something that sounded like "faster," and his corded legs started pumping as if he was biking up hill. Hard. Stuart got out of bed and sat in the chair at the vanity, watching to see if Bobby'd win this midnight race. Suddenly, Bobby jerked upright in bed, arms reaching for him, startled and scared, and then he saw him sitting just feet away from him and he whispered, "Stu? C'mon back to bed." Bobby shook his head to clear the ghosts that seemed to linger there, and Stuart climbed onto the mattress and into his warm embrace.

"I can't sleep without my boy," he said into Stuart's mussed hair. "I can't sleep without my big cock." Bobby took Stuart's swelling erection in his hand and guided it to him. Cock to cock, Stuart fell over him and let Bobby hold him until his breathing grew deep and even, and then he pulled away from him and stared at the ceiling. The plaster above him was covered with tiny sparkles that caught the light from cars driving by outside. He watched the glittering ceiling and thought about what had just happened to him, and what it meant. He had just participated in his first orgy, with the members of Razor, of all things, and Ben and Bobby were right in the thick of it. But, as always, he had ended up the night in bed with Bobby. Bobby would not leave him alone, not for long. Bobby was insatiable. And it seemed to Stuart if he wasn't fucking Bobby, he was getting fucked by Ben. He was being held captive in Malibu!

Stuart thought he had seen everything. He had thought he was sexy, and dirty when need be, and hot. Definitely hot. But nothing had prepared him for this. These guys, and their friends, the Razor, were beyond anything he'd even fantasized about.

He got up and went to the bathroom. After taking a pee, he stood before the vanity and looked at his reflection in the mirror. For the first time he felt he looked like his aunt did after a heavy night, flushed and ready, blushing and hot. Stuart would watch her sit in front of her dressing table, slowly wiping the traces of lipstick from her much-kissed mouth, sliding her fingers along her cheekbones and seeing the way she must look to the men who paid her for sex.

As much as he liked what he did with Bobby – and especially with Ben – there was something not quite right about it. How Ben would drag his nails down his back while he held Stuart, kissing him in the hollow of his neck, biting him where it would hurt...but hurt good. It was bad-good, like something so hot it was cold, so sour it was sweet. But it was also sickening, too, because there was no end to it, no end to their needs.

Bobby was the one who really needed him, not Ben. Stuart was intrigued by the way Bobby looked at him, the haunted look in Bobby's eyes. The desire. It came off him in waves, like his Halston cologne, the sweetest scent. And mingled with it was the smell of fear. Bobby feared losing Stuart; Bobby feared losing Ben. To Stuart, that was good, very good, that fear. He should be afraid. Afraid of losing either one of them. They were what kept Bobby going.

But Ben was what kept Stuart going. Big Ben, always hard, always ready. Ben would lie naked on the bed and tease Stuart. Stuart would stand beside the bed, looking down at the stud's hairy body, at the cock. His master's cock.

"Okay, now," Ben would torment him. "Pinch your other nipple. Harder this time. I want your nipples to be throbbing with heat and fire. I want you to bite down on your bottom lip to stifle the cry. That hurts more than you thought it would, doesn't it? As soon as you let go, the feeling is replaced, right? By something entirely different. A flood of sensations, sort of swollen, but tingling. It feels different, doesn't it, Stuart? It feels...good. Oh, yessss. Come closer to me. Sit yourself down right on the edge of the bed. I want you to look at my cock, Stuart. I want you to stare at it, want it. Want it more than anything.

"Now pinch those nipples again. Both at the same time. Keep holding. I'll tell you when you can stop. Stare at my cock while you're doing it. And tell me, tell me.... What do you see?"

"A cock. The biggest cock I've ever seen."

"You know what I see? I see a naughty little boy. I see a slut, a whore, a kid who worked the streets, someone who deserves to be punished. You know that, though, don't you? Of course you do. I can read it in your eyes. Even if you thought you were this big stud. Even if you thought you were the one who'd be in charge. You're not in charge now, are you? You're not telling ME what to do, are you? See how easy that is? That switch. The slide, the shift. But the power is not in the cock, boy. Now, it's in the mind.

"You're confused, aren't you? I understand that. Bobby wants your cock. I want your ass. You're torn between his love and my need. My need for that ass. But don't worry. You're supposed to be confused by us. All I'm doing is giving you what you really want. What you need. I'm giving you what you deserve. You've known for a long time. I can tell.

"You're remembering that time at school, of bending over the desk, having the teacher bare your ass and then whip you. Gets worse, doesn't it? The whole class is watching, aren't they? All those eyes on you, watching as you were whipped bloody and then fucked by the teacher. Yes, that was your fantasy."

Yes, Ben was right, right about Stuart. Stuart had never met anyone like Ben. He was hungry for Ben. Ben made him want him. Ben was so talented, his mouth, his tongue taking him to the edge of forever in a matter of strokes. No one had ever known Stuart so quickly, found out the rhythm that he needed, the powerful fucking that took him higher and higher. Stuart would lose his fingers in Ben's hair while Ben fucked him. He would say his name in a husky whisper as the fucking continued, growing stronger and faster and better.

"Oh, Ben," Stuart would moan in a croak of pleasure, uncontainable, uncontrollable. "Ben...."

Stuart had to admit he was wrong. This affair didn't start that day Ben picked him up. It didn't start when Stuart first shook Bobby's hand. It started before he ever met these guys. Stuart was waiting for them. And they were waiting for him.

Stuart went back into the bedroom and his tongue started on a magic trip. Soon he was out of control, his breathing becoming shattered, his eyelids fluttering as he licked Bobby's luscious flesh.

"Oh, I want to say it," he thought to himself, "I want to tell Bobby, tell him about Ben, see if he feels the same way. But I know he does. I've seen them together. They love each other, but not in the conventional sense. They need each other, feed off each other."

He made love to Bobby, imagining that it was Ben in his place, fingers tightening, almost painfully, gripping the boy's buttocks, fucking him. Bobby had already been gang-banged but he still wanted it, welcomed it.

Then, after Stuart came, Bobby lay curled, kitten-like in his arms, breathing in that deep, rhythmic way that signified total bliss. Total bliss.

Stuart stroked his hair, and laid his hand palm down on the nape of his neck to feel his warmth. And he looked long and hard above his bent head, wondering when he would see the halo that he just knew lingered there. For Bobby had become Stuart's angel.

FIVE

Stuart finished showering and came back into the bedroom, quietly dressing by the sliver of light that stole in through the blinds, casting a few glances of Bobby as he lay there, already deep asleep again.

Ben, who slept in Kyle's old bedroom, the master suite, bounced into the room. He said he had to get to the office, he was shooting another celebrity in the studio. He didn't say who it was.

Ben stood behind Stuart, massaging his ass as Stuart climbed into his jeans. No, there simply wasn't time to think "sex." But Ben did think "sex," all the time. Especially now, seeing Bobby asleep, so satisfied with Stuart.

"You said I could ride into town with you?"

"Of course."

"There's some ... personal business there I'd like to take care of."

"Of course. I'd be ... er ... delighted. If there's anything else you need ..." He smiled magnanimously.

Bobby had told Ben to take the Porsche. He wouldn't be leaving Bird's Eye today.

As if to cooperate fully, the weather was crisp, bright and blue. There wasn't a cloud to be seen, and they lowered the top.

Ben was in a happy mood. He was happier than Stuart had ever seen him. "You know," Ben said, "The odds of this working are too overwhelming."

"What is?"

"You...this...us. The three of us."

"Oh?"

"I think we've proved something." His voice broke, and tears began to slide down his cheeks. They were tears of happiness. "I don't know what else to say except...I'll never forget what you've done for me – for us."

"I don't understand."

"Of course you don't. Bobby and I go way back. I knew him before any of it happened really. He was just starting. But he was so in love with Kyle, I couldn't get through to him, not really. Then Kyle died and...well, Bobby needed me."

Stuart smiled across the seat at him. "Thank you for the ride."

Ben shrugged. "My pleasure."

In town, his legs half out of the car, Stuart turned around to face Ben. He smiled.

"Where will you be?" Ben asked.

"I'll come over to your studio."

"By five. Be there by five."

"Yes, sir."

Stuart stood on Santa Monica watching Ben drive away. He took a deep breath and smiled. And slowly, reluctantly, he made his way up the hill.

- - -

For a while, Stuart stood down the street, waiting for Darrell to leave the house for the work-out at the spa that he performed faithfully four afternoons a week, before the phones started ringing with calls from johns looking for tricks.

Finally Darrell left the building and Stuart watched him turn the corner before he went to the house at the end of the street. He tilted his head back and sighed as he unlocked the front door. He whispered into empty house: "I'll bet you missed me, you bastard."

Then slowly, wearily, he trudged upstairs. His room had been stripped. Everything he owned had been put in a big suitcase in the closet. He suddenly felt tired. He didn't ever remember having been this tired in all his life. It was as if all the sleep he had missed during the past several weeks was catching up with him. By the time he got to the bedroom, he was exhausted. He sprawled out on the bed.

He remembered the first time. Stuart knew the man was following him. He feared the man. He had no reason to, the man was fairly handsome, tall, slender, mid-40s, nicely dressed. But somehow he just anticipated his sex would be violent. The man would have his way with him, Stuart knew, and there was nothing he could do about it.

The man called himself Darrell, and he tied Stuart up.

"Three fingers?"

He was pushing in, bending his wrist a funny way. "I'm gonna loosen you up for my cock. I got a big one, you know." Stuart went with him and hadn't seen his cock, didn't know it would be so big, so unmanageable. It was a power that Stuart understood. He understood the amazing power of the penis. Darrell still hadn't seen Stuart's. Once he did, he knew he'd found his perfect slave.

"I don't get fucked," Stuart protested, but Darrell kept pushing his hand into him.

Darrell did fuck Stuart. When Stuart awoke Darrell said he was sorry. He grinned a lot while massaging Stuart's smooth skin and kissing his asscheeks. "Didn't I tell you it would be great?" He rubbed his wrists, almost gently, one in each of his big hands. "Didn't I tell you?"

Stuart stretched, and Darrell began to rub his ankles where the ropes had reddened them. "You're such a beauty. We'll make a lot of money together." His eyes got big as he imagined the cash Stuart would bring home. "But nobody fucks it but me. Okay?"

Stuart gulped. "Yeah, sure."

And Darrell did fuck it. Twice a week, like clockwork. Repeatedly reminding Stuart that his ass belonged to him – and only to him. He told Stuart he would fuck the boy every night, but he didn't want to wear it out. For that, Stuart was thankful.

When Stuart would fight, Darrell slapped him. "No respect," Darrell screamed at him. Stuart didn't speak, couldn't speak, because Darrell had gagged him, gagged him so tightly he had trouble breathing.

"What if I tossed you back on the street? Would you like that?" Darrell struck him hard, a glancing blow to the head.

Stuart's wrists ached. He complained that Darrell might be breaking his wrist and Darrell swatted him hard across the ass, then entered him.

As the fuckings continued, Stuart always realized it was better to be safe here, rather than on the street.

Stuart set Darrell off like no one else. It seemed he hated Stuart beyond reason. Why had he saved him? Why him?

"It sure as hell wasn't charity," he would say, and then he fucked him more urgently. He slammed into him as if he wanted to kill him.

He didn't want to hurt him too much, he said, but he didn't want to give Stuart over to too much pleasure.

"I'm going to fuck you to death, and you're gonna to love it." In the beginning, Stuart did try to struggle – Darrell told him to – but it seemed to make so little difference that he immediately wished he hadn't. After a time, hopelessness closed in and he began to accept the violent buffeting his body took. Most nights, he was driven past pain and into a sweet delirium where he could no longer struggle...

Suddenly Stuart awoke. He felt an icy, sickening panic shuddering through his bones. The rushing of his blood and the pounding of his heart screamed through his body. His jeans had been pulled down and he was being held down with considerable force, and a cock, a too-familiar cock, was slamming in and out of his ass.

His face against the pillow, Stuart whimpered, "Don't, Darrell, please."

"Where you been?"

"Don't! Stop!"

"You're gonna get the fuck of your life, pretty boy. The fuck of your life."

"No!" The adrenalin rushed potently through him and, with a cry of rage, he flung himself off the bed. Pulling his pants up, he hurled himself towards the open door, his attacker in swift pursuit. Stuart ran to the kitchen. Darrell lunged into the room, began battering Stuart in the ribs. Stuart pulled away, snatching up the first weapon which caught his eye – a butcher knife.

Darrell's mouth hung wide with surprise as Stuart leapt at him, bringing the knife arcing down with all the force and speed Stuart could muster. Darrell saw it coming, but too late. He let out a shriek as the knife entered his back. His eyes rolled upwards in their sockets and he crumpled to the floor. Stunned, Stuart stood over Darrell. But he told himself to hurry, to gather his things and get the hell out of there. He washed the blood from his body and the knife, dressed, packed his suitcase, and hurried from the house. He went out the back, then backtracked to Santa Monica, then walked to the six blocks to the studio. There was the Porsche, red and gleaming, parked right outside. He stood beside it, bent over and breathed deep, noisy, grateful lungfulls of air. Never before had air in Los Angeles tasted quite so rich and sweet.

"What are my chances at modeling?" Stuart asked.

Stuart had listened as Ben gave him a tour of studio as he might have listened to the speech of an exotic foreigner or the song of an exotic bird. Surely Ben was, as Bobby had said of him, a "master." Ben did not envy the boy the prospect of the adventure of his new profession – the very thought of "peddling" one's looks in public dismayed him – but he did envy him the brash vitality of his youth. He had no doubt that, if he did not give up too quickly, he might very well succeed.

Ben showed Stuart the portfolio of photographs of the latest "big thing" in modeling, a guy named Seth. "I just thought, you know, you might be curious," Ben said. Most of the photographs, he explained, as Stuart turned the pages slowly, were a series of test shots. Ben was delighted with Stuart's face, how it exuded an innocent, boyish quality that was so far from the truth of it. Ben poured himself a drink. Stuart was engrossed in examining the glossy photographs in sequence, thoughtfully, as if they were – as, indeed, perhaps they were – works of art. Stuart found himself staring at a particularly fetching photograph of the very blond, very arrogant-looking young stranger posed leaning against a Jaguar sports car parked amid the dunes, the point of the photograph being, evidently, the Armani suit the young man modeled, with exaggerated shoulders and a slim waist and wide lapels.

"He's really fine," Stuart said.

He turned the page and there was the formidable young blond man posing in jodhpurs and a polo shirt that fitted his slender yet muscular torso tightly; there was the young blond man in a fashionable ribbed sweater and blue jeans and running shoes; then, lounging on sunlit stone steps redolent of the Mediterranean , his hair glaringly blond – his eyebrows nearly white, eyes obscured by tinted Polo glasses. In one photograph, over which Stuart chose to linger, he was nearly naked – wearing only snugly fitting briefs. "Is he good in bed?" Stuart asked, unwilling to tear his eyes away from the photograph.

"I don't know. He's one I missed."

"The only one, I'll bet."

"I really didn't want him. He's dumb as a post."

Stuart looked expectantly up at Ben, who, standing with a strong vodka in one hand, his other hand crooked at his waist, elbow akimbo, was looking at him. "Do you," Stuart asked, with a gesture toward the portfolio, "do you think I have a future there, Ben?"

"Well, it is an exciting life, but it's tough, too – like, you know, 'dog eat dog'; you're in such immediate and continuous competition with other models, I sort of wonder whether your nerves can stand it."

Ben took a long swallow of his vodka.

"Can I have one of those?" Stuart asked. It all came back to him now, what he had just done to another human being. His heart began pounding heavily, and the portfolio dropped to the floor.

"Sure," Ben said, stepping over to the bar.

Stuart gulped the drink. Ben had never seen him drink much. Mostly he enjoyed Bobby's weed.

"You okay?"

Stuart nodded and finished the drink. Excited, Ben pulled the black turtleneck sweater off over Stuart's head and let it drop. He bent and pressed his lips to the bare, nearly hairless chest, his mouth dry with anticipation.

196

Afterward he would not remember precisely how he came to get Stuart naked on the conference table, but it was like a dream in teasing fragments, the emotional tone of it and not details or images or uttered words. He did remember that, with his eyes filling with tears, tears of joy, it was their best sex yet. In a state of ecstasy, nearly blinded, he knelt over Stuart and kissed him full on the mouth.

- — -

Back at Bird's Eye, Bobby was in a reflective mood. He was still excited about having been to an orgy, but he was disturbed.

"They didn't know who I was," he kept muttering.

Ben shook his head in disgust. "You haven't done anything in almost two years, Bobby. What do you expect?"

SIX

Now that Stuart was at Bird's Eye, Bobby didn't see any need to leave. He thought of cancelling his invitation to go back to Texas for Christmas, then Ben said he was going to New York for the holidays and, because Bobby was going to Texas, he was planning on taking Stuart with him. That settled it.

To Bobby, it didn't seem like the holidays at all, those few days in Texas. He was lonely. He kept thinking of Ben fucking Stuart in New York.

Bobby found a new restraint with his mom, Kate. He felt them somehow moving apart, drifting like clumsy logs in a pond, no real direction, but still tearing apart from each other. Bobby guessed he'd just grown up, but now he was so lonely. Bobby knew he'd always have a home there but could never stay.

Like a ghost, Bobby walked the corridors of the old hotel, remembering the men he had visited in their rooms over the years.

He began when he was barely a teen, slipping into those dingy rooms, sucking the cocks of an endless succession of traveling men. When men told him that they deliberately came back to the hotel just to see him, Bobby realized he had found freedom. He had found power. He had found his talent.

They all wanted him, and then wanted more of him. Even as they were registering, Bobby could tell their circuits were buzzing, signaling him that they wanted him. They were all good, they were all the same. None of them was enough. He retreated into his fantasies of the hottest young singer/actor of the day, Kyle Cartwright. That's why, when Kyle came to town to film "El Dorado," using the stages at the nearby Alamo Movie Location, Bobby was ecstatic, never expecting Kyle would meet him, let alone want him, then fall in love with him.

As the weeks of the filming went on, Bobby couldn't understand what the situation really was – it seemed Kyle was with Vinnie, a cinematographer whom he brought along to the location from Hollywood. Yet Vinnie was smitten with Bobby's mother. And Kyle was taking Bobby to bed, taking his cherry. It was all too much.

Upon his return to Texas, Bobby and his stepfather Vinnie had little to say to each other and all of that was superficial. But he felt the hum of something deeper, something akin to love, when they discussed Vinnie's trip to L.A. and Kyle's death. Kyle had loved Vinnie dearly, and Vinnie had cared for Kyle. There was a small flame, like a candlelight, of something warm and pleasant in their talk. There their perspectives on beauty crossed. Vinnie could soften (though Bobby could never call him a difficult man) and they could relate. There was something beyond sex – there was love. Bobby guessed he would have seduced Vinnie again, if given half a chance, but instead he avoided it, went for a long walk.

Late one afternoon, a man picked Bobby up. The man knew exactly what Bobby wanted. He said he wanted to "butt fuck" him and told Bobby to touch his crotch and Bobby did. While he man was driving Bobby rubbed his crotch – it was big. The man had just been released from prison, he said, and had a motel room. They went there and very soon they were at it – Bobby sucking him, sitting on his cock. The man turned Bobby over and fucked like he said he did his inmate lover. Then he had Bobby suck him awhile, followed by more fucking. Finally he held Bobby's head down on this large uncut cock and said "drink my cum – I want you to take it all."

Bobby enjoyed being used by the stranger, just a hole for his passion. He shoved it down Bobby's throat to come and held it there till Bobby was faint and then Bobby came. The man rubbed that big penis in Bobby's face and made him suck his balls, then he propped the pillow behind his head to face-fuck him with it. He used Bobby's throat to stimulate himself, not caring about teeth. Bobby heard him gasp as he came sharply into the side of Bobby's throat, nearly choking him.

He took Bobby back to where he'd found him. He wasn't ungrateful, but, because Bobby never asked for money, the man didn't give him any.

SEVEN

During their time in Manhattan, Stuart began thinking he would like, really, to be a real model. Ben had more or less convinced him that a boy with his energy and temperament and imagination, above all, dignity, could not be so passive, so much putty-in-the-hands like the other models (those narcissistic assholes, pretty-boys crazy in love with their own reflections).

Ben agreed to photograph him. Thus Stuart gritted his teeth, and smiled, and tried hard, showing how serious he truly was, how eager to cooperate. Ben had another photographer do some stills and, during one of the breaks Stuart began thinking perhaps he should be a photographer instead of a model. He started asking the photographer about his background, what kinds of work he did, what kinds of contracts were necessary, and was photography school actually a good or necessary thing or could you sort of pick it up on your own – "Provided you had good advice, I mean."

"Of course," the photographer said, paying him little mind.

Stuart was pleased with the stills and Ben promised to get him some work once they returned to Los Angeles.

That night, when Ben assured Stuart that he did not have to participate, but could simply add to the energy by being a voyeur, and that he would stick close to him or see to it he was comfortable if he were busy, Stuart said yes he'd go to the party a friend of Ben's was giving.

The "party" was held in an old warehouse. It was a large room, filled with heavy-beat but not intrusive music. Pools of light accentuated tables, slings, vertical and horizontal bars, whipping posts, or some bondage display – a human form spread-eagled in suspension by ropes and clamps. In varying numbers and stages of undress, some twenty studs clustered around one piece of equipment or another, much like the stations in a medieval miracle play. On, in, or at each piece of equipment a single body, a bottom, would be the intense concern of one or more tops who sought to arouse him by whatever appropriate and creative means.

Stuart had to admit it was a smorgasbord of delight. All he had to do was choose a scene and watch, like a porn video come to life. All around them, bottoms were tortured exquisitely and – usually an eternity later – released extravagantly into sexual fulfillment.

Before long, Ben was pressing his body into Stuart's until his nipples were pressing against Stuart, erect and hard underneath his black T-shirt. Every time Stuart swayed and brushed against them, Ben moaned and arched his back. Every time Ben arched him back, Stuart pressed his thigh between his legs and rocked him back into him. Stuart's fingers found a tangle in his hair, wrapped around it. With every sharp tug, they ground against each other, private pain amid one man's voice after another. They fucked at each other during hard rocking songs, and caressed each other during slower country songs. Stuart wanted to cover every inch of Ben during one ballad that was so sweet it made him like country for the first time. He was shocked to find that he was tremendously excited – aching with desire for Ben, long and hard and crazy. Just from dancing! He was wondering why he had waited so long to do this, to dance like this with Ben, when his voice brought him back to the present. "I need you," Ben whispered sharply in his ear. As usual, those words sent an immediate message to Stuart's body, and Stuart was ready to lay him down right there, except that there wasn't any room. He heard the presence of other men around them now, several of them talking and none of them fucking, but they didn't care. It didn't matter that Stuart had never been there, didn't know anyone, and hadn't ever just fucked like a sex-starved lunatic in front of perfect strangers. It didn't matter that it was dark and uncomfortable – this sensation was absolutely new. For once, control was just not part of the equation.

Nothing was on their minds but getting off. Ben opened his jeans after pulling off Stuart's. He grabbed onto Stuart's dick, and felt the warm slipperiness brought on by the precum. Stuart tried to grab for Ben's cock, and Ben let him. Ben moaned as Stuart straddled his body, and Ben leaned back against a wall, lowering his hips so Stuart could climb over him, fill himself with Ben's enormous manhood. When Stuart settled with a hard slam, they both gasped, and their faces screwed up in mutual orgasm. Stuart didn't have time to reflect on how this was a first for such an event, he was too busy coming.

Ben's head snapped back. He didn't even feel the brick wall, he was so gone. He thrust up, deeper into Stuart, and wrapped his arms tightly around his waist, pulling him to him like the perfect sex-

John Patrick

toy he was. It was violent and it was harsh, and every jerk of his body made Ben growl and Stuart scream. As Stuart panted and fought to catch his breath, he was conscious of several pairs of eyes glinting through the darkness, and knew that they had become the entertainment focus of the room. But Stuart didn't care. All he knew was that one series of spasms wasn't going to be enough for him. Ben turned awkwardly, keeping himself inside Stuart, and pressed him against the wall. Stuart started to slide down and, staying with him, Ben ended up on the floor, braced over him, while he moaned and gasped and started to whimper. Catching his legs, Ben pulled them up, his thighs now braced from Ben's hips up to his waist. His ass lifted off the floor, and Ben could see his asshole filled with his cock. The sight alone was enough to send Ben into yet another spiral of ecstasy.

"I'm not finished with you!" Ben snarled, pulling back to slam in again. Stuart's wails hit a new high note as Ben pumped, and the shifting position of his cock was just perfect for the rhythmic fucking style that he was justly famous for, giving him some more time before another orgasm made the partner insane. Stuart tried to grab for Ben, and Ben caught his wrists and slammed them down against the floor. They fucked until Ben couldn't breathe anymore, until sweat matted his shirt to his back and the pool of slickness between them seemed like a thin layer of oil spread over their entire bodies. When Ben pulled out of Stuart's ass, Stuart screamed and clutched at the empty air, and Ben stood and watched him writhe in the final throes of an agonizing series of delirious shakes which almost – but not quite – got Ben horny again. Ben wiped himself off with his back-pocket hanky and tossed it to Stuart.

"Cool," said a voice from behind Ben.

"Way cool," said another. Amid a few snickers, they heard gentle clapping. Ben blushed, because of all the reactions he'd ever gotten for fucking, no one had ever applauded!

Ben helped Stuart up and held him. Stuart was trembling. He had never had public sex before. Ben soothed him with a reminder that the night wasn't over yet. Stuart said he was not in the mood for any new adventures that night.

Back at the apartment, they were on the couch, and Ben was kissing Stuart, a sweet series of "let's-go-to-bed" kisses. Although Stuart started out feeling annoyed and snippy, having been fucked in front of perfect strangers, Stuart had to admit that his caresses were

201

nice. Stuart was not used to having someone make these soft, romantic overtures on him. In his sex-for-pay scenes there was little opportunity, or desire, to get into that. But for the first time, it seemed nice, it seemed right. Stuart let him unbutton his shirt, take his nipples into his mouth and then run his fingers down Stuart's back.

Ben moved onto the floor first, on his knees, and Stuart followed him, running his fingers through his hair for a change. Stuart began to kiss Ben's ass. He sucked on the skin. Ben moaned, determined to let Stuart play until he decided he'd like it better for Ben to take his usual role. Stuart hesitated from time to time, and Ben knew he was waiting for him to make his move. The longer Ben delayed, the bolder Stuart got.

Soon, Ben was on his back – not an odd position for him. In fact, it was one of his favorites, having an eager boy on top, bouncing up and down on his prick. Instead of telling him to get his cock up and into him and amuse him, Ben stayed silent, leaving it up to him. Stuart stripped off what remained of his clothes. Ben sighed when he saw Stuart's cock, a cock nearly as big as his own, was hard and glistening, arching toward his belly. Then, slowly, Stuart mounted Ben and slid his cock into him. He slowly rocked on Ben, building until he was at a steady swaying movement that pleased him, instead of the rough staccato thrusts which Ben was famous for. Different, definitely different. But not without its charms. A bottom fucking a top. Stuart arched his back once, pushing up into Ben, and he leaned forward and caught Ben's wrists, as easily as Ben had caught his. Ben's eyes opened wide – this would normally be a moment where he would wrestle free, turn him over onto his back and hurt him until he apologized for such a possessive, dominant move. Instead, Ben smiled and leaned back, surrendering. "Go ahead, you little slut," Ben taunted. "Take it. Take it deep."

"Fuck," Stuart snarled, this time in frustration, and then pushed himself up for better leverage. While Ben infuriated him by smiling and keeping utterly still, Stuart rose and fell against Ben, harder and harder, until Ben could see and feel the familiar signs of his approaching orgasm. He grabbed Ben's cock and stroked it. When Ben started to pant, Stuart pushed up, turned his body sharply, and pulled out of him. Ben screamed and clutched for Stuart, but the loss of balance pushed him well out of reach of Stuart's drippy cock. His hands flew down to his cock, but Stuart caught them and held onto them, and laughed out loud as Ben's entire body shook and his cock throbbed in the shattering throes of orgasm interruptus. Stuart knew that sensation – the start of the pulsing mingled with the swift fading of intensity, and the need for something more. And Stuart gave it to him, slamming back in. Stuart kept on until Ben was wild with orgasm once again. This time, he let Ben come, he came himself.

Wrapped in Ben's strong arms, Stuart realized he was tired of promiscuity, tired of desperate passion. He was tired of his violent anger and wished it was not a part of his life, of his personality. His heart yearned to be more gentle. He needed Ben to make sense of an alienating world.

EIGHT

Bobby was alone. He would have to smoke the whole joint by himself. Life was tough, he thought. His first drag filled his lungs with bitter, delicious smoke. He dragged deeply on it. He held his breath for a long time. He sighed out a great plume of smoke and leaned back. He thought about the call he had received earlier from his agent, Macaulay Kinton. Mac had had an offer for Bobby to do another TV series. "It's where the money is – " Mac insisted.

Bobby knew that was true. Jay Julian had told him he had made millions producing movies at Paramount but it wasn't until he got into television in the '50s that he really made the money, money that just kept rolling in. Jay told him, "See, everything in my life has been luck, and nobody will believe me; everybody thinks, oh, well, he's talented. Luck. You got to be at the right place at the right time. In television, you got to get the right time slot, you got to get the right casting." Jay patted Bobby's ass. "And you're the right casting, Bobby." And Bobby knew what part Jay was talking about; it was a role he was born to play: a rich man's kept boy.

Jay said that they didn't make TV for Beverly Hills or the Bel Air circuit. "We make it for people out there. People on those tour buses outside my house. TV is so much closer to them than the movies. You're in your home watching it. You could take any big TV star and have him walk down the street with four movie stars and see where the people run to. They'll run to that TV star. He's there every week for them. He's a member of the family. I can't stand it when there are buses outside, but I'll go over and talk to them. After all, they built that house."

Jay showed Bobby a copy of a Los Angeles Times article about him that seemed to imply that he had engaged in illegal activity to obtain his wealth. He sued, won an apology. "I know this sounds corny," he says, "but I believe it: You've got to follow your dream. It's better than living your life in harsh reality, as I found out."

When he first got to Los Angeles, Jay weathered desperate times. "I was out here starving," he said, "doing things I shouldn't do, like stealing Sunday papers off porches and selling them. It was really horrible."

Jay was indulgent with Bobby, saying Bobby should never want for anything. Not Bobby. Not his beautiful little Bobby. And now he didn't. He told Mac, "I just don't want to deal with mediocrity anymore. The only reason to do a series is to make money, and I don't need any more money."

Jay always reminded Bobby how lucky he was. "Bogart never made more than $200,000 from a picture," Jay was fond of saying. "With all the merchandising and the points, hell, you've made twenty million," he told Bobby. But Bobby knew that he never would have gotten anything near that if Jay's lawyers hadn't seen to it. Jay was no saint, but he was Bobby's savior.

Still, Mac pressed Bobby about the series. Mac wasn't making a dime unless Bobby was working, and it was exasperating to them both.

"But," Bobby protested, "the stuff today is so lousy. It's just not worth my time. I want to be able to go to New York when I want to."

"Then go," Mac said, slamming down the phone.

By the time half of the joint was gone Bobby decided he would go to New York. When he had finished the joint, he decided he would stay in L.A. He didn't know what he wanted. All he knew was, he was crazy with missing Ben and Stuart.

Persistent, Mac called again. He'd just been invited to a party, he wanted Bobby to come along. Bobby was tired of talking about Hollywood, and the talk of his lack of work. It was too painful. It seemed he couldn't take another second of aloneness. He surprised himself by getting dressed up and driving into West Hollywood.

He went to Hunter's bar, and saw the boy right off. He was alone, and he was gorgeous. He was taller than Bobby, with blond, stylishly trimmed hair and incredible blue eyes. The boy watched Bobby glance around the room, and when their eyes met, Bobby quickly looked away. The next thing Bobby knew, the blond was on the stool next to his. "Bud Light," he told the bartender. His voice was low and sexy. It was what Bobby was drinking too. Bobby finished what was left in his can and got up to go.

"Please," the boy said, wrapping his hand around Bobby's wrist.

This surprised Bobby and he turned to stare at the boy. "Please, don't go," the boy said. Then he laughed as if he'd embarrassed himself. "I mean, if you do, then someone else will come sit here, and I just don't feel like dealing with all that tonight."

"All what?" Bobby asked, still standing.

"You know. Another john. I'm just not in the mood for that. It takes so much energy."

"I wouldn't know," Bobby said, looking away, trying hard not to laugh.

The bartender came with the beer and the boy motioned for him to bring another.

"No, really, I was just leaving," Bobby said, turning in a sterling performance at this point, because he had no intention of leaving.

"Only because I came and sat beside you," the youth pouted.

Now Bobby laughed. "No, hardly."

"I'm glad. Most guys, well, you know – "

"No, I don't. Really. I've never been in here in my life."

"I'm Alan," he said, extending a warm, large hand.

"Bob," Bobby answered. Bobby was having trouble looking directly at the boy. His eyes were such a startling blue that he felt he could look right through him. It was an odd sensation, not entirely unpleasant, but still, rather unsettling. His smile appeared sincere and his voice was soothing, and before Bobby knew it, he found himself having a good time, relishing this role as a stranger in a strange place. Bobby blushed when Alan began stroking his crotch. He dropped his hand over Alan's, stopping him. "Not here," Bobby said.

"Do you dance?" Alan asked.

"No," Bobby answered quickly. "I mean, not for a long time. I used to." Bobby blushed. He had danced actually, in that ill-fated disco movie Steve Sommers had produced, "Movin' On." Bobby had never seen the entire movie. The movie was so bad he couldn't bring himself to sit through it to the end.

Alan nodded and Bobby was grateful he didn't press the issue about dancing. In an hour, after two more beers, they were at Studio One and Bobby was dancing. He was halfway to the dance floor when he realized what he was doing. By then, there was no turning back. It was a fast song, for which he was grateful, and he found myself enjoying the pounding rhythm that seemed to pulsate upward from the dance floor. Alan was a good dancer, free and easy, with a style all his own. Bobby's body responded as naturally to the music as if he'd been born for this moment. When the song changed, neither of them hesitated for a second. Alan took command of Bobby, taking him in his arms and they sailed around the room, unaware of the others dancing beside them. The room was dark, with weird strobe lights that pulsed to the tempo of the music. When the song changed again, Alan did not let Bobby go, and though their feet had slowed to a near stop, their bodies continued to move with the music, swaying against each other with thinly disguised and mounting passion. Bobby had not expected to feel this, had not really wanted it, but was unable to resist it.

Alan's hands traveled to Bobby's hips, and he pulled Bobby into him so that when he thrust his hips forward, Bobby let out an unexpected gasp of pleasure. Alan's lips found Bobby's. He was insistent, and Bobby could not pull away, did not want to, even though they were no longer exactly dancing. Only when the music finally came to a halt was Bobby able to pull himself away from Alan's fevered embrace. Alan grabbed Bobby, tried to force his lips on Bobby's, and then Bobby pushed him away. Shoved him, hard. The look on Alan's face, the hurt, the anger there, shocked Bobby. He stood helpless on the dance floor, watching Alan disappear through the crowd.

Bobby waited for a few moments, then left the club. In the parking lot, he was unlocking the Porsche when he noticed someone standing in the shadows. It was Alan.

"I'm sorry," Bobby said.

"Which part?" Alan asked, coming up to Bobby. At six-two he towered over Bobby.

"Which part what?"

Even in the light from the streetlamps, those blue eyes had Bobby pinned like a trapped animal. Bobby leaned against the car door.

"Which part are you sorry about? Dancing with me, kissing me or shoving me? Not that it matters, I guess. I'm just curious." Beneath the casual humor there was real anger in his voice. Alan was truly hot, Bobby decided, even more so now that his self-assured, street boy demeanor had been replaced a sweet vulnerability.

"I'm afraid I got carried away." Bobby could see the boy's dazzling eyes were wet with tears. Bobby felt his throat tighten with emotion. "I never meant to shove you away," Bobby said. "I wasn't angry at you. I was angry at myself."

"For what?" he asked.

"For locking myself up for two years."

Alan looked at the car. "I get the picture. A sugar daddy."

"Yes, I guess you could say that." Bobby knew there was no way this small-time hustler could comprehend what had happened to him, the secret of his success.

Bobby reached up to wipe at the tears which had started to slide down Alan's cheeks. Alan leaned over and pulled Bobby's face to his. They kissed, and Bobby lost himself in the boy's warm, impossibly sensual embrace.

Now Alan acted as if he and Bobby were somehow on a par. Bobby's having a sugar daddy was about the same as Alan pulling tricks out of the bar. In fact, Alan asked Bobby if he had ever worked the streets. Having just returned from Texas where he was, literally, on the street when he was picked up, perhaps that was truer than Bobby cared to admit. Yet Bobby relished his new role as a higher class of hooker. He began to relate stories he remembered the boys Kyle and he picked up had told him. He ceased to be Bobby Richards, teenaged star of TV and two blockbuster movies, and became Bob, Bozo of Beverly Hills.

Alan directed Bobby through the late night traffic to a seedy apartment complex in Hollywood. While Bobby steered the car, Alan couldn't keep his hands off Bobby, finally unzipping his pants and going down on him.

Alan was as good a cocksucker as Kyle, Bobby decided, and Bobby came for him in the parking lot. Gobs and gobs of cum.

"Thanks for the lift," Alan said, wiping the cum from his chin.

Dazed, Bobby watched as Alan lifted himself from the Porsche and slammed the door. After all that, Bobby was to be left limp and alone in front of this squalid building? He lowered the window. "Hey," he cried after Alan's back, but Alan did not stop.

NINE

The date had been set. Stuart would be modeling underwear, posing with Seth, "starting at the top," Ben said.

At the shoot, Seth was all smiles. He attempted to joke with Greg, the photographer, trying to turn their relationship into something warm, something real, something other than the merely commercial. Seth was from Savannah and he could pour on the Southern charm when he needed to.

Greg, as a favor to Ben, was fussing over Stuart, trying to get a good pose out of him. Seth was a pro; Greg didn't worry about him hitting his mark when he was told to.

"Isn't one enough?" Seth asked Stuart, obviously annoyed that Greg was showing more attention to Stuart than to him.

"What?"

"You have Ben. Leave something for the rest of us."

The shoot wrapped early. Seth invited Greg for a drink. The photographer said he had a date. That left Seth at loose ends. Seth decided to invite Stuart, who accepted. Stuart had been aching for Seth all afternoon; the prospect of sex with Seth excited him. The prospect of any sex excited him.

Seth said he wanted to stop at his apartment for a minute before they went to the bar. They were scarcely inside the apartment when Seth turned and offered up his mouth for a kiss. Stuart didn't hesitate. Their lips met with an almost audible crackle of electricity, and Stuart circled Seth's tiny waist with one arm while the other hand slid up to the hollow between his shoulder blades and just behind his heart, and pressed. Seth melted into Stuart, lips softening and parting to welcome Stuart's tongue. Seth's lips followed Stuart's hungrily. His hands reached up to Stuart's face, fingers weaving their way around his ears and into his hair as he urged Stuart's mouth to a tighter fit against his lips. A low sound escaped Stuart's throat, and Seth answered it with a muffled "um-hmm" of assent and stepped closer until their legs were intertwined, the strength of his desire a match with Stuart's own. Stuart's fingers kneaded the muscles of Seth's back, moving slowly down his spine, and he pressed himself tightly against the length of Stuart, continuing to move against him as his arms wound sinuously around his neck, fingers still combing and stroking his hair.

Seth's hand strayed to Stuart's swelling cock. Stuart felt him shudder and a chuckle welled up from deep in Stuart's throat. Seth wriggled in joyful response. Finally Stuart tore his mouth away to catch a breath, and to suggest they go to bed.

Seth led Stuart down a hallway to the bedroom. The door was open and the room was dark. Seth meant to point out where the bathroom was, but Stuart was eager, his mouth was on Seth's again, and his arms wrapped themselves around him, gripping him tightly. Seth gave in to his demanding guest as Stuart lifted and swung the model toward the bed and let him take him down.

Stuart nibbled at Seth's mouth with his lips and teeth and his hands tugged impatiently at his shirt. He quickly unbuttoned Seth's shirt and slipped it off. He freed his mouth from Seth's and began a line of kisses that inched their way down from his collarbone in the general direction of his cock. Stuart took his time. When he unzipped Seth's trousers, his uncut cock sprang out. When Stuart's tongue finally met the cockhead, Seth gasped, wrapping his fingers in Stuart's hair and clenching his hand into a fist. Stuart sucked the erect cock and Seth moaned and moved against him, his hands in his hair tightening their grip convulsively. Stuart's mouth closed around the cock and he sucked it hard while fondling his balls. Stuart slid his open hand across Seth's hard belly, fingers outstretched. Then reluctantly Stuart sat up and gave his attention to getting the linen trousers off Seth, along with his fine Italian shoes.

When Seth was naked, he said, "Now you." He rose to his knees on the bed and undressed Stuart, taking time to lick and nibble on the cock when it was finally exposed. Seth was enchanted with the huge cock, as everyone was. He now worked slowly and deliberately, sucking Stuart until he was hard and precum was oozing from the tip. Stuart moaned and strained against him, his back arched in pleasure.

When Seth sensed Stuart was close, he got up and, as he applied some lube to his ass, said, "I've gotta have that up my ass. I've just gotta."

Stuart sat up and Seth mounted him. Seth shuddered as he slowly lowered himself over the prick. As he watched Seth's delight as he fucked himself, Stuart gulped and the breath suddenly caught in his throat. He felt a stifling wave of heat, and for an instant, the present merged with the past. For the first time, he noticed just how much Seth looked like Darrell. His heart skipped a beat and then pounded on heavily. For a moment the most intense joy and the deepest sorrow he had ever felt washed over him and merged, bittersweet and painful, a feeling so tremendously powerful that he did not know if he could survive it. He inspected him more closely, stroking the blond hair out of his eyes. No, it was not an illusion; he could see that now. He was a young version of Darrell, an eerie reincarnation. Strange that he should only notice that now. Why hadn't he seen it before? Dozens of conflicting emotions were bombarding him because he was coming, coming deep inside Seth. Seth was ready, and jacked himself off.

It was perhaps the beginning but, more than likely, just a nice stop along the way. He could see that plainly now. He had just fucked Seth, the most popular male model in the world. As Ben had said, he had truly started at the top.

As Ben drove to the studio to fetch Stuart, all he could think of was sex. His thoughts, instead of focusing on the traffic, were set on sex with Stuart. He would have him again on the conference table, without Bobby around to lure Stuart away. He could almost feel the warm flesh of Stuart's thighs, the wetness of his tight asshole after he'd eaten it out. He tried to push the images from his mind, but they flowed, unbidden: Stuart bending over the table to let Ben suck his ass. Ben roughly shoving his shirt upwards, bunching the material at his breast, going for his ass quickly, the front door still partially open, the shades still up...not caring about anything but the place where their bodies joined and became one.

Sex. It was all Ben could think of as he pulled into his parking space and rode the elevator to the top floor. His secretary, Abby, greeted him with the announcement that the shoot was over. Had been over for an hour.

Abby noted Ben's flushed expression, perhaps reading something in his ragged breathing pattern, and asked, "Are you all right, Ben?"

"I'm fine," Ben assured her, moving quickly past her desk and to the studio. But he wasn't fine. Stuart was gone. Seth was gone. The studio was empty. Ben left the studio in a huff.

"You're very naughty," Ben said later, "A very naughty boy."

Stuart flushed, staring into Ben's dark brown eyes and realizing that he'd just fucked someone else. Stuart had never felt like this before, as if he had cheated on a lover. But Ben was Bobby's lover, not his, at least not so you'd notice. Not really.

Ben spoke in an unbelievably calm voice, but his words made Stuart shudder just the same. Ben had driven to Seth's building, called his apartment on the intercom, demanded that Stuart come down to the lobby. When Stuart got to the lobby, he saw Ben sitting in the Porsche in front of the building.

Now Ben said, "I wanted to fuck you at the studio, after the session."

"We can go back," Stuart said hopefully.

Ben stared, unbelieving. He didn't know him, couldn't comprehend the fact that Stuart had just fucked Seth.

There weren't many words after that. They went back to the studio. Abby had gone for the day so they were alone. Ben simply grabbed Stuart by the wrist and led him to the conference room. He undressed him, shoved him over the table. His legs spread apart, Stuart endured another tongue bath. When Ben discovered that Seth had not been there before him, he became even more energetic in his tonguing. He was also pleased to feel Stuart's cock harden. After the click of Ben's belt buckle, his jeans fell down, not off, and Ben was in him, quickly, the door to the conference room wide open, the shades open as well.

"You like that, don't you?" Ben hissed, slamming the huge cock deep inside the boy.

"Yesss..." a moan.

Ben's hand was wrapped in Stuart's hair, grabbing a fistful of it and pulling his head back so that he could whisper into Stuart's ear.

They were rocking the table, forcing it forward and against the wall. Stuart came, and Ben pulled out and went down on his knees behind him, smearing his face in his sticky cum, rubbing his chin and lips and tongue against Stuart to drink up every drop of his juices. Stuart sighed, climaxing again against the forceful rhythm of his tongue. Now Ben quickly stood and rolled Stuart onto his back, sliding his tongue in and out of his hole again, making sweet love to his asslips.

Ben suddenly stopped. His enormous cock was hard and ready. Stuart glanced up at his face. Ben's cockhead was almost touching his chin. He lowered his head, his teeth scraping Ben lightly as his cock started searching for pleasure in Stuart's mouth. His hands were on Ben's thighs, his breath warm on Ben's pubic hair. Stuart's tongue fluttered around nervously. Saliva drooled from his lips and trickled down his chin. Ben grabbed the back of his head and pushed him down on the cock as it suddenly began spurting wildly, Ben's heart pounding against his ribs as Ben came in his mouth. When it was over, Stuart glanced up at Ben. A couple of drops of cum were at the left side of his mouth.

"So, how was Seth?"

Stuart shook his head in mock disgust; he knew enough not to bother to answer such a stupid question.

To Ben, it was an obvious question. He had enjoyed his time with Seth. In fact, he had been responsible for Seth being in Los Angeles. He had lied to Stuart. Ben had been intimate with Seth on several occasions.

The relationship between photographer and model on a shoot can become a love affair of sorts. The photographer is commanding, coaxing and shooting constantly, the model is shifting and shading moods from pose to pose, and, occasionally, if everything goes right between the shutter's first click and the final flash of the strobes, a certain magic occurs that produces an unforgettable photograph. When it does, it is one of the most gratifying, electrifying experiences for a photographer. The model is less effected, because he doesn't see the picture until much later. Thus Seth did not know that what Ben considered his most provocative photograph had been snapped while Seth was posing for a Calvin Klein cologne ad. He had been casually snapping away when he caught Seth from behind, with Seth playfully lowering his briefs to expose the crack.

Ben knew he had some great shots and, for the first time, he asked one of his models out for a drink after the shoot. He had as not yet moved to Los Angeles himself, but he was toying with the idea of becoming truly bicoastal. Seth was more interested in becoming an actor than a famous model and he got Ben talking about Hollywood and all the people Ben had met through his relationship with Kyle and Bobby.

Later, in Ben's apartment, his fingers were sure and steady as he unzipped the secret pocket and went about preparing his toot. Kyle had taught him well. Tonight he used the tiny gold spoon he'd given him, and tapping it full he put it up to one nostril. Sniff. Then the other. Sniff. Ahhhh. The express elevator was zooming him up to the one hundred and fiftieth floor again. Wheee, look, no hands. It was fantastic. All the depression in Los Angeles with Bobby shattered after Kyle's death didn't exist here. Up here there was nothing but this soaring feeling that he was great and getting greater, freer, all the time. Slightly bemused, Seth wasn't interested in the drugs. He wanted Ben's cock. "I know how to make you stop," he said.

Still smiling himself, Seth muffled Ben's laughter with his mouth, and in that brief contact, the smile became a kiss, abruptly strong and demanding. "Oh, Seth," he muttered, "there's nothing even a little funny about the way I feel." Relaxed in his arms and still flushed with the warmth of laughter, Ben found it entirely natural to pull the young model closer, to return his kisses beyond thought.

When the kisses and touching ceased to be enough for them, when the weight of Seth's body upon his nudged his own stirring response, they shed their clothes. Ben was drinking in the sight of Seth, caressing each bit of sensitive flesh he exposed until he was naked in his arms. Then he gave his fingers and his mouth and his tongue and finally his cock over to the task of learning to pleasure Seth. Seth's skin felt familiar to Ben, smooth and sweet-smelling like Bobby's, and his lovemaking comforted and replenished him.

"So," Ben asked Stuart, "what do we do now? Or, to paraphrase an old rock song, 'Where do we go from here?'"

Ben couldn't tell from Stuart's eyes – there was no expression at all in his eyes, except...fear. But Ben didn't understand the fear. How could he?

"I guess we go back to Malibu," Stuart said softly. "To Bobby."

"You like Bobby don't you?"

"Yes."

"And you like me, too, right?"

"In a different way, yes."

"Well, we both like you, Stuart. We want you to stay. We worked out our thing with Kyle. I'm sure we can work it out with you."

These were the words that Stuart had longed to hear for so many weeks. He tried to process the situation. None of it made any sense to him. It might have been the alcohol he'd drunk before they left, but he didn't think so.

"I've been hurt too many times..." Stuart offered.

"Let's just let it happen. Just let it happen slowly. Don't worry about anything."

Stuart was going to say, "That's easy for you to say," but he didn't.

Back at Bird's Eye, Bobby was waiting. Soon his body and Stuart's body were topsy-turvy on the bed, wrapped in the crisp white sheets, rolling over and over until they were partially on the floor, partially on the bed, as they tore at each other. Standing, moving, turning, thrusting, Bobby at last finding himself on the bed with his legs parted and his ankles on Stuart's shoulders.

As Stuart thrusted into Bobby, he asked himself, Where was the feeling? Where was the intensity of what he had with Ben? Bobby's eyes opened and stared at him, those eyes that he'd wanted to see look at him like that for so long. He'd wanted somebody to look at him the way Bobby and Ben did. He needed it. He knew that. He had hoped for it. He had prayed for it. It was love. At this moment, Bobby loved him. Ben did too. He knew it now. Through his lovemaking abilities, he was able to make these two beautiful guys love him.

Bobby's eyes closed again, his fingers gripping into Stuart's arms as the brutal fuck went on, his mouth slightly opened, tongue flicking out between parted teeth. Bobby breathed a husky sigh, saying Stuart's name.

On the bed, in his arms, feeling the lull of Bobby's body against his, tight against him, Stuart rested his chin on the top of Bobby's head, turning his face to the side to feel his hair on his skin. As Stuart came deep inside Bobby's ass, he whispered, almost crooning to him, "I love you."

Now, after the fucking was over, Bobby knew Stuart was begging for promises he couldn't make. All Bobby could say now was, "Sure you do."

TEN

The phone rang. Bobby, enjoying a mid-afternoon nude swim with Stuart, thought about not answering it, yet he knew it would only start ringing again. He climbed from the pool, lifted the phone to his face. "Bobby?" A worried voice not far from tears. Ben's voice. Bobby had never heard Ben's voice like this.

"What's wrong?" Bobby asked.

"It's about Stuart. The police were just here."

"What about Stuart?"

"They suspect he killed somebody."

"What?" The phone nearly slipped from Bobby's moist, now trembling hand.

"Just get him out of there. Get rid of the evidence. You know what I mean."

"Yeah."

"Do it now!"

Bobby was shaking as he hung up the phone. "Stuart!" he screamed. His voice broke. He was trying to appear angry but it was really a sob.

By the time Ben arrived at Bird's Eye, the police had come and gone. One of the cops was a local one who had given Bobby several speeding tickets. He was very nice until he found out that the boy they were looking for was no longer there. Bobby had time to flush the pot down the toilet. Stuart had had time to run. Bobby told the cops he had no idea where Stuart was, that he had been there in the morning, but they had words and Stuart left in a huff. Bobby was proud of his performance; he didn't break down until the police left the house.

Ben went to Bobby immediately, tried to comfort him, but Bobby was hysterical. He let Ben kiss him, softening for a moment. "I can't believe it," Bobby kept saying, as Ben massaged his neck and back, trying to calm him.

Ben told Bobby that when the ad appeared in the newspaper with Stuart and Seth in their underwear, another hustler who was under suspicion recognized Stuart and went to the cops. Through the newspaper, the police found the ad agency and they told them who the photographer was.

"What are we going to do?" Bobby said finally.

"Nothing. We're going to stay out of it... "

"And hope he doesn't come back."

"Oh, I don't think he'll do that. Did you notice, there's a car parked down the street?"

This news caused Bobby to break down completely. Ben decided they both needed a stiff drink.

Later, after they had drunk two vodka martinis and an entire bottle of wine, they lay together. Bobby felt filthy, not having showered since Stuart had fucked him that morning before their swim. Standing under the jets, he scrubbed himself, lathering face and body as though it were impossible to wash himself clean. He held his

215

mouth open under the pelting spray and spat out the lingering taste of Stuart, until his nostrils stung with water. Still it seemed the smell of Stuart would not leave him. He even gave himself an enema, but Stuart seemed to linger. Ben glowered at Bobby, sitting on the toilet, sobbing.

Bobby gave his lover an anxious glance. "You're not angry with me, are you?"

"No, of course I'm not angry. Why in hell would I be angry with you?"

"I can't get it together." Bobby stood, uneasily, and fell into Ben's welcoming embrace. With his hair still wet and clinging to his forehead, his eyes swollen, and traces of tears drying on his cheeks, he had the look of a sulky six-year-old, oddly tall for his age. Hardly the image of a teen heartthrob he once was.

Ben let go of him, and said, "You get a good night's rest, and you'll feel brand-new by morning." Ben took a sleeping pill from the bottle and left the bottle on the vanity. "Take that," he said.

Without looking back, Ben closed the door softly behind him. Bobby stared at the door, deathly still. He began trembling again, with fear. Stuart, what if he tried to come back? No, he was being foolish, just as Ben said, and stupid. He was safe. Then he began to sob again, choking the sound with his hands, his body trembling as chill after chill shook him. He was so cold. He had to get warm, and, after taking a pill, went to Ben's bedroom. He found Ben fast sleep. He lay next to him, clung to him. He would not be afraid. What happened today was frightening. He was gripped by a feeling of loss and sadness. Something had been torn away from him today, something irretrievable, and while he wasn't sure exactly what it was, somehow he knew that no matter how many showers he took, or how many blankets he hid under, he would feel filthy for some time to come.

ELEVEN

Now there are hundreds of possibilities, none of them particularly pleasant.

"Anything could've happened," Bobby sighed, pouring his first cup of coffee.

"Yes, of course," Ben said, buttering his toast.

Bobby detected a jarring, discordant note in Ben's tone. "What's wrong?" Bobby asked. He became breathtakingly tender.

Ben said nothing, became embarrassed, and turned his head away. "I brought him in this house. It was me."

"You mustn't blame yourself. I thought he was so beautiful. But, come to think of it, I've always been afraid of him. He'd always been so grave, so sneaky in a way."

For the first time, Ben's voice trembled with some hidden emotion and, at the same time, he tried to smile. "All I wanted to do was please you, Bobby."

"You did. He was a beautiful boy."

"He is a beautiful boy. He's on the run, not dead."

"I know. We'll do everything we can."

"Yes, if they ever catch him, we'll do everything we can."

They kissed, somehow managing to overcome their anguish. Then Bobby looked at Ben closely. There was a strange look in Ben's eyes.

"I know sometimes I may not show it, but I love you, Bobby. That's just the way it is. Now you know everything." He shrugged hopelessly.

"Why do you ... I mean, how is it that ... Ah, God, I don't know what I'm saying. But you ..." He became completely confused. His cheeks were on fire; he lowered his eyes. "You were simply sorry for me. You really loved Kyle. And then Stuart. You loved Stuart."

"No," Ben shook his head. "I love you. It's always only been you. Only you. Everything has been said now, hasn't it? Right?"

"Right."

"Now I have to go." He pushed away his breakfast dishes.

"Do you have to?"

"Unlike you, I have a job."

He stood in the doorway, defiant now.

Bobby looked away. "Now that this has happened, I'm giving up the pot. I'm going to be a good little soldier. No drugs."

"It doesn't really matter to me, but if that's what you want."

"I don't know what I want."

"When you find out, call me. I'll be in New York, at your apartment."

COME Again, Volume 1

TWELVE

A journalist called and asked Bobby what he was doing. And instead of admitting he was doing nothing and producing a headline "THE END OF A SHORT CAREER," he chose to say that he was writing a book – not about him but about Kyle. In friendly commiseration, the reporter said that was a good idea. "It's good to tell the truth yourself, or else place the press in such a position that they would have to write their own version."

That got it all started.

Soon everybody was asking about The Book and Bobby became afraid. Terrified, actually. Mac was upset with him that he'd even mention doing such a thing. He spoke to Bobby as if he was a child. They agreed to meet. By the time Bobby got to the restaurant, he was at the edge of tears. He sat in his Porsche, longing for Ben to be there, to comfort him, whisper into his ear that he mustn't worry. That he understood. That everything will be all right.

Mac had already had a shrimp sandwich, and there was a bit of mayonnaise at the corner of his mouth. Bobby dropped his gaze, stared into the Coke the waitress brought and blinked to keep back the tears. He told Mac he could no longer stand the pressure of all the demands. He said something really nasty and cutting, but Mac just nodded, went on eating his dessert. Bobby spilled a little Coke on the table (his hands were shaking) and promised to stop the idiocy of writing a book. He was thinking of all the money Mac had made on him and wondered what I'd done to deserve this. Maybe I should have given him a blowjob when he wanted one, Bobby thought.

Finally at home, in his solitude, Bobby continued to sit for hours going through the photos, the mementos of Kyle's short but spectacular career as a singer and actor in westerns.

Seeing pictures of Kyle when he was young made Bobby sad. He was so cute, Bobby thought, his eyes are happy and full of expectation. Why doesn't life turn out as we hope and plan? Kyle proved it may all be over tomorrow.

Bobby enjoyed re-reading his diary entries, starting with the one shortly after Kyle died.

The heat is buzzing in my head. I am looking out over Los Angeles, seeing how the city is enveloped in visible fumes, but at the same time feeling how the sun is doing my body good – it is then that I know that I am alive. This is also reality.

I think of my sudden fame. Unexpected and for me still inexplicable. I don't know if it has made me happier. People were always around me. At times because they were paid to do so, owned a percentage of me or had invested in my future possibilities. But more often they just took advantage of me, knew I was seeking admiration, and I was trading on my charm. I had no time to worry, to wonder what happens when I was no longer a desirable commodity? Now I may still be desirable to some, but I no longer desire all that. But the emptiness is enormous. The loneliness becomes unbearable, because it is in such contrast to that which was.

And I miss the constant tension about sex. Kyle's hunger for togetherness, for fucking, was insatiable. That hunger became a vital necessity for me. We opened to each other so completely. Not only physically, not only sexually – but like human beings related in a secret way, we bound ourselves together. After a short time I was confronted with his jealousy, violent and without bounds. I had never experienced such a thing before. Now all doors were closed, barred. Friends and family, my co-stars, even memories, became a threat to our relationship. Terrified, I felt I only had him. But our needs were impossible to satisfy. That became our hell. Our drama. Nothing existed outside ourselves. I never realized it until too late that we were so much alike. What he had not known about himself he began to see in me – as if in a mirror – despite the fact that I was so much younger and perhaps unlike him in ways that he didn't know. But in the mirror he saw himself as he was, and he began to hate what he saw. He was forced to leave that other person who will always be a reminder of what one no longer wishes to be.

It was all so crazy. I had to sneak out of a hotel room and run down the back stairs because there were photographers waiting at the main entrance. Dark glasses could not hide my terror. I was chased everywhere. In my dramatic way I experienced the situation symbolically and decided that I couldn't spend the rest of my life like this. Among garbage cans.

Something broke inside me. The boy within me wept and wept. I was a little thirteen-year-old again.

It became more difficult to walk in the streets without being recognized. Strangers would come up to me and say, "Excuse me. Aren't you Travis Thompson (my character in 'Space Travelers')?" I had not accomplished anything fantastic, but I had experienced and understood a lot for someone so young. At times my conscience no longer bothered me because of all that I did not do and did not know. I found pleasure in my new-found fame. But it became a struggle against everything around me: fans, television programs, films, newspapers. I used to be able to sleep anywhere at any time, but now I often lay awake.

Then Bobby re-read the diary entries from when he was making the sequel to "Space Travelers."

Kyle is back from his tour and we are on the beach in Malibu, frying mussels and drinking wine. Everything is white: the houses, the sand, the wine; even the air. We make a big bonfire on the beach, even though it is the middle of the day. Someone plays a guitar and sings. A pretty, slim boy dances for us. I pretend I am little again and I run with Kyle along the water's edge laughing at the waves. We inspect the shells that are washed ashore. Later we have a long soak in the Jacuzzi and fuck under the stars.

The next day, strange, warm hands touch me all over my body. It is terribly hot in the studio. I am nervous and forget my lines. Bud slept badly and was impatient with me; he wants me to spend the night but I tell him Kyle is home. The extras give me dubious looks when we have to repeat take after take because I keep making mistakes.

Some of them sigh when I forget a line. There are mutterings among the group that I am not professional.

I am furious at Bud, who lets me go through this, and when the bell sounds for lunch I race out of the studio, only to find Bud's wife coming in. I force myself to nod pleasantly, but she does not acknowledge my presence. When I return to my trailer from lunch, Bud is sitting in a corner wearing a strange little smile, and nothing else.

"Lock the fuckin' door," he says.

"Do you promise to remember your lines this afternoon?" he asks as I settle myself between his outstretched thighs.

"Oh, yes," I say, stroking his erection.

"Okay, then you can suck it."

"Thank you," I say. It's a game we began long ago that I never grow tired of. I am his little cocksucker and, if I am good, I can suck it all day if I want to. But today we have only fifteen minutes. I bend forward and start nibbling, sucking and chewing on the hard candy.

I don't talk about his wife, that she might still be hanging around. He never mentions Kyle so I don't mention her. Nothing matters but this moment. Nothing matters but Bud's cock. If I don't have him right now I will burst and maybe even die. With my heart beating in my throat like a big bullfrog, the lick it, from the tip to the balls. Bud leans back slightly, letting his weight settle into the suck. But after awhile, he can't stand it: he has to kiss me. He puts his mouth down on mine and I realize he is about the most kissable man I ever met in my whole life. Bud sucks, nibbles, bites, chews, licks, rubs, strokes, caresses and damn near dances with those lips.

My knees get all rubbery, and I think they'd give out on me for sure. Then he lets me go back to the cock, which is just made for sucking on. He presses my head into his crotch harder and harder 'til I damn near choke on that huge meat. I take him in all the way, and it seemed to get bigger and bigger with each touch, each lick.

Bud catches his breath in the sweetest little gasp, like it was the first time anyone had ever sucked him that deep before. Some cocks are just made for loving, and Bud's is one of them, that's for sure. I make him come twice in those fifteen minutes and he's happy the rest of the day. I have no more trouble remembering my lines.

Leafing through his notes, he came to the diary entries he made when he went to Europe with Bud.

Dinner for four hundred in Cannes. We eat lobsters and drink champagne. Hands loaded with diamonds and pearls bring lobster claws to mouths. Celebrities are at every table. I am here too. Little me, among all the heavyweights. The actress next to me, whose bosoms are falling out of her dress, talks eagerly, unconcerned that I don't understand a word. Twice I tell her that the little French I learned at school has long since flown out of my head. But she continues on. Sometimes I smile coldly at her and nod my head. Now and then I turn aside a little and drink a toast with a handsome man at the next table. He keeps looking at me through half-closed eyes, and isn't eating his lobster claws. Outside is the soft French night. I want to walk out into it. From the noise in the brilliantly lit dining room — and then out into the stillness and the warmth and the sound of the sea.

I remember other dinners, all too many; if I hadn't been with Bud I would have gotten up and slipped out and away. All those white, made-up faces and then all the bronzed ones. People with time

COME Again, Volume 1

and money to follow summer all the year. Hands covered with rings nervously fluttering over the food, the wineglasses.

From the next table a champagne glass is again raised to me. His eyelids have almost closed. He admires himself in his spoon. The lights are turned down. Outside, rockets are being fired and it is unbelievably beautiful. And we get up from the table and say goodbye to each other. I escape from the unknown admirer, who is approaching me rather unsteadily, but first I send him a passionate look, so that he will understand how much I will suffer by this painful and sudden departure with my stud, the producer of my movie and my orgasms.

To our hotel by limousine, still being spoken to in French, this time by the driver, with whom Bud is having a conversation. And then at last I am alone. There is a little rap on the door separating Bud's suite from mine. He doesn't wait for a response. He doesn't wait for permission. He just takes what he wants, as always.

The next day, I reach Kyle by phone. He is very unhappy that I am in Cannes and he is in Malibu. I hang up the telephone and I feel sad. Bud studies me and asks if it was a stupid conversation. I nod and feel a need to cry my eyes out. And that is what I do.

Home from London. Bud stayed on to do more promotions for the picture. It was a long flight by myself. Jay has sent the limo for me. I fling myself into the back. There is press briefing at Jay's office. My head is throbbing with weariness. I arrive a quarter of an hour late. Smile to right and left. Afraid of inconveniencing Jay. Jay pats my knee, squeezes my thigh, says he missed me. Afraid the reporters may think me vain because I was in Europe being made much of. I forget they don't know the life I've been living, and I'm glad of that. The trip is already a dream.

The press briefing over, I run on. A television producer is waiting in the Brown Derby. They are to make a program with me the following week. In the limo, I phone home. Kyle says he misses me. Pangs of conscience seize me. Promise things I'll do. The tirade stops at the other end.

My meeting with the television people is disposed of in an hour. I rush on. My lawyer needs a signature on various papers. I ride to Mac's office. Phone home again. Notice that the tone of Kyle's voice is rather cool. A photographer has managed to get past the security and is suddenly there in the doorway. "Just wanted a picture," he says. Another man has painted a portrait of me from a photograph and insists that he be allowed to present it to me. A young girl has sent me a poem she has written. An editor from a teen magazine calls; surely we can meet and talk about the new movie for five minutes? I don't have five minutes, not today. Scripts lie unread on Mac's desk. I have promised to give my reactions by a certain date and have no idea of what I should say. Tears aren't far away.

At last at home I cover myself with Kyle's happy mouth. As we make love, I look into the mirror: I am both sad and happy.

After it is over, Kyle falls asleep. I have no idea what we said to each other. There has been a telephone call from Bud. I know he is having a difficult time, but I just can't call him back. Tonight I need to sleep.

Eventually, Bobby was able to articulate what his life was like after Kyle, with Ben. He wrote:

I decide that I have to get some work done, regardless of whether I want to or not. I can't let sex dominate my life completely.

Besides, it's important for me to work, to edit my notes. I know this book will never be published, but I will have it. It's not so much a financial situation for me – I have plenty of money – but a need to keep at least one part of my life regimented. To keep one corner of my world in order. I force myself to spend all of afternoon at my little typewriter. It's not much punishment, though, because I can go to my window and look out onto the pool and see Stuart taking the sun. I catch him jacking off, but he doesn't look up to see me watching.

I almost tap my finger against the glass to get his attention. But I stop myself just in time. I want to fling open the door and scream his name. But, instead, I bite my tongue and force myself to go back to work.

Of course, only moments later, I creep back to the window and look out again.

It is dark when I go to the chaise. Stuart has his arms over his head, as if in a communion with the night sky and the silver crescent moon above.

"Well...?" I ask.

He cocked his head, as if he hasn't heard me quite clearly, or as if he doesn't know what I want. But he knows.

"Yeah?" he asks, hands still over his head, stretching his body out in one long, lovely line. He's a good swimmer, and his legs were taut, his stomach flat to the point of being concave, his cock splendid in its semi-flaccid state, lazy against his thigh.

"Close your eyes."

He does as I say, but still keeps his hands over his head.

I get on my knees before him, extremely aware Ben has just returned to the house and is standing on the other side of the pool watching us. I press my face into his crotch, nuzzling forward with my mouth and chin, breathing in deeply. Smelling him. He sighs and lowers one hand to the back of my head, pressing me firmly against him. I hear Ben come up behind me and his low intake of breath, and I keep going, now bringing my hands to his cock. "Is this okay?" I murmur, my face against the now-erect cock. "Do you want this?"

Of course he does. I didn't need additional permission. I lap quickly at the drops of pre-cum that fall free. He is divine, ripe and ready for me to snack on. I feel a hand on my shoulder and Ben has his nerve revived along with his cock, after a bruising fuck earlier this morning. He is behind me, playing with my asslips. I mount Stuart, open myself for Ben. Ben is soon entering me. His powerful body feels solid as he slides in deep, and soon the three of us are rocking with the motion of his thrusts. Ben comes, pulls out. He stands over us with his hand wrapped around his cum-glistening cock, watching. Stuart gets up, pushing me down. Ben stands over us, shooting a second load all over Stuart's back, suddenly talkative as his balls were emptied onto the hustler's moonlit skin. "Oh, yeah, I can feel it coming...." His voice growing louder with each word. "Ohhhhh!"

Somehow the sound of his voice and the feel of Stuart's cock inside my ass and the rhythm of the night take me over the top. For the first time in ages, I come without any help from my hand.

THIRTEEN

Reading his diary rekindled Bobby's desire for Bud. There was just something so scandalous about a married man, Bobby thought, giving him what he couldn't get at home. Then he saw an item in Daily Variety about Bud signing to direct a film adaptation of a novel called "Youth in Revolt." It wasn't a toga epic, it wasn't a sci-fi thriller, it was just a minor project about drugged-out hippies in the '60s. Surely there was a part for him. He called Bud. Bud agreed to come for lunch. "Just like old times," Bud said.

"Yeah," Bobby said, suddenly realizing it had been two years since he had last been with Bud. Bobby had grown tired of it. Every time they got together, Bud kept playing Mary MacGregor's "Torn Between Two Lovers," and Bud's wife was becoming impossible. Bud said, "Wives know these things. I've told her I've been busy with the picture but she knows it's not the same when we're in bed together.

"I've had little flings before, with starlets, but nothing has ever been like this... " He smiled and caressed Bobby's cheek. He had a way of saying things very quietly and seriously, hardly moving his lips at all, making Bobby stop to really listen to what he was saying. He rarely smiled or paid compliments so Bobby knew when he did, he meant it. Right at the beginning of their relationship Bud had told Bobby he was the best cocksucker in the world. That Bobby was the only one who could coax more than one orgasm out of him during a session.

Said Bobby, "I'm glad you like it."

"But because it's so different. You're right, it's scary. I think I've always wondered what it would like, I just had to find the right person to do it with."

"Well, now that you've done it... "

He took Bobby in his arms. "I want to keep on seeing you, Bobby. I really do. But what can we do, we're both married?"

"Yeah," Bobby said, looking away. He tried not to think of Kyle while he was with Bud but it was impossible.

"By the way, where is Kyle?"

"He's on tour. Now he's back in New York."

He nodded and looked away, mumbling, "You love him, I know."

"Yes. But it's different with him. He was the first man I ever really loved. I loved him even before I met him. I had his poster on the back of my door in my bedroom. I used to listen to his records all the time. Then he came to Brackettville – "

"Please," Bud said. He didn't want to hear any more about Kyle. He pulled away from Bobby and slid out of the bed. He stood still, breathing deeply. "I don't want this to end but it has to, you know that."

He said nothing more, just went to the bathroom. When he came out, he began dressing and Bobby lay there watching him. He

225

looked so sad Bobby began to cry, not sobbing, just tears running down his cheeks.

When Bud was dressed, he lowered himself to the bed and swept Bobby up into his arms again. "Don't do this," he said. "Please, stop crying. Don't make it worse than it is. Who knows, maybe tomorrow everything will be different. I'd still like to see you – if you'll let me."

Bobby nodded and laid his head on Bud's chest. Hugging him to him, Bobby said, "You better go now. Your wife will be wondering what's happened to you."

But Bud couldn't stay away from Bobby. His cock soon began to miss those blowjobs.

One time after Kyle came home to find Bud in his pool, naked, Kyle admonished Bobby: "It's just that you're so public about it...fucking your fucking director, for chrissakes. A fucking married man. Even I've never done that! And he's the biggest fucking director in the fucking business right now! How much more fucking public can you get?"

Bobby tried to remain calm. "We didn't do it in public."

"You might as well have. Everyone in town knows about it. How do you think that makes me feel?"

"I'm sorry. I didn't think you had any feelings left for me that could be hurt. You watched guys fuck me, you sent me to be fucked by old men... "

"I'm sorry. I didn't know I was hurting you. You acted as if you were enjoying it. Every fucking minute of it."

"I didn't say that. I did enjoy it, but it seemed as if you just gave me up to them."

Kyle shook his head violently. "No, no! Look, I found you, I brought you here. You're mine. I'll never, ever give you up."

Bobby at that point agreed to give up Bud; but he lied. Bobby knew it was a terrible thing to lie but at that moment he thought it was best. He knew he couldn't stop seeing Bud. He didn't want to stop seeing Bud. He couldn't explain why to himself, let alone to Kyle.

Eventually, Bud changed. He wasn't satisfied with just a blowjob, no matter how expert. He also wanted the fuck that only Bobby could give him. Bud would come for lunch. First he would fuck Bobby, taking him missionary. Then, after lunch, it was Bobby's turn. Bobby would bind him up with leather and fuck him from behind. Bud delighted in watching them in the mirror. He came again while Bobby was doing it, then finish by taking Bobby's cum in his mouth. They rested, and talked. Bobby agreed to go to Rome with him, to stay with him while he scouted locations for his next film, a costume epic. Happy that Bobby accepted his invitation, they got into the sixty-nine position and stayed like that, sucking, and licking and kissing, until Bobby came again. As Bobby came, Bud was moaning and groaning, not wanting to give it up. "God you taste good," he said, trying to arouse him again.

After Kyle's death, Bobby saw Bud as one of the reasons their relationship had been strained. And then with Ben in residence, Bobby seemed to have no time for Bud. Still, Bud never lost interest. He called occasionally, to see if Bobby were "free for lunch." But Bobby never was. He thought Bud was only interested in the sex. Finally Bud stopped calling. He had many film projects, but Bobby wasn't cast. He wasn't even offered the few roles that might have been suitable.

Now he was going to press Bud. He felt Bud owed him something – "for old times' sake," was how Ben put it. Ben knew all about Bud, but Bobby waited until Ben was safely on assignment in New York before calling Bud.

In fact, Ben had been gone two days before Bud came to Bird's Eye. Bobby was so horny he wanted to jump Bud right in the driveway. Still, he held back, feeling his way with his old flame.

Bud was pleasant, but his agitation at being kept waiting for two years began to show. He was in no hurry to jump into bed. Bobby had fixed the tuna salad he knew Bud favored and served it with garlic toast and white wine.

Bud talked about his projects, but wasn't offering Bobby anything.

"What have you been doing with yourself?" Bud asked finally.

"Feeling sorry for myself," Bobby said.

"I'm sorry to hear that."

"It was such a shock – "

"I know."

"And I didn't have to work. And then Jay died. It was just too much."

"So you went to New York?"

"Yes."

"And came back with Ben."

227

"No, Ben had been here. He just stayed."

"He's made quite a name for himself."

"He's a very good photographer."

Bud winced. "I'm sure it doesn't stop there."

"No."

"What I mean is, I'm sure he's very good at everything."

Bobby knew enough not to even honor that remark with a retort. Instead, he poured the rest of the wine in their goblets.

Bud looked out across the pool. "I talk to your agent occasionally."

"Oh?"

"He says you don't want to work."

"I don't really, but I think I need to. Ben thinks I need to."

"What do you think?"

"I don't want to do TV again, but I wouldn't mind making a film – if you were directing."

"I don't think that would work."

"Why?"

"My wife would find out."

"Her again."

"She's never forgiven me. I had to promise to give you up."

"I'm sorry."

Bud shook his head. "I don't regret a thing. It was so much fun, really, but I just don't know if I'm ready to go through all that again."

"Well, I guess that's that." Bobby got up and took his glass and plate into the kitchen. Bud followed him, as Bobby knew he would. Bobby stood at the sink, rinsing the dishes.

"You fire the help?"

"No, it's Anna May's day off."

"And Ben is in New York?"

"Yes."

Bud embraced Bobby from behind, his erection rubbing against Bobby's ass. Bud kissed Bobby on the neck, then said, "And here we are, just like old times."

"Not quite. Now I'm 21 years old and all washed up."

Bud chuckled, turned him around, hugged him. "We'll see just how washed-up you are."

Poolside, Bobby proved he was certainly not washed-up as a cocksucker. It was good sucking Bud's prick again. Bobby wrapped his fingers around the hefty organ, then licked the swollen head. Bud put his hand on Bobby's head, pushing his mouth onto the cock. Bobby gagged slightly as his lips pressed against the base of the prick. Bud rocked his hips forward and back, sliding the whole length of his cock slowly in and out of Bobby's throat. Gradually, he began thrusting into Bobby's mouth harder and faster, until his heavy balls slapped against Bobby's chin. Bud moaned loudly through clenched teeth, his fingers digging into the back of Bobby's head. "I'm gonna come!" Bud roared. The big cock was even more responsive than Bobby had remembered, and the cum incredibly delicious as Bud's first orgasm gushed from it. Bobby swallowed it all, then lay across the chaise as Bud recovered. Bud ran his hand through Bobby's hair and asked, "Can we go to bedroom?"

"Sure," Bobby said, kissing the shaft of the semi-hard prick before he stood.

Bobby pulled the curtains in the bedroom but there was still enough light for Bud to enjoy what he called "the show," watching in the mirror as he fucked Bobby's ass. Bobby stripped off his Speedo and got on his knees on the bed. Bud was fully hard again; there would be no need for preliminaries today. Bud took some grease from the tube on the nightstand and two wet fingers were suddenly jammed into Bobby's ass. "Oh, same tight ass," Bud growled, holding his fingers deep in Bobby's hole, shaking them to loosen him, then withdrawing them slowly. Bobby looked back over his shoulder to see Bud pressing the head of his massive cock against his boy-pussy. Bud smiled, then turned so he could watch in the mirror as he slid his greased cock into Bobby. Bobby pushed his ass against him, and groaned in shock as Bud drove all the way into him. Bud's hands locked onto Bobby's hips and held his ass in place as he began the fuck. He had always asked if he was hurting Bobby, but he did not do that today; he was in a hurry. "That feels so good, kid. I'm sorry I can't stay all afternoon," he grunted as he quickened his pace. Bobby jacked himself and thought of other times, times when they took their time. He recalled how Bud loved it, couldn't get enough. But now, Bud was in a hurry. Bobby didn't mind, not today, so lonely was he, but whatever thoughts he had of rekindling any kind of relationship with the director were now banished as Bud took his selfish pleasure. In this position, Bobby was denied the deep kissing, the caressing, the sucking of his nipples while Bud fucked him. Bobby knew he could have been anybody.

Even as horny as he was, Bobby couldn't seem to come. Actor that he was, however, he pretended that he came, just as Bud was filling him with his spunk. Then Bud pulled off and went to the bathroom to wash. Bobby lay still, feeling cheapened by the experience. Moments later, Bud was dressed. "I'll call you," Bud said, kissing Bobby on the top of his head.

"Right," Bobby said, his eyes glazing over.

FOURTEEN

The search for Stuart continued and now Bobby's life in Malibu became a waking nightmare. Every time Bobby left the house, the police tailed him. He complained to Mac, who told him that the cops figured he knew where Stuart had gone and would eventually lead them to him.

One day the officers came to the door, having followed Anna May up the drive. The maid agreed to answer their questions and let them in the house. Bobby knew the officers had used this interview as a pretext to get into the house, and he again turned in what he considered was a sterling performance. He wanted to cooperate; he didn't want to be taken to police headquarters. He remembered what one of the hustlers he and Kyle picked up told him about the cops' interrogation routine: "What they do is take you in a room, with a good cop and a bad cop taking turns questioning you. One's real nasty, smacking you and all, then the other one comes in and he says he wants to help you, that if you tell the truth, he'll get the other guy to let up. But if you don't give them the answers he wants, then the bad cop comes in and beats you up some more. They keep this up until they get the answers they want."

No, Bobby didn't want that. He answered every question in a forthright manner, and all of his answers seemed to be satisfactory.

Bobby crumbled only when one of the officers said, "You know he killed somebody else, don't you?"

"No."

"Yeah, in Florida, a year or so ago. We're beginning to put together quite a file on this kid."

Bobby told the police Stuart had told him he had come to California from Ohio. He had never mentioned Florida.

"I doubt he would have," the cop said, matter-of-factly.

230

Stuart hadn't been in Florida a day before he went down to the beach. It was what he had come there for. It was warm but overcast and he found a great emptiness there. At first it seemed he was alone, so late on an uncertain day. Then he saw a stranger, tall, lean, and deeply tanned, wearing a pair of yellow shorts, mirrored sun-glasses, and a wide-brimmed straw hat.

They connected immediately, the boy and the older man. They passed each other, then each turned around to cruise the other. The older man stopped. Stuart stopped. The older man wiped his brow with the back of his hand. "Whew, it's hot. How 'bout a drink?" Gesturing grandly with his right arm, he went on, "My place is just down the beach a bit."

Stuart accepted without hesitation. He thought the stranger looked prosperous, very distinguished, surely a man of independent means and, whenever possible, he drank on someone else's bar tab.

On the way, they introduced themselves. Stuart, "in Florida on a little vacation..."

"Good to meet you. I'm Frank."

They climbed the wooden stairs to the balcony of Frank's beach house. Stuart was fascinated by the ultra-modern look of the place. Living in such a house meant that Frank could easily afford what Stuart had for sale.

While Frank mixed martinis, Stuart looked about him. The living room was small, but the soaring cathedral ceiling made it seem large and commodious. One wall was lined with books, most of them beautifully bound, stacked haphazardly, as if they were being read, not bought by the linear foot by a decorator. Yes, he thought, Frank could pay for what he offered, and keep on paying for as long as it took for him to get his own place.

Frank found Stuart's halting, hesitant manner endearing. Stuart seemed to Frank to be a delicate child with large, doleful eyes and wispy, streaked blond hair. A wild little fawn who didn't know whether to come to the outstretched hand or flee. Stuart seemed to alternate between being flirtatious, then standoffish, even aloof.

Before long, as they sat on the couch in the living room finishing their drinks, the sliding glass doors open to the vespered wind, the waves crashing relentlessly against the shore, Frank's fingers opened Stuart's shirt and his tongue burned the boy's neck and his hairless chest. His hands caressed the inside of his thighs.

Stuart lay back, closed his eyes tightly, spread his thighs in irresistible invitation.

Frank saw the stupendous bulge of the boy's crotch and rubbed it lightly with one hand while he kissed Stuart's ear and his other hand stroked his hair.

There was no doubt now what the story was. Frank began to feel intense affection for the lad, but it was an affection he did not feel comfortable with. A dull, mysterious dread came over him. While he kept getting older, his lovers kept getting younger. He had much trouble lately maintaining his erections. It had driven him to distraction.

He pulled back saying, "I feel entirely too paternal toward you." He was lying. It was not paternal. He could not deny it. It was carnal. He pulled him close again. Odd as it seemed, he thought this boy might do it, might restore his faith in his manhood. There was no doubt he desired the boy. Earlier he couldn't keep his eyes off the small, firm ass. Adorable. He was moved to tenderness. He wanted to fuck it in the worst way, but he knew that was risky.

The prospect of what was between Stuart's legs had him more excited than he had been in some time. And here Stuart was, clearly intending to stay if Frank would have him.

Eagerly, he unzipped Stuart's jeans and let the cock pop into view. "My, god!" Frank gasped.

Stuart opened his eyes to watch Frank stare at the thick, nearly ten-inch long pecker that had seen him through many a hard time. As Frank took the bulbous head in his mouth, Stuart's hands went to older man's head and shoved. Before long, Frank was choking on it.

Frank simply had to have the cock up his ass. He got some lube, then got undressed and got back on the couch. Stuart prepared his cock and slowly entered the older man. Frank was so tight that, for a moment, Stuart thought Frank was going to scream. Instead, he stiffened and made several tiny, funny gasps. Quickly the gasps changed to moans and he began to move with Stuart, finally wrapping his legs around him. The longer Stuart labored over him the more intense Frank's desire became until he thought he might blackout. He began to squirm under Stuart in such obvious pleasure that it pleased Stuart more than anything he had experienced in some time and, in a blinding rush of adrenaline, he came and crashed to the couch on top of Frank. Startled, Frank came, then clutched the boy's now damp hair and tightly gripped his body with his thighs.

Stuart had resisted at first, not wanting to give too much of himself too soon, to keep the older man interested. But now he saw that was not going to be the problem. "Paternal" he had said. Yes, he did remind Stuart in some ways of his stepfather. When Frank first touched him, it rekindled his memories of his stepfather...when Stuart was eleven and how the old man touched him. And the nightmare that ensued when he had gone screaming to his mother. The touch was the same. He had grown to expect it and know what to do about it, to bend an older man's will to achieve his own ends.

Frank showed Stuart to his loft bedroom and told him to get some sleep, there were guests coming for the weekend. He didn't tell Stuart there were always guests coming for the weekend. Weekends at Frank's house had no structure, a constant ebb and flow, a babble of people, all vying for his attention and affection. And there were drugs. Suddenly, Stuart felt himself hurtling down into the same old abyss, feeling the strange, insidious chemicals rearranging his blood, and his demons possessing him again.

Frank didn't really want to know too much about Stuart's background so he never asked Stuart about much of anything. Instead, he made many assumptions about the boy, creating the life he wished for him. Stuart had a simple politeness and slow gentleness that was pleasant to be around, unlike some of the tortured, sociopathic boys he had entertained through the years. He said he understood them, for he too seemed to be a broken, much-mended thing. Though he became unlovely he was never unloved, nor did he indulge in self-pity. He continued to proclaim his membership of an elite group, the elite of a fantasy world occupied by rich old men. Often he even began to think in terms of a more permanent relationship with his boys. But Frank realized that was out of the question in Stuart's case. The boy seemed to have no ambition. Frank would say, "You've gotta have a plan," but the only plans Stuart made were to get high. Stuart found that sharing a joint was easy when you lived at the beach.

Yet Frank's love for Stuart remained unchanged no matter how extreme the behavior, like the love between parent and child.

There were days when Stuart felt he had to do something to break out of what seemed to him a downward spiral. While Frank was doing whatever it was he did at the bank, Stuart would spend hours packing his bag but then leave it by the door, waiting for Frank to return to take him to the bus station. Frank would come into the house and say nothing, just pick up the bag and return it to the loft.

There began to be something rebellious in the way Stuart began to dress, or, rather, undress. He didn't need clothes to attract attention, especially in his crowd, yet he delighted in appearing with next-to-nothing on even at the beginning of the weekend. Frank was charmed with the way his guests reacted to the sight of Stuart's awesome crotch and his "adorable" butt.

At Frank's weekend parties, on drugs, Stuart began to act like a perverse child, flirting outrageously, but never letting anyone get too close. He was a tease beyond compare, in Frank's view, and he reveled in this, knowing that when everyone was gone, Stuart would be in his bed, over him, stuffing his penis in Frank's hungry mouth.

As the days passed, Frank began to understand he had created a monster. He thought of nothing all day at the bank except coming home and either sucking or being fucked by that huge cock. And that was trouble; Frank had to admit it. He was beginning to feel trapped, the way he did with all his lost boys, and he began fantasizing about how some of his friends would react to having a piece of his action. He ached to show off what made Stuart such a prize. But not just any friends would be permitted this delicacy. He began to plot what might happen when his pals from Chicago arrived. These men were strangers to Stuart, but no strangers to Frank. The trio, Barry, Greg, and Spence, traveled in a pack in Chicago, a quartet when they were in Florida, with Frank. They haunted the sleaze bars, the toilets, the baths. In their own small realm, they were infamous. When they were in Florida on vacation, they were ravenous.

Finally, at his party on a rainy Sunday just before Christmas, Stuart felt unusually uncomfortable, more than ever a lamb among a pack of wolves. Even when they were laughing, it seemed they had conspiratorial airs about them, as if every action hid a devious, secret motive. As if Frank had put out the word. Stuart was introduced to the trio from Chicago and he didn't like the look of them.

Some time after midnight, as he passed the coffee table, Stuart leaned over and dipped his forefinger into the small pile of very pure cocaine, then rubbed the powder on his gums.

"Careful, dear boy," Frank said. He turned to one of his pals and said, "He was just in the kitchen taking his magic pill...number four. He gets real quiet after that one. Some days I can hardly wait for number four to kick in!"

"I know what I'd like to kick in!" Barry, the biggest and most lascivious of the bunch, said.

They shared the laugh.

Upstairs, in the marble and gilt bathroom, Stuart chugged off his bikini, pissed, then stood before the mirror. The heavy shadows under his eyes made his eyes seem larger, like a raccoon's, he thought. Disgustedly, he dug his fingers into the jar of Frank's expensive cream on the table and slathered it on his face.

He quickly became exasperated and went to the nightstand in the bedroom where a bottle of Tattinger champagne from the night before sat in an antique pewter ice bucket. He brought the bottle to his lips and gulped it. The fizz had gone out of it and it tasted sickly sweet. He spat into the bucket, then coughed.

After letting the bottle drop from his hand and roll under the bed, he pounced onto the bed and pulled the satin sheet over his naked body.

He lay there, wide-eyed, physically tired yet full of unspent energy. He heard the men downstairs, talking in a hushed, conspiratorial tone. He could not make out what they were saying. Then they laughed. High, derisive laughter. He closed his eyes and tried to rise above the scene, to concentrate on how wonderful it felt to be floating in an anesthetized oblivion of drugs.

After a few moments, he heard footsteps. Suddenly, Frank appeared at the foot of the bed and Barry stood beside the bed. Tall, broad-shouldered, quiet, with a shock of black hair, Barry was a formidable stud. Greg loomed over him forbiddingly, his crotch only inches from his face. He could smell the bourbon on the man's breath. He squeezed his eyes shut. Although he thought he was too high to be surprised about anything, he began to feel uneasy when he heard yet another zipper being pulled down. Through the fabric of the sheet, he could feel sweaty, rough palms rub his legs, part them. As Frank climbed onto the bed and pulled the sheet from Stuart's body, Stuart felt his hot breath against his skin. He gasped as Frank started sucking his cock, then squirmed as someone pressed a greased finger into him. In a harsh, raspy voice, Barry said, "Tight, baby, tight."

"No, no," Stuart protested, "I don't get fucked – "

But the man ignored him, continued shoving his finger in. Stuart fought him. He pushed hard, then harder, but it was no use. There were four of them against him. Two held him down while Frank was tugging on his cock and Barry was fingerfucking his ass.

: climbed over Stuart's body and shoved his cock in the boy's moutn. Stuart accepted; it was a hard, big cock and tasted good.

It began to hurt Stuart when two, then three fingers were shoved in roughly. Stuart struggled to get up off the fidgeting hand, but Frank's tight grip on his cock would not permit it. After a few moments, Stuart began to weaken and his thigh muscles relaxed and the fingers slid even deeper into his tingling ass. Suddenly, Spence was coming. He made Stuart take his load before he removed his cock. Greg climbed on the bed and took Spence's place at Stuart's mouth, despite Stuart's feeble efforts to prevent it. Stuart squirmed restlessly over the fingers tickling in his ass; Greg held him down, forcing him to suck his cock.

Then Barry squeezed some more lube onto his middle finger out of a small container that Frank kept on the nightstand. He touched his greasy finger against the puckered asshole. Massaging it around the now-aching opening rapidly, he maneuvered two fingers inside again. After Stuart calmed down a bit, Barry removed his fingers and squirted some more grease on the tip, then directed it back to the already slippery cavity, forcing most of the lube down into Stuart's asshole, following it with the full length of his fingers. As he slowly prepared the asshole, it spasmed around Barry's finger.

Finally Barry was aiming his thick cock at Stuart's asshole.

"Oh, your virgin ass is ready for it now, baby," Frank whispered as Barry yanked his finger out and squeezed more lube onto the head of his throbbing cock.

Barry snarled, "You're about to get the ass-fuck of your life, kid!"

Barry lifted Stuart's ankles up onto his shoulders and leaned into the saddle Stuart's upraised thighs formed. Wrapping both of his arms around his elevated thighs to hold him in place, Barry aimed his hard cock directly at the well-lubricated hole. He brushed the opening with the tip of his cock, smearing the grease and his pre-cum around together. Now he flexed his hips forward, effortlessly penetrating Stuart while he pushed the kid's legs even higher into the air. Inch by inch, Barry's cock was eased into the asshole, all the while Frank cheering him on, tugging on Stuart's now steely-hard sex.

Stuart had become resigned to his situation. Besides, he had never enjoyed sensations so incredible. He was sucking a nice dick, being alternately jerked off and sucked by Frank, and at last being fucked by a thick, hard cock. It was something he had fantasized about, but he knew he would have to be high in order to endure it. Even when he had been tempted to let a john fuck him, the john seemed only interested in sucking his cock. This bunch seemed to care less about his cock, letting Frank have it all while they pleasured themselves elsewhere.

Barry inserted only about three inches before he stopped, then pulled his cock out slightly, and poked it back in gently, still not exceeding the three inches. It was as if he knew he was taking a virgin and was, amazingly enough, showing mercy. After a short wait, Stuart relaxed a little and Barry pushed further into him.

Just then, Greg pulled out of Stuart's mouth, released Stuart's wrists, and began to come, blasting the boy's face with his load. Stuart could stand it no longer; he came into Frank's waiting mouth.

His mouth dripping cum, Frank left the cock and began to suck on Stuart's nipples. Then he bit at his hard pecs, kissed his chest and up his neck and into his ear. Stuart could tell by the intensity of Barry's thrusts and his heavy breathing that he was close to orgasm. Frank started to jack Stuart off again. Every nerve ending in his throbbing cock was alive and extremely sensitive, and with just a few strokes, he shot another load onto his stomach. Then Stuart wiped away Greg's goo to look down and helplessly watch Frank give his rigid cock a couple of vigorous jerks, forcing more of the sticky fluid out onto his belly. Frank gripped the cock as Barry slipped in smoothly all the way to the hilt, not stopping until his pubic hair brushed Stuart's sweaty ass. He began to deliver short strokes, then extended his strokes pulling his cock almost all the way out until only the head remained inside. Stuart's head rolled from side to side as he humped his ass up against the older man. He had surrendered completely.

Frank scrambled up on the bed to shove his semi-hard prick into Stuart's mouth while Barry finished. Then Spence replaced Barry at the ass, and soon he was concentrating on maintaining steady glides up Stuart's now steamy ass, trying to sense the movement of his butt, timing his strokes to match the involuntary upward thrust of Stuart's hips and ass. The tempo accelerated as both of them became lost in the sheer ecstasy of the fuck.

When Spence's strong arms pushed down on Stuart's knees, Stuart's asscheeks were spread wide open while his slick cock slid smoothly back and forth with each upward thrust of Stuart's hips.

The dick pistoned steadily in and out of the asshole that was finally accepting, indeed demanding, all he could offer.

By the time Spence came, Greg was hard again and ready. Greg held Stuart firmly as he began lunging his probing dick into the boy, who twisted and turned his ass to take it from different angles.

Meanwhile, Stuart sucked on Frank's cock, but the cock would only get semi-hard. Frank pulled himself away, permitting Stuart to watch as Greg continued relentlessly for quite a while. Then Stuart felt Greg's cock throbbing and bursting, shooting a second load, this time up his ass. After Greg spurted deep in his quivering hole, Stuart continued to reach with his ass for more hard thrusts, more deep insertions, more fucking. But Greg pulled out and Stuart opened his eyes to see it was Frank over him, ready to shove his half-hard cock into him. Stuart whimpered, "No, Frank."

"It'll be okay, kid," Frank said. But the entry was difficult because, despite Stuart's sucking, Frank was not fully hard. Eventually Frank was successful at shoving the head and a couple inches of shaft in and as he gradually increased in speed and depth, Stuart lay his head on his shoulder. Even in his hazy muddle he realized the trio had disappeared and he was at last alone with Frank.

"Please, it hurts," Stuart said, trying to push Frank off.

"Stay still."

"No, I can't take any more."

Frank gripped Stuart's wrists and forced his arms up, pinning him to the mattress as he continued attempts to fuck. Stuart's agony turned Frank on and his cock hardened a bit, but not enough to prevent the pain that now had Stuart incensed.

Stuart did not know the others, he could forgive them, but for Frank to be so callous was the last affront to his dignity. Stuart pushed him away, and Frank reluctantly left the boy alone, saying, "I'll be back, asshole. I'm gonna fuck you like you've never been fucked."

"Go to hell, Frank," Stuart snapped, tossing one of the pillows at the door as Frank made his exit.

Stuart lay still for a few minutes. Doors slammed. A car started up. Then the house became quiet except for the soft nag of the surf. Stuart's temples throbbed. His eyeballs burned. He felt like crying, laughing, and screaming at the top of his lungs, all at the same time. He somehow found strength and stumbled to his feet. He scrubbed himself in the bathroom but couldn't wash away the smell of their filthy sex. His asshole ached and he cursed them all.

He went to the edge of the loft. The moon was full and reflected on the rippling water. He sensed a sadness to the rhythm of the stars as they danced their last flickering recognition of the night. Tears gathered in his eyes and he thought of jumping. But no, he decided, he would only hurt himself.

Suddenly, Frank was behind him, still naked, still half-hard, forcing himself on him. Stuart pulled away violently. Frank laughed. A piercing, maniacal laugh. He lunged for the boy, jamming his hand against Stuart's mouth to silence him as the boy began to scream. With his other hand, Frank grabbed his wrist and turned his arm around behind his back. Stuart twisted away from Frank and drove his elbow into his stomach, knocking the wind out of Frank.

"You ungrateful shit," Frank muttered at the boy, and lunged for him again, but Stuart stepped out of the way, grabbing Frank as he hit the railing, then shoving him over. Frank screamed as he plunged into the living room below, narrowly missing the flocked Christmas tree.

Stuart was momentarily stunned. Then he staggered downstairs. In the living room, he saw the men had finished the cocaine. He stumbled into the kitchen and gulped the last of his pills. Returning to the living room, he fluffed the cushions of the couch...the same couch on which he had fucked Frank the first time...a time which now seemed as remote as his childhood. He sat down on the couch and stared at Frank's motionless body. Bleary-eyed, he struggled to get his circuits composed. And suddenly he could hear Frank telling him, "You've gotta have a plan, boy..."

Now, leaving Malibu in haste, Stuart's plan was to get to San Francisco, where he knew he could easily get lost in the crowd. Within a hour of fleeing Bird's Eye with his suitcase in hand, he was picked up by a man who could not take his eyes off the bulge in Stuart's jeans. The man said he was going only as far as Sacramento.

"That's far enough," Stuart sighed.

- — -

Meanwhile, in Malibu, Bobby was having that nightmare again. Whenever he slept alone, Bobby would have the nightmare. Kyle was in his bedroom, the place where they had been happiest, and he was jacking off, thinking of Bobby, wishing he were there. The next instant he was gone, swallowed up by fire. Bobby could hear

Kyle's wild, shrill, madness-filled laughter reverberating from the angrily crackling flames. Then nothing more could be heard but sounds of the fire. And Bobby woke up screaming.

FIFTEEN

"I'll be at your apartment," Ben had said before he left. He made quite a point of it, in fact. Thanks to Jay Julian, Bobby did have an apartment in Manhattan. But only Ben was using it. It wasn't fair. He decided to surprise Ben. After his time with Bud, Bobby felt like getting out of town. All the wishes in the world couldn't change his impossible situation, but he was free to travel. He doubted the cops would follow him to New York.

As soon as Bobby was safely in the apartment, the memories began to haunt him. He had been incredibly happy here. With Kyle, surely, but mostly with Jay. Kyle had disappointed Jay by making an unholy mess of his life, then by dying so young. But Bobby never disappointed Jay. Jay had become the father Bobby never knew. It was Jay who made it possible for Bobby never to have to work again if he didn't want to. It was Jay who was so grateful for Bobby's "little boy-pussy" that Jay was willing to pay for the privilege in every way he could. Jay enjoyed Bobby's blowjobs as much as Bud, but, more than anything, he wanted to make love to Bobby's ass, sucking it, fucking it. Jay would call Bobby's ass his "boy-cunt" while he fucked it, saying it was better than any woman's he'd ever known. Later on, when Jay couldn't fuck it, he still delighted in eating it out while Bobby masturbated. Jay would get between the perfect mounds and spend an hour making a pig of himself. It was Jay who showered Bobby with attention, showing him what the world offered. Jay took Bobby to the museums, the galleries, the fancy restaurants.

And travel was just not the same anymore, without Jay's Gulf stream jet, the limos, the best tables at the restaurants, recognition wherever they went.

Bobby had even met Jay's widow, Angela. After the funeral, he had gone to her mansion in Beverly Hills. He had been summoned there. Bobby found it curious but "the wife" wanted to meet him, give him some things Jay wanted him to have. Bobby was nervous, but once inside the sumptuous palace of a house, Angela was quite nice. She was far more attractive than Bobby had imagined; he had seen photos of her but they didn't do her justice.

After exchanging pleasantries, the woman, whom Bobby found to be elegant and gracious, said she could see why her husband had loved Bobby so much.

"Thank you," Bobby said, realizing the woman would never know why Jay really loved him. Or why Bobby really loved Jay. The things Jay wanted Bobby to have were mementos of Jay's days at Paramount, before Adolph Zukor sold the studio to Charlie Bluhdorn, a man Jay thought was "a monumental pain in the ass." Jay eventually had Charlie buy out his contract, netting Jay another forty million for doing nothing at all.

"Jay said these will be worth a lot some day," Angela said, handing the large box to Bobby. There were original shooting scripts of some of Jay's films and framed photos of Jay with the biggest stars of the era. To think all of this pertained to a time before Bobby was even born made him realize how ancient the guy really was. God, Bobby thought, the guy was 73 when he died, a pixie-frail figure, but his energy was incredible – even if the past few months hadn't been the easiest for him.

As Bobby was leaving, Angela said, "You're such a nice boy. You must come to our place in the mountains. Jay loved it there."

Bobby could not remember Jay ever even mentioning a place in the mountains.

"You do ride don't you?" she asked.

"Ride?"

"Horses."

"Oh, yes. In fact, I was in a western once. With Kyle."

"Oh, yes, Kyle," she said, frowning for the first time. "That was so tragic."

"Yes."

She was not a woman to dwell on unpleasant things. She smiled, "Yes, you must come up to the mountains one day. Jay loved going on picnics up in the mountains. It was a wonderful way to spend a day. A long ride up into the hills, a swim in the stream, then a nice picnic." She looked off into the distance, beyond Bobby's Porsche parked in front of the mansion, perhaps visualizing their mountain retreat.

Bobby nodded appreciate, but he found it hard to imagine Jay ever riding a horse. "Did Jay enjoy riding?" Bobby asked.

The wife chuckled. "Oh, no, Jay joined us for lunch in the helicopter, then flew back afterward."

241

When he related this story to Mac, the agent said that Angela undoubtedly knew about her husband's secret passions and was thankful that she didn't have to put out.

"And speaking of putting out," Bobby said, "any fresh meat?"

"If I did, I wouldn't tell you!"

Bobby sighed. "I guess you've given up on me."

"I know when I'm welcome. But I haven't given up on you entirely. I bring your name up all the time, but everybody knows you don't wanna work."

"It's not that I don't want to – "

"Someday, honey, you'll be hungry. I can hardly wait."

Thinking about that conversation now reminded Bobby just how hungry he was – for Ben. He had come three thousand miles to get fucked by Ben, but Ben wasn't at the apartment. Besides, there was no sign that he'd ever been there.

Bobby called Ben's studio. The secretary said he had gone on location to Fire Island and she had no idea when he would be back. "Weather," she said, curtly.

Bobby smoked a Marlboro, a poor substitute for a joint, showered, changed into his New York outfit of leather jacket, black jeans and Doc Martens and left the apartment. Although it was cool in Manhattan, the sun was warm and Bobby stripped off the jacket, revealing his skintight white T-shirt. He would catch his reflection in shop windows as he walked along and admire himself. His work-out regimen was turning him into a stud. Yes, he decided, he was becoming a young stud, if a bottom could be ever be considered that. Even when he was fucking Kyle, he could never think of himself as a top.

Before long, Bobby found himself in the Village, in front of C.C.'s apartment building. He stood across the street, remembering the many times he had come here, on his mission to meet the man again.

After Kyle's final tour, Kyle stayed on in New York. He had actually been living with a black man, C.C., his accompanist. Bobby went there in an effort to patch things up, but Kyle could talk about nothing but C.C. "Hey," Kyle said on the way over to the apartment, "you always wanted a big black one. Now's your chance."

They arrived at C.C.'s and the pianist was out. "He has his friends. I don't ask," Kyle said.

They weren't in the cramped apartment in the Village ten minutes before they were in bed, but Kyle held back. "I've treated you like shit," he said. "Now I want you to treat me like shit!" He got on the bed, nude, begging Bobby to fuck him. Bobby rolled him over and started swatting his ass. He reached between his legs, caressed his asshole. His ass twitched. He was furious with him for staying away so long; he wanted to hurt him, but he was nice about it. He slapped his ass, spanking hard, soft, and in between, until both sides were warm, red.

Then Kyle produced a black dildo, enormous. He said he found it in a shop down the street.

"Is C.C. as big as this?" Bobby had to ask.

"It's not that he's big, it's just that he's – well, you'll see."

The years of trouble between them let go as Bobby fucked Kyle with the dildo. Bobby had never really hurt Kyle but he was hurting him now. Kyle howled as the dildo went all the way in, was pulled out nearly all the way, then sunk in again.

Bobby's fingers went in next. Kyle was crying out, groaning, loving every minute of it. Then Bobby got in position so that Kyle could blow him while Bobby was fisting him.

Later, C.C. finally arrived. Bobby had seen him on stage during Kyle's little show at Max's Kansas City, but he was unprepared for the smoothness, the pleasantness of the Negro. They went to dinner at David's Pot Belly, sat in the window, as if they were on a stage. They laughed at the passing parade on Christopher Street, and for the first time Bobby felt good to be out in public with Kyle.

When they returned to the apartment, Kyle went into the bedroom and closed the door, leaving C.C. and Bobby in the living room. C.C. put Kyle's first album on the stereo.

"He really is good," C.C. said, sitting across from Bobby on the couch, kicking off his shoes.

"When he works at it," Bobby said. "What's he doing in there?" he asked, pointing to the bedroom.

"Doing some lines, getting ready." He rubbed his crotch, stared at him, his large dark eyes glistening in the moody light of the single table lamp.

Bobby looked at his suitcases, still by the front door. "I think I'd better go."

"Oh?"

"It's got nothing to do with you. I find you very nice and, well... "

"I understand."

"At another time, another place, I'd be all over you in a minute."

"I would like that."

"I know I would like it, but not like this."

He nodded. "Do you have a place to go?"

"Yes. I'll just go back to the hotel." Bobby stood and stepped towards the door.

"You're sure?" he asked, following Bobby.

"Yes." Bobby turned and C.C. took him in his long arms. He towered over Bobby, and was all muscle. Bobby hugged him, lay his head on his chest. C.C.'s heart was beating very fast.

"Tesoro," Bobby said.

"What?"

"Oh, it all happened so quickly. Sometimes I don't think I can deal with it. This is one of those times." He looked up into his handsome, smiling face. "Please understand."

He nodded. "Another time, another place," he said, putting his finger under Bobby's chin and tilting his head back.

They kissed. It was a short, friendly kiss.

"Kiss him goodbye for me," Bobby said, pulling away from him.

"I will. He loves you, you know. You're his little boy."

"I know. I'll always be his little boy."

Bobby left Kyle in C.C.'s apartment, getting ready in the bedroom. He would never see Kyle again.

Often Bobby thought about C.C., wondered about how that night would have gone had he stayed. His fascination with men of color had never been satisfied. He remembered the night in Vegas, when they were staying at the Hilton, and had just seen Sammy Davis Jr. performing. Bobby was thinking about Sammy and asked Kyle, "Is it true about Negroes, you know, that they have such big dicks?"

And Jay was with them in the elevator and he laughed. "Ask Kyle. He should know. He had one in New York that I'll never forget."

Later, in the living room of the suite, Kyle put on some music and entertained them with the entire scene as he remembered it. Bobby often jacked off to the story of Kyle being fucked by the giant black in front of a crowd of people, but he imagined that if he ever went with a black it would have to be C.C.

Every time he was in New York Bobby went to the apartment but C.C. was never there. He felt messages in the mail box. C.C. never called.

Now, standing across the street, Bobby could not believe his luck. There, walking toward the front door, was C.C., looking better than ever. Bobby raced across the street and greeted C.C. with a cheery, "Hi."

C.C. was speechless. He looked Bobby up and down and then, shook his head. Although Bobby had never forgotten C.C., the pianist had obviously not spent the years thinking about Bobby. "Do I know you?" he asked.

"I'm Bobby, Kyle's lover." It was the first time in so long that Bobby had introduced himself that way that it stunned him.

But, true to form, C.C. was hardly fazed. Calmly, he opened the door wide and said, "Took you long enough... "

C.C. took Bobby back to David's Pot Belly where they had dined with Kyle. Bobby so wanted to talk. C.C. got him to vocalize and Bobby thanked him profusely for trying to understand him. "Oh," C.C. said, "I understand all right."

On the way home from the restaurant, they held one another. C.C. had an arm around Bobby's shoulder. Even in the Village, guys stared. C.C. muttered something about "prejudiced motherfuckers," and Bobby said they were just jealous and they laughed.

They walked as if in a drunken haze, like walking through clouds, with no idea of what was going on around them. They stopped, chatted without moving from the spot, then set off walking again.

C.C. said, "Oh, man, look at the sky: it will be a wonderful day tomorrow."

"It's a wonderful night tonight." Bobby said, pressing himself against C.C. in a strange way. He took C.C.'s hand: C.C.'s hand was sweaty. Perhaps C.C. was more anxious about this encounter than Bobby had thought. Bobby looked at C.C. Bobby pressed himself even closer to C.C. Then, with the speed of lightning, C.C.'s arms were around his neck, and before Bobby knew what had happened, he felt his passionate kiss.

There was no question of what Bobby wanted, and C.C. wasted no time when they were safely back in his apartment. There

245

were no preliminaries. They kissed and went at each other violently, as if consumed with the desperate need of horniness and loneliness. C.C. pushed Bobby to his knees before him and Bobby began kissing the bulge in C.C.'s jeans. C.C. let Bobby lower the zipper. Bobby gasped when the thick cock was revealed. The huge smooth head felt like heaven in Bobby's eager mouth. C.C.'s cock was large, but not larger than Ben's. Still, it was a fearsome organ if ever there was one, and Bobby couldn't take it all without gagging.

Then C.C. got nasty with his cock, played it across Bobby's face and it felt even bigger and slick and warm and ready.

C.C. held Bobby's head and his dominance thrilled Bobby. C.C. forced the boy to lick his balls, then started jamming and rocking when the cock was in Bobby's mouth again. He came and Bobby was slow to part from it.

C.C. went his bedroom and lit some love candles – a dozen or so, wax half burnt down in saucers. Flickering candlelight lit their shadows across the walls. They stripped naked against the backdrop of this romantic flame, and by the moonlight and neon rays of street lamps outside the window. French kissing, his tongue dipped into Bobby's mouth. C.C. parted Bobby's thighs and licked his butt. Soon his fingers went into him and he began screwing him with his fingers. There was not much resistance from his ass muscles. Once inside, C.C. romanced him, stroked his tits with his other hand, toyed with his erection. They kissed, they played; a few minutes passed in which Bobby had an orgasm in C.C.'s mouth. Bobby was excited, sweating, and C.C. knew he wanted to be fucked very much.

Candles melted away into oblivion as C.C. began finger-fucking Bobby. Sweat ran off Bobby's skin as he pressed his nose to C.C.'s neck, inhaling the sweet aroma of the black stud. C.C. pushed his fingers in Bobby, starting with two, then three, four.

Bobby grunted, tears forming. C.C. was firm, kept right on. Bobby recalled the times near the end when he fisted Kyle. C.C. probably fisted Kyle. Right here in this very bedroom, he fisted Kyle. The thought of it nearly got Bobby off, but he held back, begged C.C. to "stick it in."

Bobby's ass expanded to fit the large part of C.C.'s hand. C.C. felt the muscles open. He pushed it further. Bobby felt so tight; his ass felt like a glove. "Ohhh," Bobby moaned. His head lay back on the pillow, tossing to and fro as he felt the ecstasy. His face changed expressions. C.C. made some slow punches. Bobby tossed and turned, sweat broke out in beads over his naked body. "Ohhh." His moans matched C.C.'s angry thrusts, evenly spaced. Then Bobby had another grand explosive orgasm in total ecstasy from the inside of his very being. Exhausted, Bobby lay on tousled sheets, a solemn expression on his face, parted lips breathing steady, slow, his dark eyes blinking. Carefully C.C. began to pull his fist out; Bobby's ass didn't want to let go easily, but when it finally was free, Bobby said, "Wow!" and lay back, drained.

C.C., however, was not finished. Not yet. He parted Bobby's thighs and finally C.C. got into position for the moment Bobby had been waiting for. C.C. spit on his cockhead and began stuffing the monster into Bobby.

As C.C. began the fuck, to Bobby it was a strange mixture of pleasure and pain. He saw the power there, a power concentrated, so undeniably potent. C.C. left no doubt he enjoyed his role. It was thrilling to be so close to something so raw, so real. Bobby saw Kyle in his place, loving this, being fucked senseless after he had been fisted. Kyle had been exciting to Bobby. He excited him as he imagined he would excite himself. They switched off on the dominant/submissive roles. Eventually the roles were just forgotten, perhaps because they were just into pleasure from all sides. Their sex play was slow and varied and only perhaps a little too calculated. They ran out of moves now and then and perhaps grew bored with each other, but their sex remained pleasurable and somehow mutually right, or satisfying. Bobby tried to discover what Kyle liked by the things Kyle did to him.

Now it was Bobby in C.C.'s bed, surrounded by things that assaulted his now heightened aesthetic sensibilities, away from the Chinese porcelain, the gilded triptychs, and Aubusson rugs of the apartment he inherited. He was also far, far away from the hilltop mansion he inherited from his lover, with its maid service, gardener, and pool service. Yet he was comfortable, because C.C. fucked him so expertly. The black stud stayed hard in him for a long time. The sex was strong, the same as he was, and Bobby loved it.

As the fucking continued, Bobby realized how much he enjoyed being a bottom when he had such a relentless top. The stud would come, stop briefly, then go back in again. His thirst for "pretty little white boy ass" could not be easily quenched. Delirious, Bobby lost count of the number of orgasms C.C. had as he did his thing.

SIXTEEN

Even having finally been with C.C. was not enough to still the need for him. He tried to lay with him, beside him, against him like a lover, but after such a long session of sex, C.C. wanted to sleep. Bobby decided to leave; he told C.C. he had to get back to the apartment, that Ben would be missing him.

But Ben wasn't missing him. Ben wasn't even there. But, exhausted by the incredible fucking he had just received, Bobby showered and then slept soundly in bed alone.

- — -

It was the morning after. The weather was bad. It was raining. C.C. didn't know shit, Bobby chuckled. The rain beat a gloomy tattoo on his window. It was dark inside the bedroom and bleak outside the windows. His head ached. Objects swam before his eyes. Fever was sneaking along his limbs.

A ray of sun that for a second had broken through a rain cloud disappeared behind it again, and everything darkened once more. Suddenly his sad and barren future flashed before him. He saw himself exactly the way he was now, fifteen years later, having aged in this very room, just as lonely, still waiting here for Ben.

Still he felt blessed for the moments of bliss and happiness he had had in these rooms, in C.C.'s bed, everywhere in Manhattan. Why isn't that enough for a whole lifetime? he asked himself as he drifted back to sleep.

Bobby'd been hurting all day. C.C.'s fuck had proven to be more merciless than he realized. He actually bled from it. He spent most of the afternoon soaking in the tub with Diana Ross' "Touch Me in the Morning" album playing in the background. He recalled how often he and Kyle had fucked to that music.

It was raining harder now and the predictions were for two more days of rain at least. Ben would be stranded on Fire Island, waiting for the sun. Even if Ben were to come in the door right now, there was no way Bobby could have sex with him. That would require too much explaining.

There was time to catch the red-eye back to L.A. He hurriedly packed and left a note, "B. – See you in Malibu! Love, B," on the table in the foyer. That oughta surprise the shit out of him, Bobby chuckled to himself.

SEVENTEEN

Back in L.A., the weather wasn't much better. It was a sad, drizzly day, without relief. Bobby was oppressed by strange thoughts and dark sensations. He had jacked-off to the image of C.C. inside him. He had jacked off to images of Stuart. And later he jacked off to images of Bud. He passed the day that way. Still, he felt empty being alone at Bird's Eye. Yet he felt he had neither the strength nor the desire to cope with his feelings now. But it was true that, without the pot, he had begun to see things with more clarity. Ben called from New York, left a message that he said he was returning to L.A. and Bobby resolved he would patch things up with him. Maybe he would even act on Ben's suggestion that he go to work for him, learning photography. He had heard of "celebrity photographers," so why not?

The next morning, when he woke up, Bobby could swear he could hear the sweet melody, heard so long ago but never forgotten. It came back to him now. He been longing for it, longing to return to that grassy slope where Kyle first sang to him. It was the most romantic moment of his life.

He rolled over and realized he was not alone. He looked right into Ben's eyes. "Oh," he started in a pitiful voice in which there was still a note of sadness.

It hadn't taken Ben long to guess that Bobby was again dreaming of Kyle. Perhaps he dreamt of Kyle every night. And it was always very awkward, arriving in Bobby's room uninvited. Worse of all lately was coming into the room while Bobby and Stuart were mid-fuck. But now Bobby became flirtatious, exposing his hard-on. "You see," he began, "I'm a bit upset with you for not waking me when you got in last night."

"People don't always make sense, remember. I thought you wanted to be alone."

Bobby did not respond, other than getting into position in the center of the bed. As Ben began to make love to him Bobby realized that it was the first time in a long time that Ben had done this, or was it he just hadn't noticed?

As Ben tenderly massaged, kissed, and licked Bobby's smooth body before actually sticking his cock into him, Bobby found his heart was overflowing with love for this big-dicked, dependable, basically good-hearted man. As Ben got ready to fuck him, Bobby wanted to pour what love he had left into him. As Ben gently eased the big dick into him, there was so much tenderness, so much friendliness, Bobby began to cry. He saw now that Ben tried so hard to make him happy.

As the fuck continued, excellent as always, with Ben taking Bobby missionary, kissing him all through it, Bobby thought, How could I have been so blind?

Strangely, Ben sensed Bobby was responding in a very new way, and he doubled the attentions he showered on Bobby, as if he wanted instinctively to give Bobby something he was longing for himself, something he feared he would never get from Bobby. Ben knew Kyle had been Bobby's great love, and then there was the married, but both of them were gone, and he was here, and it was he who was fucking Bobby, fucking him expertly, as he had always done.

It was as if Bobby grasped finally that Ben was deeply in love with him, and completely devoted to him. How insensitive to Ben's needs Bobby had been in his two years of self-imposed exile. Bobby met Ben when he was just becoming famous, and Ben stayed, all through the celebrity of the teen fan magazines and the movies, and then after. Ben didn't care whether Bobby was famous or not. He was with him because he loved him, as Kyle was. Bobby could see that now. Bobby also saw that he had mythologized Kyle, forgetting bad times, remembering only the good times. Ben was the one, Bobby knew now; he was finally free of Kyle's shackles.

Ben jacked Bobby off before he came himself, as he always did, savoring the beauty of Bobby's spurting cock. He kept jacking Bobby all through his own violent orgasm, then lay back, panting, but still stroking his younger lover.

"Yes," Bobby said, "God sent you to me, really, I mean it. I can't imagine what would have become of me without you."

"Oh, c'mon."

"It's true. But why, why are you here? Why do you stay?"

"How do I know? I want to be here, that's all. Always have."

"Why?"

"Because I belong here. Because you're my fucking lover, that's why. How do I know? That's just how I feel."

They both began to tremble. Bobby didn't know how to respond, it was uncharacteristic of Ben. Ben just managed to suppress a desire to cry. He made a great effort to control the idiotic tears that otherwise would have spurted from his eyes. Instead, he pulled Bobby into his arms and buried his head in the pillow next to Bobby's. Bobby reached down and began to stroke his lover's slimy cock. In moments, Ben was ready again and Bobby maneuvered to take it. When it was all the way in, Ben began kissing Bobby, and the kisses didn't stop until each of them had come again.

- – -

Bobby put "Celebration" by Kool and the Gang on the stereo and poured champagne.

"Champagne for breakfast?" Ben asked.

"I feel like celebrating – "

Ben tugged Bobby back down to the bed. "I feel like fucking," he said, kissing Bobby.

Soon Bobby was being taken warmly, lovingly to bed again. Ben was relentless, each orgasm more explosive than the last.

Later they sipped their champagne and Ben said he was glad to be home. He hadn't had a very good time in New York; the talk was all about a disease that was going around that was killing gay males. "It may be linked to drug abuse," Ben said, and he related how it made everybody on the Island cautious.

"I'm glad I gave up the pot," Bobby said wistfully.

"I am, too," Ben said. "I gave up the coke, too. Now we're both addicted to only one thing."

"Yeah," Bobby beamed, stroking Ben's cock to hardness again. His dark eyes gleamed with anticipation.

As Ben entered him and began plowed into Bobby again, it began to hurt and Bobby couldn't help but think of himself as damaged goods. He feared he might start bleeding again. But, Bobby remembered, C.C. felt so damn good. It had been worth it.

But so did this. Ben was, all things considered, simply the best. As Bobby came again, his cum reduced to a trickle now, he felt gloriously alive with Ben, who was, he decided, everything he ever wanted – father, brother, lover, best friend.

As Ben came inside him, Bobby never felt so infinitely valued, so cherished as now. He watched his lover slip into a post-orgasmic snooze. And as though to reaffirm his faith in these new feelings, he touched Ben softly. Instinctively strengthening his hold on him, Ben mumbled something unintelligible out of his sleep, and then, coming further awake, said, "Oh, Bobby, I thought I dreamed you." He kissed the boy drowsily, and returning his kiss, Bobby touched his cock again and felt him tauten instantly under his fingers.

He nuzzled his face in the pubic hair. Then, as Bobby began to suck his penis, Ben drew in his breath sharply. "Oh, god, Bobby! My baby!"

"Oh, Ben, I love your cock. I love you! I really do!"

As he sucked Ben's cock with greater joy than ever before, Bobby realized this was a beginning and, in a way, the end, too. The end of yet another portion of Bobby's life. That was what life was after all – an endless series of adventures unfolding before him. What was important now was that he had Ben here with him, and their future together loomed large and bright and glorious. He could see that plainly now.

Ben got into position between his thighs and entered him. Bobby gasped. And despite the pain he was now feeling as Ben continued to take his pleasure the way so many other men had, this was the best of all worlds, and he had been born under the luckiest of lucky stars.

CONTRIBUTORS

Frank Brooks

The author is a regular contributor to gay magazines. In addition to writing, his interests include figure drawing from the live model and mountain hiking.

Leo Cardini

The celebrated author of the best-selling Mineshaft Nights, Leo's short stories and theatre-related articles have appeared in numerous magazines. An enthusiastic nudist, he reports that, "A hundred and fifty thousand people have seen me naked, but I only had sex with half of them."

William Cozad

The author is a regular contributor to gay magazines and his startling memoirs were published by STARbooks Press in Lover Boys and Boys of the Night. Another of his books," The Preacher's Boy," appeared in Secret Passions.

Keith Davis

The author resides in New York and has contributed many stories to gay sex magazines. He also has a story in Boys of the Night from STARbooks.

Thomas C. Humphrey

The author, who resides in Florida, is working on his first novel, All the Difference, and has contributed stories to First Hand publications. His superb memoir of his youth on the farm appeared in Juniors.

Bud O'Donnell

The author's stories have appeared in Lover Boys and Secret Passions, as well as Hand jobs magazine.

Carl St. John

This is the first story for STARbooks by this esteemed author.

Dan Veen

The author's first stories were based on his experiences as a hustler in San Francisco and New Orleans. He has written erotic fiction for Honcho, Mandate, Playguy, Torso, Inches, and First Hand magazines. He writes regular film articles and erotic video reviews for Honcho under the name of V.C. Rand. He has a PhD. in English Literature and Germanic Languages.

ABOUT THE EDITOR

John Patrick is a prolific, prize-winning author of fiction and non-fiction. One of his short stories, "The Well," was honored by PEN American Center as one of the best of 1987. His novels and anthologies, as well as his non-fiction works, including Legends and The Best of the Superstars series, continue to gain him new fans every day. One of his most famous short stories appears in the Badboy collection Southern Comfort.

A divorced father of two, the author is a longtime member of the American Booksellers Association, the Florida Publishers' Association, American Civil Liberties Union, and the Adult Video Association. He resides in Florida.

aring any underwear. "Excuse me," I said, having a hard time look
inded by that bulge in his crotch, "but don't I know you?" "Maybe
nd of t   bout a
ith Ra   God, y
loser?   in?" h
id. "Lik   s stron
e body   e on G
ly, he   I ever
up to t   any ide
staking   e sam
, I coul   ery lo
ood rac   he sw
ng with   c in s
we go   behin
ill see   in pu
ed?" he   vent to
rivacy,   grabb
hard. I
k, tracing   t, so
ed it, ha
with my   bing
obing,   n coc
e sound of unzipping filled the small space. I don't know who's
, but before I knew it, I had his rod in my hand, and mine was in h
t to do?" he asked, his tone challenging. I knew exactly, and sank